GANG GIRL

Lora Menotti is five feet five of concentrated sex, one hundred twenty-five pounds of undiluted viciousness. She is sixteen. She is deadly. Her parents know it, and they are afraid of her. Her older brother knows it, and he tries never to turn his back on her. Her neighbors know it, and they keep their distance. The other kids in the gang, the Scarlet Sinners, they know it, too. They fear her, and because of that they respect her. In a teen gang, fear equals respect. There is no other law. This is Lora's story, a girl who thrills at the thought of death, embraces sex with each new leader of the gang, and who controls her world the only way she can—by pitting each member against the other, with her body as bait.

SEX BUM

Johnny Price has big plans. Only 19, he already knows what he wants, and he isn't going to find it delivering groceries in a small town in upstate New York. So when he gets a chance to help a couple of local gangsters take out the competition, he jumps at the opportunity. Suddenly, he's in, a member of the Syndicate. Johnny is on his way. Now he's got plenty of money, a new car— and lots of women. And that suits him fine, because Johnny knows how to please them all. But Johnny wants more—more power, classier ladies—like the slinky, sophisticated Marie. But Marie is Rizzo's woman. To take Marie, he has to go all the way to New York City. And to get there, he has to betray his own bosses. Good thing for Johnny he has a plan.

Gang Girl
Sex Bum

TWO HARDBOILED CLASSICS BY
DON ELLIOTT

Stark House Press • Eureka California

GANG GIRL / SEX BUM

Published by Stark House Press
1315 H Street
Eureka, CA 95501, USA
griffinskye3@sbcglobal.net
www.starkhousepress.com

ISBN: 1-933586-34-6
ISBN-13: 978-1-933586-34-2

Cover design and layout by Mark Shepard, SHEPGRAPHICS.COM
Proofreading by Rick Ollerman

First Stark House Press Edition: April 2011

THOSE GOOD OLD SOFT-CORE DAYS

By Robert Silverberg

This is how I might write it if I were writing it today:

"Come on," she said, her green eyes wild with hunger for it. "Are you ready to fuck or aren't you?"

Her clothes dropped away and instantly, at the sight of her full, hard-nippled breasts and the dense, dark thatch of hair at the base of her belly, his cock sprang up into aching rigidity. She grinned and came toward him and knelt before him, slipping one hand under his balls and grasping his stiff shaft with the other.

"Go on," Holman said hoarsely. "Suck it! Oh, Jesus, suck it, babe!"

She tickled the tip of his dick with her tongue and rubbed it voluptuously for a moment or two between the heavy mounds of her tits, and then her lips slid over him and she took him into her mouth. Deep. Amazingly deep. And moved slowly back and forth, back and forth, wringing moans from him, driving him wild with sensation. Her mouth was as soft and as sweet as a velvet cunt. She squeezed his balls lightly as she sucked. He could feel the jism starting to pulse within him, on the verge of leaping forth into her throat. But then she pulled back and spread herself for him, and an instant later, to his amazement and delight, his hard cock was plunging into the hot, throbbing depths of her moist pussy, and —

The year was 1959, though, and the American government's ideas of what was permissible to print and sell through normal commercial channels was very different, so this is what I actually wrote:

She undid the garter-belt herself, and rolled down the stockings, and then she was nude, and he stood up, dropping his trousers, and she reached out and caught his arm and pulled him down again, and they rolled off the couch together, down onto the carpeted floor.

For what might have been an hour they lay there, side by side, lips glued, hands roaming up and down bodies, breath coming shorter and shorter. Holman opened his eyes and saw her staring at him, her eyes moist and the pupils that peculiar shade of green again. He smiled into her eyes and brought his fingers lightly down the small of her back, pausing at the dimples just above her firm, swelling buttocks.

It was like pulling a trigger. She began to gasp excitedly, and she dragged him over on top of her, her eyes going tight shut, her lips drooping open, moist and passionate. "Now, darling! Take me now!"

She shuddered convulsively as the moment of union came. Her thighs tightened around him, and she began to writhe and moan — an animal moan, low and deep in her throat, coming from the same place that those deep, sad blues came from.

Holman clenched his teeth and gripped her shoulders tight, and she cried out three times, a whimper of excitement following, and then they were thundering away together on a tornado of passion, and she dug her fingernails into the skin of his back and gasped out breathlessly, "Oh oh oh *oh*," and Holman felt the explosion in his loins, and then they were lying quietly all of a sudden, limp and sweat-soaked, and he could feel the pounding of her heart when he touched her breasts, and the fireworks stopped.

It was over.

Hot stuff, yes? Well, actually it is, in its quaint fashion. No tits or cocks or cunts are mentioned, or any other nasty Anglo-Saxon words, no clits, no moist pussies, no vivid descriptions whatsoever of genital organs, erect or otherwise — not even of pubic hair; and an orgasm isn't a fountain of hot jism or anything else anatomically specific, it's a metaphorical "explosion in the loins." People don't fuck or screw, they experience "union." The tone is very antiseptic, almost prim, you would say. Even so, all the basic ingredients of the good old beast with two backs are there, the moans and groans, whimpers of excitement, and, yes, the explosion in the loins — everything you would want in a scene describing passionate sex, if you were living in 1959. But the difference between the hot stuff of 1959 and today's pornographic fiction is the difference between the lightning bug and the lightning.

The 1959 passage that begins with the undoing of the garter-belt was, in fact, the opening erotic scene in *Love Addict*, published by Nightstand Books of Chicago in October of that year — the first of about a hundred and fifty novels of what we now would regard as very innocent soft-core porn that I would write over the next five years for Nightstand under the pseudonym of "Don Elliott."

That's right. One hundred fifty full-length novels in five years. Thirty books a year, better than one every two weeks, month in and month out, between 1959 and 1964. Written on a manual typewriter, no less. (Writers didn't use computers then. The IBM Selectric typewriter, once considered a fast futuristic device, had not yet been invented, either.) Other writers who, as I did, went on to significant careers in other fields, were turning out similar soft-core books at almost the same sizzling pace. We were *fast*, in those days. But of course we were very young.

I was 24 years old when I stumbled, much to my surprise, into a career of writing sex novels. I was then, as I am now, primarily known as a science-fiction writer. But in 1958, as a result of a behind-the-scenes convulsion in the magazine-distribution business, the whole s-f publishing world went belly up. A dozen or so magazines for which I had been writing regularly ceased publication overnight; and as for the tiny market for s-f novels (two paperback houses and one hardcover) it suddenly became so tight that unless you were one of the first-magnitude stars like Robert Heinlein or Isaac Asimov you were out of luck.

I had been earning a very nice living writing science fiction since my graduation from college a few years earlier. I had a posh five-room apartment on Manhattan's exclusive West End Avenue ($150 a month rent — a fortune then!), I had fallen into the habit of spending my summer vacations in places like London and Paris, I ate at the best restaurants, I was learning something about fine wines. And suddenly two thirds of the magazines I wrote for were out of business, with a slew of older and better established writers competing for the few remaining slots. Most of the reliable writing income on which I had come to depend disappeared overnight.

But I was fast on my feet, and I had some good friends. One of them was Harlan Ellison, a science-fiction writer of my own age, who — seeing the handwriting on the wall in the s-f world — had left New York to accept a job in Chicago as editor of *Rogue*, an early men's magazine that was trying with some success to compete with its crosstown neighbor, *Playboy*. The publisher of *Rogue* was William L. Hamling, a clean-cut young Chicago suburbanite whose first great love, like Harlan's and mine, had been science fiction. Bill Hamling had published an s-f magazine called *Imagination*, which bought one of my first stories in 1954. From 1956 on, he had paid me $500 a month to churn out fast-paced epics of the spaceways for him on a contract basis. Now, though, *Imagination* was gone, and Hamling's only remaining publishing endeavor was his bi-monthly girlie magazine.

Harlan, soon after going to work for him, convinced Bill that the future lay in paperback erotic novels. Hamling thought about it for about six minutes and agreed. And then Harlan called me.

"I have a deal for you, if you're interested," he said. "One sex novel a month, 50,000 words. $600 per book. We need the first one by the end of July." It was then the *beginning* of July. I didn't hesitate. $600 a month was big money in those days, especially when you were a young writer at your wits' end because all your regular markets had crashed and burned. One book would pay four months' rent. They were going to publish two paperbacks a month, and I was being offered a chance to write half the list myself. "You bet," I said. By the end of July Harlan had *Love Addict* — a searing novel of hopeless hungers, demanding bodies, girls trapped in a torment of their own making, et cetera, et cetera. (I'm quoting from the jacket copy.)

Bill Hamling loved *Love Addict*. By return mail came my six hundred bucks and a request for more books. I couldn't do a second one immediately because I was heading off to Canada for a holiday from New York City's summer heat, but when I returned after Labor Day I wrote *Gang Girl*, the first of the two novels reprinted here. It would be published that fall as Nightstand Book 1504.

Gang Girl belongs to the once-popular genre of kid-gang novels. The first of them, I think, was Evan Hunter's best-seller *The Blackboard Jungle*, which created a vocabulary of juvenile-delinquent concepts and jargon that a host of imitators quickly turned into a formula. Magazines like *Manhunt*, *Trapped*, and *Guilty* specialized in kid-gang stories. I wrote for many of those magazines myself, dozens of pseudonymous stories about tough kids prowling the urban jungles. One of them was a 10,000-worder called "New Girl in the Gang," which appeared in the September, 1959 issue of *Guilty* under the byline of "Ray McKenzie." It was no great technical challenge to expand it to the 50,000-word length of a Nightstand book. I turned *Gang Girl* in in mid-September, just as its magazine version was leaving the newsstands. In October I did *The Love Goddess* for Nightstand. Later that month I wrote *Summertime Affair* also. Two novels the same month? Why not? I was fast, I was hungry, I was good.

That same month of October saw the first two Nightstand Books going on sale — mine and one called *Lust Club*, by another young writer who also was making a quick adaptation to changes in his writing markets. His book, like mine, was really pretty tame stuff. What we were writing, basically, were straightforward novels of contemporary life, with very mild interludes of sexual activity every twenty or thirty pages. But the characters actually did go to bed with each other, and we did try to describe what they were doing and how they felt in as much detail as the government would allow.

At that time, fairly rigid censorship still prevailed in American publishing. It was illegal to publish or sell such classics of erotic literature as *Tropic of Cancer* or *Lady Chatterley's Lover*, and even the presence of words like "fuck" or "cunt" in a book could bring its publisher a call from the district attorney's office. To a reading public eager for vicarious sexual thrills, Bill

Hamling's Nightstand Books, which were openly and widely distributed, offered a commodity that was in instant and enormous demand. Incredible quantities of the first two books were sold. It was impossible to reprint them fast enough.

Hamling sent me a bonus of $200 for each book I had written thus far, and raised my price to $800 from then on. And he decided to publish four titles a month instead of two. "Can you possibly write two books every month for us?" he asked.

A Nightstand Book, you understand, was a 212-page double-spaced manuscript. I was setting myself up for an unthinkable amount of typing — not to mention the problem of inventing plots, characters, setting, all that stuff. But I didn't hesitate to say yes. I could type quickly and I could think quickly. I had just demonstrated to myself that I could indeed do two Nightstand jobs a month, and, since they took only six working days apiece, I would still have time left over for other projects. And I had arrived at a perfect formula for these books. Apart from the kid-gang books, which were a subgenre of their own, most of them were stories about ordinary people who were in the grip of powerful sexual obsessions that got them into trouble.

What I did was take a sympathetic character (male or female, it made no difference) who has normal, healthy sexual desires that are somehow being frustrated — the hard-working husband who suddenly feels a powerful need to have an affair, the woman who unexpectedly discovers that drinking too much makes her want to let go of her sexual inhibitions. Removing the obstacles to the fulfillment of the desires leads to complications and then more complications, which create tensions that can best be satisfied by more sex, and so on and on, in and out of bed and in and out of trouble, until in the end everything is resolved and the protagonist's life shows signs of becoming calmer. (Or spirals into a disastrous crash.)

Any setting would do. I just had to pick my characters and set them in motion against a vivid background. I told tales of illicit goings-on at plush Caribbean resorts, of nice high school kids learning interesting things to do with their bodies, of suburban swap clubs. Where I could make use of my own experiences, such as they had been at the age of 25 or so, I did. The rest I spun out of whole cloth, or out of my own teeming, steamy fantasies. (I had grown up in the repressed Fifties, and had plenty to fantasize about.)

I wrote *Pawn of Lust* and *Nudist Camp* in November, 1959. I wrote *Warped Lusts* and *Suburban Wife* in December. January produced only *Sin on Wheels*, but in February came *Sin Ranch* and *Trap of Desire*. And so on and so on, month after month. Each book took me exactly six days: one stint of sixteen to eighteen pages before lunch, another of the same amount after lunch, fifteen or sixteen manuscript pages to a chapter, fourteen chapters and 212 pages in all. No book came out short and none, of course, ran long: I became adept in moving my characters around in such a way that the climax of the plot always arrived on schedule in Chapter Fourteen. The books sold well and more retroactive bonuses were paid me for the early titles. Now I was getting $1200 a book for the new ones. That was an income of better than a thousand dollars a week at a time when dinner for two at the finest restaurant in New York cost about $40, including a bottle of first-rate French wine. My new career in soft-core erotica was rapidly making me rich.

I felt absolutely unabashed about what I was doing. Writing was my job, and I was working hard and telling crisp, exciting stories. What difference did it make, really, that they were stories about people caught in tense sexual situations instead of people exploring the slime-pits of Aldebaran IX? I experienced the joy — and there is one, believe me — of working hard and steadily, long hours sitting at a typing table under the summer sun, creating scenes of erotic tension as fast as my fingers could move. Of course, what I was writing was not "respectable," not even slightly, and so when people asked me what I did for a living I told them I was a science-fiction writer. (I was still writing some of that, too, as a sideline.) I could hardly tell my neighbors in my elegant suburban community that I was a professional pornographer.

But was what I was writing really pornography?

Not if your definition of pornography involves the use of "obscene" words or graphic physiological description. As the sample I quoted above should show, the stuff was really laughably chaste and demure. Everything was done by euphemism and metaphor. No explicit anatomical descriptions were allowed, no naughty words. About as far as you could go was a phrase like "they were lying together, and he felt the urgent thrust of her body against him, and his aroused maleness was penetrating her, and he felt the warm soft moist clasping and the tightening...."

Unmistakably these people are Doing It. But his "maleness" is what's penetrating her, not his cock or his prick or his dick, and *something* is clasping and tightening, presumably a vagina, but we aren't told that in so many syllables. Characters didn't "come" — they reached "the moment of ecstasy." Men had neither cocks nor balls; they had "loins." Foreplay was a matter of cupping breasts and letting a hand "slip lower on her body." Anal sex? No such concept. Dildos and other sex toys? Forget it. Oral sex was indicated by saying, "He kissed her here and he kissed her there, and then he kissed her there." And so forth. None of it was much spicier than Peter Rabbit.

I limited myself to words that were in the standard dictionary because I had been warned at the outset that the publisher would not tolerate what he termed "vulgarisms." One reason for this was that he genuinely didn't like them — he was basically a very earnest and straight type of guy, who would much rather have been publishing science fiction — but also he knew that he might very well go to jail if he started printing them. *Jail*, yes — no matter what the First Amendment might say. (And eventually he did, many years later — not for publishing sexy novels, but for violating the postal code by sending an advertisement for an illustrated history of erotic art and literature through the mails!)

The list of what was a "vulgarism," though, kept changing in line with various court actions and rulings affecting Nightstand's competitors in the rapidly expanding erotic-book business. All across the nation, bluenosed civic authorities were trying to stamp out this new plague of smut. Whenever a liberal-minded judge threw out a censor's case, the word came down to us that we could take a few more risks in what we wrote, although our prose remained exceedingly pure by later publishing standards. But whenever some unfortunate publisher was hit by a fine, the word was passed to the little crew of Nightstand regulars that we had to try to be more proper.

One day the word "it" became a vulgarism. *"It"* as in *"'Do it,' she cried,"* I mean. By this time Harlan Ellison had moved along to Hollywood, and my Nightstand editor in Chicago was Algis Budrys, another top science-fiction writer who had found it necessary after the s-f crash to switch from freelance writing to editing. Budrys phoned me to say that I must restrict my use of "it" from now on. I took a look at a recently published book of mine and saw that they had indeed changed all my "it"s to "that"s, creating stuff like: *"'Do that,' she cried. 'I want that! I want that!'"*

This sounded nuts to me, and I told Budrys I would refuse to abide by it. To prove it, I turned in a book in which "it" was just about every other word: *"Give it to me! I want it! It! It! I must have it!"* I was the star of the line, the first and most reliable and prolific writer they had, and I got my way. "It" was removed from the list of vulgarisms.

By this time — it was about 1962 — I was turning out *three* Nightstand books a month. It was a fantastic amount of work to do, but I had no choice. Like many writers (Sir Walter Scott, for example, or Mark Twain) I had gone in for owning fancy real estate. I had bought myself an enormous mansion in the finest residential neighborhood of New York City, close to the Westchester County line, for the immense sum (then) of $80,000. The place had 20 rooms, all of which needed to be painted and furnished, and then too I had to think about the heating bill, property taxes, etc., etc. So I upped the output. The record for June, 1962, for example, shows *Unnatural, Illicit Joys,* and *The Flesh is Willing* — a typically productive month. That month the plumbing in the house broke down and I remember a team of five plumbers digging around in the back yard, simply trying to locate the water main, while I sat upstairs trying to turn out words fast enough to earn more than their combined hourly rate. And did.

One way I managed to keep up this amazing level of output was to assemble a sheaf of what I called "modules" — prefabricated sex scenes that I could simply plug into any book. Plots and characters had to change from book to book, of course, but under the highly restrictive rules we were forced to use there were only so many ways to describe what my people were up to in bed, and so I extracted relevant scenes from my books — a basic seduction scene, a copulation scene, a voyeurism scene, a rape scene, a Lesbian scene, and so on — and recycled them into the new manuscripts in the appropriate places, as needed. Nobody ever objected. (If computers had existed then, I could have done it all with a single keystroke. Instead I had to type it all out, over and over.)

Where I could, I would expand something I had written before. I still had a considerable backlog of crime stories that I had done in the late 50s for *Trapped* and *Guilty*, and, since these all dealt with people in extreme situations, it was easy enough to build one up to book length. That was what I did in December, 1962 with a novelet called "Mobster on the Make," from the August, 1958 issue of *Trapped*, which I turned into a novel I called *Sex Hoodlum*, and which Earl Kemp, who by that time had replaced Budrys as my Nightstand editor, renamed *Sex Bum*. (Earl almost always changed my titles.) It came out in May, 1963 as Midnight Reader 489.

The Nightstand line now was running to eight or ten books a month, maybe more, and as the list grew, a lot of other clever young men joined the roster of writers. (Entry to the list was by invitation only — the publisher didn't want to deal with amateurs, only with crafty young pros.) In an insecure career like freelance writing, those guaranteed monthly checks were very tempting. You would probably be astonished at how many eventually-famous writers were among my colleagues at Nightstand. We were like a bunch of future major-leaguers getting a chance to sharpen our skills in Triple-A minor-league baseball.

I won't name names, because it's not my place to do so. But I can tell you that two writers who became widely admired mystery novelists, enormously popular and successful, were Nightstand regulars under the names of "Andrew Shaw" and "Alan Marshall." Their work for Nightstand usually had a broadly comic touch, which mine never did. (Sex was always Serious Stuff to me.) Another, who wrote under the name of "J.X. Williams," became a major best-selling author of historical novels, and I mean *major*, specializing in American history. The author of the "Don Bellmore" books went on to a career as a Hollywood writer. "Clyde Allison" was the pseudonym used by a brilliant young mainstream novelist who died of alcoholism while still in his thirties. And, though I have no proof of this, I was told on good authority long ago that one of the Nightstand writers was a man who was *already* a best-selling author even then, and who was knocking out Nightstands on the side for the fun of it, without his wife's knowledge (or his regular publisher's) and having the payments sent to the mistress he was keeping.

We were all working hard, and having fun, and making plenty of money. (So was the publisher, who left Chicago for a Palm Springs estate.) Of course, all sorts of governmental units right up to the Federal level were trying to put us out of business, and there were indictments all over the place, and a nasty censorship trial in Houston. Since we writers worked under pseudonyms, and got our checks from a dummy corporation, we weren't involved in that.

But one day two F.B.I. agents came to talk to me. It was all very silly. I received them in the paneled library of my imposing mansion. We chatted about my writing — my *science fiction* writing. I showed them a few recent books on archaeology and science for young readers I had written — I was doing that too, in my spare time, and I just happened to have the books close at hand. The word "pornography" was never mentioned. They did ask me if I had ever done business with a company called Such-and-Such Enterprises. Evidently that was one of the dummy corporations that paid the writers for the Nightstand lines; but it so happened that my checks came from This-and-That Enterprises instead, a *different* dummy corporation, and the nice F.B.I. men had gotten things mixed up. "No," I said, absolutely truthfully. "I've never done business with Such-and-Such. I've never even heard of them." And that was that. The F.B.I. men left, probably thinking there was some case of mistaken identity here, and no one ever bothered me again.

But I did stop writing for Nightstand a year or so later — not because I was afraid of more government harassment, but because after 150 erotic novels in five years I was getting pretty tired of marching my characters in and out of bedrooms. I wanted to get back to the intellectual challenge of science fiction, which was making a strong commercial recovery after its slump of the late Fifties. And my non-fiction books on archaeology and science were very successful too; I wanted time to do more of those. So in a final flurry — *E for Eros, One Night Stand, Sin Kitten* — I went out of the business of writing erotic novels.

But I have no regrets about those five years in the sex-book factory — none. I don't think any of us who wrote Nightstands do. It isn't just that I earned enough by writing them to pay for that big house and my trips to Europe. I developed and honed important professional skills, too, while I was pounding out all those books.

Working at fantastic speeds (I once did a complete novel in 3-1/2 days, just to see if I could) I mastered the knack of improvising plots from scratch and making everything work out neatly at the required 50,000-word length: a wonderful exercise in structural discipline that has stood me in good stead ever since. I think the experience was useful for my colleagues, too. There was no time to make mistakes: we had to get it right on the first draft, and we did, telling good stories in crisp, no-nonsense prose. And because we all worked under pen names, we were free to let our inhibitions drop away and push our characters to their limits, without worrying about what anyone else — friends, relatives, book reviewers — might say or think about our work. We had ourselves a ball, and got paid nicely while we were doing it.

And also we never forgot that we were doing the fundamental thing that writers are supposed to do: providing pleasure and entertainment for readers who genuinely loved our work. Huge numbers of the books were snapped up as fast as they came from the presses, which meant that they filled a need, that *somebody* appreciated them a whole lot. It meant something to me to know that my novels were brightening the lives of a vast host of people in those dim dark days of fifty-plus years ago when puritanism was riding high and sex was in chains.

One hundred fifty novels! *Passion Patsy! Flesh Flames! Sin Hellion! The Orgy Boys!* Writing those books was a terrific experience and I look back fondly on it without shame, without apologies.

OAKLAND, CA
OCTOBER 2010

Gang Girl

By Don Elliott

CHAPTER ONE

Lora Menotti was five feet five of concentrated sex, one hundred twenty-five pounds of undiluted viciousness. She was sixteen.

She was deadly.

Her parents knew it, and they were afraid of her. Her older brother knew it, and he tried never to turn his back on her. Her neighbors knew it, and they kept their distance.

The other kids in the gang, the Scarlet Sinners, they had known it too. They feared her, and because of that they respected her. In a teen gang, fear equals respect. There is no other law.

Lora paced around the apartment, still fresh and bare and new-smelling. Her parents were busy getting the place fixed up. Her mother was hanging up the drapes, her father and brother were putting the furniture where it belonged. Lora just stood by and watched. Nobody asked her to do anything. She just stood by.

This was the first day down here, in the big new housing project on the Lower East Side. Before that, the Menotti family had lived in the upper reaches of the Bronx, the four of them crammed together in a squalid little three-room apartment on the fifth floor of a rundown walkup building. But Mr. Menotti had been on the waiting list at this new project for the last two years, and he had finally received the long brown envelope telling him to come sign for his apartment and move in.

So now they had four and a half rooms with nice new white paint on the walls. They were on the fourteenth floor, facing east, and on a nice clear day you could see clear across the river into Queens. Lora had an entire room to herself, and so did her brother Chick. It was the first time in their lives that they hadn't had to sleep in the same room.

Lora knew why the move had been made. It hadn't just been so things wouldn't be as cramped. She had heard her parents talking about it, late one night soon after the new lease had been signed.

Her mother had been saying, "Thank God we're getting out of this neighborhood! Maybe now Lora will stop running with those wild kids. Those—what do they call themselves?—the Scarlet Sinners."

"I hope so," her father had said. "Damn crazy kid. Maybe in a decent neighborhood she'll settle down before it's too late. Turn into a normal human being instead of a wildcat."

"She's only sixteen, Leo. It isn't too late for her to change. The new neighborhood—"

"Let's hope. Let's hope it isn't too late."

Lying on her bed in the next room, Lora had smiled to herself. In an apartment that small it wasn't easy to keep a conversation secret, and she knew her parents had probably intended that she overhear. They didn't dare lecture her directly about running with the teen gang, but they could let her overhear.

She made a scornful face and silently mouthed an obscenity. So the big move was all aimed at her, eh? So the idea was to pull her away from the gang environment and let her straighten out? Hell, she thought, if the old dopes thought they were going to get her away from the gang life by moving to another part of New York City, they damn jolly well had another thing coming. Lora was a gang girl from the word go. Nobody was going to turn *her* into a square! Nobody was going to make a Sunday School sweetheart out of Lora Menotti, she vowed grimly.

The next day, she had gone looking for Danny the Limp. A crip like Danny got all around the city, and nobody paid very much attention to him. Danny always had the information you wanted.

"Guess what," Lora told him. "I'm moving out next month."

"No crap? How come?"

"Parents. They want a change of air."

Danny's ugly face became intently curious. "You told Spook about it yet?"

"Uh-uh."

"Gonna tell him?"

"Whaddya think? Sure I'll tell him. I'll tell him tonight."

"Spook's gonna miss you," the cripple said. His filmy, pale eyes focused hungrily on the upthrusting mounds of Lora's breasts, pushing outward against the straining fabric of her sweater. "Spook thinks real big of you, Lora. He's gonna miss you."

Lora shrugged, ignoring the hungriness in Danny's eyes. The ugly cripple would probably have gladly given his one good leg for half an hour in the hay with her, but the idea disgusted her. She didn't mind laying for top men, but not for dirty crips. She said casually, "There's plenty of other tail in Scarlet Sinner turf. I ain't the only one. Spook'll survive."

"Yeah, sure. But he'll miss you."

"Hell with that. I want some info, Danny."

"Sure," the cripple said eagerly. He was always ready with information, hoping to barter it for a kiss or a feel. "What you want to know?"

"I'm moving down to the Lower East Side. Project called the Bryson Houses."

"Yeah. I know the place."

"You know everything, Danny. Tell me—they got any action down there?"

"What kinda action?"

"You know goddam well. That's gang turf down there, ain't it?"

Danny closed his eyes a moment. "Yeah," he said, after sifting through the card-file of his mind. "Yeah, they got a gang down there. Name of Cougars."

"What kind of cruddy name is that?"

"It's a kind of animal," Danny said. "Kind of a wildcat, like."

"Cougars, huh," Lora repeated. "They any good, Danny?"

"They're okay. They're pretty tough."

"Where do I find them?"

"Fourth Street and Avenue C," the cripple replied immediately. "They hang out in a candy store called—uh—Sid's. They got a clubhouse, too, but I don't know where that is." The cripple smiled hopefully. "I know a lot, huh, Lora?"

"You're a goddam encyclopedia."

"A guy like me, I gotta be good for something."

Danny held up his withered right hand, looked down at his shrivelled right leg, and grinned sadly, revealing yellow straggly teeth. "I don't use a knife so good, I can't fight at all. So I remember. I squirrel around town and learn things."

"You're a wonder, crip."

"Lora?"

"Huh?"

"How about a favor?"

She turned her eyes to ice. "What you mean, a favor?"

The cripple shuffled closer. "Just let me touch you, Lora. Just once."

"You crazy?"

"Just once," Danny pleaded. His left hand snaked out, trembling, and paused midway between his body and hers. "Please, Lora. I'll lick your boots if you want. Just let me touch you. Nobody can see. Nobody'll ever find out."

She frowned. "Just a touch."

"That's all."

"Quick," she snapped.

The hand moved forward, hovering over the rounded globe of her left breast. The hand descended. For one moment it cupped the breast, and the firm flesh quivered a little beneath the touch. Then Danny drew the hand away, as quickly as though he had put it down on a hot stove. He looked at it strangely. Then he looked at Lora. His eyes were wet with tears of gratitude.

"Thanks," he whispered. "Jeez, thanks!"

And he turned and shuffled away, doing his sideways crabdance and getting away from her as fast as he possibly could. Lora stared after him, shaking her head. What a creep, she thought! One quick feel and he's probably had his kicks for the year. She shrugged. The poor goof had been drooling to do that for three years. Now he could die happy, she thought.

Well, he had earned the squeeze. She had gotten from him the information she wanted. The name of the gang in her new territory, and the name and address of the place where they hung out. The rest she could do for herself. There was always room in a gang for a girl with a size thirty-nine bust.

That night, at the Scarlet Sinner clubhouse, Lora passed the bad news along to Spook. Spook was the president of the Scarlet Sinners, and he and Lora had been shacking up steady for the past six months. His real name was Mario, but they called him Spook because he moved so fast when he was in a knife-fight. He was like a ghost, vanishing and reappearing again where his opponent didn't expect him to be. He was tall and lean, without an extra ounce of fat on his body, and he wore his hair swept back straight in a big shiny pompadour.

Lora said, "I'm leaving first of the month, Spook."

"Leaving where?"

"Moving out. My folks got a new apartment way the hell downtown."

Spook's eyes glinted angrily. "You gonna go with them, Lora?"

"You got any better ideas?"

"Can't you find someone in the neighborhood you can live with?"

"Like who? Nobody'd give me a room. Anyway, my folks wouldn't let me. They'd put the police on me. I ain't old enough to move out on them."

Spook licked his lips nervously. He put his hands around Lora's waist, slipped them under the hem of her sweater, and brought them up her back to the catch of her bra. He pushed open the catch and the cups dropped away from her breasts. His long, tapering hands slid around the heavy, ripe melons that were her breasts, and his fingers toyed with her stiff nipples. He contracted his hands suddenly, tightening breathtakingly around her breasts.

"I'm gonna miss them," Spook whispered. "I'm gonna miss all of you, honey."

"Come move down too."

"Can't. My old lady's too sick to be left alone."

"Since when you care about her?" Lora asked, leaning back and starting to open his trousers. "You never used to, Spook."

"It's different now. She's sick. And she's my mother. I can't just leave her."

"Not even for me?"

"Uh-uh."

Lora smiled. It was a funny streak in Spook, this mother stuff. He'd killed two guys and he hadn't worried much about *their* mothers, but he was half crazy ever since his own had had that stroke. Well, she thought, chalk off Spook. He'd find somebody else, and so would she.

She wriggled out of her pants. One of his hands left her breasts and travelled down the silky smoothness of her belly, coming to rest for a moment on her thigh, then wandering over her flesh. Lora began to gasp. She spun around suddenly, pressing herself up against Spook, ripping away his clothing, pulling his lean hard body down against hers, twining her legs around his hips, throwing back her head, crying out in ecstasy as his aroused passion transfixed her....

That had been last month. Lora smiled, remembering it, remembering that whole final month with Spook. They had made it practically around the clock the last week, as though when she was gone he wasn't ever going to get any more of it from anybody. She could still feel the tingling sensation of his hands against her breasts, could still remember the taste of his mouth and the way he quivered and moaned right at the biggest moment. The way his fingers dug into her shoulders in a kind of agony of delight.

And that was all Spook was for her, now, she thought—just a bundle of memories, to be blotted out soon by somebody else. It was an hour trip by subway from this neighborhood back to Scarlet Sinner turf, and that meant it was as far away as the next planet. New York was criscrossed with dozens of gang turfs, each one rigidly marked out, each boundary sternly defended. Gang kids generally didn't go outside the few square blocks of their own turf, let alone take a trip all the way up to the Bronx from the Lower East Side. Only the rare exception like Danny the Limp could go threading his way through the territories of rival gangs without getting into any trouble. It was worth a Scarlet Sinner's life to cross Webster Avenue into the territory of the Golden Avengers, and vice versa.

So Lora wouldn't be returning to the old grounds. And Spook was just a handful of fading memories.

She walked to the window of the new apartment and looked out, over the river. She could see factories in Queens, and a bridge. And down there to the right was Brooklyn. She had lived in New York all her life, and she had never been in Brooklyn or Queens. They had other gangs over there, she knew. The Jolly Rogers, the Counts, the Slayers. Only names to her, names brought back by Danny the Limp. But it was a strange world to her, on the other side of the river.

It was time to get out of the apartment and start hunting up the Cougars, she decided abruptly. She was getting fidgety, watching all the unpacking going on around her. She had to get out.

She walked into the next room, where her mother was working.

"What time is it, Ma?"

"Quarter to two."

Lora nodded. "I'm going out."

There was a moment of silence. Then her mother said, "Out where?"

"Out looking."

"Why can't you stay here and help us with the unpacking? Why—"

"I'm going out, Ma."

A look of defeat crossed her mother's tired face. The older woman shrugged heavily and turned away, back to the drapes. Lora grinned in triumph. The flat words, *I'm going out, Ma,* had carried menace with them. Nobody dared talk back to her, not even her own mother, Lora thought.

Lora walked toward the door. As she put her hand on the knob, her mother said, "What time you going to come back?"

"I'll be back."

"Supper's at six-thirty."

"I ain't got a watch, Ma. How can I help it if I ain't back on time?"

"We won't wait. The roast will get spoiled if we wait for you."

"I ain't gonna be gone all night," Lora said boredly. "I just want to take a look around."

"Lora—"

She opened the door part way. "Yeah, Ma?"

"Lora, don't get into any trouble, hear me? This is a new neighborhood. Start off right."

"Skip the preach, Ma. Seeya around."

She walked out, slamming the door behind her. When she was in the hall, she turned and put her thumb to her nose. Sometimes she did it to her mother's face, but right now she wasn't looking for much of a fuss. She just wanted to get out.

It was the middle of September, and the first tang of autumn was in the air. Lora had registered at the new high school earlier that day; there hadn't been any classes, just an hour of registration. Classes didn't start till later in the week. She hadn't paid any attention to her fellow students in the morning. For all she knew, she was in the same class as some of the Cougars. Well, the high school jazz wouldn't be going on much longer, anyway. Another ten months and she'd be seventeen, and she could quit. It was just a matter of waiting it out.

The elevator reached the ground floor and Lora stepped out. It was almost a full block to the street; the housing project consisted of a lot of identical twenty-story buildings placed catacorner from one another, and interspersed with little playgrounds and lawns. The idea was to make a little city within the city, with no traffic going through the project area. Lora walked briskly toward the nearest exit. She emerged on Avenue B.

Danny had said the candy store where the Cougars hung out was on Fourth Street and Avenue C. A place named Sid's. Nodding, Lora strolled down to Fourth Street and turned east. She smiled. The Cougars didn't know it yet, but Lora Menotti was on her way to apply for membership.

CHAPTER TWO

The candy store was on Fourth, about an eighth of a block past the intersection of Fourth and C. It looked kind of dumpy: a faded orange awning out in front, and a red-painted wooden box with all the newspapers held down by a weighted wooden rod. A neon sign buzzed in the unwashed window: ICE CREAM — SODAS — NEWSPAPERS. In faded white letters across the front of the awning were the words: SID'S — LUNCHEONETTE, NEWSTAND, SODA FOUNTAIN. Lora stood outside for a moment, sizing the place up. It was the place, all right. She wondered how many of the Cougars would be inside. Warily, she looked around. On the other side of the street, facing Avenue C, two boys were leaning against the wall. They looked like Cougars. They had the black leather jackets and the blue jeans and the duck-tail haircuts. They stood with their hands in their pockets, teetering back and forth on the balls of their feet, shoulders scrunched up high toward their ears, eyes glinting. They were looking Lora over, she knew. They were the lookouts, guarding the turf, posted there to survey any strangers who might happen to approach the headquarters of the gang.

She turned, giving them the eye in return, looking back at them long and slow to show them that they weren't bugging her any. Then she pushed open the door of the candy store and walked in.

She was wearing blue jeans that clung to her legs and wide hips and full buttocks as though the fabric had been sprayed onto her skin. Her red sweater had deliberately been bought two sizes too small. Lora walked in with her shoulders drawn back, her lungs inflated, her breasts thrust forward. She knew she had a good body. She was big in the bust, flat in the belly. She had fluid-drive hips and bedroom thighs. She wasn't easy to overlook when she walked by.

She stepped in. Sid's Candy Store, from the inside, looked pretty much like the place that served as the Scarlet Sinners' hangout uptown. These places were all the same. There was the long pink imitation marble soda-counter, the five or six upholstered booths in the back, the racks at the side with the pocketbooks and the dogeared magazines. Nobody ever bought the magazines, in the gang. They looked them over for free, lamping all the pictures and putting them back in the rack. The proprietor never complained about the library bit. He was too smart to raise a fuss. When you had a gang using your place as its headquarters, you didn't go out of your way to rock the boat.

Lora smiled quietly. There were some kids jammed into the booths in back, sipping malteds and cracking jokes in loud voices. Just as Lora stepped in, the place seemed to erupt with laughter, high and clear over the loud rock-'n-roll number that the jukebox was bellowing forth. Lora didn't pay any attention.

She ambled over to the soda-counter and plunked herself down. The soda-jerk came over. He was a fat, red-faced, worried-looking little man with a comic little fringe of sandy hair sprouting around the base of his bald head.

"What's yours, Miss?" he asked hoarsely.

"Vanilla milkshake," Lora said.

"One milkshake, coming up."

The soda-jerk turned away and started going through the complicated motions of assembling the milkshake and placing it on the mixing machine. Lora spun on her seat and took a long, slow look around the Cougar hangout. She saw five teenagers in the booth in back, three fellows, two girls, laughing. They looked like gang kids. They wore the right clothes, they had the right look in their eyes. This was the right place, sure enough. Danny the Limp hadn't given her the wrong scoop. These were some of the Cougars.

The soda-jerk came back. "Here's your shake."

"How much?"

"Thirty."

Lora dropped a nickel on the counter, followed it with a worn two-bit piece, and picked up her milkshake glass in one hand and the metal mixing container in the other. She started across the floor pushing her breasts out as far as she could and giving it plenty of hip action by way of accompaniment.

She strutted past the booth of Cougars. Somebody whistled at her. She grinned.

Somebody else muttered, "Hey, dig that pair of knockers, willya!"

Lora grinned even harder.

Lora sat down two booths behind the group of Cougars, and without paying the slightest attention to them she began to pour out her milkshake, slowly and deliberately, into the glass. She sipped it.

The bait had been cast. No girl comes into a gang headquarters alone and in a tight sweater unless she wants to be seen. They had seen her. Now to see if the Cougars took the hook—

Yeah.

Yeah, they were interested.

One of them was getting up and coming over to talk to her. He paused in front of her booth and leaned down, planting his hands in the middle of the table.

"Hey, gorgeous," he said. "You anti-social?"

"Who me?"

"Yeah, you," he said.

The fellow who was talking to her was big and pretty rugged-looking, with a strong face and high, sharp cheekbones. He had a little white scar on his cheek that began near his jaw and went up across one cheekbone. His black hair was swept back into a greasy d.a. style hairdo. He wore a shiny black leather jacket with a pair of olive-colored gloves thrust through the shoulder-loop. He leaned over a little further and said, "Well?"

"Well what?"

"How about coming over and joining us? Don't make like a lone cat."

Lora looked up at him and turned on the sex smile. It was the come-to-bed smile, the come-squeeze-my-knobs smile, the ain't-you-a-great-big-hunk-of-man smile. She said softly, "I'm a stranger around here, Daddy-o, and I ain't dumb. I don't go pushing myself in anyplace without invite."

"Well, I'm giving you an invite, doll! Come on over. We got room!"

"I won't be crowding you none?"

"For something like you we can always find room, baby. Come on."

"Okay," Lora said.

She grinned her secret smile triumph as she slid out from the booth. This was only the beginning, and they were already falling all over themselves to invite her to join them. She knew she had it made. In no time at all, she'd be in like Flynn with the Cougars, running the show the way she ran it when she was with the Scarlet Sinners.

She followed the big fellow back to where the others were sitting. The booth was the extra wide kind, holding three on each side of the table. There was one couple sitting on each side of the booth now. The big fellow who had invited her to join them sat down on one end, and Lora slipped in opposite him, putting her milkshake down in front of her.

Lora took a quick look at the other four in the booth, measuring them for size. The fellows were okay, nothing special worth noticing. One of them had a lot of yellow hair hanging in his eyes; the other one was thin and mean-looking. Lora chalked them off as second-raters in the Cougar hierarchy.

The girls weren't in her league at all, either. They were both pretty flat-chested, and both of them had plenty of pimples. One had long stringy red hair and the other had short frizzy black hair. The black-haired one had more bust than the redhead, but judging from how thin her arms were, Lora figured that there was mostly cotton in the brunette's bra. Lora knew when a girl was faking. She didn't need to fake, herself.

Lora grinned inwardly. She felt pretty good about things. If the rest of the Cougar debs were as chinchy-looking as these two, she wouldn't have any trouble at all moving into this gang and running things the way she wanted to.

She sipped her milkshake and waited for somebody else to start talking. After a couple of seconds the guy to her right, the yellow-haired one, said, "You new around here, huh?"

"Yeah," Lora said.

"Where you from?"

"East Bronx."

"There a gang there?"

"Scarlet Sinners," she said. "They're okay. I ran with them two years."

"What's your name?"

Lora took a coolly deliberate sip of her milkshake. Her voice was chilly as she answered, "You ask a hell of a lot of questions, don't you?"

The blonde boy scowled and shifted his weight. "I just wanta know your name."

"Lora," she said. "Lora Menotti." She shook her head, giving her jet-black hair a shake. She had long hair, and she was proud of it. Right now she had it in a pony-tail that dangled practically all the way to her buttocks. "You from the Cougars?" she asked.

"Yeah," said the boy who had invited her over to join them. "We're the Cougars."

She nodded. "So maybe you ought to tell me your names now, huh?"

"Call me Squirrel," said the fellow who invited her over, the one who was at the table stag. He pointed at the other two studs. "That's Marty," he said, indicating Yellowhair. "And that's Pug," he said, pointing to the ratty-looking one.

The girls' names were Claire—the redhead—and Dolores. Lora filed all the names away carefully in the back of her head. She didn't like to forget a name or anything else that might be useful. When you're making a play for the top rung, it helps to have a pretty damned good memory, Lora had discovered.

"Tell me something," Squirrel said, leaning across the table and speaking in a low voice. "You got a regular hookup?"

"I *had* one, in the Scarlet Sinners."

"Finished now?" Squirrel asked. His eyes were riveted on the twin jutting mounds of her bosom, thrusting stiffly out at him.

"Yeah. We broke it up because I was moving away. He was the President of the Scarlet Sinners."

"Yeah?"

"Name of Spook. Okay guy. But I couldn't ask a guy to cross enemy turf and travel for an hour just to come see me."

"So you ain't tied up now," Squirrel said, still eyeing her breasts avidly. There was a speculative glint in his eyes.

Lora didn't miss it. "No, I'm not tied up now. Why—you interested?"

Squirrel smiled strangely, without saying anything, and leaned back again. Grinning, the girl named Claire looked at him and said, "You better go talk to Mae before you start snooping around new debs, Squirrel."

Squirrel glared angrily at her. His face went pale and the thin white scar stood out. "Shut your stupid mouth, Claire."

Pugs's cold eyes glimmered. "You ain't talking to my deb that way, Squirrel."

"She asked for it, didn't she?" Squirrel shot back hotly. "Who tells her to go shooting her goddam mouth off about Mae, huh? If I want to bust things up with Mae, I'll bust up, and it's none of your goddam business in the first place."

Lora had watched the angry interchange with amusement. Now she decided it was time to cut in.

"Hold on a sec," she said slowly. "I didn't say I was interested in getting tied up with anybody right away, did I? I'm new around this place. I want to take my time about things. Find out what goes down here, first. Okay?"

"Nobody's rushing you," Squirrel said irritably.

"Good." Lora flashed the sex smile again, just to keep him encouraged. "Who's the Prez of the Cougars, somebody tell me."

"A guy named Whitey," Squirrel told her. "He oughta be here in half an hour or so."

"I'll bet she's gonna be interested in Whitey," Dolores said. "These new girls always come butting in and make a play for the top man."

Lora turned around to face the skinny girl. "You want your ears chopped off, honey?"

"I don't know what—"

"Seems to me you're making a lot of noise out of turn. Why don't you clam up?"

"Why you—"

"Hold it!" Squirrel snapped. "Hold down the noise, dammit!" He shook his head. "Jesus Christ. Let a new girl walk into the turf and all of a sudden the whole place is jumping. Look," he said more quietly to Lora. "Let me fill you in on the pitch, and don't hop to any quick conclusions."

"Shoot."

"Right now everybody in the Cougars is coupled off. We got eighteen guys, eighteen debs. You wanta move into the gang, fine. But if you come in, somebody else has gotta get bumped out. So you can expect plenty of trouble, girlie."

"I can handle myself okay," Lora said.

"Okay. Just so you know."

"Sure. But if it's so tight, why'd you invite me over?"

"Just to be friendly, like," Squirrel said. His eyes came to rest again just below her throat, on the big globes of her breasts. "I didn't say there wasn't no room for you. I just wanted to let you know that you've gotta make room for yourself."

"I get the pitch," Lora said. "Okay. Okay."

After that, the talk at the table died down for awhile. Lora concentrated on finishing up her milkshake. She could see that her presence was being felt in the Cougar rank already.

They were all coupled off, eh? So she was going to have to push somebody aside. She'd done it before, and she wasn't worried about doing it again.

She remembered how she had come up the ranks in the Scarlet Sinners. The Sinners were a big gang, fifty or sixty members. They were divided into two sections, the Big People and the Little People. The Little People were the guys under fourteen and the older guys who didn't get around so fast. Lora had started out Little People when she was around thirteen, but then her breasts started to sprout, and she knew she was heading for the top. Not too many of the older guys in the gang noticed her then, even though she was developing fast. She had lost her cherry when she was twelve, but most of the older guys in the gang didn't like to make time with the Little People. So Lora laid for some of the other kids in the gang, but that was all.

Then when she was fourteen she decided it was time to move up to the senior division of the gang. She got her break when Johnny Diablo's girl Lola got knocked up. She went into a back alley to have the baby and she died from blood poisoning. Johnny Diablo was looking around for a new deb. He was the War Counselor of the Scarlet Sinners, the Number Three man—short and wiry, quick with a switchblade.

She walked into the clubhouse one day when Johnny Diablo was alone. Johnny was pretty moody after Lola died. He was sitting by himself with a jug of sneaky pete, and Lora walked up to him.

"Hi, Johnny."

"H'lo." Johnny knew her only in passing; he didn't have much to do with the junior members of the Scarlet Sinners.

"Still mooning about Lola?" she asked.

Johnny's face darkened. "Listen, kid, how come you're bothering me?"

"Got something to show you," she said.

"What?"

"These," Lora said. She put her hands to her collar and unbuttoned her shirt. She wasn't wearing any bra underneath. The shirt fell open and her young breasts were bared, firm and round and tender, with the nipples standing up stiffly like little towers on the high curved hemispheres.

Johnny's jaw dropped. His dead girl had had a big pair, and everybody knew he liked them that way. But he had never noticed Lora.

"Christ," he whispered. "All this time I thought you were stuffing your bra."

"They're real, Johnny. Take hold and squeeze, if you don't think so."

He had come forward, hands outstretched to cup her breasts, and she had flattened herself up against him and for an hour they made wild love, and that night it was announced in the clubhouse that Lora Menotti was Big People from now on, that she was Johnny Diablo's new deb. That had been the beginning of her rise. She had made it with Johnny for almost a year, till he got sent to reformatory for slashing a cop. It was no trouble at all for her to elbow right up to the Number One spot then, and become the deb of Geronimo, the President. And when Geronimo got cooled off in the rumble with the Huns and Spook became top man of the gang, she shifted over and became Spook's deb, making him drop the girl he'd had.

Now she had to start all over. But she was sixteen, not fourteen, and she was crafty. She knew she'd get where she wanted to go.

This Squirrel looked okay, she thought. He was big and strong and he wasn't bad-looking. Right now he was making it with some deb named Mae, but Lora knew it wouldn't be any sweat at all to cut into that situation. Well, no sense jumping into anything too fast, she decided. Might as well wait and see the whole gang before making a move. That was the cool way to play it. Wait and see.

CHAPTER THREE

Lora bided her time. Marty put a coin in the jukebox to keep it going, and he and Dolores started to dance. They were dancing the fish—just standing pressed tight against each other, chest to chest, belly to belly, thighs to thighs, rhythmically grinding their hips in beat with the music. Lora recalled how she and Spook had been real good at the fish. They would dance it for half an hour at a stretch, until they were both so heated up that Spook would drag her into one of the little rooms at the back of the clubhouse, and they would rip off their clothes in a mutual frenzy of desire.

But right now Lora was not interested in dancing. Squirrel looked at her and jerked his head toward the dance area, but she shook him off with an almost invisible sidewise motion of her head, and remained sitting where she was.

After about twenty minutes had gone by, the door opened and some more Cougars came in, each of them accompanied by his deb. Leading the rest of the group was a short, dark-eyed boy with a hard face and the blondest hair Lora had ever seen. His hair was so yellow it looked practically white. He came in with a girl who was a little taller than he was—a big-breasted girl in a soft, fuzzy sweater. She looked untidy and sullen. Lora thought quietly that there were all kinds of figures. Some girls with big breasts just looked like cows, the way this one did. Others stopped traffic. There were all kinds.

Three other couples followed the short boy in. He came immediately over to the table in back where Lora was sitting. Squirrel turned and gave him a big smile.

"Hi, Whitey," Squirrel said.

Whitey ignored the greeting, not even bothering to acknowledge it with a nod. He looked straight at Lora. His eyes were flinty and piercing, digging right through her sweater like a dentist's drill.

"Who's this?" he asked.

Lora met his glance evenly. "The name is Lora Menotti," she said. "I'm new to Cougar turf. Squirrel invited me over to sit here."

Whitey laughed harshly. "Invited you, huh? He wouldn't pull a stunt like that if Mae was around. Huh, Squirrel? Wouldya?"

Lora saw the black anger rise suddenly in Squirrel's face. But the big boy throttled it back with an effort. Squirrel seemed afraid of Whitey, even though he was half a foot taller than the gang leader. Everyone in the place seemed afraid of Whitey. You could sense it in the air, from the way they gave him anxious little smiles, from the way they made him the center of the stage. Whitey was holding court.

But there was one person in the room who wasn't afraid of Whitey. Lora looked up at him boldly and said, "I told you my name. Now who are you?"

Whitey seemed amused by her outspokenness. "I'm the Prez of the Cougars. Whitey. You going to move in on our turf, Menotti?"

Lora nodded. "My folks just moved here. Down from the Bronx."

"That's interesting."

"I ran with the Scarlet Sinners up there. You know them?"

"I've heard," Whitey said. "An okay outfit."

"I'd like to become a Cougar deb," Lora said.

Whitey grinned at her in cold appraisal. "We gotta think about that for a while."

"You know there ain't no room for no more debs in the gang, Whitey," said the plump, sloppy-looking girl who had come in with him.

Fire flared in the sawed-off gang leader's eyes. He snapped, "Since when are you running the show around here, Donna?"

"I only said—"

Whitey went tense, and his fist balled. He looked like a cobra about to strike. "Shut up, you hear me, Donna?"

"But—"

"Shut your blubbery yap!"

The fist-hand trembled as if about to break loose. Donna closed her mouth tight, in a hurry. Whitey relaxed, and said to Lora, "I'll think about it, Lora. That okay?"

"Yeah," she said. "You think about it, Whitey." She gave him a slow smile, the smile with all the stops pulled out, the smile that said *I'm yours any-time you want me,* and gave him a wink. The shadow of a smile crossed Whitey's face. Lora knew she wasn't going to have any troubles at all making Whitey do what she wanted him to do.

The door opened again, and a couple more Cougars came in, one and two at a time, until the candy store was full of them. Lora recognized the two lookouts from across the street; they walked in, nudged each other as they saw Lora, and tapped two fellows to go outside and replace them.

The place was pretty full now. The jukebox kept going steadily, and there were six or seven couples out on the dance floor all the time. Squirrel asked her to dance again, and this time she accepted. Whitey was dancing with his cow Donna, and Lora knew she could move in on that situation any time she pleased. So it was safe to dance with Squirrel.

They moved out onto the floor and for a few seconds they did an ordi-nary rhumba, but after a couple of steps Squirrel pulled her up close to dance the fish with her. She didn't object. They planted their feet and locked arms around each other's waists, and began to move their hips, belly against belly. Despite the fast tempo of the music behind them, they moved slowly, maintaining a relation to the beat but picking it up at their own private tempo. Lora rubbed her breasts against Squirrel's shirt, and felt him quiver a little in pleasure. It took her only a moment of expert writhing to arouse him to full desire. His hands slipped down over her belt, curving into the back pockets of her jeans. His powerful fingers dug into the flesh of her buttocks, separated from him only by a few layers of cloth.

Out of the corner of her eye she caught sight of Whitey dancing with Donna. But Whitey's mind wasn't on Donna. Whitey was watching *her.* Lora pressed herself even more tightly against Squirrel. There wasn't any quicker way to get Whitey interested than to make him jealous of Squirrel.

But it wasn't smart to overdo it, right at the beginning. When the record ended, Lora smiled politely at Squirrel and made her way back to the booth. Squirrel started for her, but then the door opened and another girl came in. Somebody nudged Squirrel and he turned around.

"Hi, Mae," he said reluctantly.

Lora's eyes narrowed as she studied the newcomer. Squirrel's deb wasn't a bad looker at all, she decided objectively. She was pretty tall, maybe five-seven or even five-eight, and she had a kind of innocent choir-girl face that probably didn't belong to her personality. Like most tall, lean girls she was on the skimpy side in the bosom department—her breasts were small and pointy against her sweater— but she moved with a sexy grace that made up for it.

Mae and Squirrel started to dance. Sitting by herself, Lora took stock of things.

This Cougar outfit looked like a pretty tight little establishment. It was smaller by far than the Scarlet Sinners, though. The Scarlet Sinners had been a full-sized gang, with close to sixty members at its biggest. It was big because it was an old gang, going back close to fifteen years. It had a junior division and a senior division, plus an alumni group of guys in their twenties and thirties who still took an interest in the gang without actually running with them. The alumni—some of them big-time mobsters now—helped out with cash or knives or bail when things got tough.

But the Cougars seemed newer and more compact. Squirrel had said there were eighteen couples. Lora counted about a dozen couples on the dance floor; there were a pair of lookouts on the corner, and the rest were probably either sick, in jail, or out looking for some kicks. There didn't seem to be any junior division. Everybody in the room looked to be at least fifteen, and a couple of the fellows seemed to be nineteen or twenty or maybe even older.

A compact outfit like this had a lot of inner loyalty, Lora knew. It was going to be a challenge to move in and take this outfit over, put herself in the position of number one woman. She wasn't worried, but she knew it was going to take some complicated maneuvering. The first thing, though, was to catch hold of Whitey. Start right at the top. Judging from the way he had grinned at her after the wink, and the way he had looked at her on the dance floor, it wasn't going to be very hard to bring Whitey to heel.

The afternoon moved along. It was half past five, now, and Lora was getting hungry. It was close to time to go home and get herself a feed. A couple of the other Cougars apparently had the same idea, because the crowd was starting to thin out.

Marty was sitting next to her. Lora said, "What generally goes here in the evenings?"

The blonde boy said, "We stick around here till Sid closes. That's eight-nine o'clock, tonight. Some nights he's open to midnight."

"Where do you go then?"

"The clubhouse," Marty said.

Lora nodded and got up out of the booth. "See you later," she said.

She headed toward the door. Whitey, who had been dancing with Donna, abandoned the plump girl unceremoniously and came over to Lora.

"Where you going?" he asked.

"Supper."

"They expecting you?"

"I told them I'd be home. I don't want to make a fuss with them the first day."

Whitey's jaw-muscles tensed. "You coming back here later?"

"You want me to?"

"You come back, hear? We're gonna be here till around half past eight. Then we go to the clubhouse for a party."

"That an invitation?"

"Suit yourself," Whitey said.

"I'll be back here by seven-thirty," Lora told him.

"See you," Whitey said.

"Yeah. See you."

Lora stepped out of the candy store, away from the blaring jukebox into the different blare of the street. It was getting chilly, and the sky was overcast, a sign of the winter moving toward them. She began to walk up Fourth Street toward the project. On the other corner of Avenue C, a young cop stood by the lamppost, twirling his nightstick. He gave Lora a good looking. She looked back, and walked on.

You couldn't tell about the fuzz, she thought. Most likely the cop was just sizing her up as somebody new in the neighborhood, a potential trouble-maker who had to be watched. But his eyes had lingered just a little too long on the fullness of her breasts and on the tight crotch of her blue jeans. Some of these young cops didn't mind tearing off a piece sometimes themselves, on the back stairs of some old brownstone house where nobody was likely to come looking. And in return for that they sometimes let the gang get away with a few things.

It was just around six when she reached her apartment. The warm smells of roasting meat and vegetables met her in the foyer. The place looked almost livable, now; the drapes were up, and many of the cartons had been unpacked. Nobody spoke to Lora as she came in. Her brother and her father were hammering something to one of the closet walls, while her mother was busy with pots and pans in the kitchen.

Dinner was equally silent. Nobody asked Lora where she had been during the day, nobody asked her how she had spent her afternoon. Nor did she begin any topics of conversation herself. For years, it had been this way. She was a stranger in her own family, somebody who could not be turned away but yet who could not be met with love either.

After dinner, she washed up, took a jacket from the closet, and started for the door.

"I'm going out," she said.

Her father looked at her helplessly. He was a thin, worn-out man, bewildered by his daughter's savagery. "Can't you stay home even on your first night in the new place?" he asked mildly.

"I'm going out," Lora repeated.

"Tomorrow's school again," her mother warned her. "Don't stay out late."

"I'll be back by eleven," she said. "Or maybe eleven thirty. See you."

She went out, slamming the door behind her.

When she reached Sid's, ten minutes later, she saw that the scene had not changed much. There were still two lookouts in front, watching for any possible invasion of the turf. Down here where the gangs were small, you could expect trouble from almost any side, from any one of three or four gangs. The Scarlet Sinners had had only one really serious regular enemy, the Huns, a Puerto Rican gang. But you had to look sharp down here or somebody would jap you.

She went in. The crowd had thinned out some; a few of the Cougars had already filtered out and gone over to the clubhouse, it seemed. But there were still some dancers. Whitey and Squirrel were still there. Whitey came over to her as she walked in.

"Dance?"

"Sure."

She had a quick dance with Whitey—not a fish, but a fast, wild dance.

He seemed to have tremendous inner resources of energy. Lora stuck with him, her breasts bobbing gaily as she gyrated at the end of Whitey's leash. After the music stopped, she noticed Donna standing in one corner, fuming like a left-out wife. And when she danced with Squirrel next, it was Mae's turn to stand around with her arms folded.

Lora knew she was stirring up the Cougar debs plenty. And that two or three of the Cougars were interested in giving her the real big play. But she had looked them over, and she was interested in only one man in the outfit.

The top man.

After a little while, Sid started making signs to indicate that he wanted to close up and go home. The Cougars started to clear out, until only about half a dozen of them remained in the candy store. Both Whitey and Squirrel stayed.

But Squirrel left, finally, taking Mae with him, leaving only Whitey, Donna, and Lora in the store. Whitey said to Donna casually, "Why don't you go on ahead. I'll meet you in the clubhouse in a couple of minutes, Donna, hear me?"

Donna looked hesitant. She knew she was in trouble. "Why don't you come now?"

Whitey's eyes became ugly, and his lower lip drew back as though he were going to snarl. "Run along, I said," he muttered quietly. *"Run along!"*

Donna nodded, quick-quick, and scuttled out of the candy store. She was scared of Whitey, you could see that. Scared green.

Now there was nobody in the place but Whitey and Lora and the proprietor. The jukebox had run out of fuel, and was quiet for once. Sid was busy mopping up the soda counter. He kept his nose out of what didn't concern him, like any smart soda-jerk who doesn't want his place busted up and his head kicked in by gang stompers. His elaborate unconcern was something he had picked up in a long career of operating the store in a slum neighborhood where tough kids abounded.

"You wanta shake it a little?" Whitey asked. "We got some time."

Lora shrugged. "Suits me."

Whitey walked over to the juke, fished a coin out of his jeans, and dumped it in. A moment later, the music started up. It wasn't rock-'n-roll this time, but a tender, reflective kind of melody, not the sort of thing Whitey might be expected to pick. The gang leader took her by the hand and led her out into the open space used for dancing.

She melted up against him, cheek to cheek, thigh to thigh. He was very short, about five feet five—exactly Lora's own height. She filed that fact away for future reference. She was pretty certain that the easiest way to bug Whitey would be to make a crack about his height.

As they moved slowly around the floor, covering an area no more than a yard in diameter, bodies pressed tightly together, hips grinding sensuously, Whitey brought his hand up from her waist and, passing it over her shoulders, slipped it between their bodies. It came to rest cupping one of her breasts. Lora made no attempt to remove the exploratory hand. Instead, she hardened the chest muscle, pushing the breast out against his palm. She felt the slow stirring of desire inside her. It would be swell to make it with Whitey, she thought. He crackled like dynamite.

"Mm. Nice," Whitey whispered. "Nice-o."

"You like?"

"You bet!"

"And it's real, all mine," Lora said, grinning at him. "No rubber, no cotton."

He tightened his grip, and his fingers tried to feel the hard little nipple beneath the cloth. "Can you prove it's all real?"

"Maybe."

"What do you mean, maybe?"

"For the right guy, I prove it."

"Am I the right guy?"

"Maybe."

"Cut the *maybe* crap," Whitey said. His hand slid lower, forcing itself down over the flat hardness of her belly, going around her hips to her buttocks. Lora wriggled in anticipation.

"Okay," she said. "Let's go someplace where we can be alone. I'll prove what I got is a hundred percent genuine."

The dance drifted to its finish. Sid looked up at them quizzically from behind his counter, not saying anything, just trying to tell them silently that if they would leave he could close up his store and go home.

As they separated, Lora said, "Another one?"

"Nah," Whitey said. "This is Sid's early night, and he's giving us the hints. Let's check out of here. I'll take you over to the clubhouse, give you a little look around the place. Okay?"

Lora smiled enticingly. "You got someplace there where we can be alone?"

He patted her buttocks in affectionate token that he was about to take possession. "I can arrange it, kiddo. Leave it to Whitey. Whitey can arrange anything around here."

CHAPTER FOUR

Night had fallen, and a nearly full moon hung overhead, white and swollen. A light sprinkling of stars could be seen—only the very brightest ones, since the rest were always blotted out by the city haze and the lights of the buildings.

Lora and Whitey walked close together, but he did not put his arm around her. They said practically nothing. He set a brisk pace and she followed at his side—down to Second Street, then over one block. The clubhouse of the Cougars was three and a half blocks from the candy store.

"Here," Whitey muttered. "This is the place, right here."

The clubhouse was a big, sprawling basement apartment in a rundown tenement building. Whitey led Lora through darkened passageways that smelled of stale garbage until they reached the clubhouse door. A single bare lightbulb illuminated the hallway.

With self-important deliberation, Whitey produced a key and guided it into the lock. Lora could hear the sounds of dance music coming through the door. He turned the key and pushed the door open, letting Lora through and closing the door quickly behind him.

Inside, the place was brightly lit. It was furnished with cheap tables and chairs and battered armchairs and sofas that looked like they had been bought from the Salvation Army, and probably had been. A portable phonograph mounted on one table was turning out the sound.

Some of the Cougars were dancing "fishing." Squirrel and Mae, Marty and Dolores among them. Dolores was standing with her back against the wall, and Marty was shoving hard against her. They ground their hips rhythmically. Their mouths were joined in a kiss that had probably been going on fifteen minutes.

Some of the others turned to stare as Whitey and Lora entered the clubhouse. A few of the dancing couples were too far gone in their own private rapture to have paid any attention, but the rest looked. Lora met the stares blandly and without embarrassment. *Let them look,* she thought. *Let 'em take a good look.*

One of the ones who turned to stare at the newcomers was the hefty, untidy-looking girl named Donna, who was Whitey's deb at the moment. Her pasty face was chalk-white and her thick lips were quivering in anger and fear. Donna knew the score, that was for certain. Right now Donna was probably deciding whether to bluff things out or just to give up and be resigned to her fate.

Whitey gestured irritably at the gapers. "Okay, go on dancing," he told them. "Don't stop and make a fuss. There ain't nothing to make a fuss about!"

Obediently, several of the couples began dancing again, moving against one another in the slow erotic motions of the "fish." But Donna had evidently made up her mind to put up a fight. She hesitated one moment more, and then came stamping heavily across to where Whitey and Lora stood at the door.

"What the crap did you bring that little tramp back here for?" Donna demanded.

Whitey glowered at her, and the muscles in his cheeks bunched up in fury. "I brought her in to show her the clubhouse," he said in a flat, level, deadly voice. "You mind?"

"Yeah, I do mind," Donna retorted.

Whitey raised his voice only a little, to show that he was starting to burn and getting ready to explode. "Who the hell are you to tell me what to do?"

"I'm your deb, ain't I?"

There was a momentary pause. Then Whitey said in a cold voice, "You used to be."

Lora felt a wild surge of triumph at the words Whitey had spoken.

"*Used* to be?" Donna screamed. "You mean you're giving me the boot for this two-bit floozie?"

"Yeah," Whitey said.

Donna's face worked convulsively. Suddenly her anger and hatred became uncontrollable, and she rushed forward toward Lora, her hands bent into curved talons, her fingernails high.

Lora sidestepped the fierce advance. Whitey reached out, grabbing Donna's arm and swinging her around, and Lora, recovering her balance, joined the attack as well. She grabbed hold of the front of Donna's sweater, bunching the cloth up tight, and ripped. At the same moment Whitey slammed a backhand blow across Donna's face.

The sweater come ripping away, Lora hanging onto the flap and yanking. Whitey stepped back, and Lora pulled the final shred of cloth away and clawed at Donna's bra. Snaps popped; the brassiere ripped hissingly and fell, and Donna's heavy, swinging breasts, sweat-flecked and fat, came into view. Donna threw one arm across her nipples, trying to shield herself, but before she covered herself Lora saw a startling sight: the initials W. B. carved into the white skin of Donna's fleshy right breast. Whitey's initials! It was a gang custom Lora had heard about, this marking of a woman, but the Scarlet Sinners had never practiced it.

Donna glanced wildly around. She spat at Whitey, who slapped her again. The force of the blow sent the big girl spinning back against the wall. Whitey moved in, planning to hit her again, but Lora elbowed her way past him and faced Donna herself. Lora's hand flicked out, and her sharp nails drew bloody lines along the heavy swell of Donna's bare breast. Donna cowered against the wall. She aimed a punch at Lora, but it went wild, and Lora retaliated with a savage kick to the other girl's crotch.

Donna dropped to her knees, against the wall, one hand gripping her loins to protect them against another kick. Her swaying breasts were dripping blood and sweat, and she was close to hysteria. Her eyes radiated mixed hatred and yellow terror.

Lora stepped back, knowing that her triumph was complete. Whitey advanced now, a small but powerful figure, looking down in scorn at the shaking, fearful Donna.

Donna put up one hand, shielding her face. "D-don't hit me, Whitey—"

"Get out of here," he said in a low, flat tone. "Pack up and scram."

Donna's lips trembled. "So I'm all through, huh? Just like that."

"You heard me. It's finished. Scoot!"

Cautiously, Donna rose, folding her left arm across the front of her body to conceal the fleshy swells of her bosom. She snatched up the tattered sweater and wrapped it ineffectually around her. Looking around at Lora, she muttered a bitter curse, and scuttled toward the door before Lora could react.

The door closed. Donna was gone.

The clubhouse was terribly silent. No one was dancing. The record had come to its end, but nobody had bothered to change it, and the needle, stuck in the last groove, was making an endless, monotonous *thunkety-thunk-thunk* sound.

Whitey shattered the silence by barking, "What the hell are you all staring at? Go on, dance! Don't mess in my business!"

His face an impartial mask, Squirrel lifted the needle from the groove, removed the record, put another disk on the turntable. Wild dance music swelled up in the clubhouse, and the dancing resumed.

Whitey said to Lora, "Let's go get a drink."

"Sure thing."

He picked up a gallon jug and filled two drinking-glasses. Lora took a sip. It was half-and-half: a fifty-fifty mixture of cheap wine and cheap whiskey. They drank a lot of it around the Scarlet Sinners, when they could afford the whiskey. The rest of the time they got along on straight sneaky pete, at 69c for a gallon jug.

Whitey grinned up over his glass. "We sure showed that Donna."

"Let's not talk about her. She's finished around here, isn't she?"

"She won't ever show her fat butt around here again." Whitey's arm slid possessively around Lora's hips. "I got me a new deb now. Huh, Lora?"

"You bet."

"Let's celebrate. Let's bust a joint, you and me. You use?"

"Just reefers," Lora said. "I stay off the hard stuff."

"Me too," Whitey grinned. "We got a couple horseheads around here. That Bozo, over there, he's a real junkie. But that's the dumb way. Me, I just bust a joint every so often. Hey, *Bozo!*"

A big, sleepy-eyed boy looked up out of the corner. "Yeah, Whitey?"

"Over here, huh?"

Bozo ambled over. Whitey stared up—Bozo was almost a foot taller— and said, "Me and Lora, we're gonna make it together. We wanta celebrate. You got any M on you, Bozo?"

"I'm carrying, yeah."

"Make with a coupla joints like a good fellow, will you?" Whitey said.

"Sure," Bozo said nervously. "Sure. Here. How many you want?"

"One apiece's enough," Whitey told him. "We ain't pigs."

Bozo reached into his shirt pocket and produced a wrinkled Lucky Strike wrapper, and shook it so the cigarette ends protruded. The cigarettes that stuck out weren't any that had ever seen the inside of the Luckies factory. They were uneven and lopsided-looking, and the paper they were rolled in was a dingy brown. Whitey selected two of the reefers and dismissed Bozo.

He held one reefer out to Lora. "Now?" he asked.

She shook her head. "Not now. Afterwards. When we got something *real* to celebrate."

Whitey smiled knowingly. "Yeah, yeah, I get you. Afterward." He put the reefers into his shirt pocket and buttoned the flap.

Lora held out her hands, and they began to dance, undulating slowly. She didn't want to smoke the reefer until after she and Whitey had been to bed. When you busted a joint, it took the edge off your sex drive. She didn't want to do that. She wanted to meet Whitey at the top of her form. They could go knitting off to dreamland afterward....

Lora had been thirteen when she first made the acquaintance of marijuana. One of the Scarlet Sinners alumni was a pusher, and when he came around to supply the gang's few heroin addicts with junk he sometimes handed out reefers, on the house. Once he had handed one to Lora. She liked the effect, the way it made her cut loose and go soaring, but she had never caught the habit. She was too brainy for that. She smoked maybe one or two a month, no more, and she stayed completely away from H and C. She didn't want any monkeys on *her* back. She had seen the way the older girls lived when they got on the heroin kick. They had to have fifteen or twenty bucks a day to pay the pusher, some of them more. There was only one way that a girl of seventeen or eighteen could make that kind of money. So they went out on the street, wearing blue jeans with nothing under them, and when they found a guy who was willing to pay they went into the dark alleys, and down came the jeans, and open went the legs. Two or three minutes of quick action and you collected two or three bucks, and if you could find seven or eight customers a day you had enough to pay the pusher.

Of course, there were risks. You stood a good chance of clap or syph or getting knocked up, or of getting nailed by the cops, or of just getting your head kicked in by a slap-happy client. And the pusher was always around, squeezing more and more out of you, while the H ate you away and turned you into a walking skeleton.

Lora had eyes and she had brains, so she didn't get mixed up with the pushers who were always hanging around the turf. But she didn't mind a reefer every now and then, every once in a while....

She squeezed up tight against Whitey, moving her hips rhythmically, feeling through her jeans his tense aroused maleness. As the wine and whiskey worked toward her head, she danced more and more torridly. Whitey had his hands under the front of her sweater now, clasping the outside of her bra. His mouth was against hers, and his tongue pushed its way between her lips, exploring her cheeks.

After a while she said, "Remember, I promised to prove something to you."

"Yeah. Yeah."

"I'm in the mood. Let's go somewhere and I'll do the proving."

"Come on," Whitey said. "Come on with me."

He took her by the hand and led her through the crowded room, around one glued-together couple and over another that had fallen into a deep embrace on the floor. They left the big room and walked down a long corridor to a room at the very end of the strung-out apartment. Lora followed him in. Whitey shut the door and slammed shut a bolt on the inside of the door.

"This room belongs to the Prez of the Cougars," Whitey explained. "Which is me. So nobody else uses this room."

Lora looked around. There were trophies on a bookshelf against the wall: lead-filled billy-clubs, lengths of chain, things like that. Standing against one wall was a souped-up air-rifle.

"We got all that stuff from other gangs," Whitey said proudly. "I took a lot of it away myself. The billy used to belong to the War Counselor of the Snakes. Big black son-of-a-bitch he was. He started to bring that big billy down on my head, and I got out of the way and cut his arm up with my shiv. He dropped the billy and ran for all he was worth." Whitey hefted the weighted club, bringing it down with a smart *crack!* against his open left palm. Then, tossing it back onto the shelf, he seemed to remember why he had come to the room.

There was a rickety old bed in the middle of the floor, an iron frame and a stained mattress covered by a single crumpled sheet. Whitey stood by the side of the bed with his arms folded.

"Take your sweater off," Whitey commanded.

Smiling, Lora obeyed, tossing the discarded garment into a trophy shelf.

"Now the bra," Whitey said.

She unhooked the bra without a moment of doubt or embarrassment and let it fall. Her breasts rose proudly, and the nipples were already going stiff with desire. Whitey nodded, eyeing the ripe melons of her breasts as though he were buying her at auction. Finally he said in a satisfied voice, "You weren't funning me. It was all real."

"I said I'd prove it."

"All real."

"Sure it's real, Whitey. And all yours, too."

"I like the way you say that. Now show me the rest of the stuff."

Lora gave him the bedroom smile. She was wearing a pair of man-style dungarees, with fly front. She unzipped the fly, and pulled the tight jeans down over her hips. It was a tough struggle. She kicked them off and started to remove her gauzy white panties.

"Don't," Whitey said. "I'll take 'em off myself."

He came toward her and put his hands on her bare breasts. His hands were cold, and sent little chills through her. Slowly, he drew his hands lower, down her chest, over the lean tautness of her belly. He hooked his fingers into the elastic waistband of her panties and rolled them down, past her navel, past the ebony triangle of womanhood, past the soft thighs and wide hips, past her knees and over her ankles. He knelt and rose, putting his lips to her and circling the swelling globe of her buttocks with tense fingers.

Then he rose and stepped back.

"Undress me now," he ordered.

She opened his shirt and took it off, unbuckled his belt, unzipped him, pulled all his clothes off. He was ready for making love. His body was squat and muscular, looking like the body of a tall man who had been somehow sawed off below the knee. He was enormously broad through the shoulders, and his arms were corded and knotted with muscle.

He grabbed her, and their bodies came together, his cold, hard one, her warmer, softer body. Then he tugged her down on the bed.

"I ain't using anything," he told her. "I don't. Not ever."

"That's okay," Lora whispered. "You do it the way you like it best."

They didn't waste time on preliminaries. They were both fully aroused. Their lips met, and then suddenly she squirmed and pulled her body around so it was underneath his, and his arms were gripping her tight, like steel bands, and her legs parted. She clasped them tight around his muscular buttocks, and there was a quick thrust and their bodies were joined, and she looked up and saw his face, a cold, killer's face, the kind of face she liked to see above her when she was making it.

Making it with Whitey was like making it with a wild stallion. He bucked and wheeled and writhed, and every motion sent an unbelievable thrill of delight through her. Lora closed her eyes and drew back her lips, and a little animal groan of ecstasy burst from her as she felt herself coming to a climax. She gasped and moaned, and Whitey gripped her swollen breasts tight and rode out the storm, and when it was over he was still riding her, and she opened her eyes and smiled and he smiled back, and then they were going again.

And again... and again... and suddenly she heard Whitey draw his breath in, making an odd scooping sound, and his hands became claws that dug into her shoulders, and for one moment he moved with uncontrollable wildness and then she heard him sob and the world stood still as he shuddered violently five times and went limp in her arms.

"Christ," he muttered hoarsely. "Christ, but I ain't never had it like that before!"

"I'm okay, huh, Whitey?"

"You're okay. Yeah."

They lay together while the thunder receded, while their exhausted bodies returned to normal. Finally Whitey left the bed and padded across to his shirt. He took out the two reefers and a pack of matches.

"Here," he said. "Let's celebrate."

"I'm with you, man."

She took the cigarette from him and put it in her mouth, and he struck a match and lit first her reefer and then his. Lora knew all about smoking M. You had to draw and draw hard, pull it all into your lungs in one long suck, because the reefer burned fast and was gone before you knew it. She dragged, pulling the harsh, sickly-sweet smoke down into her throat, sucking the reefer until it was a burning coal. She tossed the last ember to the floor and flopped back onto the bed, and Whitey was next to her with his cold hand making a cup for her breast, and the ceiling began to spin, and Lora let out a wild gale of laughter as the M took hold and swept her way out into the distant galaxies, and it was the real kick, really the most, to be lying here in her skin with this hard little man next to her, lying here and floating to the stars all at the same time, and plenty more kicks where these came from....

CHAPTER FIVE

Perhaps half an hour later, she started coming back to Earth. She opened her eyes and saw Whitey leaning against the headboard, his legs crossed, his hands behind his head. He was grinning.

"Well?" he said.

"That was the greatest."

"Want to bust another one?"

She shook her head. She still had the marijuana-taste in her mouth, sweet and rough. "One's enough for me. One at a time."

"Okay," he said. He put his hands on her shoulders and drew them quickly across her breasts. "One at a time." He rolled lithely off the bed and began putting on his clothes. The reefer had done its work; he wasn't interested in taking another tumble in the hay with her right now.

Slowly, Lora dressed, pulling on the bra and panties, slipping the sweater over her head, zipping up the fly-front dungarees. She still felt loose and dreamy from the reefer. And she felt the man-imprint, the lust-imprint on her body, the warm masculine smell.

Whitey opened the bolt and they left the room, going back down the hall to the big room. The phonograph was still blaring. A couple of the smaller rooms along the narrow hallway had their doors closed, and Lora figured that the rooms were in use. That was the way most clubhouse evenings had ended up in the Scarlet Sinners, with everybody loving like crazy, and it wasn't surprising to find the same thing here. Nobody in a gang ever had to worry much about sex. You got all you wanted.

Heads turned and nodded as Whitey and Lora walked into the room. Nobody in the Cougars needed to be told about the new set-up that had been established. It was perfectly obvious to everybody. Donna had been given the boot, and Lora, the new girl in the gang, had gone straight to the top in one seven-league leap. She was Whitey's deb, now. She made it with the Prez.

Whitey circulated, laughing it up, slapping backs and pouring drinks. They smiled back at him, no matter how they felt about the treatment Donna had received. A deb could get kicked out of a gang just that unceremoniously any time. Everyone in the Cougars was trying hard to forget the nasty scene that had taken place earlier. So far as they were concerned, Donna had never existed, had never been a Cougar, and Lora had always been Whitey's deb. Anyone who thought otherwise and happened to let his thoughts be known was asking for big trouble at Whitey's hands.

Lora poured another glassful of half-and-half and drank it slowly. She didn't need the drink—the reefer and the session in bed had left her without any tensions that a drink would ease—but it made her feel even more relaxed to have something she could hold in her hand. She felt pleased with herself. In just one eventful day, she had been able to work her way into the Cougars—and to push her way right to the top.

It was a good day's work.

But, thought Lora, she wasn't through yet. She smiled inwardly. She wasn't satisfied just by being Whitey's deb. Judging by the way he had treated Donna, Whitey thought of a deb as just someone to keep him warm in bed and to be tossed away like an old shoe when something better came along. Lora wasn't going to put up with any such status. She wouldn't be satisfied until she had demonstrated that she was the real power in the Cougars, who made all the others sit up and take notice. She was going to be Whitey's boss, not his slave and concubine.

It had been that way in the Scarlet Sinners, she remembered. First with Johnny Diablo, then with Geronimo, then finally with Spook. Oh, they had *thought* they were running things, but they weren't. Not at all. Lora had pulled the puppet-strings from behind the scenes. She had worked up rumbles, she had created and resolved little frictions in the gang, she had shaped and guided gang policy. Johnny Diablo and Geronimo and Spook had spoken the words, but Lora had put them in their mouths herself.

That was going to be the way it would be with Whitey and the Cougars, Lora thought. Whether Whitey liked it or not.

She walked over to him. He was standing in the corner with Squirrel and one of the other gang boys, who was called Conch. Conch was showing them a knife he had just bought—not a switchblade, but the newest kind, a gravity knife. The shank came out with a twist of the wrist, and snapped into place. Conch was demonstrating—whipping the harmless butt out of his pocket, snapping his wrist to bring the blade sliding out. Whitey was watching with keen interest.

Lora said, "I'm skiing out."

"Wait a while."

"It's eleven o'clock," she said. "I gotta get home. I'm playing it cool, these first couple of days here."

"Another half hour," Whitey said.

"Now. You gonna walk me?"

Whitey glanced at her in surprise. But his eyes narrowed and clouded, and the surprise went away. "You afraid of going back alone?"

She shrugged. "I'm new here. I don't know who's who. You want me to get japped?"

"Nobody would—"

"Walk me, Whitey," she said wheedlingly.

The halfpint gang leader hesitated a moment. Then he said, "Okay. Okay." He looked around. "Pug! Conch! Come on with me. I'm takin' Lora home."

The four of them left the clubhouse together—Whitey and Lora up ahead, Conch and Pug trailing behind as a bodyguard. Even Whitey didn't want to walk around the streets alone late at night. You never could be sure who was hiding in the dark alleyways, crouched down behind the garbage can. Some stud from another gang could win plenty of prestige if he could brag that he had slipped into Cougar turf and japped the famous Whitey. So Conch and Pug went along, just in case.

Whitey's arm was tight around Lora's waist, with his fingers thrust into her back pocket. But he was tense, ready to break loose and defend himself. In the jungle of the night streets, you didn't ever relax your guard, not if you wanted to live to see the next morning.

They came to the entrance to the project. The towering buildings loomed up beyond the wall like giant beacon towers.

Whitey said, "This is far enough."

"Yeah. I can manage it the rest of the way myself, Whitey."

He took her and they spun around inside the wall, standing in the shadows, and he grabbed her tight when they were hidden from view. He thrust his body up against hers, and his hands seized her breasts so hard she became dizzy. He thrust his leg between her thighs and they kissed goodnight, up against that wall, tongues meeting, lips hard and tight. It was a savage goodnight, an animal goodnight.

And then he was gone, without a word.

Lora turned and trudged through the little playground area into her building. Alone in the elevator, she tucked her sweater in, tightened her belt, and generally tidied up.

Her parents hadn't had an extra key made for her yet. That was one of the reasons why she took care to get home at a decent hour. She rang the doorbell.

For a long moment, nothing happened. Then the door opened and her brother looked out at her. He was wearing a bathrobe and a pair of pajamas.

"About time," he said.

"What the hell, it's still before midnight, ain't it?"

"You got school tomorrow," he muttered, closing the door and locking it. "Ma and Pa asleep?"

"What do you think? Eleven-thirty and they been working to fix this place up all day. And what have you been doing, huh?"

"Never you mind," Lora said sullenly. She glared at her brother with hatred in her eyes. He was eighteen, and he was going to graduate from high school next June and go into the army. He didn't mix with the gangs, any. In the Scarlet Sinner territory, he had been known as a "coolie." An outsider, a shunner of the gangs. Most of the Scarlet Sinners had respected Chick. They didn't razz Lora because her brother was a coolie. They knew that he just didn't need the day-by-day kicks that the gang boys did. But Lora hated him for his quiet assumption of superiority, for his withdrawal from street life.

He knew she hated him. And, though he was a powerful six-footer, he was afraid of her. When they were younger, he had hit her, sometimes. But he hadn't touched her since she was thirteen.

Lora remembered that last incident vividly. She had rifled his wallet to pay for one of her early reefers, and he had discovered it. That night, in their bedroom, he had confronted her with the loss. And then, angrily, he had grabbed her, hauled her across his knee, yanked down her pajama bottoms, and brought the palm of his hand down again and again on the pink, already sensuous flesh of her buttocks.

Lora hadn't cried out, hadn't even whimpered, though the pain was great and the humiliation even greater. But the next day she had come home from school and slashed up Chick's books. He had a library of auto repair manuals that he had bought over a two-year period, saving out of his odd-job money. Lora methodically reduced them to waste-paper with a kitchen knife, and defiantly left them strewn on Chick's bed.

He hadn't punished her, that time. He didn't dare, because he knew now that she was no longer afraid of him—and from that day, he became afraid of *her.*

Now he padded silently past her into his bedroom. Turning, he whispered, "Don't forget to set your alarm clock. There's school tomorrow."

"Sure, creep." She scowled contemptuously at him and went into her own room.

It was a novelty, having a room of her own. It was the first time she had had a whole bedroom all to herself. Up in the Bronx, she and Chick had always shared a bedroom, right up until the time they moved. She remembered when they were kids, how they had been so interested in each other's bodies. But then Chick had started to mature, and he stopped letting Lora look at him. And once Lora herself ripened into womanhood, Chick became very fussy. He always refused to get undressed in front of her or to let her undress with him in the room.

That had made life a little complicated. And she had delighted in embarrassing him, in walking around the room without any bra on, or naked below the waist. Chick got upset. She couldn't figure him out. She knew he laid girls sometimes, because he kept contraceptives in his drawer and every few months there was a new box there. But he wouldn't look at her.

Hell, Lora knew a lot of kids who didn't mind looking at their sisters. A lot of kids slept right in the same beds with their teen-age sisters, because there wasn't any room anywhere else for them to sleep. You could bet that plenty went on between brother and sister that way. There were even some girls who got knocked up by their own brothers, sometimes. But even Lora thought that was going a little too far.

She closed her bedroom door, wriggled out of her clothes, and, putting on her robe, went into the bathroom to take a shower. Then she got into bed, snapping out the little light on the wall.

The alarm went off at seven. Lora came groping up out of deep sleep, but it was fifteen minutes before she got out of bed. Chick was in the bathroom by then. She waited for him impatiently, banging on the door a couple of times.

Breakfast was a quick meal—juice, toast, coffee. They ate in a hurry. Chick left first—he had to take the subway to his vocational high school. He hadn't needed to change schools when the family moved; he was actually closer to his school now than he had been when they lived in the Bronx.

By eight-thirty, Lora was dressed and on her way out to school herself. Her old school, in the Bronx, had been built in the Year One; down here, though, she had transferred to a school that was only two or three years old, built to accommodate the overflow of the neighborhood caused by all the new housing projects. The fact that this new school had unbroken windows and brightly-lit halls didn't matter a damn to her, though. The day she was seventeen, she was quitting, and to hell with brightly-lit halls.

Her school day passed slowly, as always. This was only the second day, and nothing much was happening yet. Lora wandered around the halls from class to class.... Spanish 5, Bookkeeping, Gym, Household Management, History, English. Lora sat in the back row of each classroom, hardly listening. She didn't care if she passed or failed; she was just waiting out her time. But usually she passed anyway, at the old school. They didn't believe in failing people, because there wasn't room in the classrooms for repeaters. Unless you were abysmally hopeless, you got a passing grade and a promotion.

Lora saw three or four of the Cougars around the school—Marty, Conch, and one named Zorro, as well as a couple of the debs. She was standing with them in the school courtyard after lunch when a fight broke out not far away. A tall negro boy had come up to a group of voluble Puerto Ricans, and, suddenly pulling one Puerto Rican away from the group, had laid open his skull with a lead pipe. The other Puerto Ricans reacted quickly, clustering around the big negro, and by the time order was restored the negro was writhing on the pavement, clutching the lower left side of his stomach, and blood was pouring from between his fingers.

"What was that all about?" Lora asked.

"The Puertos went out raiding last night and raped a couple colored girls," Marty explained. "Maybe they got the sister of the big guy."

"What gangs are they?" Lora wanted to know.

"Those Puertos were from the Magicians," Conch said. "And I think the black boy was an Ace." He shrugged. "There's gonna be a rumble, I can feel it."

"Us too?" Lora asked.

"Maybe," Conch told her. "We been tight with the Aces a long time. Almost a brother club. If the Magicians make trouble, maybe we'll do a little bopping."

"There ain't been a decent rumble in a long time," said Zorro. "Two-three months."

"Damn fuzz clamping down," Conch said. "But the time's coming, I tell you truly."

The police had arrived, now, and an ambulance had come for the two wounded boys. Little knots of Puerto Ricans and negroes had gathered, and were muttering angrily at each other across a boundary line of teachers. Lora watched, drinking in the excitement of the possible explosion. She would have liked nothing better than to see a full-scale outbreak right now.

But the police broke things up, sending everyone inside. There was word, later in the day, of some fighting in the washrooms, but Lora had seen nothing by the time school was out.

She stopped off at home just long enough to drop off her notebook and nod curtly at her mother. Then she left, heading for the Cougar clubhouse. She hoped someone would be there. Whitey had told her that Cougar debs weren't allowed to have keys to the clubhouse, only the studs—a rule which Lora hoped to change a little, in the near future.

The place was empty except for Pug and Dolores. Pug let her in and went back to the couch, where Dolores was waiting. Her skirt was up above her knees and her blouse was open, and they were obviously a little annoyed that their privacy had been disturbed. But they didn't say anything. Not to Whitey's deb, they didn't. They didn't dare.

Lora roamed around the place, taking advantage of its emptiness to inspect it. There was a kitchen, a big livingroom, and four bedrooms, each with its own little bolt to insure a measure of privacy. It wasn't a bad set-up at all. The windows were below street level, opening out onto a kind of subterranean courtyard. Little light filtered in, and they were covered with criscrossed iron bars to prevent entry from outside.

A couple of empty wine jugs were sitting around, but it had all been killed the night before. There was nothing to drink except some cans of beer in the yellowed refrigerator. Lora opened one up, carried it into the livingroom, and sat down. Without a word, Pug and Dolores rose and went into one of the bedrooms. Lora heard springs squeaking a few minutes later.

During the next half hour, the rest of the Cougars began to troop in, with and without their debs. About half the gang went to school, more or less; three or four had jobs, and the rest said they were "out of work," meaning either that nobody would hire them or that they were currently preferring to loaf. By four o'clock the place was getting crowded. A lot of bedroom action was going on; most of the Cougars liked to sneak in a quick lay in the middle of the afternoon, and then tear off another piece at night.

Whitey came in around four-thirty. Whitey was in the "out of work" category right now. He was carrying two big jugs of wine in paper bags—bought legally, since he was over eighteen. Lora went to him.

They had some wine, and then they went to the President's room in back. Whitey was the only stud in the gang who didn't have to wait in line for a bedroom during the afternoon rush, because the room at the end of the corridor was reserved for the Prez's exclusive use. The rest of the Cougars had to wait their turns for one of the other three rooms, if they were in love-making moods, and they were standing around outside the locked bedrooms yelling derisive, foul-mouthed orders telling the couple within to hurry things up.

Whitey closed the door and shot the bolt. He sat down on the bed. While they were undressing, he said, "There's one thing I been meaning to talk to you about, now that you're my deb."

"Yeah?"

"You remember yesterday, when you yanked Donna's sweater off, what you saw on her—over here?" Whitey put one finger heavily on the firm swelling fullness of her right breast.

Lora's jaw tightened. "Yeah. Initials. W. B."

"Yeah. My initials, get it? Whitey Barone. It's kind of a requirement I have. Any girl who makes it with Whitey, she gotta wear my initials in two places. Here and here, I mean." He touched her breast again, and her left hip.

Lora nibbled her lip uncertainly. "Do all the Cougars mark up their girls that way?"

Whitey shrugged. "Only a couple. But I do."

"We didn't do it that way in the Scarlet Sinners," Lora said tentatively, testing him.

"You ain't in the Scarlet Sinners now." There was just a faint hint of menace in Whitey's voice. "And you're my deb, ain't you?"

"Sure, Whitey."

"Then you'll let me put my mark on you."

Lora was silent, thinking about that. She was proud of her body. She knew it was a good one, full and lush, with white, flawless skin. Kid-gang or no kid-gang, she wasn't aiming to get it messed up. It just wasn't worth it. She wasn't going to be making it with Whitey forever, and for that matter she wasn't going on being a gang girl all the rest of her life, either. She had plans. Maybe in two years or so, when she was eighteen, she could graduate into the big leagues, getting hooked up with one of the call-girl syndicates. There were some Scarlet Sinners alumni who might be able to work out a deal for her. Why lay for free, in basement tenement apartments, when she could be doing it for fifty or a hundred bucks a night, high class? It was a good niche to aim for. But nobody would want to hire a call-girl who was marked up with initials on her hip and on one of her breasts.

Lora said, "Will it hurt much?"

"We dope you up first. You get some booze or a reefer, or maybe some pot if you want, and you don't feel a thing."

"How do you mark?"

Whitey shrugged. "Cigarettes or knife. If we do it with lighted cigarettes, it hurts a long time. It's quicker with the knife, but that way you might get infected."

She frowned. "It don't sound nice."

"You gotta have it, though. This I insist."

"You in any hurry to get me marked up?" she asked troubledly.

"Nah, no hurry. Today, tomorrow, the day after. Whenever you want. Just so it gets done, is all. Once I got my mark on you, you're the absolute Number One deb of the Cougars."

Yeah, Lora thought sourly. *The way Donna was the absolute Number One of the Cougars. Until she got elbowed out into the cold.*

She said, "Okay. Just gimme a day or two to get used to the idea, huh? I'll let you know when I'm ready. I'll let you know."

CHAPTER SIX

They let the matter drop right there. So far as Whitey was concerned, the matter was ended. Lora would get marked, period.

But Lora had other ideas. She wasn't putting initials on her body, not for anybody. Whitey was in for some surprises, she thought. Let him think she was giving in. He'd have to think twice.

Right now, she knew how she could keep him from talking about it. She reached out for him, drawing him tight against her. His body stiffened, his hands encircled the steep globes of her breasts. Smoothly, now, without all the tumultuous violence of the first time, they began to move into the rhythms of passion, Lora gliding beneath his tense body and quivering with delight as shock after shock of ecstasy rippled through her. Skillfully Whitey built her up to one peak of delight after another, until she could no longer contain herself. She gripped his body convulsively with her pistoning thighs; his shoulder presented itself, and she dug her teeth in, breaking the skin. Whitey made no protest, felt no pain. He only held her tighter, moved with more urgent force.

And then she could hold back no longer. The floodgates were lowered; she threw her head back, gasping, "Now, Whitey! Now! Ride me!"

He gasped too, and they were silent for thirty seconds of fierce activity, and then it was over, their sweat-soaked bodies glued tight, and she could feel the thunder of his heart pounding near her own. His hand touched her breasts lightly and they both relaxed.

"Christ, baby," he muttered. "Christ, it's the greatest."

"You're it, Whitey," she told him. "Like a stick of dynamite, man."

They lay quietly. Lora's thoughts went back a few years, as she mentally compared Whitey with the other studs who had taken her. She always did that, stacking one man up against another.

They had all been pretty good. Johnny Diablo, Geronimo, Spook, Whitey—they were four of a kind, lean, dangerous men who had excitement bottled up inside them, excitement that they discharged into a woman's body. They had all been good, one a little better than the one before him, Whitey the best of all.

Lora thought back before Johnny Diablo. She could remember the day she lost her cherry, as clearly as though it had happened last week instead of four years ago. It had been when she was twelve, one of the littlest of the Scarlet Sinner Little People. She had been getting her periods for a couple of months, but her breasts were just unformed little nubbins then, and she didn't have much hair on her body. She remembered how it had happened. She had come into the Scarlet Sinner clubhouse on a Saturday morning, a month or two after she had joined the gang. She was tough and hard, but she didn't have too good an idea of what it was all about.

The Sinner clubhouse was in an old brownstone building. It was a two-story building that was paid for by the gang's alumni. Lora had walked in. There was nobody there but a kid named Saint. Saint was around fourteen, thin and gangly, with pimples all over his face. He was just standing around doing nothing, and Lora said, "Come on, man, let's get some kicks."

Just for the hell of it. Not even knowing what it was all about.

Saint was surprised, but they went into one of the upstairs rooms and shut the door, and Lora peeled out of her clothes before she knew what she was getting into. She stood there nude in front of him, feeling ashamed of her little breasts and narrow boyish hips.

Saint looked her over and said, "What the hell, kid. You old enough to bleed yet?"

"Don't worry none about me. You gonna do it or are you queer, man?"

Saint smiled a funny smile. "You want to lose your cherry, huh?"

"You talk too much. Come here and lie down." Saint dropped his trousers and came over to her, and got on top of her and started to move. Right then, Lora had thought of him as a big wheel, but as she looked back she realized he'd been almost as scared as she was. She felt him touching her body, and then there was a moment of sudden white-hot pain. Saint moved briefly and let out his breath, and then he rose from her.

She glared at him, unsatisfied. "That all?"

"What you expect?"

"More than that, man."

"Maybe next time," he told her.

She was sharply disappointed. She was bleeding and sore, and there was no pleasure in it. But she tried again, with somebody else. It was better that time. And then her body began to ripen, the last vestiges of girlishness leaving it, and she became full-breasted and hippy and sensuous, and the next time she and Saint made it together it was something, something big.

Then after that she moved into the Big People, as Johnny Diablo's deb. Johnny taught her a few things about making it. Johnny knew plenty. So when she moved over to Geronimo, she was an expert, and Spook just put the trimming on top. And now Whitey.

Lora smiled, thinking about Saint. The dumb goof. He was doing twenty years upstate because he raped some ten-year-old. Caught her on the street, dragged her into a cellar and broke her cherry. The cops found her wandering around dazed and half-naked, but not so dazed that she couldn't describe Saint. They picked him up and put him away upstate.

Poor Saint, Lora thought. *Some guys like the weirdest kicks.*

Whitey looked over at her. "What you thinking about so much?"

"My first lay," she said. "Just remembering. You remember yours?"

Whitey chuckled harshly. "Crap, I must have been nine years old. How am I supposed to remember? Come on—let's go get something to drink."

They rejoined the gang, and had a few drinks, and then went out, ten or eleven of them, to take a stroll around the turf. They stopped into Sid's, then walked south to the boundary. The Aces and the Magicians were supposed to be getting shaped up for a rumble, any day now. The Cougars just wanted to keep an eye out, so they knew how the wind was blowing.

For the next couple of days, the routine went along the same way. The Cougars generally came to the clubhouse along around three or four in the afternoon, except for the guys who were working steadily and couldn't make it till later. After a couple of hours of drinking and lovemaking, the gang split up, around six, going to their homes to grab a meal. About half the gang lived in one of the several big housing projects in the neighborhood; the rest lived in the rundown tenements on Third and Fourth Streets.

And in the evening, as soon as the members could get away from home, they wandered down to Sid's candy store to meet, kid around, and dance. They had a lot of time on their hands. You couldn't drink and love and fight right around the clock. They were bored silly a lot of times.

After they left Sid's, a general patrol of the turf was in order. This was heavy gang territory. There was the Puerto Rican Magicians and the negro Aces, just to the south. Over to the west was an Irish gang, the Ravens, who were the traditional enemy of the Cougars. The Cougars had to keep on their toes to make sure the Ravens didn't come around looking for trouble. There hadn't been a serious rumble with the Ravens in over a year, nor even any minor skirmishes in the last couple of months, but it was impossible to relax guard.

Sometimes in the evening the gang would take in a movie. The dragstrip movies were the favorites. Nobody in the gang owned a car—you didn't have any place to park it, and the cops made trouble for you if you couldn't prove you were insured, and insurance cost a regular fortune. So they ate up the hotrod movies. Usually there were fights in the theater, to liven things up. When there was no movie playing worth seeing, and when the Cougars were particularly bored, they would wander around their turf on a bopping expedition, making trouble for anyone who was alone and didn't seem to be carrying a weapon. They took care never to do any real damage, like a killing or a rape. These days when a gang stamped somebody to death just for the hell of it, there was an outcry in the papers, and a tight police net, and trials. The Cougars didn't want any of that jazz. So they kept their bopping expeditions limited to a little mugging and a little stomping, nothing really vicious, and watched out when it came to the real brutality. That only flared up at the big rumbles.

The routine, Lora saw, was pretty much like the Scarlet Sinner routine. Drinking and laying, guarding the turf, movies, bopping, every now and then a rumble. It wasn't much of a life—but what the hell, it was better than sitting around on your butt with a bunch of schoolbooks.

During those first few days of breaking in with the gang, Lora bided her time. She kept her eyes open, getting to know everybody in the gang, sizing them up, learning their strengths, their weaknesses, finding out how she might be able to use them.

There was one complication that she had not planned on when first entering the Cougars. That was Whitey's insistence on putting his mark on her.

"When you gonna let me initial you?" he asked her several times.

She gave a noncommittal shrug. "A day or two, man. Don't bug me."

"Get me, this is important. You gotta wear my mark if you're gonna be my deb."

"Couple of days, Whitey."

"You chicken to be cut?" he demanded. "Come on, I wanna know. You chicken to be cut?"

"Just give me a coupla days," she pleaded, ducking the question at that point by clasping him in a hot embrace.

She kept on ducking the question that way for three or four days. She was trying hard to figure out her strategy, to figure out some way of coping with his stubborn insistence on marking her up. It was a rough problem. She knew he wouldn't be shaken from his desire, not for anything. If she didn't let him mark her, he would toss her out.

She had to come up with something. Had to figure out some way of continuing as the gang president's deb while not having her body marked up messily with anybody's initials.

On the fifth day of her membership in the Cougars, the answer came to her.

It was very simple, after all.

All she had to do, she reasoned, was eliminate Whitey as gang president.

She thought about it from six or seven different angles. Whitey was okay, good in bed, tough and hard. *Too* tough. She could see already that he wouldn't give in and let himself be swayed by her. So he was going to have to be shoved aside. Somebody a little more pliable would have to be found and put in Whitey's place, and it would have to be done soon, before Whitey got any more rambunctious and decided he wouldn't wait any longer before marking her up.

Ordinarily she could wait and take a chance that Whitey would be killed in a rumble. But no rumbles were coming up, and she couldn't wait.

She had to move fast.

She spent an hour thinking over the qualities of the other Cougars, one by one, trying to figure out who would be a likely successor for Whitey. Whitey had been the boss of the Cougars for two years. That was a long time, in gang annals. His control seemed absolute. There weren't many guys in the club who could even consider the idea of overthrowing him and taking over.

But there was one who might fit the bill, Lora decided finally.

Squirrel.

The more she thought about it, the more she liked the idea. Despite his nickname, Squirrel was one of the best-looking of the Cougars. She wouldn't mind shacking with him as a regular thing. Squirrel was handy with a knife, too, according to his reputation. He was tremendously loyal to Whitey. But, unlike most of the other Cougars, Squirrel wasn't afraid of Whitey to the point of boot-licking. Squirrel respected Whitey—anybody in his right mind would—but he wasn't scared spitless by the idea of crossing him.

So it would be Squirrel, then.

The operation, Lora reasoned, would have to be carried out in two sections. The first part of the maneuver would be for her to get between Squirrel and his deb Mae. That part taken care of, the next step would be to work Squirrel up until he found enough heart to challenge Whitey for the gang leadership in a two-man stand.

The first part of the project wouldn't be very hard at all. It had been Squirrel, after all, who had first approached Lora when she walked into the candy store that day. He had made eyes at her from then on. He had given ground reluctantly only because Whitey had chosen her as his deb, and he wasn't anxious to stir up trouble with the boss. But it wouldn't be much trouble to reawaken Squirrel's interest in her. It was easy to see that he didn't have much interest in Mae any more. Squirrel could be maneuvered. Lora was sure of it.

Once she had formed her plan, she waited no longer. She grabbed the opportunity when it came, a day later.

It was a stroke of luck that when she walked into the clubhouse she found Squirrel in the clubhouse alone. Squirrel usually got there early, after his last class of the day, and so did Lora. But this was the first time she had been alone with him, with neither Whitey or Mae around.

Squirrel was in the kitchen, getting himself a can of beer from the noisy old refrigerator, when Lora came in and greeted him.

"Hello there," she said, giving him a special smile that rocked him immediately.

"H-hi."

"Open one for me?"

"Sure," he said, and took another beer out of the icebox. Lora was wearing her tightest sweater, and her breasts jutted forward provocatively. Squirrel looked disturbed. He tried not to glance at her bosom. Her smile had unsettled him, and he was pretending not to be interested, forcing himself not to look at her closely. Lora knew that was just discipline on his part. He expected Whitey to walk in soon, and he wasn't aiming to get into trouble with him.

But Lora thought she could change all that.

As he handed her the opened can of beer, she let her hands graze his for a moment. Then, crossing around behind him, she lightly touched the tips of her breasts to his back and flattened her loins against his hard buttocks. Startled, he pulled away from her, but she went after him.

"Squirrel?" she murmured.

"What do you want?"

"We're all alone in here, you and me."

"What of it?" he said hesitantly, still not looking at her.

"Take me into the bedroom."

He swung round to face her, his eyes wide with surprise—and desire, Lora saw. "*Huh?*" he snorted. "Hey, you lookin' to get me in hot water with Whitey, Lora?"

"Are you afraid of him?" she asked mockingly.

"Whitey's the Prez. It isn't a matter of being afraid or not being afraid. I just don't go cutting in on his deb, that's all." His face was pale and he looked uneasy.

"Even if the deb wants you to?" she teased. "Wants you real bad?"

He looked at her queerly. "Listen, you playing some kinda fool game with me? I ain't gonna play. I don't know what you're trying to get—"

"You. That's what I want. You're chicken, Squirrel. Chicken!"

"Like hell!"

"I say you're chicken!" she taunted. "A girl comes up to you and says, come on, let's make it, you and me, and you don't have the guts to do it."

"Who says?"

"Prove otherwise."

Squirrel moistened his lips. "I ain't chicken," he said in a dull voice. "Whitey put you up to this, didn't he? He wants to see if I'll listen to you."

"Uh-uh," Lora grinned. "Whitey would flip if he knew this was going on. Listen. Whitey wants to cut his initials into me."

"Sure. He does it to all his debs."

"Well, this is one deb who don't go for that kind of crud. Nobody's marking me up, hear? So I'm gonna give Whitey the boot. If he don't want me without marks, I'm gonna move over to somebody who can take care of a girl without wanting to cut her up, is all. You get the scoop now?"

Squirrel nodded slowly. Color was coming back into his face. He wasn't dumb, was Squirrel.

"You're dumping Whitey," he said. "Okay. Okay, I get it. And you want me—"

"Yeah, Squirrel. Yeah."

"But I'll hafta have a stand with Whitey on account of you, then. He won't just let you walk out on him and come over to me."

Lora grinned. Once again, she asked the question that a gang kid could only answer in one way. "Do you have heart, Squirrel? Or are you chicken to stand with Whitey, man?"

Squirrel's jaws worked tensely. "I ain't chicken," he said. "I'll show you. You come on with me, Lora. I'll show you."

He took her by the wrist and led her along the hall—not into one of the bedrooms reserved for rank-and-file Cougars, but into the end room, the room that was supposed to be used only by the President. Lora's heart surged. Squirrel was taking the challenge. Squirrel wanted her bad enough to be willing to face Whitey's deadly blade. Lora felt the excitement coursing through her now. This was the greatest kick of all, to be able to manipulate men, to force them to fight and kill one another for the privilege of having her.

Squirrel shut the door. He slammed home the bolt. By the time he turned around, Lora was half undressed.

CHAPTER SEVEN

Squirrel looked a little bit dazed by his sudden good fortune. His lips were open, his eyes wide, his hands dangling slackly. Lora could hear the harsh uneven rasping of his breath.

She pulled the sweater off and tossed it carelessly into the furthest corner. Then, while Squirrel's eyeballs threatened to bug out of their sockets, she opened the bra. Her breasts, unconfined, rose and expanded, and her nipples jutted upward at an angle, pointing toward Squirrel.

Lora stood with her hands on her hips, her eyes bright with lust, her breasts bare in open and unconditional invitation.

"Come on," she murmured. "What the hell are you waiting for, Squirrel? Come here and help me get the rest of it off."

Squirrel took a couple of uncertain steps toward her. He walked stiffly, more like a marionette than like a man. Lora felt the thrill of knowing she had conquered him, that she had turned him into just another of the men she could manipulate like a puppet.

His hands shook a little as he fumbled for the zipper of her jeans. He pulled them off, and then, growing more eager as the stiff urgency of desire drove all thoughts of caution from his mind, he slipped his hands under the waistband of her panties, and his cold palms flattened against the sizzling skin of her buttocks, and after a brief caress he removed her final garment.

Lora flung herself on him, practically ripping his clothing off, and they tumbled together to the unmade bed. Their lips met. His hands—still cold with tension—roved her body, now gripping her breasts, now tracing gut-tingling pathways across her buttocks and belly and the soft flesh of her inner thighs. She writhed and moaned, her tongue touching his, her hips working in a steady rhythm.

"Squirrel... " she whimpered. "Squirrel... " and in a sudden quick motion she imprisoned his body with her own.

Squirrel's big, powerful body pressed down on her heavily, and he held her tightly enfolded in his strong arms as they made it. He was calmer, less explosively dynamic in bed than was Whitey, but in his own strong, unspectacular way he was good, very good. Lora felt thrill after thrill go rippling through her loins, and still it continued. After Whitey's crazy madman way of loving, this was a welcome contrast. You didn't feel that you were likely to be burned by the sheer blast of intensity, with Squirrel. You just let yourself be held tight, and let the pleasure go coursing through every muscle and nerve of your body.

She heard Squirrel gulp in breath hoarsely, and she knew they were coming to the grand finale. Her legs locked tight around his body, and his arms doubled their crushing hold on her back, and for one long moment of frantic action time and space and the universe was blotted out completely, and then it was over and they were coming back down from the top of Mount Everest together.

Neither of them spoke. Squirrel rolled over and lay alongside her, slipping her hand inside his. Idly and without passion, he stroked the side of her thigh, while his ragged breathing slowly returned to a normal rhythm.

After a long while Lora said, "How am I?"

"Out of this world, baby."

"Worth fighting Whitey for?"

"Worth fighting ten Whiteys." His hand wandered toward her breasts. She turned over on her side, so the heavy globes of her breasts faced him, and he curled up, burying his face in the deep, warm valley formed by the two full mounds.

After a while desire began to stir in Squirrel again. Lora was starting to feel drowsy, but she made no protest as Squirrel clasped her to him.

This time their lovemaking was brief: a few moments of quick, urgent action and desire was satisfied for both of them. Lora closed her eyes, feeling warm and cozy and fulfilled. It was better with Squirrel than with Whitey, she decided. Whitey was like a hurricane, coming along and ripping your guts apart. Squirrel was more like a breeze—a gentle, cool breeze, blowing steadily and without interruption, giving you pleasure and relief. For one time only, she'd rather have a Whitey than a Squirrel. But as a steady thing, she preferred to keep away from hurricanes.

And a different sort of hurricane was brewing, she thought. When Whitey found out what was going on in the President's room, there was going to be a big storm, all right. A blaster.

Maybe half an hour went by. Squirrel had dozed a little, but he was awake now, and starting to get amorous for the third time. His hands were beginning to roam around Lora's body. She felt detached, half a million miles from anywhere. She didn't mind if Squirrel wanted to make it again, but she would rather just lie quietly, feeling the warmth of his strong body against hers on the bed.

Suddenly there came an interruption. A barrage of loud angry knocking, five blows of a pummelling fist against the solid wood of the door.

Whitey!

Lora heard him angrily demanding, "Who in hell's in my room, huh?"

Squirrel sat up, abruptly tense and ready for action. "Me," he said, in a deep, newly commanding tone of voice. "Me, Squirrel. I'm in here."

Outside, Whitey was silent for a moment. Then, incredulously, he asked, "You out of your everlovin' head, man? You can't go using my room—"

"Sure I can, Daddy-o," Squirrel replied evenly, sitting up on one elbow and facing the bolted door. "I'm taking over the Cougars, Whitey. And I got Lora in here with me."

"You *what?*" Whitey screamed apoplectically. His fists rained wild thunder on the door. "Get that goddam door open or I'll bust it down, you hear me, Squirrel? Get it open!"

"Keep your britches on," Squirrel said.

He seemed calm. He rose from the bed and began to put his clothes back on. Glancing over at Lora, who lay sprawled out nude, satisfied and sleepy, he ordered sharply, "Get your clothes back on."

She sat up. "You gonna fight him, Squirrel? There gonna be a stand?"

"What the hell do you think?"

"You think it's smart to fight him now?" she asked, half genuinely worried and half baiting him on. "I mean, we been making it pretty hard, man. It takes a lot outa you. You oughtn't fight a stud like Whitey when you ain't fresh."

"Don't worry about me," Squirrel said. "I'll take care of him."

He grinned, and he seemed to be trying hard to make the grin look like a confident, devil-may-care one. But Lora could see past the cockiness to the numbing tenseness beneath the grin. Probably, she thought, Squirrel was just now beginning to wonder what he had let himself in for by challenging Whitey. Up to now he had been carried away by the hypnotism of her body, by the blinding impact of her bare breasts and white thighs. But now his desire was satisfied, for the moment—and now there was Whitey to answer to.

Lora felt a rising sweep of excitement as the tension mounted. If Squirrel came out victorious in the stand, she wouldn't have to worry about any initials being cut into her breasts. And if Whitey won—well, she thought hesitantly, she could always make up some story about Squirrel forcing her. Whitey could be made to believe that, and no denial from Squirrel would do a damned bit of good. And then, when she got the chance, she thought, she would kill Whitey herself, before he could succeed in putting his initials on her. The thought of killing made her blood pound faster. Lora had never killed anyone that she knew about. She had done some slashing and stomping, but she hadn't been able to find out whether her victims had died.

She wanted to kill. And she *would* kill, if she had to. If Whitey survived the stand.

Rising from the bed, she found her bra and put it on, wriggled into her sweater, slipped on her panties and blue jeans. Squirrel was dressed also. Lora heard the little clicking sound that was his switchblade snapping into position.

Whitey pounded on the door again. His voice was screaming practically at hysteria pitch as he roared, "You motherlover, come on out of there!"

"I'm coming, Whitey," Squirrel said. "Don't flip, man. I'm opening up."

Squirrel's hand went to the bolt. He hesitated a fraction of a second. Then he unbolted the door and threw it open.

Whitey waited outside.

There was a switchblade in the gang leader's hand, and as the door opened the blade came flicking swiftly into position. Whitey's face was utterly white, bloodless with sheer hatred. His beady little eyes were narrowed to terrifying slits, and his thin lips were tightly compressed. Bands of muscles were quivering in his cheeks.

Whitey looked horribly ugly just now, Lora thought. His beak of a nose jutted out, and his adam's-apple bulked in his throat. Whitey was a tough little punk, the kind who drives unstoppably to the top of the heap, riding along on the intensity of his furious anger at the world of bigger people. Right now Whitey Barone looked like the incarnation of every deadly, ruthless killer the world had ever known.

But he was keeping his fury rigidly in check. In an oddly soft voice, Whitey asked, "What the hell you want to do a thing like this for, Squirrel? Man, you got a good head on your shoulders, I always thought. What made that head swell up, man? What the hell you want to fool around with my girl for?"

Squirrel remained silent. Lora stared at the broad back in the doorway, and at the knife held stiff in Squirrel's hand.

Kill, she thought. *Kill and slice and destroy!*

Words tumbled out of Whitey, soft-spoken words. "You musta been way up on pot, man. Why you wanta take over the Cougars, huh? I never bugged you any. You had it good. And now you've gone and crapped yourself up, Squirrel. Now I'm gonna have to kill you, Squirrel. You know that, don't you? Now I gotta put the knife in your belly and rip you open."

"You talk a lot, Whitey," Squirrel said in a hoarse voice. "Shut your mouth and let's see you make the knife talk for you."

"Okay, man. Come out of that room," Whitey said, his voice still feather-soft.

Squirrel stepped forward, knife high.

He crossed the threshold, and, the moment he was out in the corridor, he sprang forward in a sudden lunge. Whitey blocked it by sweeping his forearm up against Squirrel's wrist. They strained for a moment, Squirrel trying to force the knife-hand past the iron barrier of Whitey's arm. Then Squirrel gave ground, lowering his blade and dropping back a bit.

Lora felt an icy chill of excitement. The stand was on, out there in the corridor that was so narrow there was hardly room to turn around in.

Whitey and Squirrel, fighting to the death—over her!

Squirrel had the size and the reach advantage; Whitey had the asset of his deadly intensity, his fierce will to succeed, which in itself could terrify an opponent, freezing his blood and leaving him open for an easy slice.

For a couple of moments after Squirrel's first lunge, nothing much happened. The antagonists edged up and down the corridor, taking each other's measure. They had fought side by side for years, but this was the first time that either had raised a blade against the other.

Lora came out of the room to watch the contest. She saw a few of the other Cougars congregating in the darkness at the other end of the corridor. They were watching with keen interest. Nobody made a move to interfere. You never broke up a two-man stand. You let them fight it out to the finish.

But neither Whitey nor Squirrel was willing to start opening up an offensive yet. Whitey made a series of little feinting jabs, never striking seriously. As for Squirrel, he danced lightly back and forth, moving well for someone so big, getting in position for a strike several times but not making it. This was the beginning of the stand, the moments of caginess.

They ended abruptly as Whitey came leaping forward. Lora saw the deadly gleam in Whitey's eyes. He was fighting to defend his position on the top, fighting to wipe out the stain of his honor. Nothing less than Squirrel's life could salvage Whitey's rep in the gang now, and both Whitey and Squirrel knew it.

Whitey's knife bored through Squirrel's guard, slipping under his arm. Lora gasped. Squirrel turned pale, but he deftly pivoted and got out of the way. The keen blade sliced harmlessly through Squirrel's sleeve, drawing no blood. Whitey's lips curled, and he vented his disappointment in an animal-like snarl.

Now it was Squirrel's turn to lunge, while Whitey was still involved in the follow-through of his attack. Squirrel made his strike, jabbing at Whitey's middle and missing.

Then Squirrel slipped.

He started to go staggering forward, arms and legs pinwheeling in what looked like an impossible attempt to regain balance. Lora felt her stomach churn as Whitey gleefully brought his knife up for the kill.

"Got you, you motherlovin' bastard!" Whitey hissed, striking forward.

But it had only been a feint. An exclamation of surprise went up from the watchers as Squirrel, already halfway past the kill-poised Whitey, unexpectedly recovered the balance that he had merely pretended to have lost.

Whitey was over-extended, in the middle of a fierce lunge toward someone who was no longer there. Squirrel had caught him with an old trick, but a trick performed better than Lora had ever seen. Squirrel's face gleamed in satisfaction.

"Kill him!" Lora screamed.

Squirrel brought his blade savagely upward.

The keen point embedded itself in the armpit of Whitey's knife-wielding arm, penetrating deep enough to sever nerves and muscles and blood vessels. Whitey who has never known defeat and who is suddenly staring it in the face.

Squirrel drew the knife out. Blood spurted. Whitey's switch dropped from his numb hand. The gang leader stared down at the blade lying on the floor. He made a tentative groping motion toward it, but his nerveless fingers would not obey. He hovered for a moment, while Squirrel stood over him, waiting now to close in for the inevitable kill.

The Cougars were murmuring in astonishment. Only Lora was smiling. This morning, Squirrel had been just another Cougar, loyal to Whitey and complacent about the way the gang was set up. And now he was a killer, about to mount the throne.

Squirrel lifted the knife.

Whitey made a little choking sound. Then he turned to run down the corridor, blood spouting from the deep wound in his armpit.

"Chicken!" Squirrel shouted.

He stuck out his foot, thrusting it between Whitey's frantically pistoning legs. Whitey pitched forward, grabbed air with his one functioning arm, and dropped into a sprawled little heap.

He stared up, and the kill-glint was gone from his eyes. He looked like what he was, now—a cornered rat. It didn't matter how many men Whitey Barone had killed in stands before. It didn't matter that for almost two years he had been undisputed Prez of the Cougars. One mistake was all it took to knock a man off his lofty perch. Squirrel had faked him out; Whitey had made the fatal mistake. Now he was just another blubbering little rat pleading for his life.

Squirrel was in no hurry. He stood over the weaponless Whitey, gloating.

Whitey's lips moved. "Squirrel, *no!* For godssake, no! Don't do it!"

"You never used to listen when guys said that to you," Squirrel reminded him.

"That was different! We're buddies, Squirrel! I'll let you be Prez! I'll let you have Lora! Just let me be, Squirrel! Let me be!"

Watching, Lora's face hardened with contempt. Whitey was breaking the gang code by begging for mercy. Here, right at the end, for the first time ever, Whitey was going chicken. It was sickening. A man couldn't live as Number Two, after he'd been on top. There was nothing for Whitey to do but die. Only Whitey was trying to weasel out of it. *So he was yellow under all the toughness,* Lora thought. *Whitey was chicken.*

"Let me be, Squirrel!" he whimpered.

"Sure, Whitey. I'll let you be."

Squirrel smiled the death-smile. He bent over, drew back his arm, and jabbed his blade into Whitey's belly, guiding it in past the hand that tried futilely to block the blow. The razor-sharp knife ripped easily through the tough belly muscles into the soft organs beneath. Squirrel sliced upward until his blade, banging against the rib cage, could go no further. He twisted sharply and pulled the blade out.

Guts slashed to ribbons, lungs punctured, Whitey tried to say something. But the blood bubbling out of his mouth made his words unintelligible, turning them into thick moist meaningless sounds. Suddenly Whitey's eyes glazed over, and he uttered one last rattling sound, and died.

Slowly, Lora released the breath she had been holding for the final half minute of the fight. Whitey was dead. Nobody would carve initials in her now. And she had demonstrated her power. Strictly with her own strength, she had compelled Squirrel to destroy the Prez and move into his place.

It was almost as though she had killed Whitey herself.

CHAPTER EIGHT

The clubhouse was awesomely quiet. The Cougars all stood in a stunned knot at one end of the corridor, not far from where Whitey had fallen. Lora stood next to Squirrel. The sound of Squirrel's breathing was all that could be heard.

After a moment Squirrel said, facing the rest of the Cougars, "Okay, you guys. Whitey and I had a little argument. Whitey lost."

"Jeez," Pug said. "You cooled him off!"

"Yeah," Squirrel agreed. He seemed to have added two inches to his stature since killing Whitey. He looked at the rest of the gang, waiting for some challenge to his new supremacy. At length he said, "Unless somebody objects, I'm gonna be the new Prez of the Cougars. I'm waiting for objections. Anybody want to object, let him open his mouth right now."

Silence.

"Well?"

Still silence.

Lora said, "Looks like you're the new Prez, huh, Squirrel?"

"Looks that way," Squirrel said. "Okay. Pug, Marty, Gimp—come here."

Frowning, the three came out of the group. Squirrel folded his arms, leader-fashion. "You three get rid of Whitey's body. Bandage him up so he don't drip blood, then stuff him inside that old trunk outside and take him into Raven turf. I want you to dump him where it'll look like it was the Ravens who cooled him. Don't get yourself mixed up in no trouble while you're across the line, neither. Dolores, Claire, Anna—get to work and clean up the mess here. Mop up all the blood. We don't want no messes around here."

The stunned Cougars moved obediently to their assignments, none of them saying a word. It had all happened so suddenly, like a quick bolt of lightning. The stand had been called, Whitey had been faked out, leadership of the gang had changed hands. The Cougars still hadn't had enough time to get used to the fact that Whitey was dead and Squirrel was the boss of the Cougars now. It hadn't sunk in yet.

Lora felt pretty good about things. She had walked cold into this gang. Right away, she had started making it with the top man. That was a pretty fast start. And then, when she decided she didn't go for some of the top man's ideas, she had picked out a likely successor and propelled *him* to the top.

That was what power meant, she thought: to be able to control people, to make them do what you wanted them to do. Lora loved the feel of power. She lived for it. And she knew beyond a doubt that right now Lora Menotti, and not Squirrel, held the real power in the Cougar organization.

Lora waited for her next chance to exert power. It came a minute later.

Mae stepped forward, Mae who had been Squirrel's deb up till now. Her lean, oddly innocent-looking face was rigidly set in an angry expression now, as she walked toward Squirrel.

"So now you're big man around this gang, huh, Squirrel?" she asked.

"That's right, Mae. You got the picture clear." Squirrel stood balancing himself lightly on the balls of his feet. He seemed to be floating half an inch off the ground. He was still feeling the kicks of the successful knife-fight, Lora thought.

Mae said, "Okay, so you're the Prez. So what happens to me?"

"What do you mean, what happens?" Squirrel asked easily, hardly looking at her.

"You cooled off Whitey. You took his job. Do you take over Whitey's deb too?"

"What do you think?"

"I want to know. Am I your deb or is Lora going to take over?"

Squirrel smiled mockingly. Contemptuously he plucked up the fabric of Mae's sweater and let it fall back, as if emphasizing the meagerness of the tall girl's bosom compared with Lora's. He said, "You've had it, girlie."

"So Lora's in," Mae said bitterly. "And I get pushed out. The way Donna did."

Squirrel shrugged. "You had yours. There ain't room enough for two in my bed, Mae. So I figure you gotta go."

Mae nodded, half-closing her eyes. She had obviously figured as much too, the moment the blade sliced into Whitey's belly.

"I'll kill that goddam whore!" Mae shrieked. With that, she went racing across the hallway, seizing Lora and grabbing hold of Lora's hair. Taken by surprise, Lora was powerless to prevent the attack. She yelled in agony as Mae tugged. Lora pummelled the taller girl with her fists, trying to break the hold. In another second, Mae would have yanked a handful of Lora's jet-black hair out by the roots.

Moving quickly, Squirrel came between them, seizing Mae's arm and twisting it. Mae released her grip. Lora stepped back, rubbing her aching scalp. Needles of pain were sleeting through her head, but no hair was missing, at least.

Squirrel held Mae out at arm's length, gripping her by the bunched-up fabric of her sweater, slapping her across the face again and again. A massive ring studded Squirrel's big hand. As the merciless slapping continued, Mae's lower lip split and a trickle of blood dribbled down across her chin, and still Squirrel kept belting her until he grew weary of it.

He let go.

Mae went sagging dizzily against the wall.

Squirrel said, "Get out of here, Mae. You've had it around here. You ain't a Cougar any more."

Mae elbowed herself away from the wall and began to shuffle toward the door. Suddenly, as she approached Lora, a gleam of fresh hatred appeared in the tall girl's pain-wracked eyes. Pursing her bleeding lips, Mae turned on Lora and spat a gobbet of saliva into Lora's eyes.

Lora recoiled, wiping her eyes. Squirrel cursed and stepped across the room, knocking Mae down with one terrific swipe of his fist. She huddled on the floor, cowering the way Whitey had cowered not very long before, one arm raised in protection.

Squirrel gestured as if to kick her. But Lora, her face set in stony vengefulness now, pulled at Squirrel's sleeve, halting the blow.

Squirrel glanced at her. "What?"

"Don't hit her."

"I gotta show her she's dirt," Squirrel said.

Lora smiled icily. "There's a better way, Squirrel. A real good way. Let's line her up."

Squirrel looked dumfounded. "But—"

"What's the matter? She too good for it?" Lora demanded. She whirled, counting. "Twelve studs here. That's enough to give her a real swell workout. What do you think, Squirrel?"

The big boy's face was darkened by doubt. He said slowly, "That's kinda drastic, Lora—"

"She's dirt. She's crud. Let's show her that she's crud."

Mae was whimpering on the floor. Lora knew that this was the first big test of her control over Squirrel. If he still had some lingering attachment for Mae, and refused to humiliate her in this fashion, Lora would be forced to exert pressure. She didn't want to have to put the squeeze on. She continued to stare steadily at Squirrel, silently daring him to give the order for the mass rape of the girl who had been his steady shack-up for nearly a year.

Squirrel wavered. Then his last wall of resistance collapsed.

"Bozo! Conch!" he snapped. He gestured toward Mae. "Pick up this crud and drag her into the first room back here."

They came forward, seizing the prostrate Mae under each arm and hauling her off into the nearest of the clubhouse bedrooms. Turning, Lora saw the other Cougar debs looking coldly at her. They didn't like the idea of Lora organizing a gang laying party that would give their men a free shot at another girl. But there wasn't a damn thing that could be done about it. Squirrel had ordered it, and it meant a knife-fight for anybody who shot off an argument now.

Lora went into the bedroom. Conch and Bozo had thrown Mae down on the bed. She was struggling to get up, kicking and scratching.

"Hold her," Lora ordered. She glanced over her shoulder and saw Squirrel watching her in perplexity, looking a little uneasy at the demon he had given power to.

Bozo gripped Mae's legs tightly. While Conch held her arms, Lora yanked the sweater up from Mae's waist and pulled it over her head. She didn't bother unhooking Mae's bra, merely ripping it loose. Mae's breasts were small but well-formed, tip-tilted and firm. Her face was contorted in fury and terror, and she was blushing down to her waist.

"Grab her legs tight," Lora said. She unzipped Mae's fly and, with some effort, pulled her jeans off. The jeans were so tight that they dragged the panties off too, and Mae was naked. Her long, lean body had none of Lora's voluptuousness, but there was a catlike sensuousness about her that explained why Squirrel had been so attracted to her.

Lora watched Squirrel's face. Only yesterday, he would have felt it necessary to fight any man who made a slighting remark about Mae. Now, because of the change in his status, he was in the position of having to stand by approvingly while her nakedness was revealed to the whole gang.

"Who's gonna be first?" Lora asked. "Squirrel, you gotta pick someone."

Squirrel shrugged. "Anybody. Conch, you be the first."

None of the debs watched, none but Lora. They were on hand at the start, but they slipped away silently as Conch began to fumble with his trousers. The Cougar men, though, stood by with keen interest.

Conch didn't have any inhibitions about doing it in front of the gang. This probably wasn't the first time the Cougars had held such a line-up, though it was certainly the first time that the victim was an ex-Cougar deb herself.

Lora could remember when the Scarlet Sinners had held these line-ups. There was one time, in Johnny Diablo's time. Johnny had said hello to a girl on the street, the sister of a "coolie" who didn't take part in gang affairs. The girl had slapped him and run away. That night, eighteen of the Scarlet Sinners had gone to her door at a time when nobody else in the family was home. When she answered, they grabbed her, dragging her out of her apartment and carrying her down to a vacant lot overgrown with weeds and bushes.

There, behind the bushes, to an audience of some twenty of the Scarlet Sinners' Little People, the gang boys had methodically stripped her and raped her. Lora had been among the watchers. She remembered the way the terrified girl had protested feebly, "No... no, I'm a virgin, don't do it...."

But nobody had listened. They had clamped a rag into her mouth to keep her quiet, and they sliced away her clothes, baring round young breasts and soft thighs to the view of the crowd. And Johnny had been the first to rape her. Lora remembered the shudder of pain, the drops of blood....

And then all the rest of the men had raped her. It took almost two hours, and when it was finished they just walked away and left the girl lying on the ground, unconscious. She was never seen in the neighborhood again. The rumor was that she had gone out of her mind, and was in a mental institution someplace.

There had been other line-ups, too. Lora remembered them. She enjoyed the sight of another person being humiliated and ruined.

Conch unzipped his trousers. He was a cheerful, heavy-set boy, and he was grinning as he walked toward the bed. He didn't seem at all bothered by revealing himself in front of a group that included Lora.

Mae moaned and tried to clamp her legs together. Conch untwined them and forced them apart with his knee. He threw himself on the lean girl, resting his elbows on her arms in such a way as to prevent her from striking out at him.

"Don't be easy on her, Conch," Lora warned.

"I'm gonna have a good time," he answered.

She tried to resist—kicking her legs furiously in the air, struggling to get her hands free. But she was helpless. Methodically, brutally, Conch took her, chuckling to himself about it. Lora kept glancing over at Squirrel. Beads of sweat made his face glitter, and his lips were tense and tight, but he wasn't making any attempt to stop what was going on.

Conch wasn't in any rush. Mae sobbed and whimpered, while the rape was going on. At last, the muscular Conch was satisfied. He rose, zipping up his trousers. Mae tried to spring from the bed, but Conch slapped her, knocking her back down. She lay there, hatred turning her face into a hideous mask.

"Zorro next," Squirrel said in an emotionless voice.

Zorro was the next, satisfying himself quickly, and then came Little Richie, Gut, and Manny. By the fifth assault, Mae wasn't fighting back any more. She lay limply, her eyes closed, making deep sobbing sounds at the base of her throat.

Eight Cougars had her... nine... ten. Lora began to lose interest in the spectacle. She tugged Squirrel by the arm.

"Come on. Let's get something to drink."

"Okay," he said, too eager to get out of the room where the brutality was taking place. They passed into the big room, where the Cougar debs were sitting, stonyfaced. A few of the Cougars who had already had Mae were in the room too.

The door opened and Pug, Marty, and Gimp came in. "We dumped him," Marty reported.

"Any trouble?" Squirrel asked.

Marty shook his head. "We got four blocks into Raven turf and planted him in an empty lot. We brought the trunk back."

"There blood in it?"

"Uh-uh. We checked."

"Go into the bedroom," Lora said. "There's some fun for you in there."

"What kinda fun?" Pug wanted to know.

"We're having a line-up," Lora said. "On Mae."

"Jeez," Pug said. He cut off any further comment. He and Marty and Gimp went down the hallway. Lora poured two glasses of thunderbird, one for her, one for Squirrel.

"Here," she said. "Drink hearty. Celebrate. You're the top man, now."

"Yeah," he said moodily.

"What's the matter?" she whispered. "You worried about Mae?"

"Christ, Lora, she meant something to me once," Squirrel said weakly.

"Well, that crap's over!" she blazed. "I'm your deb now. And she's dirt. Just dirt."

Squirrel downed his drink and managed to grin.

"Yeah," he said. "She's gettin' what she deserved. Pullin' your hair and spittin' like that—"

"She's lucky I'm letting her off alive," Lora said. She winked at Squirrel. "Don't you go get into the line-up, though. You save yourself for me, hear?"

"Sure, Lora-babe. Sure."

"Go ask Bozo for some M, now. I feel like blasting a joint, Squirrel."

Squirrel called to the hophead, who came shuffling over. The new gang leader ordered Bozo to produce two reefers. Bozo handed them over, and Squirrel gave him a dollar.

Lora said, "Let's save 'em till later. After Mae's outa here."

"Yeah. Yeah," Squirrel said, putting the reefers in his pocket.

Gimp came limping out of the bedroom, buttoning his fly and grinning. Gimp had been a cripple ever since getting the tendons behind his right knee slashed in a rumble a year and a half back. He was tremendously powerful, and despite his handicap he was still a feared man in a battle.

He said now, "We gonna have seconds?"

"That's up to you," Squirrel said. "How's Mae?"

"She passed out a long time ago. Marty's giving it to her now. He's the last one."

The rape continued for another hour, while those who wanted a second turn with Mae satisfied themselves. She was conscious only for occasional moments, looking dazed and feverish. At last, when nobody else in the gang expressed an interest in raping her, Lora went in to make a final inspection of her former rival.

Somebody had thrown a towel over Mae's waist. She was dimly conscious again, her eyes red with weeping, her face bruised and bloody from the beating Squirrel had administered. Her lips were moving slowly, but no words were coming out.

Lora scowled. "Put some clothes on this crud and get it out of here," she said.

Claire and Dolores came forward, hesitantly. Lifting Mae's limp, tormented body, they carefully put her sweater and jeans back on, not bothering with any underthings. Mae's head lolled as the two debs carried their outcast comrade to the door.

"Dump her in an alley," Squirrel ordered.

Lora grinned triumphantly as the door closed. She was conquering everyone. First Whitey, then Squirrel. First Donna, then Mae.

Nobody could stand in her way!

Nobody!

CHAPTER NINE

The next day, at school, there was more trouble between the negroes and the Puerto Ricans. It started, so the word got around, in the boys' locker room during a first-period gym class. A Magician and an Ace had a scuffle because the Magician thought he was getting deliberately overcrowded in the locker. There was a quick fist-fight and the Puerto Rican, the Magician, was knocked down, cutting open his cheek badly on the sharp edge of one of the lockers.

Lora heard the story from Conch in the halls between the first and second period. "There's gonna be trouble," Conch whispered. "The Magicians are out to get the Aces, and they ain't stopping till there's a rumble."

Lora smiled. That was just what she wanted—a rumble. Maiming and killing!

There wasn't any doubt in her mind that the Cougars would get dragged into the feud sooner or later. Most of the Cougars were of Italian ancestry, but they had been friendly with the negro gang, the Aces, ever since Whitey had negotiated a "cool" between the two gangs the summer before. The way it worked, the Cougars would help the Aces out whenever the Aces' traditional enemies, the Magicians, got rambunctious. And if the Ravens, the Irish gang that had it in for the Cougars, started acting up, the Aces would step in on the Cougars' side.

Of course, you couldn't count on any such alliances. You never knew when the Aces might negotiate a "cool" with the Ravens themselves, and turn around and jap the Cougars some day. You had to be constantly on guard against some such shift of loyalty. There wasn't any percentage in trusting anybody too much, in the kid-gang jungle.

But the tension was rising. Ugly storm-clouds were gathering. The Aces and the Magicians would be at each other's throats any day.

During her third-period gym class, Lora was treated to a skirmish incident herself. The class of several hundred girls was getting into gym suits in the locker room, the gym suits being skimpy one-piece outfits of green linen. Lora was getting into hers when she heard violent cursing erupt suddenly in the aisle immediately to her left. She went to have a look.

A towering negro girl, stark naked, was standing at bay there, bellowing defiance. The girl was, Lora knew, an Ace deb named Hollie. She was practically six feet tall, a statuesque girl with skin so black it almost seemed to be purple. She was fending off three much shorter Puerto Rican girls who were clustered around her like hounds trying to bring down a bear. They were screaming at her in Spanish, and she was lashing out with fists and feet, trying to keep them away. Her gigantic breasts bounced and quivered with each motion. Sweat rolled down her body, making the dark skin gleam, giving a strange sheen to the great bowls of her breasts and to the massive columns of her thighs.

As Lora watched, one of the Puerto Rican girls darted forward, nails held high, and, reaching up, clawed the negro girl's bosom. Hollie shrieked. Three parallel lines of bright red sprang up against the black skin, crossing her right breast just above the nipple. A fourth Puerto Rican girl had joined the assault now, and there were no other colored girls in sight. Rivers of sweat were coursing down the enormous black body, mingling with the blood flowing from the wounded melon-sized breast.

Lora grinned. This was time for some action!

Wearing only a pair of panties herself, she cruised toward the aisle. She came plowing into the little group of attackers, scattering them to right and left. The negro girl glanced down at her in surprise.

"I'm a Cougar deb," Lora explained.

Hollie grinned her thanks.

They stood side by side, the fiery, bare-breasted Italian girl and the monumental negress, and began to take the offensive in the skirmish. Hollie seized one of the Puerto Rican girls and hurled her back against a locker, stunning her and reducing the sides to only three against two. At the same moment, Lora sprang upon another of the Magician debs and bore her to the ground. They rolled over twice, and then Lora emerged on top. She seized the Puerto Rican's abundant hair and began to pound her head against the concrete floor of the locker room. Only when the girl went limp did Lora rise.

She turned to see Hollie holding off the two remaining Magician debs with some difficulty. Lora rejoined the fray, and for a moment the four of them tangled together, sweaty, naked bodies inextricably locked. A bare, tawny breast presented itself suddenly; grinning savagely, Lora bit it, and was rewarded with a howling outcry of agony and a string of Spanish profanity. The tangled heap writhed round and round; Lora found herself lying crosswise atop Hollie's firm, titanic buttocks, with one Puerto Rican girl at the bottom of the heap and the other sprawled across Hollie's back. Lora's nails raked out, drawing lines of blood across the back and buttocks of one of the Magician debs. There was another scream of pain. And then whistles were blowing, and the other girls in the locker room, up till now only interested bystanders, began to mill around chaotically, to protect the combatants from discovery.

Magically, the heap of struggling flesh dissolved. Limping and rubbing their wounds, the Puerto Rican girls slipped off into the crowd. Lora and Hollie got to their feet and rapidly faded from the aisle, just a moment before two furious gym teachers came striding past in an effort to discover the culprits.

The huge negress grinned at Lora. "You sure saved my ass that time, cat."

"Why'd they jump you?"

"My man split open some Puerto's face first period. They just gettin' even."

Lora wriggled into her gym suit. The colored girl imprisoned the vast globes of her breasts in the top of her green suit and began to button it. She was really king-size, Lora thought. A size 45 bust, maybe, and the rest of the proportions to match. Not fat or sloppy, though. Just *big*.

There were no incidents during the gym session, and the Puerto Rican girls kept their distance at the end of the period when everyone was changing back into street clothes. At lunchtime, Lora met Marty and Squirrel in the cafeteria and told them about the fight.

Squirrel looked worried. "There's gonna be a rumble. Those Magicians are out for blood now."

"So?" Lora asked. "So there'll be a rumble. Crap, it's been quiet around here long enough, hasn't it, Squirrel?"

"Yeah. Yeah. It ain't gonna be quiet for long, though."

Word travels fast on the high-school grapevine. The fight in the girls' locker room was being whispered all over the school by the fifth period. Lora grinned to herself as she heard the story being told.

"*...and this big nigger girl was jumped by four spics—Aces against Magicians, you know. You shoulda seen the girl. Tits like a coupla basketballs, I hear. Anyway, then this new Cougar girl got into the fight, and she and the Ace wiped up the floor with the four spics....*"

It was getting around. A Cougar deb had helped an Ace deb fight off four Magician debs. Now there wouldn't be any doubt of the alliance between the Cougars and the Aces. So the Cougars would inevitably be drawn into the coming rumble.

And that was exactly what Lora wanted. She wanted action.

The action started at ten after two, when the early-shift kids were leaving the school. Lora missed it, because she had gone out the side entrance. As Marty told her later that afternoon, it had been a continuation of the locker-room fight of the first period. One of the Magicians, a friend of the boy whose face had been cut, had accosted two Aces as they left the school. There had been a quick scuffle and one of the Aces got knifed. The Magician, Marty said, escaped; the Ace was in the hospital, having been stabbed in the abdomen.

Lora went home in high excitement. She tossed her books on her bed and went into the kitchen to get the three o'clock news broadcast. You could always depend on the radio announcers to give you the latest gang news soon as it happened.

Sure enough. *"...a new outbreak of teenage violence erupted on the Lower East Side today, when 17-year-old John Thompson was stabbed while leaving Nathan Harley High School. Thompson, who has a record as a juvenile offender, was taken to Bellevue Hospital in critical condition. His assailant escaped. School authorities said the stabbing was an outgrowth of recent mounting friction between negro and Puerto Rican teenage gangs in the past several days...."*

Lora snapped the radio off. The rumble wasn't far away, now. Not with one of the Aces in the hospital with a Magician knife-hole in his belly.

She pulled off her skirt—girls weren't allowed to wear jeans to school now and took a tight pair of dungarees out of the closet. She pulled them on and went out.

Most of the Cougars were at the clubhouse already, discussing the events of the day. It was all they could talk about. Nobody was making out, hardly anybody was drinking. Today the excitement of the coming rumble took the place of sex and drinking. The recent struggle for power within the gang was forgotten, too. The possibility of a rumble blotted out all else.

Squirrel came over to her. "You hear about the stabbing?"

"Yeah. Marty told me on the way home. Then I heard it on the radio at three."

"Looks like the Aces are gonna be out for a rumble," Squirrel said. "Looks like we'll be in it too."

"High time we had some action," Lora said.

Gimp came limping up. "Hey, Squirrel?"

"Yeah."

"Coupla visitors outside."

"What kind?"

"They're from the Aces," Gimp said. "I made 'em wait. I told 'em you might be busy with Lora."

"Who are they?" Squirrel asked.

"China and the Bishop, they said. They wanta talk about a rumble."

Squirrel shrugged. "Let 'em in."

The two Aces were dressed to kill. China was the Prez of the Aces, and also the stud who made it with the negress Hollie. He looked like he could handle a girl that size. He was tremendous, six feet four or five, and his shoulders were almost as wide as the doorway. He was dressed in a dark beige topcoat with black velvet collar, a striped orange-and-black jacket, a blue dacron shirt, and black, peg-top trousers. He put out his hand to take Squirrel's, and though Squirrel had a big hand it was swallowed up and dwarfed by the great mahogany paw of the Ace leader.

The Bishop was the War Counselor of the Aces, and he, too, was decked out in his fanciest garb. He had on a deep blue gabardine coat, a bright red silk shirt, sleek black pegged trousers, and black woven-leather pumps. It was a sharp contrast with the khaki trousers and black leather jacket that was his usual uniform. He contrasted physically with China, too: while the gang leader was brutally massive, the war counselor was slim and agile, with a dancer's nimble grace.

China said, in a rumbling basso, "Which one of these debs is Lora?"

"I am."

"My woman tol' me about the fight today," China boomed. "She says you were okay. Real okay."

"She was okay too," Lora said. "That's one hell of a lot of woman you got there, China."

Squirrel said, "You hear from the hospital about Spider?"

The Bishop nodded. "Yeah, his mother called up. They sewin' him up now. He got a big hole in his gut, and they don't think he gonna live till tomorrow."

China said, "That's why we come over. We wanta parley. We're building up a rumble, man."

Squirrel's eyes narrowed. The rest of the Cougars stared intently at the two visitors. Lora's gaze rested sharply on the Cougar Prez.

Squirrel said slowly, "We always been pretty friendly with you Aces."

"We know it, man," the Bishop said. "So we come over to fill you in on our plans. We want you in on it when we jump the Puertos."

Marty said, "The area's gonna be crawling with the fuzz tonight, after the stabbing. You ain't starting nothing tonight, are you, man?"

The Bishop shrugged elegantly. "Not tonight, cat. Tomorrow. We gonna keep things calm and slow tonight while the fuzz come poking. But tomorrow—"

"Where?" Squirrel asked.

"You really want to know?" the Bishop asked lazily. He wasn't going to reveal any strategic information until he knew exactly where the Cougars stood.

"Go on, lay it out," Squirrel said, irritated. "We ain't gonna leak it."

The Bishop smiled. "We gonna jap 'em in their own turf. We gonna teach them spic bastards once and for all. There ain't gonna be nothing fair about this rumble, man."

"They expect a rumble," Gimp put in. "They won't be nappin'."

China nodded. "Sure, they'll be waitin'. But they only got twenty men. We got twenty-eight. And if you guys go along with us—"

"We got seventeen," Squirrel said.

"You with us, man?"

Squirrel hesitated, but only for a moment. He knew that as the new head of the gang it was important to prove his strength by leading the gang into battle. And the odds sounded good this time.

"Yeah," Squirrel said. "We're with you."

"Okay," the Bishop said. "We're gonna go down on them around nine tomorrow."

"Where do we meet you?"

"Lou's Billiards," the Bishop said. "We start from there. I got everything worked out. We gonna waste them, man. We gonna use them all up."

It was agreed, then. The two Ace emissaries stayed around long enough to have a couple of drinks with the Cougars; then they left, heading back south to their own turf. The alliance had been forged.

Lora felt pleased. By stepping to the aid of Hollie, she had practically volunteered the help of the Cougars singlehanded. Now the Cougars were definitely in the rumble.

The rumble would be a one-sided slaughter, she thought happily. And, a few weeks later, after the police foofaraw had died down, it would be possible to make use of the alliance for a return favor. The Cougars could provoke the Ravens into a rumble, too. The Irish gang was a big one, but they wouldn't be able to withstand the combined strength of the Cougars and the Aces.

It was interesting, Lora thought, that neither China nor the Bishop had said one word about Whitey. It had been Whitey who had arranged the original "cool" between the two gangs, the year before. But now Squirrel was in charge, and the two Aces had accepted the situation without even bothering to ask what had happened to Whitey. That was the way it had to be. Whitey was out of the way, finished, somebody who didn't count any more. You were only looking for trouble if you mentioned him.

She poured herself a drink. Squirrel came over to her, looking serious.

"What's the matter?" she asked. "You look all stirred up."

"Gimme a drink."

"Sure, man. What's bugging you?"

"Nothing," Squirrel insisted.

"It's the rumble, ain't it?" she said in a low voice.

"Nothing's bugging me," Squirrel muttered angrily.

She shook her head, smiling knowingly. Pouring him a drink, she picked it up and began to walk out of the room with it.

"Hey," Squirrel yelled. "Where you going?"

"In back," she answered. "Come on along, man."

She went into the President's room and put down the drinks on top of the trophy shelf. Squirrel followed her in, still frowning, and bolted the door.

She looked up at him. "You trying to mess yourself up, man?"

"What the hell you mean?"

"I mean the long faces you're pulling."

"I don't dig," Squirrel said.

"Lemme spell it out for you, then. We got ourselves into a rumble. You don't look happy about it. What's the matter, Squirrel? You scared?"

"Who ever said—"

"Nobody. It's just the way you look. You look like you don't wanta be mixed up in the rumble."

He stared uncomfortably at his shoes. "I dunno," he muttered. "I just can't get excited about mixing up with the Aces and the Magicians."

"Listen to me," she said fiercely. "You're the top man here, now. You killed a man to get on top, and now that you're there you gotta act like a boss! You want this rumble, man. And you're gonna fight like crazy when it comes off. You're gonna kill spics, and you're gonna let everybody in the gang see it."

Squirrel smiled. "Yeah, Lora."

"You cooled off Whitey, remember? Now you gotta fill his shoes. You can't just follow along any more. A leader's gotta *lead,* Squirrel. If he don't, he'll wake up with a hole in his guts."

With a sudden wrench she yanked her sweater off. A moment later the bra dropped to the floor. She threw her shoulders back, thrusting her high, round breasts outward at him. Her nipples rose stiffly, telling him of her desire.

"You see these?" she demanded. "They're yours, Squirrel. But you gotta earn 'em. You killed to get 'em—now you've gotta kill to keep 'em!"

Lust glinted brightly in Squirrel's eyes. Lora's words had cut deep. He was on fire, now, burning with the same flame that had led him on to triumph over Whitey. Lora smiled. She had done it at last; she had stirred him on to be a real leader.

Squirrel stepped forward. His hands shot out, grabbing her breasts tightly, bruising her nipples. She flattened herself against him. Their lips met; she ground her hips against his, felt his hands leave her breasts and grasp the firm flesh of her buttocks. She began to pant. Breaking away from him, she ripped off her clothing and flung herself on the bed.

She held out her arms to him. He came toward her, shedding his clothing, aroused and eager. Their bodies met, and he took her violently, overpoweringly, and they went sweeping off to ecstasy together.

CHAPTER TEN

Nathan Harley High School was quiet the next day, but it was a deceptive quiet, an uneasy quiet. The different racial groups kept well apart. What little conversation there was, was carried on in whispers and gestures. Trouble was about to break, and this was the calm before the storm.

There were cops all over the place, standing on the corners facing the school, hanging around near the entrance to the schoolyard, even coming onto the school grounds themselves. But nobody gave them provocation. The real trouble would start later, after dark. The Magicians gave no sign of suspecting that a rumble was brewing, though; several times they attempted to taunt the Aces, but each time they were met with a cold, chilly silence.

Word had come that the wounded Ace, Spider, had died during the night. After that, the Magicians quieted down considerably. They didn't want to get picked up for questioning by the prowling police.

It was agreed that nobody would go to the clubhouse before evening. They scattered, spending the afternoon at home. Lora took the opportunity to catch up a little with her homework.

At dinner, her parents discussed little but the Thompson killing. Her father was particularly bitter.

"You spend all you have to make a new home for your family," he complained. "And then the week you move, it's the same old thing all over again. Killings and fightings in my daughter's school."

"The thing we ought to do is move out of this city altogether," Mrs. Menotti said.

"That won't help," her husband said broodingly. "The kids in the suburbs are just as bad. A pack of wolves, this whole generation. A pack of wolves. And my own daughter one of them."

Lora said nothing and tried not to smirk. The old creeps, she thought! Jabbering away about how terrible things were today. They didn't do anything about it, didn't try to make things any better. They just talked.

Round and round and round, the same old jabber. *How terrible. How shocking. How frightful it all is!*

She left soon after dinner, without a word, and headed for the Cougar clubhouse. Most of the Cougars were there already, and their debs. Everybody was armed, in one way or another. Conch had a sawed-off shotgun. Squirrel had a Beretta, a deadly little Italian pistol. Most of the others had zip-guns that fired .22 caliber bullets. They were all carrying switchblades or gravity knives in reserve, of course.

The Cougars were in battle dress. Heavy leather jackets that served as armor against all but the most vicious thrusts. Heavy hobnailed boots that came in handy when you were stomping a fallen adversary. Brass-studded garrison belts that made dandy face-smashers when other weapons failed.

Squirrel looked eager and unafraid. He kept looking at his watch. A bottle of sneaky pete was going round and round, and everybody was taking deep pulls to increase their courage.

All of the Cougars were there, including the debs. The debs were going along on this rumble, all except a few who were short-winded and couldn't be trusted to make a quick getaway.

Squirrel said, "Conch, give the debs their aerials."

From a locked closet Conch produced a sheaf of snapped-off automobile radio aerials. They were handy weapons. Most of them telescoped up small enough to be carried under a jacket, and each of the debs carried one. Used as a whip, they could put out eyes and cut a face open to the bone. Used as spears, they could jab through stomach-linings or lungs. The debs would congregate around the borders of the rumble area, using the aerials whenever an unwary enemy ventured close enough.

At eight o'clock Squirrel said, "Okay, let's get on the move. Lou's Billiards on First Street. Groups of twos and threes, and keep it scattered. Don't look for trouble on the way down."

Lora folded her aerial up and shoved it under her jacket. She and Squirrel left the clubhouse and started to stroll south into Ace turf.

The border was First Street. Below that, the area was held by the Aces and, to the west of them, the Magicians. In fifteen minutes, she and Squirrel had reached the poolroom that was the headquarters of the negro gang. About half of the Cougars had already arrived. In the basement of the poolroom, the Aces had congregated, waiting for their allies to show up.

It was eight-thirty before everyone was on hand. As war counselor of the larger gang, the Bishop was in charge of the meeting. In his soft voice he explained his strategy.

"We got this one car, y'see," he told the Cougars. "We gonna load that up and drive it right past the Magician hangout and have them fire off some shots. Meantime while the Magicians are all fussed up about the car, the rest of us come outa the side streets and jap 'em. I figure the whole thing oughta take two-three minutes, then we beat it. And it's finish for the Magicians after tonight."

They started out, dribbling westward in little groups. It was important not to look menacing, because the neighborhood was saturated with cops. If they got picked up on suspicion of a rumble, they could get the book thrown at them—illegal possession of weapons and all the rest.

First Avenue was the borderline between Ace turf and Magician turf. By threes and fours, the combined gangs slipped toward First Avenue on different side streets, following the master plan that the Bishop had devised. Squirrel and China led their respective gangs onward. The Bishop was riding in the car that would provide the diversionary action.

Lora went along up front, right beside Squirrel. Her heart was racing. The Scarlet Sinners had kept the debs out of the rumbles, most of the times. The debs just stood to one side, ready to receive their studs' weapons and hide them if the police threatened. But now she had a weapon of her own.

The Cougars and Aces began to take positions in the first block of Magician turf, just back of the street where the Magician hangout was. It was a quiet lateSeptember night, warm and mild. From the next block came the raucous bellowing of a jukebox, belting out the current Spanish-language hits. The Magicians were living it up, it seemed. They didn't know what was in store for them yet.

Lora tensed. Suddenly, from the next block, came the sound of roaring motors—followed by the flat boom of a sawed-off shotgun. There was the tinkle of store-windows smashing under the hail of lead.

"Come on!" Squirrel yelled.

"Shake your tails," boomed the giant China.

Nearly fifty gang kids sprang forward, heading for the corner and rounding it. The Ace auto had reached the end of the block and was turning round to take another potshot at the Magician hangout. Heads were sticking out of every window on the black. A dozen astounded Magicians had come out into the street and were hurling vivid imprecations at the passing auto. Lora heard the Bishop's high-pitched voice returning the curses as the old car zoomed past again.

"Now!" China yelled.

"Let 'em have it!" Squirrel bellowed.

The combined gangs swept down on the ambushed Magicians. The Puerto Ricans turned, stunned, caught in a crossfire between the auto and the ambushers. The shotgun blasted again. The Cougars and Aces each surrounded the outnumbered Puerto Ricans. Switchblades clicked; zip-guns whined, and screams of pain split the night.

Lora, feverish with excitement, saw other Puerto Ricans come running from Second Avenue. She uncoiled her aerial and, as the first one came past, swung out backhand in a vicious slash. The singing wire slapped sharply into a Magician's throat, nearly wrapping itself around it. Lora pulled back; a deep bloody line was indented in the Puerto Rican's skin. A moment later, a zip-gun bullet slashed into his arm, spinning him around and knocking him down.

Conch and one of the Aces had caught hold of a Puerto Rican in a flamboyant silk jacket. The Ace dragged the Magician to his knees, and Conch kicked him, hard, making him double up and clutch his groin. Conch kicked him again, and this time the heavy boot landed in the Puerto Rican's face.

By now the street was a scene of wild confusion. Magicians were lying everywhere. The Magician debs were screaming frantically. Grinning, Lora saw the titanic Hollie claw the flimsy blouse off a Puerto Rican girl and slash her across the bare breasts with a car radio antenna. The girl went spinning away on her knees, clutching her nipples.

Cut, slash, stomp, shoot... cut, slash, stomp shoot... Milling combatants filled the street, and over it all came the screams of the wounded.

Sirens wailed suddenly.

"Scram! It's the fuzz!" came the voice of China, rising like thunder over the melee.

Sirens screamed louder.

The invaders melted away. Lora slipped into a side alley and began to run quickly eastward, keeping her eyes open so she wouldn't run full tilt into a policeman. When she had crossed First Avenue she stopped to catch her breath. She proceeded more slowly, now, not looking back. At the next block she stopped and took the car aerial out. It was bloody. She dropped it in a trashcan and kept going. It was better not to be carrying it. The gang could always get more, any time they needed them—just snap them off the parked cars in the street.

Behind her, the sirens' wail continued. Probably some passer-by had phoned in the alarm, and police cars were converging from all over. Lora wondered how many of the Cougars would get caught. She wondered how much damage had been inflicted on the Puerto Rican gang. Plenty, she thought. She had seen with her own eyes one of the Puerto Ricans with his head practically blown off by a shotgun blast, and another who had been stabbed in the chest a couple of dozen times.

No sense going back to the clubhouse now. It was a lot safer just to go home. The cops would be roaming the whole area all night, picking up anybody suspicious-looking for questioning. Lora had heard about the way the cops sometimes questioned. Other gang members had told stories of the bare rooms with the naked light-bulbs overhead, of the bullying detectives, of the almost-torture that was used. Of the girls who had been stripped to the waist and slapped across the nipples until they answered questions. Of naked boys with cigarettes held near their most delicate parts. Lora didn't know whether the torture stories were true or not. She didn't want to find out first-hand, that was all.

It was half past nine now. The whole rumble had lasted only a few minutes. It had seemed like hours, while it was going on.

Funny, she thought. For weeks you hang around, doing nothing. Then when the action finally comes, it's suddenly over, and you wait for weeks to live it up again.

She reached the project. It was still warm out, and people were sitting out front, reading newspapers, drinking beer. They didn't know that a dozen blocks away a grim war had just taken place. Right here, everything was deceptively peaceful.

She went upstairs. Her parents were watching television and her brother was doing homework. They blinked at her in surprise, not able to understand why she had come home so early this night.

"You sick?" her mother asked.

Lora shrugged. "There wasn't nothin' doing, so I came home. You mind?"

She didn't answer. Lora walked past her and went on into her room. Kicking off her shoes, she stretched out on her bed.

The excitement still tingled through her. She had drawn blood; she had fought, she had maimed, she had escaped. She went over the details of the rumble again and again, recalling the ambush, the surprised looks on the faces of the Magicians as forty gang boys and two dozen debs came bursting out at them from hiding. They had really creamed.

Now the Magicians were finished as a gang. Some of them were dead, practically all of them were cut up in some way. The Aces would get most of the credit for the wipe-out job, but the other gangs would know that the Cougars, under their new leader, had taken a big part in the operation too. The Cougar rep would grow, and Squirrel would become a big man in the city. You were automatically a big man if you cooled off someone like Whitey, but now he would be *real* big.

And next, Lora thought gleefully, would be the rumble with the Ravens.

She was jumpy with excitement. She wanted to go down, to hurry over to the clubhouse and find out the score. But she knew it would be a mistake to venture out again tonight. It would be asking for trouble, and when you asked for it you got it. She pictured herself in a police station, sitting in a chair with her hands tied behind her back, naked to the waist, and three drooling cops standing over her giving her a smack across the nipples every time she refused to answer a question the right way.

Uh-uh, Lora thought. Not for me.

For an hour she lay stretched out, eyes closed, reliving the fight. Then there was a timid knock on her bedroom door.

"Yeah?"

"Can I come in?" her mother asked.

"If you want to."

The door opened. Her mother stood in the doorway, looking fearful and uncertain. Her lips moved for a moment before words came out. "Lora—"

"Yeah?"

"We just heard the news on the television, Lora. There was a gang fight down here tonight."

"Do tell."

"Lora—" The old lady's tongue flicked nervously across her lips. "It was a terrible fight. Some Puerto Rican boys got killed and a lot got taken away to the hospital."

"Gee," Lora said emotionlessly.

"You came home early tonight," her mother said. "Lora, were you in that fight?"

"Me, Ma?"

"I want to know. We don't want you in those terrible gangs, Lora."

Lora smiled. "I wasn't in no fight tonight, Ma. I came home early because nobody much was around. Honest, Ma."

Her mother frowned, as though trying to look behind Lora's glib protestations of innocence. But then her eyes filmed in the dull cast of defeat. Shrugging, she turned and walked out, closing the door of the bedroom behind her.

Lora grinned triumphantly. She had the old lady bulldozed!

She got up and began to undress, tossing her clothes negligently on the chair. She was sweaty from her earlier running.

She paused in front of the mirror, critically eyeing the soft swells of her breasts, the tapering curves of her thighs. She liked to look at her own body. She put her hands under her breasts, lifting them, feeling their warm heaviness. It amused her, the way boys went wild when they saw her breasts. She could make them do anything she wanted, just by taking her bra off for them.

Then she went on into the shower. She was under the water a long time, making it good and cold. She felt the throbbing in her loins, the itch of desire. It was lousy to come running home after a rumble, she thought. It would have been better to go back to the clubhouse with Squirrel and make it there, twine her body around his and mingle sweat and blood and saliva. But the clubhouse was probably empty. It wouldn't be safe to congregate in the neighborhood for a couple of days.

She toweled dry, put on her robe, and left the bathroom. Her brother was waiting outside.

"About time you came out," he muttered.

"Doncha want me to be clean?"

"It would take more than a shower," he snapped.

Lora grinned at him. Deliberately, provocatively, she let her robe fall open, exposing the whiteness of her breasts. Chick took a fast involuntary look, and then he hurried past her into the bathroom. Lora laughed derisively at him. She wondered what it would be like, making it with her own brother. He probably wasn't much good in bed. But it would be a switch.

Yeah, she thought. Only the creep would probably have a fit. He damn near had apoplexy when she opened her robe.

The creep, she thought. What the hell was so wrong with making it with your own sister, anyway? You'd think she had the plague or something. Why, she knew plenty who did it all the time.

Shaking her head, she went into her bedroom and closed the door.

CHAPTER ELEVEN

Lora woke late the next morning, because it was Saturday. It was past ten when she got up, and the apartment was empty. She knew where the others were. Her brother had a job on Saturdays, to supplement the slim family income. Her mother was probably out doing the Saturday morning marketing. And her father, most likely, was over in the park playing checkers. He played a lot of checkers. When they lived in the Bronx, he would spend practically all weekend playing checkers with men in the park, and now that they had moved down here he would undoubtedly find a new park, new checker-playing opponents. It was a funny way to keep happy, Lora thought, but what the hell—it took all sorts of people to make a world.

She put on a robe and slouched into the kitchen to brew some coffee. Taking advantage of the fact that she was alone, she turned on the radio and dialed in a news broadcast to find out about the rumble.

After a couple of minutes of foreign news, she got what she wanted to hear:

"...Manhattan police are still probing last night's newest outbreak of juvenile savagery on the Lower East Side. In what police described as a 'carefully organized raid,' a predominantly negro gang descended on a candy store frequented by a rival gang made up largely of boys of Puerto Rican ancestry. The pitched battle, which saw the use of shotguns and pistols as well as knives, cost the lives of four of the Puerto Rican boys. A fifth, Orlando Dominguez, 18, is in critical condition as a result of multiple stab wounds, and is not expected to live. Eight more members of the Puerto Rican gang are listed as being in 'serious' condition, while four others suffered minor wounds. There were no casualties on the part of the attackers.

"Police last night arrested five members of an East side gang known as the Aces, charging them with homicide in connection with the slayings. Police Commissioner O'Brien said this morning that the troubled area would receive extra patrols until all of the attackers had been taken into custody, and that there will be an intensified crackdown on juvenile crime areas throughout the city...."

Smiling, Lora reached across and snapped the radio off just as the announcer began to talk about the weather. Four Magicians killed, one dying! Eight more in the hospital! The back of the gang had been broken.

Five Aces arrested, though. She frowned over that. Would they talk? Would they drag the Cougars into the situation?

After breakfast, Lora dressed and went over to Sid's. The candy-store proprietor looked even more harried than ever. As Lora walked in, he came quickly to the door and blocked her.

"What kinda jazz is this?" she asked.

Sid's pasty face looked fishbelly white. "Listen," he said in a husky voice. "Do me a favor, huh? Don't come in here today."

"Of all the crud—"

"I know, I know. Squirrel was here and I told him the same thing." The candy-store man looked about ready to get down on his knees to Lora. "Look, the cops have been around here all morning. It's for your own good as well as mine. If all you kids hang around together here, they'll arrest you. The cops are out to make trouble today. The Chief of Police is making it hot for them, and they're passing it right along."

"Where's Squirrel now?"

"He left when I told him," Sid said. "What I mean is, stay off the streets a couple days, till this thing blows over. You hang around here, the cops'll come in, and I'll get into the papers because I let you hang around my place. They can put me out of business. Look, I been okay, no? I let you all stay here even though all my old customers they won't come in here any more. So look, just go easy on me, keep away for a couple of days till the cops cool down—"

"Okay, okay," Lora said contemptuously. Sid was quivering with fright. "We'll keep out."

"Thanks a million. I can't tell you—"

"Okay, mac. Skip the blubbering."

She turned and walked out. The candy-store man's pathetic pleas left her with a queasy feeling in her stomach. She didn't like to see a man go so yellow. But Sid was scared, now. Voluntarily or not, he had allowed his place to be used as a kid-gang hangout, and now he was afraid that some of the outcry against teenage gangs would rebound on him. Well, okay, she thought—it was smart anyway for the Cougars to avoid congregating in public places, just for now.

She went over to the clubhouse.

Squirrel and a half dozen other Cougars were there. They had all the morning papers spread out in the main room, and they were reading the accounts of the rumble, laboriously spelling out the big words.

"I just came from Sid's," Lora said. "He told me he don't want us around for a few days."

Squirrel nodded. "He told me the same. I'm passing it around. No sense getting the dumb kook in trouble, is there?"

She pointed to the papers. "What do they say?"

"They play it up like World War Five," Gimp snorted. "Christ, you'd think we used tanks."

"We killed four," Squirrel said. "And Piggy Dominguez is about to make it five. His lungs are all cut up and he can't last."

"I heard it on the radio," Lora said. "What about these five Aces they arrested?"

Squirrel moistened his lips nervously. "Five dopes. They ran the wrong way and got grabbed by the fuzz on Second Avenue."

"You know who they are?"

"One of them was Shark," Squirrel said. "I don't know the others. But I talked to China and he said they weren't any of the big men in the club."

"But they'll fry," Pug said nervously. "They'll cook like turkeys."

"They asked for it, the dumb kooks!" Conch said scornfully. "You gotta know your ass from your elbow if you wanta go bopping and come back safe. What the hell were they doing running to Second Avenue?"

"So they got mixed up," Pug retorted. "Crap, in a rumble like that anybody could get mixed up. Bodies all over the place and the fuzz sirens going off every which way you turned—"

"We got away safe, didn't we?" Squirrel demanded. "They coulda too, if they had any brains."

"It don't matter how dumb they were," Lora cut in. "It's what's gonna happen now. Suppose they tell the cops that we were in on the rumble? Christ, suppose they give them all our names?"

Squirrel leaned back and picked up a glass of wine. "Don't worry about that," he said expansively.

"I'm glad you *ain't* worried," Lora said.

Squirrel took a long gulp and said, "I cleared it with China. Those five guys are too dumb to squeal. They don't even know our names. All they'd be able to say is that some white guys from up here were in on the rumble. That ain't good enough for a convention. Besides, Marty's got a theory that says the fuzz won't even *try* to make arrests."

Lora turned to the blonde boy, who was generally considered the most scholarly of the Cougar studs. "You got a theory, Marty?"

"Yeah," he said slowly. "Looka: the D.A. wants to make convictions. He wants to send guys to the chair or to Sing Sing. Right?"

"Yeah, sure. But—"

"I been following all the other big gang trials. The Farmer case, the Guzman thing, some of the others. How many guys do they put on trial? They don't round up a whole gang. Nah, they take six or seven guys and try them—and let half of them go. You can't try fifty guys for one rumble. It would just overflow the crappin' courtroom and nobody could figure out what was what. So look—they got five Aces now. Maybe they'll pick up two or three more this week. The D.A. has a nice clean case, a black gang against a Spanish gang. He ain't gonna cloud things up by dragging in a bunch of Guineas like us. He don't even want any more Aces up there on the stand. Five, six, seven and he can get a conviction. More than that and he just has a scramble on his hands."

Lora nodded doubtfully. "Yeah, okay. It *sounds* pretty good. Let's just hope you're right, now. I ain't keen on rotting in the pen."

Squirrel said, "Meantime I been giving orders. For the next couple days nobody goes to Sid's. And nobody hangs around in bunches of more than three or four. We gotta play it cool, now."

"Okay," Lora said. "Cool."

She walked over and poured herself a drink, the first one of the day. It was sweet red wine, thick and syrupy and pretty lousy.

Somebody put a record on. Marty and Dolores started to dance a cha-cha.

"Come on," Squirrel said. "Put down the drink and let's shake it a little."

"Hold everything, man." Lora belted away the wine in three greasy gulps and set the glass down. Cheap wine went to the head fast. She was wobbling a little as Squirrel pulled her out onto the floor. But the dancing cleared her head as the alcohol was burned out of her system by exertion.

The dancing got wilder. Lora didn't bother to go home for lunch. The Cougars were coming in steadily, filling up the place. The rumble was a thing of the past, now. This was the victory celebration. They lived it up.

Around one o'clock things got livelier when Zorro came in brandishing a fifth of rye, unopened, worth at least four bucks.

"Hey, where'd you get that, man?" Conch yelled out jubilantly.

"My old man," Zorro said. "He found some in the closet he didn't even know he had."

"And gave it to you for a present, huh?"

"He'll never miss it," Zorro laughed. He tossed the bottle football-fashion to Conch, who tucked it under his arm and ran for a touchdown down the full length of the room, shouldering aside the dancing couples as if they were opposition blockers. The Cougars crowded round him. He opened the bottle and handed it back to Zorro, who took the first pull. Then it got passed round.

The fifth didn't last long—but the party was a lot wilder when it was finished. The dancing took on a frenzied tone. Lora and Squirrel did a dizzying merengue in the middle of the floor, and she practically went into orbit as she gyrated madly around, her breasts bouncing like baseballs in her sweater.

Then another couple took over the floor—Cocoa, a short, stubby muscular boy, and his deb Lulu. She was short too, and pretty thick through the hips. She had big breasts and a heavy backside, and she was always laughing. She laughed plenty now. She was very drunk. She went reeling up and down the floor, while Cocoa deadpanned and went through dance steps. Suddenly, still giggling, Lulu yelled out, "Too crappin' hot in here." And, pulling her hand free from Cocoa, she yanked her sweater off and tossed it into the corner.

A cheer went up. That seemed to encourage her. Zorro yelled, "Take it off!" and the cry was picked up by everybody in the room, even Cocoa.

"Take it off! Take it off!"

Lulu responded. This was her big moment, the first time she had ever had the complete attention of the gang, and she had her mind set on making the most of it. Weaving drunkenly in vague contact with the rhythm of the music, she unsnapped her bra and let it drop. Her heavy, sweat-beaded breasts tumbled loose. On such a short girl, big breasts like that didn't seem right, Lora thought. They were big balls of fat tipped with dark rimmed jutting nipples.

Lulu clapped her hands over her head and wiggled her shoulders, making her breasts bounce and leap. She was rewarded with wild cheering.

"Take off some more!" Zorro boomed.

Lulu threw back her head and giggled. She was enjoying every minute of this.

She groped at her belt, trying to undo the catch with her drink-scrambled fingers. Finally she got it open and managed to yank the zipper. She pulled the jeans off. Underneath, she was wearing black panties. Her plump belly rippled out over the elastic waistband, and her buttocks jiggled and jounced with every motion. She went round and round the room, her body glistening with sweat now, her eyes glassy. Moisture rolled down the valley between her breasts.

The cheering rose tumultuously as she pulled off her final garment. She waltzed round the room, showing every side of herself. Nobody dared reach out to touch her—that would be inviting a fight with Cocoa—but everybody looked and everybody laughed, even Cocoa.

Then he stepped forward, rolling a little, because he was pretty well lit too. He grabbed the nude Lulu by the wrist.

"C'mere, babe. We're gonna have some fun."

He dropped his trousers and yanked Lulu to the floor. She giggled, yelling, "Hey, I'm gonna get splinters in my tail!"

But Cocoa forced her down and they began to make love while an interested audience of Cougars looked on. Lora had seen things like this at the Scarlet Sinners, too. In the wake of a big victory, it was frequent to have a mass orgy or a public display like this.

The idea was catching. Nobody was bothering about the bedrooms now. Half the girls in the room were bare to the waist all of a sudden, and their studs were busily removing the rest of their clothing, while those couples who had not yet started petting themselves remained in the middle of the room cheering Lulu and Cocoa on. In the midst of the wild melee, Lora staggered to the bar and put a jug of thunderbird to her lips. The warmth was immediate. She turned back.

On the floor, Lulu and Cocoa were in the last stages of delight, their bodies clamped together, Cocoa clutching the bobbling globes of Lulu's breasts. Elsewhere, half a dozen couples had begun to make love, on the floor, on the couches, on the chairs.

Squirrel reached out uncertainly for her and dragged her with him to the floor. They lay there a minute, giggling wildly over nothing at all, and then she felt his hands pawing her thighs in an attempt to find the fly of her jeans. He couldn't manage it. She unzipped them herself and wriggled free.

He slipped his hands up under her sweater to grab her breasts, and lowered his weight on top of her. For fifteen minutes Lora neither saw nor heard anything going on around. It was only Squirrel, Squirrel, Squirrel, and the rest of the universe didn't matter a damn....

And then the gasping moment of passion was gone.

She curled up against him, not troubled at all by the fact that she was naked below the waist. He put his hand between her thighs and they dozed off.

It was more than an hour before Lora woke. She opened her eyes, slid free of Squirrel, and stood up. Cool air touched her buttocks, and she looked down, surprised to discover that she was half-naked. She blinked, remembering. Her panties and jeans lay a few feet away.

She glanced around the room. Nearly everybody was asleep or lying still. A few couples had fallen asleep still locked in the position of love. Most were naked or half-naked, sprawled carelessly around the room. A jumbled litter of clothes was piled in the middle.

Off to the left was Lulu, who had started it all. She was mother-naked, lying on her back. Her mouth sagged open. Her heavy breasts had flattened out of their own weight in her position. She was snoring.

A stink of alcohol and sex was heavy over everything. Lora looked at her watch. Five in the afternoon. They had the whole evening ahead of them for more of the same, if they wanted.

She slipped her panties on and started to put on her dungarees. She felt very calm, very loose and free and easy. There had been plenty of kicks in the past couple of days.

Stepping over the slumbering bodies, she got up and walked into the bathroom. The door was half open, and she pushed her way in without looking. Someone was in there—Bozo, the tall, skinny junkie. He was wearing only a pair of striped shorts. He was sitting on the edge of the grimy bathtub, holding a tablespoon in his shaking hand. He looked up, startled.

"Oh—excuse me," Lora muttered.

"Hold it," Bozo said. There was an eerie intensity about his eyes. "Do me a favor, Lora?"

"What?"

"Strike a match. I'm gonna shoot up."

He pointed to a book of matches on the sink. She struck one and handed it to him, and he held it under the bell of the spoon, boiling a whitish powder.

Lora knew what the powder was.

H. Horse. Heroin.

She watched in chilled fascination as Bozo produced a hypodermic syringe, sucked up the contents of the spoon, and poised the needle over his fleshless, scarred arm. He had tied a piece of rubber tubing around his arm to make the vein stand out. Hesitating just a moment, he plunged the needle into one of the few places on the arm that was not covered with festering scabs. He waited a moment, then drew back on the plunger. The syringe filled up with blood. That intensified the kick of the heroin, Lora knew. Bozo plunged the contents of the syringe back into his vein and pulled the needle out. There was a faint smile on his face. The strange intensity seemed to die away. He shivered a little, but there was no other reaction.

"That's all?" Lora asked.

"That's all," Bozo said in a barely audible whisper.

"But where's the kick?"

He shook his head sadly. "Not any more. I don't feel the kick these days. I just feel lousy when I *don't* take the stuff. I gotta have it to feel like I felt all the time before I got hooked."

Lora felt sick to her stomach at the sight of Bozo, scarred arms, bloodshot eyes, fleshless body. And he fed $20 a day to the pusher to feed the monkey on his back. She felt something like pity. She thought that it would be a good thing for Bozo if he got killed in the next rumble. Put him out of his misery.

He went lurching out of the bathroom. Lora closed the door and used the john. When she came out, she saw Bozo sitting on the floor, starting to go to sleep in the middle of all the other sleepers.

She shook her head. She walked over to the table and finished off what was left of the wine, and stretched out again next to Squirrel.

CHAPTER TWELVE

She didn't bother to go home for dinner, either. With all the wine in her, she didn't feel very hungry, and she wasn't in the mood for staring across the kitchen table at the silently reproachful faces of her parents and her brother. They hardly ever said a word to her, but she could feel the unvoiced pressure of their disapproving thoughts all the time.

Screw 'em, she thought. Life was short and it was only as much fun as you could grab. There wasn't any sense in playing it the square way, working hard and going to school and getting a job and getting married, and then having kids and wearing yourself to the bone to keep them fed and clothed. Where did that get you, anyway? Did you get any kicks out of life? Crap, no. You kept your nose to the grindstone and your kids grew up, and they started the whole routine over again, studying and working and sweating to support *their* kids.

And so on forever.

What the hell for?

What the friggin' *good* was it all?

It was a lot better this way, Lora thought. To run free and wild, to feel power, real power, in your hand. To drink and fight and smoke M. To have sex whenever you want, instead of saving it like the squares did for their wedding night. Sure, you could get killed in a rumble. What of it? Live fast, die young. It was a lot better to get sliced up in battle than to creep along for seventy sleepy years of squareness. Or suppose you got knocked up. Well, that was tough. You had an operation, or else you had the baby and you gave it to a foundling home or something like that. It was the chance you took. It was still a lot better than doing without altogether, out of fear.

Instead of going home for dinner, Lora went out to the drugstore on the corner and called home. She didn't want them to get scared and send the police out looking for her, after all.

Her brother answered the phone. "Hello?"

"Tell Ma I ain't gonna be home till late tonight, you hear?"

"Who's this—Lora?"

"Who you think?"

"Where you going to be?"

"None of your friggin' business. I'm with some friends and I'll be home late."

"What about dinner?"

"I'll skip it," Lora said.

"Hey, but—"

She hung up the phone, cutting off his tinny squawk. Let him explain things, she thought. Her parents wouldn't raise the roof about having one less mouth to feed at dinner time. In fact, she suspected, they would be more pleased than angry if she someday packed her things and cleared out for good. They didn't like her around. They were afraid of her.

Well, it won't be long, she thought. She had to wait till she was eighteen. The syndicates wouldn't touch a girl under eighteen; they didn't want any statutory rape crap tacked on to white-slavery charges. But once she was eighteen the Scarlet Sinner alumni could get her set up in business. Two or three hundred bucks a week for doing what she did for free, now.

That's a lot of bread, she thought. With all that green in her jeans, she wouldn't be drinking thunderbird any more. Uh-uh. Champagne and martinis for her, and caviar and filet mignon. It wasn't hard to get somewhere in the world. You just had to put your mind to it, to know the right people and have the right kind of body, and you could get every single goddam friggin' thing you wanted.

She strolled back to the clubhouse and let herself in with the key she had wheedled from Squirrel. The party was going strong again. A lot of the sleepers who had passed out were up on their feet again with their second winds. People were putting their clothes back on and feeling a little shamefaced about the orgy. Lulu was still out cold, though, stark naked, a round little ball of soft pink flesh in the middle of the floor, oblivious to all that was going on around it.

Zorro said, "Hey, let's wake her up and make her dance again!"

"Pour some water on her!" Conch suggested.

Bozo picked up an empty wine bottle and went into the bathroom with it. He returned a few minutes later with a jugful of cold water.

"Should I?" he asked doubtfully, looking at Cocoa.

"Go on," Cocoa said.

Bozo inverted the jug. Water came gurgling out, showering down. At the first icy contact, Lulu gasped and drew her body together in a tight fetal ball. But the waterfall continued, drenching her breasts and thighs and stomach, and she sat up, thumbing open her eyes, looking around in amazement.

"Hey," she yelled. "What's the big idea—"

Everyone was roaring. Suddenly she realized she was naked and everyone in the gang was staring at her. Sober now, she turned beet-red and tried simultaneously to shield her breasts, her buttocks, and her loins with her hands. Failing that, she snatched up her clothes and ran down the corridor into one of the bedrooms, followed by laughter.

She came back in a few minutes, dressed. She looked angry. "Lousy bastards," she muttered. "Pour water all over somebody when they're asleep."

She sat down, complaining to herself, and poured herself a drink. She was starting all over.

Squirrel was awake now. He went into the john to freshen up, and when he came out he was anxious to dance. Lora danced with him. They did the fish for a while, and some cha-chas, and another merengue. They had some more drinks. The drink supply was running low, now. They were down to the last jug of wine. By nine o'clock they were on the last inch of that jug, and then there was no more.

Squirrel held up the empty jug, banging it against the wall to get some order.

"We're outa wine," he said. "Let's see some dough, huh?"

Nickels and dimes came forth. Squirrel collected it and counted through it. "A buck eighty," he announced finally. "We oughta get a couple gallons of muscatel outa that easy. Who's gonna go?"

"Let's you and me go, Squirrel," Lora said. "I can use the fresh air."

"Okay," he said, pocketing the change.

They stepped outside, going up to the street level. The night was cool, and there was only a sliver of moon. They walked together, holding hands, not saying much. The liquor store was two blocks away. The owner always asked to see draft registration cards, but Squirrel was past eighteen and could buy liquor legitimately.

They were a block from the store when the policeman stopped them.

He came out of the shadows suddenly, stepping out from between two tenements.

"Hold it, you two."

Lora went tense. She felt Squirrel's hand tighten on hers so painfully that she wanted to cry out.

"Yeah, officer?" Squirrel managed to say, keeping his voice calm. "You want something?"

The cop was a young one. He looked like he was around twenty-five, and he was shorter than Squirrel and not very hefty. But he had a gun and a belt-full of cartridges, and that made a lot of difference.

He said, "Where are you two going?"

"Just for a walk, officer," Squirrel said. "There ain't no law against that, is there?"

"Not yet, but there oughta be. This was supposed to be my night off, except I'm on double time on account of that crap yesterday."

"Jeez, that's a tough break," Squirrel sympathized.

"I bet you're all broken up. Let's have your names," the cop said.

"Now, hold on," Squirrel objected. "We're just out for a walk, my girl and me—"

"Don't make a court case out of it, goof," Lora said quietly. "We ain't done nothing wrong." She smiled at the cop and pushed her breasts out. "My name is Lora Menotti. I live in the Bryson Houses over here. And this is my boyfriend, Edward Santangelo."

"That your name, Santangelo?"

"Why—yeah. Yeah," Squirrel said. "Edward Santangelo, that's me."

"You know where there's a party going on around here tonight?" the cop asked.

Squirrel shrugged. "Jeez, no. Me and Lora, we were just going over to the park for a while—"

"Okay, okay. Where were you last night?"

"We were in the park," Squirrel said.

"Can you prove that?"

"Jeez," Squirrel said. "How can you prove something like that? We was there, that's all. Huh, Lora?"

She nodded. "Just sitting there on the bench, officer. There ain't no law, is there?"

The cop's lips firmed. "What do you know about the rumble last night?"

"The what?" Squirrel said.

"Don't play dumb. The *rumble.*"

Again Squirrel shrugged. "Just what I heard. A bunch of niggers jumped a bunch of spics over near First Avenue. That's all I know."

"You don't know very much, do you, Santangelo. How old are you?"

"Eighteen."

"You go to school?"

"Nathan Harley."

"Eighteen and you're still in school?"

"I wanta graduate. You mind?"

"Skip it. How about you, sweetie."

"Sixteen," Lora said. "I go to Harley too."

"You belong to any gangs?"

"Huh?" Squirrel said in innocent outrage.

"Social organizations?" the cop said.

Squirrel grinned. "We ain't the type."

"I bet," the cop said. "Okay, one more thing. You got a knife on you?"

"What do you mean, like a pen-knife?"

"I mean like a switchblade."

"You kidding, officer?" Squirrel yelped. "Those things are against the law!"

"Let's see your pockets anyway."

"For Christ's sake—"

"Don't make a fuss," Lora said. "Show him."

Squirrel turned out his pockets, revealing the liquor money, a wallet, and some keys, but no knife. He wasn't dumb enough to carry a piece around with him in the streets during a time when the cops were clamping down.

"Okay. What about you, baby?"

Lora spread her arms. "I ain't got any pocketbook to keep one in. Maybe I got one hidden in my bra, though. You wanta go look?"

"Never mind," the cop grated. "All right, beat it. You're pretty wise, both of you."

"Goodnight, officer," Lora said courteously. Squirrel slipped his arm around her waist, and they began to stroll away.

"Damn snotnose punk," Squirrel muttered. "I shoulda belted him."

"And get your head shot off? Uh-uh, Squirrel. You gotta cooperate with the fuzz. Especially when they can't pin anything on you."

Squirrel began to cross the street. Lora tugged him back.

"This way," she said. "Over to the park."

"But the wine—"

"Screw the wine," she whispered harshly. "We told the fuzz we were going to the park. Suppose he's watching us, numbhead?"

It wouldn't be good at all if the cop trailed them, just on general suspicions, and saw them going into a liquor store instead of the park. It would be a lot worse if he kept on trailing them and followed them all the way back to the Cougar clubhouse.

So they went to the park. "The park" was a one-block-square oasis of greenery in the neighborhood—trees, bushes, grass, benches, checkertables. It wasn't the safest place in the world at night, since the Cougars sometimes went roaring through it bopping everyone in sight. Lora and Squirrel picked out an empty bench.

He put his arm around her.

"Pet a little," she hissed. "Just in case we're being watched."

Their lips met. He slipped his hand under the hem of her sweater, working it up until the entire firm ripeness of her left breast lay in his hand. Slowly, he maneuvered his fingers under the tight fabric of her bra, and touched the stiff nipple. They remained that way a long while, Squirrel fondling her breasts. That was about as far as it was safe to go in the park. The cops didn't like too much hot stuff taking place.

"C'mere, baby," Squirrel murmured.

"Don't be a goofhead. We can do better things back in the clubhouse. That cop's gone."

"You sure?"

"He watched us from outside the railing for fifteen minutes. I guess he decided we were okay."

Cautiously, they left the park, looking around for the policeman before continuing on to the liquor store. Lora waited outside while Squirrel made the purchase. He came out carrying a big paper bag.

"He ask you for an ID?"

"Nah. He knows me by now."

"What you buy?"

"Muscatel." Squirrel adjusted the grip on the package. "He says the cops are really choking him. They been in the store five times today to make sure he ain't selling to minors."

"He don't, don't he?"

"The cops want to make sure," Squirrel said.

They headed back to the clubhouse by a roundabout route, and got there without interference from the police.

The Cougars had been worried. Conch said, "Christ, man, you been gone an hour, you know? We was sure you got japped by the Ravens."

"We got japped by a cop," Squirrel said. "Dumb fuzz was asking questions half an hour. Searched me, everything. Then we had to go stall in the park till he went away." He set the bottles down. "Three bottles of muscatel. That oughta last."

There was a general rush for the bottles. The party, which had calmed down in the absence of an alcohol supply, grew gay again. A couple of the Cougars passed quietly out, and their debs, not caring, danced with each other. And Zorro got sick and heaved up his guts loudly, making it to the john just in the nick of time. Conch made a pass at Zorro's deb, putting his hand in her sweater and feeling her up, but Zorro was too greenfaced to notice.

Around midnight the wine started to give out again. Nobody felt much like chipping in for more, so the party began to peter out. The Cougars and their debs were strewn around the room. A sweetish haze of reefer smoke filtered upward. There was no repetition of the wild orgy of the afternoon. Instead, there was quieter petting, and the occasional harsh breath-sounds of a couple in rut.

"Time to ski out," Lora said when things got really quiet. She nudged Squirrel awake. "Come on. Take me home."

"Go home yourself."

She jabbed her toe into his shin. "You hunk of crud, what the hell you say?"

He opened both eyes. "Huh?"

"You're too drunk to understand me. I said I want to go home."

"Oh. Oh."

He rose, swaying uncertainly, his eyes cloudy and sleep-fogged and bloodshot. It took him almost five minutes to get his mind clear. Finally they left the clubhouse.

They stood for a while just inside the gates of the project, hugging in the darkness. He pawed her breasts and tried to open her jeans, but she wouldn't let him, and finally he decided that enough was enough for one day. He lurched away from her.

"See you tomorrow?" he mumbled.

"Yeah."

"G'night."

"G'night."

She waved to him and went inside.

She felt tired. The elevator rose, sixth floor, seventh, eighth. It had been a long day. She didn't remember how many times she and Squirrel had made it, but it was plenty. She felt like every square inch of her body had been pawed a dozen times. And reefers, and cheap wine, and half-and-half—yeah, a busy day.

A good day. Plenty of kicks.

Squirrel was okay, she thought. But he didn't have much spark. He wasn't a dynamo like Whitey. He was just a big strong guy, handy with a knife, easy to lead around with a ring through his nose.

Well, that wasn't too bad, she figured. Whitey would have been impossible to control. Squirrel was more docile. Lora smiled. She had a few notions, as soon as the flap died down over the Magician rumble. A rumble with the Ravens, for one thing. And maybe a special deal—the Cougar debs fighting the debs of some other gang. Plenty of kicks in that.

She opened her apartment door. Everybody was asleep, but they had left a light on for her.

She didn't bother to wash up. She peeled off her sweat-soaked clothes and tumbled into bed. She had plans, she thought. Big plans.

She was asleep almost immediately.

CHAPTER THIRTEEN

Sunday morning was quiet. Sunlight woke Lora around eleven. Her head was throbbing and her tongue felt thick and fuzzy. She sat on the edge of the bed for a while, thumbing her eyeballs.

That was the trouble with a big night, she thought ruefully. You felt like somebody's old shoe the next day. What the hell, though. In this world you don't get anything for nothing. If you want kicks, you got to pay the price. The price for screwing around indiscriminately is the chance of getting knocked up. The price for drinking cheap wine and smoking M is the way you felt the next day.

She padded into the kitchen and put some coffee on. There was no one else home. Mr. & Mrs. Menotti and Chick had been gone for an hour, at least. Off to church. They went every Sunday. Lora hadn't been to church since her confirmation, and the Menottis had long since stopped trying to force her. It didn't get you anywhere to try to force Lora into anything.

She chuckled, trying to picture what would happen if she were to go to church next Sunday. The poor priest's ears would sizzle as Lora unloaded three years of sinning. She would have to spend hours in the confessional, and even then she would never get the whole story told.

The day was a warm one. Lora spent it at the clubhouse, mostly. She sat in the park with Squirrel for a while. There were still plenty of cops patrolling the neighborhood, ready to start swinging their sticks at the first sign of any trouble.

The cops were still hanging around on Monday at school. The high school was a quiet place, though. The members of the Puerto Rican gang were conspicuous by their absence, and none of the Aces showed up either—probably awarding themselves a day off because of their triumph.

The police pressure continued for a whole week. Wherever you turned in the neighborhood, there was a cop, balancing on the balls of his toes, ready to go into action the moment he saw anything going on that he didn't particularly like. The cops didn't have much to do, though. As Marty had predicted, no further arrests were made in the rumble case. The five Aces were going to stand trial for murder soon.

On Tuesday of the following week there was a kid-gang outbreak in East Harlem. In classic gangland style, a carload of gang boys swept down on a group of idlers from a rival gang and cut them down with a shotgun. Two were killed, three more were seriously injured, and grim reprisals were being threatened by the attacked gang.

It was the relief from pressure that the Cougars had been hoping for.

Since all was quiet on the Lower East Side, the floating supply of extra policemen was quickly transferred to the Harlem troublespot. Cougar turf was once again patrolled only by the normal complement of officers.

Which left Lora free to begin planning the rumble with the Ravens.

She began to talk up the idea with Squirrel. Both she and Squirrel now knew plainly who it was who ran the Cougars: it was Lora Menotti. Squirrel gave the actual orders, but it was Lora who told him, in the privacy of his locked room, what he was going to say.

Squirrel was strong physically, and he was pretty smart, but he could be easily led. That was why he had been content to play second fiddle to Whitey for so long—and that was also why Lora had been able to whip him up into something as rash as challenging his leader for Cougar supremacy.

And now, he listened to her suggestions and acted on them. Thus Lora was in the catbird seat, running the Cougars through her puppet Squirrel. The raw feel of power tingled in her hands.

"We oughta move against the Ravens now," she said. "While we're still kicked up by the Magician rumble. We'll get the Aces in on it and we'll sweep into the Raven turf before anybody knows what's happening."

"But the Ravens ain't done nothing to us lately," Squirrel protested weakly. "They been keeping on their side of the turf. They haven't been messing around any. We ain't got no cause to go off out of nowhere and bop them."

"The cause is that we want to!" Lora said fiercely. "We got to show those Irish bastards that they got to knuckle under to us."

Squirrel was perplexed. He could understand violence in the name of revenge easily enough, and he could comprehend violence that gained you some real advantage—as had his stand with Whitey. He could also see violence for pure kicks, violence that didn't run you any risks—like racing through the park knocking over people.

But this—a savage rumble, murder, possibly jail or bloody death, for no reason at all? He couldn't see it. But he didn't dare speak up. Lora swept him along on the power of her desire for blood.

So it was understood. A rumble with the Ravens was in the works. Squirrel would start thinking about it and getting it planned.

A couple of days went by. The top men of the gang were told of the forthcoming rumble. Plans started to take shape.

And then came another event that Lora seized and twisted to her own desires. It was the day when Pug walked into the clubhouse and announced that he was resigning from the Cougars.

It was early in the afternoon, in the middle of the week. Squirrel wasn't in the clubhouse at the time. Pug came in with his deb Claire, the redhead.

Pug was dressed in ordinary slacks and a plain jacket, and somehow he looked very different from the thin, ratty-looking boy he had seemed to be.

He was very pale and tense-looking. He glanced around the clubhouse. Lora was there, and a handful of the other Cougars.

Pug said, "Is Squirrel around?"

There was something peculiar about the way he said it, something nervous and halting, that made Lora suspect something unusual was up. Frowning, she sat up to pay close attention.

She said, "He won't be here for another half an hour, maybe an hour, Pug. You got anything special on your mind?"

"Yeah," Pug said, running his tongue around the rim of his mouth. "Yeah."

"What is it?"

"I gotta tell Squirrel about it."

"You can tell me. Anything for Squirrel, I can know about too."

Pug squirmed. "It's kinda personal."

"Come on. Out with it!"

"Well—" Pug gulped in air. "We came to say goodbye. Claire and me. We're gonna resign from the Cougars, both of us."

Lora blinked in surprise. You didn't *quit* a club like the Cougars. Maybe you got thrown out for punking off in a rumble, or you got drafted or put in jail. But you didn't just quit.

She said, "What you saying, man?"

Pug nodded. He fidgeted in embarrassment and his face turned so red that the blush practically hid his acne scars. "We're quittin'. I been thinking about it a long time, Lora. I'm gonna be seventeen tomorrow, y'see. That's old enough to quit school. And, well, I figure it's time to get out of the gang and try to get myself a good job. Mechanic or something, you know."

"And if he can't find a job," Claire said, her thin bosom puffed up with pride, "he'll go into the army for two years. And when he gets out we're gonna get married. Huh, Pug?"

"Sure, honey." Pug smiled sappily and slipped his arm around the skinny girl's waist.

Lora leaned forward, her lips curved in a mocking sneer. "Ain't that sweet! Ain't that an absolute gas! So you're gonna quit on us, both of you, huh?" Her voice suddenly snapped like a bullwhip. "Who the hell said you could quit the Cougars ever?"

"Who said—" Pug shook his head. "Hold on, Lora. We don't need any goddam permission to check out of the Cougars if we want to."

"You sure as hell do!" she blazed. "You need my permission—and Squirrel's. You ain't pulling out as easy as this, Pug."

From his seat in the far corner, Marty put in mildly, "Crap, Lora, if the man simply don't *want* to be in the gang any more—"

"Shut up," Lora snapped at him in the same bullwhip voice. "Shut up and keep shut. He can't just pick up and leave, you got that? He gotta ask permission. That's the way, hear?"

"First I ever heard—" Pug began.

Lora grinned. She knew that everyone in the room was watching her, and that everyone was afraid of her—not only because she was Squirrel's woman but because she held power in her own right. She felt the joy of control, the ecstasy of being able to manipulate people, to tell them what they could or could not do.

"You wait till Squirrel finds out," she said ominously. "You ain't just gonna walk out."

"When's he gettin' here, then?" Pug demanded truculently.

"I told you. Half an hour, maybe an hour. You just sit here and wait."

"We got things to do, Lora."

"*Sit here and wait.*"

They sat. Nobody spoke. Lora went to the icebox and got herself a beer, and sipped it slowly. Fifteen minutes went by, and then the front door opened and Squirrel came in, with a bottle of wine in a paper bag. Pug leaped up immediately to say something, but Lora cut him off before he got a couple of words out.

"Shut your mouth, Pug."

"But—"

"What the hell's going on?" Squirrel demanded, putting down the bottle and looking around in bewilderment.

"Come on into the bedroom," Lora said. "I gotta talk to you, Squirrel."

"What about?"

"Inside," she said. "It's private."

Squirrel shrugged and slicked back his hair in confusion. He followed Lora down the hall into the trophy-lined bedroom, and closed the door behind him.

"Okay," he said. "What's all the mystery crap about, huh?"

She smiled coldly. "Pug and Claire want to check out of the Cougars. I bet they're gonna turn stoolie on us, Squirrel. They're gonna spill their guts."

"Huh? I don't dig."

"Pug and Claire come in around twenty minutes ago. You see how they're all dressed up. And he puts on that crud-eating grin of his and says, I'm quitting the Cougars. I'm gonna get me a good job or else I'm gonna go into the army, and when I get out Claire and me are gonna get married."

"So?"

"So plenty! Listen, Squirrel, I never liked either of that pair. And now I know we gotta do something. They ain't just quitting all of a sudden out of the blue for no reason. You know Pug a long time. D'ya ever remember him talking about quitting and getting a job?"

"No, but—"

"I tell you the cops have been messing with him and Claire! Maybe they wanted to arrest him, and told him he'd get clear if he squealed. I bet the only reason he's quitting the gang is so he don't get messed up when we get arrested. He'll testify against us. He's gonna go running to them soon as he gets outa here, and sing. Maybe they've already been singing—singing about Whitey, about the rumble, about lots of things."

Squirrel frowned. "You ain't got no proof."

"Why else would he quit?" she demanded intensely. "He ain't got no reason! Unless he wants to turn us all in!"

"What you think I ought to do? If you're right, I mean."

"Cool him off," Lora said savagely. "Burn him!"

Squirrel looked shocked. "But Pug's okay! I been with him years. He's—"

"He's a *stoolie!* Take him out in the back alley and cut his guts out. That'll be a tip to the others, if they got the same idea. Nobody quits the Cougars! Nobody crosses up Squirrel!"

Squirrel hesitated for a moment, but Lora saw that she had him in the palm of her hand. Sure, Pug was an old friend of his. Sure, Squirrel had no real reason for suspecting Pug of treachery. Yet Lora had her hooks in Squirrel, and the big boy was powerless to resist. His face remained emotionless. Lora was silent, waiting for the decision to become fixed.

He said finally, slowly, "Maybe I better do something about Pug."

"Maybe you better. Unless you wanta fry in Sing Sing. Cool him off, Squirrel!"

"Yeah," he said, his eyes brightening. "Yeah. I better do that. Yeah."

Slowly, he walked back into the other room. It became very silent. Lora stood behind Squirrel, just at his elbow, as he walked over to Pug.

Squirrel said quietly, "I hear you plan to leave us, you and your deb. That so, Pug?"

"Now, listen, Squirrel, I ain't lookin' for no trouble with you, you understand that—"

"Are you quittin' the gang?"

Courage flickered on Pug's ratty face. He licked his lips. His knobby adam's-apple went up-down in a great gulp.

"Yeah," he said. Pug's voice was shaky. "It ain't nothin' personal, Squirrel. Just that Claire and me, we talked it over, and we decided we wanted to check out and make a clean break."

Squirrel nodded calmly. "That's very interesting, Pug. Quitting the gang, and all. Why don't you just come outside around back and discuss it with me, huh, man? A nice friendly discussion."

"Now, look, Squirrel—"

"I said let's go out back and discuss it! You hear me, man?"

In a barely audible voice Pug said, "What kinda crazy things did Lora tell you? Listen, Squirrel, I just want to check out—"

"You coming out back or do I hafta drag you?" Squirrel thundered.

Pug's face was dead white now. The acne scars stood out like lighthouse beacons on his hollow cheeks. In a trembling voice he said, "What you want to talk about out there, Squirrel?"

"You'll see. Come on."

Pug rose shakily and they went out through the side door, into the little courtyard in back. It was bordered by blank walls, and nobody could see what was going on in it. Pug walked out into the middle of it and turned around. Squirrel and Lora had followed him out. The rest of the Cougars gathered at the doorway.

"No!" Claire whimpered suddenly. "Stop him! He's going to—"

"Shut her up," Lora hissed. Automatically, Conch glided over and clamped one meaty hand over Claire's mouth. She tried to claw it away without success. Pug flicked a glance at her, but did not move.

Squirrel took out his blade and snapped it open. With deliberate coolness he began to clean under his fingernails.

He said, "I hear you're gonna turn into an opera star, Pug. You're gonna sing and sing and sing."

"That's crazy, Squirrel! Who ever told you that I was—"

"A little birdie told me," Squirrel murmured. He took a couple of steps toward the terrified Pug. "You don't like our company, huh, Pug?"

"You got this all cockeyed, man. I ain't no stoolie. I just wanted to quit and get a job."

"Get your knife out, Pug."

"I ain't carrying it."

"Give him a knife, somebody."

Zorro flipped a switchblade across to Pug. Pug was so shaky he fumbled the catch, and the knife went skittering to the ground. He picked it up and thumbed it open, and stood there letting the blade dangle limply in his hand. He was dazed and confused.

"Now fight," Squirrel said.

It was over almost before it could get started. Even at the best of times, Pug would have been no match for Squirrel, and now Pug was so punked-out that he could hardly hold his knife. As Squirrel advanced smoothly toward him, Pug yelled and tried to run. But there was no place he could run to. On three sides, there was nothing but blank unscaleable brick walls. On the fourth side, there was Squirrel and a waiting shiv.

"Come here, chicken," Squirrel ordered.

Pug turned, with his back to the wall. He lifted his knife and made a wild, hysterical charge, rushing forward like a madman. Squirrel easily sidestepped the clumsy assault.

Then, easily, Squirrel moved into the offensive. He took four zigzagging steps toward Pug and, timing the shift of his weight perfectly, drove the knife past Pug's guard on the fourth zag. The blade slipped into Pug's gut. Squirrel gave it the deadly upward twist and yanked it out.

Pug's knees sagged and his eyes went glassy. A great gout of purplish blood cascaded from his belly. He made the futile gesture of all who are so wounded, trying to hold the flow back with his fingers. He crumpled into a little dead heap.

Squirrel smiled proudly, looking down at his victim. This was his second kill, now. It wasn't as glorious as the first, but it was a kill. An execution, really. His face was gleaming. Lora knew that he had enjoyed the kill, every minute of it.

Claire had fainted. Conch was holding her.

Squirrel said, "Zorro, Cocoa—get Pug wrapped up and dump him over in Raven turf, the way we dumped Whitey. Maybe we'll let him be found and use that as our excuse for japping them."

They set to work, cleaning up. Conch carried Claire inside and someone poured water over her until she woke up. She looked blank-eyed and numb.

Squirrel said, "You're gonna scram, now. And you're gonna keep your mouth shut about what you just saw, hear me? Because if you don't, I'll cut your friggin' tongue out. I'll yank it out by the roots. You understand what I'm saying to you?"

"Yeah... yeah...."

"Then get."

Claire left. Squirrel poured out a drink for himself. Lora took one too.

She felt the warmth of satisfaction, of fulfillment. These Cougars were so many dumb marionettes dancing to her whims, she thought. It had been the easiest thing in the world to make Squirrel kill Pug. And probably Squirrel was starting to think that the killing had been all his own idea, now. Lora grinned. She could manipulate these Cougars into doing just about anything she wanted. Anything. Anything at all.

CHAPTER FOURTEEN

The gang was a little subdued after the killing. They had a kind of party, but it was a quiet one. Lora and Squirrel went into the bedroom and he undressed her, and there was still some blood on his fingers and she made him wipe the blood off on her nipples and then lick them clean. After that they made love, and the killing seemed to double Squirrel's vitality. She clung to him, her nails digging into his back, and they panted out their ecstasy together.

For a long time afterward they lay together quietly, Squirrel's hand gently encircling the rising mound of her breast, toying with the nipples. Then she felt desire again, and pulled him over on top of her, and for the second time their bodies ran the course of passion....

That night Lora got back to her apartment about half past eight. The Cougars had decided to break up early, just in case the calling-off of the police was just temporary. With Pug's body being found in Raven turf, it would be the signal for a new crackdown, maybe.

Her parents hardly looked up as she came in. She went straight into her room, deciding to spend a little time with her neglected schoolwork. She dragged the textbooks out—she hadn't cracked a couple of them yet that term—and stared boredly at the pages.

But her mind wasn't in it. She was too filled up with the kicks of having made one Cougar kill another. She was pleased with the way she held a whole gang in the palm of her hand. She was pleased with the way Squirrel had turned to putty for her.

Why bother with schoolwork, she asked herself, shoving the books away. She wasn't going to stay in school any longer than she had to. She was heading for better things than that. And if they wanted to flunk her, well, let them just go ahead and flunk her. You didn't need a high-school diploma to be a call-girl for one of the big syndicates. All you needed was an educated body. Breasts that could score 100% on any exam, thighs that rated a straight A Plus. And Lora had those. She didn't need a diploma too.

She stretched out, closing her eyes, daydreaming about what her life would be like once she was past the magic age of eighteen. She'd quit the Cougars, for one thing. Just like Pug had tried to do, only she'd be able to make it stick.

The Cougars were okay, but they didn't have any future for her. She'd hook up with those Scarlet Sinner alumni. Maybe they wouldn't remember her, but the moment she unpeeled her blouse and showed them the jutting white globes of her breasts they'd remember her fast enough—and they'd take her on.

That would be a good life. Fancy gowns, an apartment someplace clean where it was safe to walk on the streets at night. Money. Good food. Dancing. And men to go to bed with—rich men, businessmen, who would pay through the gut for the chance to grapple with her. No more worries about getting knocked up, either. It didn't happen—and if it did, the syndicate would take care of her operation, and they wouldn't get her some old drunken crud for a doctor, either. They'd buy her the best talent there was, because her body would be important to them and they wouldn't want it messed up.

Lora smiled. That would be the life. Maybe she would go on trips with the clients. Mexico, Palm Beach, Florida—all the warm sunny places, palm trees, cocktails under the starry sky. She'd wear lowcut gowns that showed everything but her nipples, and the big shots would stand around trying to get a peek. But all she would show would be the tops of her knockers. Anybody who wanted to see the rest, well, they would pay, man, *pay.*

Lora closed her eyes and kicked her legs in delight. She was lucky, having looks like these. She had a figure in a million—lean in the belly, big in the breasts, and a face that made you turn around for a second look. It was a hit combination. And it was going to pay off big for her.

Around nine o'clock, she heard the telephone ringing in the other room. Her mother picked it up on the third ring and spoke briefly. Then she came to Lora's door and pushed it open without knocking.

Mother and daughter stared at each other coldly for a second. Then her mother said—practically the first words she had spoken to Lora all day—"It's for you. One of your friends."

"Which one?"

"They didn't say who."

Lora frowned and elbowed up from the bed. She didn't get many phonecalls. She couldn't imagine who this might be. She went out into the hall, to the telephone.

"Hello?"

"Lora? This is Dolores."

"Yeah?"

"Listen, Lora," Dolores said in a hesitant voice. "Can you come to the clubhouse right away?"

"The clubhouse?" Lora repeated. "Yeah—yeah, I guess so. What's the rush?"

"It's—it's Squirrel," Dolores said. Her voice sounded distant and strange. "He kind of got hurt this evening."

"Squirrel hurt? How?"

"He went out into Raven turf. Scouting, or something. But he got fouled up with a Raven stomping party. They caught him and worked him over in a big way and dumped him in Cougar turf."

"How is he?"

"He's hurt pretty bad. He wants to see you fast as you can get here."

"Oh. I guess I better hurry, then."

"Yeah. He's calling for you, Lora."

"I'll be right there."

She hung up. She went back into her room and picked up her street jacket, nibbling her lip in anxiety. She felt agitated and upset about Squirrel. Why did the big goof have to go off and mess with the Ravens? Why didn't he take a bunch of guys with him to protect him? He was probably all puffed up with killing Pug, she thought. He thought he was superman or something, and no Raven would dare touch him. So now he was all crapped up.

She went into the hallway. Her mother looked up from the television set.

"Going out?"

"Yeah."

"But it's late. I thought you were staying home tonight, anyway."

"It's only nine. I'll be back by eleven. It's important."

Without further explanation, she left. On the way over to the clubhouse, she started rearranging her future with the Cougars. If Squirrel died, she would have to pick someone else out to run the Cougars and be her stud. Conch, she wondered? Zorro? Marty? They all had their good points, and they had weaknesses too.

What if Squirrel was just crippled, though? Suppose he tried to stay boss of the gang? She didn't want to shack with a crip. If he got badly messed up, she would have to dispose of him. She would pick his successor and maneuver something. Then she'd have to get rid of the extra deb, she thought. But that could be managed. She had power. Big power.

She reached the clubhouse building, going down into the basement and across the hallway. She let herself in with the key Squirrel had given her. In the clubhouse living room she saw Dolores, Anna, Mary, and Betty. They looked very solemn. None of the Cougar men were around, just the four debs, Lora noticed. That was a little peculiar, she thought. Unless all the men were with Squirrel.

"Where is he?" she asked excitedly. "Where's Squirrel? Is he in his room?"

"Nice of you to come," Betty said in a slow voice, ignoring Lora's agitated question.

"Yeah, but where's Squirrel?" she repeated, irritated.

Dolores looked up. "Squirrel ain't here, Lora," she said quietly.

Lora squinted in surprise, not understanding. "But—you said—"

"He ain't here at all."

"Where is he, then? The hospital?"

"He ain't hurt, Lora," Dolores went on, in the same flat, quiet voice.

Now Lora was utterly mystified. "He ain't hurt?" she snapped. "Listen, what kind of crap—"

"It was just talk," Anna said. "Just a little something to get you over here."

Lora looked at the four girls—skinny Dolores, busty little Anna, Betty with the big behind, and lean, panther-like Mary. She didn't dig this. She didn't dig it one little bit. And she wasn't used to being in a situation that she couldn't dig.

Figures appeared, emerging from the shadows in the back of the apartment. Lora's eyes widened in amazement as she saw who the girls were.

Donna, Whitey's deb.

Mae, Squirrel's ex-deb.

Claire, Pug's deb.

Two gang "widows" and one cast-off. Lora gasped in outrage. "What the hell are you three cruds doing here? You ain't Cougar debs any more! You don't belong in the clubhouse!"

"We were invited," Donna said.

Lora glanced around, at the seven girls facing her. She began to feel uneasy. Little cold prickles were creeping up and down her spine. Other girls were emerging now from the rooms in back. All of the Cougar debs were here, as well as the three girls whose men were either dead or had pushed them aside. Three girls who had plenty of reason for hating Lora.

And none of the Cougar men were there.

And someone had slipped around behind to lock the door. Lora was hemmed in.

Donna came forward, hatred and cold rage on her plump face. "This gang was okay till you marched your pretty ass into it," she said. "Whitey was boss and I was his deb. Then you had to come busting in. The big wheel from the Bronx."

"Whitey threw you out because he couldn't stand your goddam ugly face!" Lora blazed defiantly, overflowing with anger and concealed fear.

Donna replied evenly, not losing her temper, "My face was *okay* for Whitey a good long time. It was okay till you came along. Then you butted in and Whitey got rid of me."

"And you weren't satisfied with that," Mae said bitterly. "Whitey was too much for you to handle, so you decided to grab Squirrel instead. So I got thrown aside on the junkheap. I got laid by everybody in the gang. That was your idea, Lora. They all gave it to me one after another. I still hurt from that."

"And you made Squirrel kill Whitey, too," Donna took up the recitation. "They were good friends until the big shot came in."

"And then you made Squirrel kill Pug too," Claire sobbed brokenly. Dark lines of anguish ringed her eyes. "He didn't mean no harm. He just wanted to check outa the Cougars and go right. So you made Squirrel slice him up with the knife."

"Things haven't been so good here since you came," Dolores summed up. "So we had a little meeting tonight, all us Cougar debs. And we decided we better stop you before you took our men away, too. We don't know who you'll go after next. But you ain't fit for being with human beings. You're a devil, Lora. So we invited Donna and Mae and Claire to come help us take care of you."

"What the crap is this, a friggin' kangaroo court?" Lora asked in sudden jellykneed terror. "What the hell you gonna do to me?"

"Nothing much," said Donna slowly. "We ain't gonna kill you, Lora."

"We're just going to fix you so you can't go around stealing men any more," Dolores said.

Lora turned and tried to bolt in sudden panic, but Anna was blocking the door and there was no way past. She began to get frantic. She was outnumbered better than fifteen to one, and there was nobody here who would help her.

Nobody at all.

She chattered wildly, "Keep away from me! Squirrel will kill you if you touch me! Put a finger on me and he'll carve up your guts!"

"He can't kill us all," Dolores said. "Anyway, the other fellows won't let him. We been talking to them too. They're pretty sore about what he did to Pug today. They liked Pug a lot. They didn't think he deserved what he got. Maybe they'll take care of Squirrel, too."

"Keep away from me," Lora warned. She felt real fright for the first time in her life. She understood now how Pug had felt cornered in the back yard this afternoon. How Whitey had felt with a hole in his side, waiting for Squirrel to finish him off. "Keep away from me," she repeated, trembling.

They laughed.

Suddenly Lora saw that they had taken all of the weapons out of the trophy collection. The chain, the billy-club, the knives, and all the rest of those devilish pain inflicters.

"No," Lora screamed. "No!"

"Remember," Dolores said, as they closed in. "We don't want to kill her."

Lora sprang to one side, her back against the wall, clawing out wildly with fists and legs, trying to keep them away from her. Her foot landed solidly on Donna's groin, sending the plump girl toppling backward, and in the same moment Lora's fist smashed into Betty's cheek. But she couldn't fight off fifteen of them at once, no matter how desperate the fury of her struggle, how savage the intensity of her desire to keep them away from her. They dragged her away from the wall.

Someone seized her by the hair. She was forced to the floor, hurled there roughly.

"Goddam pigs... get off me," she rasped thickly.

They ignored her.

They were ripping open her clothes. She felt the eager hands shredding off her sweater, breaking the straps of her bra, laying bare the high, full mounds of her breasts. They were pulling her jeans off, tearing off her panties, stripping her bare, exposing her thighs, her deep loins, her full buttocks....

And then the fury broke in full vehemence. They swept over the naked Lora like avenging demons. She struggled futilely. She felt them trampling her, stomping her, kicking her.

Her eyes wild and demonic, Donna sat straddle-legged over Lora while the other girls held her down. Donna's hands grasped the fleshy roundness of Lora's breast, not cupping it tenderly but gripping it roughly, and suddenly Lora saw the knife, gasped as it descended to the pale white globe of flesh, felt the sudden hot agony as the knife slashed through the tender mound, as Donna carved the dead Whitey's initials in her breast. And then it was Claire's turn, carving Pug's initials in the roundness of Lora's thighs. The pain made her wild; she tried to break loose, feeling fire in her breast, fire on her thigh, but the Cougar debs were not through with her yet. The knife descended, leaving indelible scars. She felt them swinging the chain, smashing it into her teeth, felt them ripping out the jet-black glory of her hair, felt the zing of aerials whipping across the silky skin of her buttocks and leaving angry, dripping red lines. She felt them kicking her, pummeling her....

And consciousness would not leave her. She screamed and sobbed madly through shattered teeth and bloody lips; with satanic force she clawed and scratched at them, but there were fifteen of them to her one, and resistance was futile. Like a flock of maddened birds they hovered over her, ripping and tearing and cutting and hurting.

Lora was learning that there were limits to her power. She was learning that you could push a group of people only so far—and then their fury would explode in consuming destructiveness.

She was one mass of pain. Numb, unable to feel the agony any more, she lay on the clubhouse floor in the widening pool of her own blood, eyes clenched shut but still conscious.

She was terribly aware that they had ruined her beauty forever. She was hideous, now.

Disfigured.

She tried to speak, but no words would pass her lips. Nothing coherent would come out, only gobbling hysteria. They laughed.

"Listen to her!" Dolores cried. "She thought she ran this outfit!"

"We showed her," Donna crowed. "We showed her what happens to a smart girl who thinks she can move in and take over the whole outfit."

"No... no... " Lora muttered thickly.

"Let's get her outa here," Mae said.

Lora felt hands under her battered and shattered body, unfriendly hands, ungentle hands, lifting her, carrying her out, up, leaving her in the moonless, darkened street. Their laughter faded away.

For a long time Lora lay there, unable to move, feeling the pain surge through her, looking down at the bloody gashes that disfigured her once-sensuous breasts and irresistible body. There wouldn't be any call-girl syndicates interested in her now. *Nobody* would be interested in the scarred, toothless hulk of Lora Menotti. She would have to pay a man to lay *her.*

She remained motionless, stark naked in the night, feeling the cold October wind whip around her bleeding breasts, her ravaged buttocks. She was practically out of her head with pain.

After a while she began to crawl aimlessly on her hands and knees, as the strength ebbed out of her. Wild, hysterical thoughts ran through her mind. The Rise and Fall of Lora Menotti. The power who ran the Cougars now crawling naked, bleeding through the night. From top to the ashheap in fifteen minutes. *Everything's all over for me,* she thought. *No more power... everything finished... why didn't they tell me that this is the price you got to pay for power? ...when you get too big, they chop you down... all finished now... finished....*

She wanted to die. All her beauty was gone, her face and body were hideously disfigured by the vengeance of the gang girls. In a few short minutes she had been transformed from a coruscating radiant sexpot to something ghastly. She didn't want to live.

Let me die, she prayed as she crawled.

She heard voices above her. "Christ, they really gave it to this one!"

"Get an ambulance, quick!"

"They can still save her if they get her to the hospital in time."

Lora tried to speak, to tell them. *Let me die,* she thought. *Let me die....*

But she was not that lucky.

THE END

Sex Bum

By Don Elliott

CHAPTER ONE

Life began for Johnny Price one stinking hot afternoon at Grogan's Poolroom, late in August. He was nineteen, then, a big, tough kid who had been out of high school for a couple of months, and who had a job running orders for a grocery in town, and whose chief hobby at the moment was making a girl named Beth, who didn't have too much in her top story but who was neatly stacked and who didn't mind coming across.

Johnny didn't like running orders for a grocery store. He didn't like the $50 a week he made, either. He didn't like the lousy nickel and dime tips he got handed, after he'd been sweating and breaking his back to deliver somebody's carton of cookies and apple juice.

What the hell, though. He needed a job for the time being. High school hadn't taught him anything worth a damn. He was shrewd and sly when he went in, shrewd and sly when he came out, but he hadn't bothered to pick up any information on quadratic equations or the French Revolution, or even anything that would help him learn a trade.

He didn't want to clutter up his mind with useless things like that.

Johnny Price had big plans for Johnny Price. They involved a lot of money being his, and girls with boobs like swollen melons, and all the good things life had to offer.

And everything started to begin that sweltering day in Grogan's Poolroom.

"Take the afternoon off, Johnny," Old Man Thompson of the grocery had said, with a big, generous sweep of his hand. "It's too damn hot to work."

"Gee, thanks," Johnny said, and he was off.

It was the hottest day Johnny could remember, the hottest day of a hot month. Nobody was coming to the grocery store in this kind of weather—it was even too hot to eat—and there was nothing at all for him to do. In a sleepy little town like Reesport, New York, you couldn't expect the grocery store to bother with anything like air-conditioning.

Uh-uh. Air-conditioning was a city trick, a newfangled gimmick. Old Man Thompson just didn't believe in it, that was all.

Grogan of Grogan's Poolroom did, though. Not real air-conditioning—that was carrying things too far—but a big fan that kept the poolhall pretty clean and fresh during the summer. Johnny made tracks for Grogan's that afternoon. He had ten bucks in his pocket, and that would see him through a couple of hours' pool and maybe even some fun in the evening, too.

He had a date with Beth that evening. He knew just how the evening would end, too. With both of them naked, and his hands tight around Beth's big hard warm breasts, and her legs wrapped around his body, and his belly flat against hers, and him gliding easily to the snug harbor of her body, and the two of them moving and moving and moving still faster until passion overwhelmed them both. It was something to look forward to, anyway. Beth was a pig when it came to love, but he didn't mind that much.

When he got to the poolroom, Johnny saw a couple of cars pulled up outside. They weren't the old clunks you usually saw around town, dilapidated Plymouths and Fords that were old when Harry Truman was Vice-President. These were shiny new cars with the big sweeping tail-fins in back that looked so flashy and expensive.

Johnny knew whose cars those were, and he was twice as glad that he had decided to come to Grogan's this afternoon. The cars belonged to Mike Lurton and Ed Kloss, two of the local bigshots. They were racketeers tied up with some big, powerful New York City Crime Syndicate. Everybody in town knew that. That was why Lurton and Kloss drove the flashiest cars in Reesport.

Ed Kloss and Mike Lurton were a couple of Johnny Price's big heroes. He wanted to be just like them. He wanted to work for the Syndicate and drive a car with fins a mile long. He wanted to drink good liquor the way they did, and sleep with slim, hot-eyed New York women whose boobs played jingle-bells as they bent over you. He was glad to see that Lurton and Kloss had come to Grogan's this afternoon.

He went inside.

Grogan was sitting at the little booth in front, where he could see who came in. He was a little, dried-up man of sixty, without an ounce of spare flesh on him anywhere. He was sweating more than usual today. Pellets of gleaming perspiration trickled steadily down his bald dome of a head. For some reason Grogan looked scared, Johnny thought. Maybe he didn't like the idea of having two bigshot mobsters playing pool on his tables.

"Afternoon, Mr. Grogan."

"Afternoon, Johnny," Grogan's voice was harsh and thin-sounding.

Johnny leaned forward and grinned. "How's business, Mr. Grogan?"

"Fair. Fair."

"I see Lurton and Moss are here already."

"Yeah," Grogan said. He jerked his head toward the door. "Be a smart kid and get the hell out of here, will you, Johnny?"

"Huh?"

"Go on," Grogan whispered hoarsely. "Get out. Fast. There's gonna be trouble around here. Don't get yourself mixed up in it, kid. Get the hell out of here before someone puts a hole in you."

Johnny blinked. He stared at the wizened poolhall proprietor and said quietly, "You tell me what kind of trouble there's gonna be, Mr. Grogan. I ain't running away so fast, I don't think."

Grogan was sweating hard. "Lurton and Kloss. They're waitin' for someone in there. When he shows up there's going to be fireworks."

Johnny's eyes widened. "Who they waiting for? Anybody I know?"

Grogan said in a hushed whisper, "Guy name of Phil McCarran. You know him?"

"Uh-uh."

"Big pinball operator out of Hudson. He's coming down here to get a payoff from Lurton and Kloss, and they aren't planning to hand it over. Go on and git, now. I said a lot too much already."

A nerve twitched somewhere in Johnny's cheek. He didn't know Phil McCarran, but he'd heard of him. McCarran was a real big operator from upstate. There would be a real explosion if Lurton and Kloss tried to give him a rough deal.

If there was going to be some gunplay, Johnny wanted in. Maybe, he thought, maybe this would be his chance to break into the big time.

He said to Grogan, "Thanks for the information. Mind if I go inside now?"

"You crazy? Go on and git home."

Johnny was obstinate. "I wanta get in there, Mr. Grogan."

He started to walk past Grogan's cubicle and into the poolroom itself. Grogan reached out a clawing hand to stop him, slithering down from his high three-legged stool and running around front to stand in Johnny's way.

Johnny grinned. Grogan was an old man and he was half Johnny's size. Johnny grabbed the poolroom owner by the scruff of his collar and sat him back up on his high stool again.

"You stay there, Mr. Grogan. It'll be safer for you up there."

Grogan sputtered something incoherent. Johnny grinned and opened the inner door and walked through, into the long, low-ceilinged room that was the poolroom.

The fan was humming quietly. Johnny saw the five baize-covered tables and the single naked light-bulb dangling from the gray dingy ceiling. But one part of the scene was missing, and conspicuously so. Johnny didn't hear the familiar click of cue against ball, of ball against ball.

There were only two men in the poolroom and neither of them was playing pool. They were sitting on opposite sides of the door, and they looked like they were expecting a hydrogen bomb to go off in the front office any minute now. One of them, Johnny knew, was Mike Lurton, and the other one was Ed Kloss.

As Johnny entered they tensed and jumped up, and said, speaking at the same time, "What the hell are *you* doing in here, kid?"

Johnny smiled pleasantly and fought back the tension rising within him. "Grogan let me in," he said. "He figured I could help you guys."

They stared at him. Mike Lurton was a big man, Johnny's size—six foot two or so, about two hundred pounds. But he was easily twelve years older than Johnny, and where the boy had firm tough muscle, Lurton mostly had wads of sagging fat.

As for Kloss, he was small and ratty-looking, with a little thin mustache and beady clever eyes. Johnny admired both of them. Lurton was supposed to be able to bend a beercan between his thumb and middle finger, just like that. And Kloss was the best poker-player in the five counties thereabouts, they said.

In a deep rumbling voice Lurton said, "Grogan must be nuts to let you in. Get the hell out of here fast, sonny. Like, *fast!*"

Johnny shook his head and didn't budge. "Listen to me, you guys. Grogan gave me the pitch—about McCarran coming here to collect, and all. McCarran's a tough character. I want to help out. Anything at all."

"We ain't interested in a junior Varsity," Kloss said in a cold voice.

"Suppose McCarran knows the score and comes prepared?" Johnny persisted. "What then? Let me help you, huh? I'll be your lookout. You won't regret it. I'm big and I can take care of myself."

Lurton didn't look impressed. He glanced casually at his wristwatch and said, "McCarran's going to be here in fifteen minutes, sonny. Get out now or I'll have to throw you out."

"You wouldn't want to do that," Johnny said, trying to get his voice down low to match Lurton's rumble. His heart was pounding hard. "You might regret it if I got on the wrong side in this thing."

Kloss said, "What the hell do you mean by that? Kid, you *threatening* us?"

"I'm trying to help out! Look—when McCarran gets here I'll be playing pool. All by myself, just practicing up on my shots. You two guys can hide in the washroom over there. I'll shoot the breeze with McCarran, and get his attention distracted, and you two can nail him easy."

Johnny saw that Lurton was thinking it over. The big man was smiling.

"Maybe the kid's got something there after all," Lurton said.

Uneasily Moss muttered, "I don't like it. Maybe the kid is part of something McCarran rigged up."

Lurton let go of a big chuckle that boomed up from deep in his belly. "Him? He's one of the local kids, Ed. Johnny something-or-other. Right?"

"John Price," Johnny said.

"Yeah. Price. Okay, Price. Get out the chalk and start making with the billiards. And be ready to duck when the time comes to duck."

Johnny felt an inward surge of glee, but didn't allow even a smile to break the surface of his face. Joy rippled within him. He told himself that this was the big break of his life. He'd have something to celebrate, tonight, when he got Beth into the hay and started muscling up those big solid boobs of hers, moving her legs for the trip to paradise. Tonight would be an occasion.

Lurton and Kloss vanished into the washroom. Johnny heard the clicking of safeties on two guns. He picked up a cue and took a couple of random shots, just cannonading the balls around without trying to play anything.

The place was deadly silent. Only the humming of the fan broke the quiet. Each carom sounded fantastically loud. Sweat rolled freely down Johnny's face. Even with the fan going, the temperature in the poolroom was eighty-five or ninety degrees, and maybe close to a hundred degrees outdoors.

The door of the poolroom opened about ten minutes later. Johnny tensed and tightened his jaws and felt a stab of uncertainty in his guts, but he stuck to his practicing without looking up.

The silence continued for a long moment.

Finally a voice said, "Hey, you. Fella."

Johnny glanced up. "Yeah?"

He saw a big, red-haired man of forty or so, standing in the entrance. He wore an open red sports shirt and slick blue pants, and his face was a pasty white color. An unlit cigar jutted from the corner of his mouth. Johnny didn't need to be told that this was Phil McCarran.

"You all alone in here, kid?"

"Yeah, damnit," Johnny said. He forced himself to grin good-naturedly. "You want try a game or two? My name's Price."

"I'm looking for a couple of friends of mine," the other man said. "They were supposed to meet me here around now. How long you been here?"

Johnny shrugged. He said, "About half hour or so. Ain't been nobody here."

On wobbly legs he walked around to the other end of his table, so he'd be out of the line of fire whenever the two mobsters in the washroom decided to shoot. Johnny wondered what the hell they were waiting for.

Then he saw, and he understood. McCarran had been chicken. He had brought some friends along.

Two cold-faced toughs stood just outside, in the hall, ready to jump in if there was any trouble.

Johnny said in a clear, loud voice, "Those guys outside—they come with you? Bring 'em in and let's have a match, huh? I'm sick and tired of playing solitaire, man."

McCarran looked annoyed, but he turned and said, "Okay. Come on in, boys."

They came in and closed the door behind them. Johnny didn't lose a stroke. He waited.

Suddenly the washroom door flew open and Lurton and Kloss appeared, firing as they came. The first shots dropped the two toughs before they knew what was happening. One went down with a red mess where his face had been, the other one clutching his belly.

McCarran was quick, though; he spun away and started to run, figuring he'd make a getaway under cover of all the confusion.

Johnny grinned and took three quick steps forward. He stuck out his cue-stick and rammed it between McCarran's legs. The big gambler stalled like a bike with a pipe stuck between its spokes.

McCarran cursed and went sprawling forward.

Johnny jumped back. A second later, a bullet from Lurton's gun took off the top of McCarran's red-haired skull.

It was messy.

For a long moment there was silence in the room, broken only by the humming of the fan. Three bloody bodies lay on the floor. Smoke rose toward the ceiling. Old Man Grogan appeared, timidly poked his nose through the door, quickly pulled back, turtle-fashion, and disappeared.

Finally Kloss said, "What was your name again, kid?"

"Price. John Price."

"You live in this town, huh?"

"Yes sir."

"Live with your parents?"

"My aunt," Johnny said. "My parents died a few years ago. I just live with my aunt."

"That's good. You're free to clear out at any time, then. How old are you?"

"Twenty-two," Johnny lied.

"Congratulations. You're now an accessory before the fact in this murder. Help us drag these bodies into the washroom and then let's get the hell out of here. Maybe we can find some use for you after all. You're pretty quick with your brains, for a guy your size."

Johnny grinned. "Thank you."

"Skip it. Let's go to work."

So that was the beginning for Johnny Price. He was a mobster on the make, a big boy with big plans. He was climbing up in the world of crime.

He helped Lurton and Kloss drag the bodies out of sight. While he was doing it, he got blood on his hands, but he was careful not to get any on his clothes, and he washed it off before he left the poolroom.

When the bodies were hidden, the three of them filed out, Kloss, then Lurton, then Johnny. Grogan was waiting, cowering, in his cubicle.

Kloss said, "Wait fifteen minutes. Then call the police. Tell them that four masked men came busting in here and murdered those three guys. You can't identify any of them, Grogan. They all had Halloween masks on, got it? They were driving a blue and white '38 Buick."

They left.

Outside the poolhall, just as Kloss and Lurton were about to get into their huge Cadillac, Lurton said, "Come see us tomorrow, kid. Okay?"

"Sure," Johnny said. "Where will you be?"

"Home. At our place on Rumsey Road. You know where it is?"

"The old Collins mansion, isn't it?"

"That's right," Lurton said. "Stop off around one in the afternoon. We'll talk some things over."

"Sure," Johnny said. "Sure."

He watched them get into their car and pull away in a cloud of smoke. He smiled.

They wanted to talk to him.

That meant they wanted to give him a job.

He was in. In like Flynn. He was on his way, all right.

A savage glee took hold of him and he felt drunk and dizzy at the thought of the new world that was opening before him. Money, power, girls—

Girls!

Not a slut like Beth, either. But really red-hot, sophisticated girls, beautiful girls, New York City type girls. They'd be his by the dozens, once he got where he was heading. He'd revel in them.

He sauntered toward his car. Heat-waves were rising from its hood. It was a tired out old Chevy, a '53 that he was holding together with baling wire and spit. He could imagine himself behind the wheel of his own Cadillac in a couple of years, and he liked the idea.

He got into the car. He thumbed the starter and the engine sputtered into life.

He took a look back at the poolhall, a shabby frame building standing a hundred yards back from the two-lane highway, in a clump of shrub oak and sumac. It was a pretty dingy place to have started a big career in, Johnny thought. But what the hell, Lincoln was born in a log cabin, wasn't he?

Johnny grinned. Then he hit the gas hard and thundered away at sixty miles an hour, the steering wheel rattling like it wanted to break off in his hand.

CHAPTER TWO

He picked Beth up at her place around seven-thirty that evening. The heat hadn't let up at all. The temperature had dropped to perhaps eighty-two with the setting of the sun, but a heavy blanket of humidity lay over the whole town, stifling it. The air was hot and hard to breathe. There was a layer of grit drifting over the town, imprisoned smoglike in the warm air.

There wasn't much to do in the town on a night like this. There was one movie theater, but it changed programs every five days, and Johnny and Beth had seen the show two days ago. There were theaters in neighboring towns, of course, but they weren't in the mood for a movie. It was too hot to go dancing. They stopped off for sodas instead.

Beth said, "Johnny?"

"Mmm?"

"You're all dreamy tonight."

"Am I?"

"You sure are."

"I didn't notice," he said.

"What are you thinking about?"

"Nothing much."

"Sure you are."

He shrugged. "I'm just thinking, that's all. Can't a guy think?"

"Sure he can," Beth said. She ran her hands over his biceps, digging her fingers in. "Maybe you're dreaming that you love me, huh?"

He didn't answer.

"You do love me, don't you?" she asked worriedly.

"Huh? Oh—oh, yeah. Yeah. You know I do, baby."

"You haven't told me so all evening."

"It's the heat," he said. "This goddamn heat. It's driving me crazy. Every day ninety, a hundred degrees. It's getting so I can't think any more."

"Why don't we go swimming?" Beth said.

"Now?"

"Sure. Right now. Bare-bottom. We can drive out to Collins Creek. Nobody's going to be there."

He looked at her. It was an amusing idea. Anything to beat the heat, he figured.

"Okay. Finish your soda and let's go."

They went outside and got into his car. She snuggled up tight against him. Beth was a short, roly-poly girl of seventeen going on eighteen. She had black hair cut in bangs, and big breasts, and a firm body that she enjoyed making good use of.

She wasn't a bad-looking girl, Johnny thought. But no beauty, either. She was just a country girl, with her snub nose and her rosy cheeks and her healthy, fullblown body. She was like all the other girls around here started getting loved at fourteen, and would continued balling around till she was maybe twenty, and then she'd get married to some guy a couple of years older than she was. Unless she happened to get pregnant sooner, in which case she'd get married sooner. They were all like that.

Johnny wasn't interested in getting married, and he especially wasn't interested in marrying a girl like Beth. She was good to make, but that was all. He had seen real women—the kind he wanted. Once for the Fourth of July he had gone down to New York City, and he had seen them walking on Fifth Avenue, women with high cheekbones and beautiful dresses and lovely legs and firm round breasts.

Women walking poodles. That was what he wanted: the kind of woman who could go around walking a poodle without looking silly.

But in the meanwhile Beth would do.

He started the car, and they drove out toward Collins Creek. It was on Route 71, to the east of Reesport, about seven and a half miles from town, and as they drove out Johnny drove past the old Collins mansion, where Lurton and Kloss now lived. Sid Collins had been a big man in Reesport forty years ago. He had owned most of the land east of town, and he not only had a creek but a lake and a small mountain named for him.

A lot of good it did him, though. He lost his dough in the market crash, and had to sell off his land, and now he was dead. So what did it matter that he had things named after him, in the long run?

Collins Creek was almost a small river. It flowed into Collins Lake, which was about half a mile across, and good for fishing and swimming. During the day, people were always using the creek and the lake, since the land around them was part of the Collins estate that no one had ever bought. But at night they could be alone.

Johnny pulled the car up. They got out. Here, outside of town, the heat was a little milder, but still uncomfortable. The moon was nearly full, lighting up the place like a floodlamp.

Beth said, "You want to swim first and do it afterward, Johnny? Or the other way around?"

"Yeah," he said.

They began to undress. Beth was always quick at getting out of her clothes. Johnny watched her as she pulled her polo shirt off. She didn't have a bra on underneath. Beth hardly ever wore bras, even though her breasts were very big, so that they wobbled and bounced around when she walked. Johnny looked at her bare breasts now. They rose like a couple of basketballs. The nipples were stiff already. It didn't take much to warm Beth up. Let her show her boobs to a boy, and she was ready to go.

She unbuckled her belt and tugged her jeans off. Now she was naked in the moonlight. He eyed her. He had seen her naked a million times. There were the heavy cones of her breasts, and then the flatness of her belly, and the deep indentation of her navel, and then her legs. She didn't have good legs. They were too short for her body, and too thick through the thighs. Her buttocks were too big, too, round and hefty, like the farm girl she was. From the waist up, she had the body of a tall woman. But she was only five feet three.

"Last one in's a rotten egg," she yelled.

Johnny kicked off his pants. But she had already turned and was running toward the water, and he didn't make any attempt to outrace her. He watched her go. His eyes studied the heavy slabs of her buttock-cheeks, with the moonlight highlighting the deep crevice between them. Her butt jiggled as she pounded toward the water. She rushed out, hip-deep, and flopped forward in a surface-dive.

Johnny waded out and stood in water up to his knees. Beth surfaced and grinned at him.

"Isn't it great!" she said. "The water's so cool! Oooh, look what I see!"

"I bet you never saw one before in your life," Johnny said.

"No, I never did. What do you use it for?"

"Later," he said. He dove forward and swam toward her.

She waited for him. Johnny caught up with her about twenty feet from shore. The water was deep here, and cold. He swam up toward her and put his hands on her buttocks, clamping them tight, drawing them upward, pushing her body against his as they trod water.

The hard tips of her breasts drilled into him.

Her lips sought his. He kissed her, jamming his tongue into her mouth, meeting the heat and the wet warmth of hers. They held the embrace for a moment. Then, laughing, she broke away from him and began to swim upstream.

He watched her. Every moment or two, her bare buttocks would break the surface as she swam, and he would see the gleaming fleshy curve. He let her get about fifteen feet ahead of him, and then he slipped beneath the surface and began to breast-stroke toward her.

Johnny was a powerful swimmer, and he could hold his breath almost indefinitely. He glided up to her, five feet below the surface. Rolling over on his back, he could look up and see her, her breasts dangling down into the dark water. He started to float upward, and he came up right beneath her, grabbing her breasts.

He rolled over, surfacing, pulling air into his lungs. Beth giggled.

"You scared me!"

"What did you think I was, a turtle?"

"Yeah! Yeah, a big snapper!"

He laughed. "You know something? You were right. I'm the biggest damn snapper you ever saw." He groped through the water at her, found her buttocks, pinched the firm quivering flesh.

"Ouch! Johnny!"

He laughed. He pinched her buttocks again, the other cheek this time.

"Cut that out!" she yelped.

"I'm a snapper," he said. He grabbed her breasts and caught the nipples between his index and middle fingers. The nipples were like hard little nuts.

He pinched them. "Snap! Snap!"

"Hey, that hurts!"

"Nuts," he said. "You love it. You go wild when I squeeze your boobs. Admit it, Beth."

He pinched her again.

"Oh, Johnny Price, if you don't stop that I'm going to fix you!"

"Fix me how?"

"Like this!"

She reached out. Now it was his turn to yelp, but she held on tight, her small, pudgy fingers gripping tightly. He retaliated by digging his hands into her buttocks again, and a moment later they were embracing.

Abruptly Johnny did not feel like fooling around. Loveplay was okay for kids. But today he had taken part in a murder, he had helped to get three men killed, and he no longer thought of himself as a kid. He was a big man now, and he wanted to play a big man's game.

"Come on," he said. "Out of the water."

"I thought you said you wanted to swim for a while first," Beth said.

"I changed my mind. We swam enough for now. We can go back in later. Let's go."

"You're the boss," Beth said, shrugging.

They paddled their way back to shore, and scrambled up onto the fringe of mud that passed for a beach there. The heat no longer seemed to be so irritating, now that they had cooled off. They stood together at the edge of the water, letting the droplets run from their bodies.

Then Johnny seized her and bore her to the ground.

They landed together, Beth at the bottom of the heap. His mouth covered hers. One of his hands cupped her left breast, and the other travelled down her body, found her, and held on there. She was ready to go. His fingers touched her.

"Johnny," she said. "Johnny, Johnny, Johnny!"

He moved his fingers around, felt her jump and heard her hiss, and touched her again. Her heart was pounding, now. The hand that cupped the heavy round of her breast felt the inner thump-thump-thump.

She tugged at him. Her hands went to him, and as the small fingers found him, he closed his eyes, caught his breath sharply.

Beth had clever fingers. She went to work on him skillfully, and he didn't interrupt her.

"Now," she said, in a muffled voice. "Come on, Johnny. Get aboard."

He didn't wait for a second invitation.

He rolled over to her as she lay with her buttocks in the cool mud, and his feet dangled in the water as he settled into position. Her body opened for him, and she welcomed him.

It was good to be there. It was the best thing in the world, he thought. To have that hidden hand enfold him and hold him tight.

He liked that. But he knew it wouldn't last. Before he had been going with Beth, he had been making it with a chick named Jane, and Jane had been nice too, until she got pregnant. She got a guy called Horace to marry her, a big hick farmer from Rumseyville, and they had a baby, which for all Johnny knew was his own.

Two weeks ago he had happened to be making a delivery in Rumseyville, and he looked Jane up. It was five months since she had had the baby, and her breasts were hard and full of milk, which Johnny liked, because in the old days Jane had never had any boobs worth noticing. Her husband wasn't around, so he took her.

But having the baby had changed everything. The old nice Jane he remembered was gone forever. She was built like a two-car garage now.

And someday it would be Beth's turn, too. But he would never find out about it, because he didn't intend to stay in Reesport that long.

His body surged and pressed hard against her. She welcomed him, her legs straining, her heels digging into the backs of his knees as she clasped him. He dug his way to the depths of her body.

"Go, man, go!" she yelled. "All the way, Johnny! Yeah! Yeah! Yeah!"

He went.

All the way.

"Harder! Faster!"

He went harder. Faster.

She quivered and jiggled and trembled. Her body arched, and her buttocks rose and slapped down into the mud again three or four times, making a sound like a beaver's tail slapping out a warning. He held her tight. He felt the surge of her, the spasm, the jolt, and he knew it was time, and he sent searing pleasure to her, and her body went rigid and he grabbed onto her breasts and squeezed them and she let out a screech of culmination.

And then it was over.

Then he was lying there naked on top of a naked girl, and his body was still throbbing with the aftereffects, and his feet were dangling in the water, and he could feel her warmth, and he knew that this had been a pretty good round.

He couldn't complain. Beth was a nice item.

But he could do a lot better than Beth, all the same. And he was planning to start improving the situation in the very near future.

They lay still. He didn't take his body from hers.

After a while she said, "Are you ready to go again?"

"You know I am."

"Yeah. So am I."

"What are we waiting for, then?"

She started to move. He matched her rhythms. Her body started to tremble.

On a good night, Johnny could make it three, four times and not feel any strain. He knew he was unusual that way, that there were guys who were still young but who couldn't make it four times a week, let alone four times a night. He felt sorry for them. And glad that he was young and strong and full of vigor.

He reared back on his knees. He got his hands on her buttocks, and pulled her with him to a standing position, their bodies still joined. Easily, he swung her upward, and she wrapped her legs around his waist.

He walked out into the water with her.

Standing in knee-deep water, he held her tight, supporting her by her buttocks. She was breathing hard, and her big, heavy breasts rose and fell rapidly. She hugged him, and put her lips to his for a moment, but the position was too awkward to maintain, and she leaned back again.

Their locked bodies moved passionately.

Grinning, Johnny swung her out and pulled her toward him, swung out, pulled in, every motion resulting in a new eddy of emotion. He could see her eyes gleaming. He enjoyed showing off this way, demonstrating his strength.

She was gasping now. Their bodies were heated to fever pitch. The moment was coming.

It arrived.

He slammed to her hard, and felt the surge and quiver of her fulfillment, and answered with the sudden burst of his own. Her buttocks writhed and her entire body went taut, and he held onto her while they spasmed together through the full fury.

Then it was over, and she was clinging limply to him, and he heard her whisper, "I love you, Johnny, I love you so much!"

He smiled and squeezed her buttocks.

"Tell me you love me," she begged.

"I love you," he said.

Words were cheap.

He was getting cold, now, standing here in the water with the sweat of his lusts still rolling down his body. Gently, he eased her down, and they stood face to face for a moment, her head barely coming up to his chin, the points of her breasts touching his belly, and then they sat down in the water, and relaxed for a while, and then drifted into the deep water and swam.

When they grew tired of swimming, they returned to shore, moving up into the high ground, where the grass grew. They lay side by side on the grass, naked. He cupped his hands over her bare breasts. She rested her hand against his body.

"This was a nice evening, Johnny."

"Mmm."

"We ought to come here more often. We can swim, and then we can make love, and swim some more."

"Yeah," he said. "Nice."

He thought of bullets ripping into Phil McCarran's head. He thought of blood oozing over a poolroom floor. He thought of a Cadillac half a block long.

Absent-mindedly, he played with Beth's naked breasts, but they didn't interest him any more. They were just roundness of flesh, nice to touch, but of no special attraction.

He yawned. "We oughta get going."

"You don't want another round?"

"Not tonight, kid. I'm bushed. All that heat, it takes a lot out of a guy."

They rose. She was in a kissing mood, so he opened his arms to her, and they stood together for a few minutes body to naked body, tongue to tongue.

Then they parted. It was time to get dressed.

She was still glowing. She pulled her polo shirt on, and stood there naked from the waist down, bright and fleshy in the moonlight, and said, "I'm so happy, Johnny. I guess I'm just about the happiest girl in the world."

He nodded. Let her have her happiness now, he thought. All she could get. She probably had some idea that he was going to ask her to marry him, but she'd get over it.

She was headed for a big disappointment, he figured.

He dressed. "Come on," he said. "Get your jeans on and let's go."

CHAPTER THREE

The next day, at lunchtime, he told Old Man Thompson he wouldn't be back in the afternoon.

"Got to see some important people," Johnny said.

"But I gave you yesterday afternoon off!" the old man sputtered. "What is this, you only work half a day now?"

"I got to see these people," Johnny said.

"There's work for you. I need you."

"Sorry," Johnny said.

He turned and walked out of the grocery store, while the old man raged and fumed behind him. Johnny figured he had just done himself out of a good job. What the hell though—he was counting on Lurton and Moss to come through for him. And even if they didn't, well, he could find some other job someplace. Digging ditches, if he had to.

He got into his car and drove out of town on Route 71, out five miles to the turnoff onto Rumsey Road. He drove a couple of hundred yards, and pulled up outside the old Collins mansion.

It was the fanciest house in the county. It was a big, three-story, fifteen-room place, colonial style, with four white pillars out front. It looked like the kind of house a bank president might have. In a county where everybody else lived in rickety frame houses a hundred years old, this imposing brick house looked like the Taj Mahal.

Johnny left his car parked out front. The car was an eyesore in front of such a fancy place, but Johnny couldn't help it. He'd have a better car as soon as he could.

He rang the bell.

He waited almost a minute, debating whether or not to ring again, and then the door opened.

A girl looked out at him.

She was one of the fanciest hunks of womanflesh he had ever seen. She was tall, five feet eight, and she had two boobs that stuck out in front of her like a pair of cannons ready to go off. Her blonde hair was done up in a gleaming bouffant heap. Her face was cool and aristocratic, with thin lips and a high-bridged, delicate nose. She was wearing a loose housecoat, a gauzy thing that left him in very little doubt about the equipment underneath.

Johnny realized he was gaping. He closed his mouth and tried not to look flabbergasted.

She said, in a husky voice, "Your name Johnny Price?"

"That's right."

"You're expected. Come on in."

She turned on her heel and walked away from the door. Johnny followed her in. His eyes travelled down the length of her back. He could plainly make out the firm cheeks of her buttocks moving under the housecoat as she walked, the deep shadowed crevice between the rounded swells of flesh. His pulse quickened. There was a throbbing in his loins. There were all kinds of rumors about this house and the things that went on inside it, but he had always assumed that they were only wild stories—until now, when he saw what kind of dame was answering the doorbell.

She led him into a room toward the left, a big study, thirty feet long and almost as wide. Lurton was sitting at an elegant desk, talking on the telephone. Kloss, at another desk, was listening in on an extension.

Johnny stared at the two hoodlums. Then at the fabulous furniture of the room. Then at the even more fabulous girl who stood by the door, the tips of her high breasts showing dark against her gauzy wrap.

Kloss put down the phone and crossed the room toward them. He nodded and said, "Hello, Johnny. You can go now, Marilyn."

The girl smiled and sauntered away. Johnny stole a quick glance after her, at the buttocks so startlingly visible beneath the thin fabric.

Kloss grinned. "You like her?"

"What do you think?"

"She works for the Syndicate," Kloss said. "She just did a big job in Rochester, and she stopped off here for a couple of days on her way back. You know what it costs to make that girl, Price?"

"Ten bucks?"

"Twenty-five," Kloss said. "Twenty-five a tumble, and more for specialties. You wouldn't mind some of that one, would you?"

"You bet!"

"Tell you what," Kloss said. "Because you did us such a good favor yesterday, I'm going to let you have her. On the house. How's that?"

"Gee, Mr. Kloss, do you mean it?"

"I never say a word I don't mean," Kloss replied thinly.

Lurton was off the telephone now. He rose and came toward them, moving slowly, heavily, with a fat man's rolling, lumbering gait.

"What are you two jabbering about?" Lurton asked.

Kloss said, "He likes Marilyn. I told him he could have a round with her on the house."

Lurton chuckled amiably. "So you're a chaser, are you, kid?"

Johnny shrugged. "It doesn't take much to go for that one."

"Yeah. Yeah. Well, okay. If you like her, you can take a crack at her. Sit down, Johnny. Ed, get some drinks, will you?"

Kloss picked up a phone and buzzed it. He said, "Marilyn, let's have three Scotch-and-sodas, huh?"

Lurton and Kloss and Johnny sat down. A couple of minutes later, Marilyn entered, handed a drink to Lurton, then to Kloss, then to Johnny. When she bent over to give him the drink, the front of her flimsy gown came open, and he could see her breasts, hanging in there like two ripe apples ready for the plucking. A kind of cold sweat burst out on him at the thought that sometime soon he was going to be with those long, tapered legs. The perfume of her almost dizzied him. He took a quick gulp of his drink.

Marilyn left the room. Lurton said, "We've decided to offer you a job, Johnny."

"What sort?"

"Chauffeur," Moss said. "That's what we'll call it, officially. Actually you'll be a kind of junior partner. Our Man Friday, sort of."

Johnny nodded. "That sounds okay."

"You're sure you want to get mixed up in stuff like this?" Lurton said.

Johnny nodded toward the door through which Marilyn had just departed. "I want to get mixed up in stuff like *that,*" he said. "And I can't have it by going straight."

"Sure you can," Moss said. "Just pay your twenty-five bucks, like everybody else."

"That's the sucker's way," Johnny said. "I'd rather get it for free. Anyway, the kind of lousy job I have, I can't afford any twenty-five buck lays."

"What kind of work do you do now?" Lurton asked.

"Delivery boy for a grocery store."

"What's your pay?"

Johnny hesitated, decided finally to tell the truth. "I make about fifty a week, including tips."

Kloss said, "We can do a little better for you. We'll pay you ninety a week. How's that?"

"Sounds good," Johnny said.

"Plus room and board," Lurton added.

"I live here?"

"Sure. How the hell are you going to be any use to us living in town?"

"Well—"

"You don't want to live in town, do you?" Kloss said.

"No. Of course not. I'm just a little stunned. The idea of living here—the Collins mansion—"

"That's one of the extras," Kloss said. "There are others now and then."

"Like Marilyn?"

"Like Marilyn," Kloss agreed.

It was all settled quickly. He would move in that night, into a room on the third floor. He would go on the mob payroll as of today. The grocery store was part of his past, now. Ancient history. Like Beth.

"You go pick up your stuff," Lurton said. "Get yourself moved in. Marilyn'll be waiting."

Johnny was in a daze as he left the building. Things were happening too fast for him, and the breaks were much too good. His salary practically doubled, and living in the fanciest mansion in town, and on his first day being offered the slickest, sleekest woman he had ever seen—

But this was just the beginning, Johnny realized deliriously.

Just the beginning.

It was almost the end, too, as he drove back along Route 71 to town. He was in such a hyped-up mood that he drove like a madman, weaving from one side of the road to another, and he took an elbow bend at 55 mph when it should never be taken higher than 30 mph, and the car started to leave the road in a lateral slide and he caught it only as it crossed the shoulder and headed for the ravine to his left. Another few yards and he'd have been wrapped around an oak tree thirty feet below the level of the road.

Steady, boy. Let's stay in one piece.

He calmed down and made it home alive. He parked the car out front of the shabby, Civil War-vintage frame house where he had been living since his parents died.

His aunt was in the back yard, gathering tomatoes. She was his father's sister, an old maid in her late fifties, who took him in only because he agreed to pay his share of the food bill every week.

She straightened up and looked at him sourly. "You're home early. What happened, get fired?"

"Nope. I've got a new job."

"That's nice," she said without enthusiasm, and went back to picking tomatoes.

"I'm moving out, Aunt Grace," he said. "The new job's in Rumseyville. It includes room and board."

She didn't look up. "When are you leaving?"

"Right now."

"Pretty fast. You want me to help you pack?"

"I can manage."

"Remember you owe me sixteen dollars," she said. "Don't think I'll forget."

"I'll give you five right now," he told her. "And the rest next week. How's that?"

"It'll do," she said, and plucked another tomato.

So that was that. She didn't care what he did, where he went. He was an adult, or practically one, and had his own life to lead.

It didn't take him long to pack. He had never gone in much for accumulating things. Two suitcases held all his possessions. He loaded them into the car, and waved to his aunt, who waved back casually.

He drove off.

Good-bye to Reesport, he thought. *So long, you stinking mudhole of a town! So long!*

He scooted back to the mansion. Lurton took him to his room. It wasn't exactly a palatial room—ten by twelve, with a sloping roof, up on the third floor in what was probably the servants' wing. What the hell, though, he didn't intend to spend much time in the room, and it was good just to be living in this house.

Lurton pointed to a box on the wall. "That's the intercom," he said. "When we want you, we'll buzz. You answer, just talk into the box. No buttons to press or anything. Okay?"

"Got it."

"All set, now?"

"Sure," Johnny said. "Where do I find Marilyn, now?"

Lurton leered at him. "Always on your mind, huh, kid?"

"Is there anything better to think about?"

"I guess you're right," Lurton said. "Well, Marilyn's right down the hall here. At the far end of the third floor Last room on the left. She's waiting for you, kid. She's all yours."

Lurton went out. Johnny's heart was racing furiously. But he made up his mind not to be too eager, not to seem like too much of a greenhorn. Both Lurton and Kloss still had a slight tendency to make fun of him. They didn't take him seriously. They still looked upon him as being wet behind the ears. He had to change that image, if he ever wanted to be anything more than a glorified errand boy for the Syndicate.

He didn't rush to Marilyn's room. He unpacked, first, and put his clothes away. Then he took a shower. He had his own private bathroom, opening off his closet. Toweling dry, he put on fresh clothes, and combed his hair, and took a close shave.

Then, and only then, did he leave his room and walk down the hall to the last door on the left.

He knocked.

"Who's there?"

"Johnny."

"Come in," Marilyn said.

Johnny reached for the doorknob. His hand was shaking a little, and he forced it to steady down. Then he pushed the door open, and let himself in, and closed the door behind him.

"Hi," Marilyn said.

She was waiting on the bed, with three pillows propped up behind her head. She was reading a paperbound book, and her knees were drawn up high.

She was nude.

Johnny stared at her, and a pounding throb of disbelief began to rise in his head. She was magnificent. She was flawless. She was as far above the thick-ankled, flabby-butted farm girls he had been laying since he was thirteen as a sleek Jaguar was above a pickup truck.

Her breasts were high and round and very close together. They weren't extravagantly big breasts, basketball-size, but she was far from being flat-chested, and what she lacked in volume she more than made up in per-fection of shape. Her breasts were like two medium-sized apples, round and firm. The nipples were tiny, little peaked points, and so were the aure-oles surrounding them.

Johnny couldn't see her middle, because she had turned her book face-down over it. But the long, flawless lines of her legs were visible, from the trim, tapered ankles past the superb calves to the firm, rounded thighs. And he could see a little bit of her buttocks underneath her, and a few tan-talizing glimmers of blondeness.

She put her book aside. She slid her feet down the length of the bed, and stretched voluptuously. Johnny eyed the sleek beauty of her, the pink and gold perfection.

Then he came toward the bed.

She said, "So they're going to let you have some fun with me, eh, sonny?"

"Don't call me sonny!"

"Why not? I'm older than you are."

"Are you bragging about it?"

She smiled patronizingly. "I'm just telling you." She stood up, unashamed of her nakedness, and he saw the enmity in her eyes. But her voice was still level as she said, "I don't mind being given away now and then. It's all part of the job. But I kind of resent it when I'm handed to a hayseed hick like you. I expect to be given to bigshots, not chauffeurs."

Johnny met her glare. "You're a friendly one, aren't you?"

"What do you want? Am I supposed to be glad? I'm a human being, not a piece of merchandise."

Johnny's lips firmed. A muscle flickered in his cheeks. "You work for the Syndicate," he said. "So do I. Your boss wants you to give me a good time. You got no call handing me all this jazz, Marilyn."

She stared at him rebelliously for a moment, one hand on her hip, her lower lip puckered thoughtfully. Then she turned and went back to the bed, and lay down on it.

She split her legs wide. She pointed to what was between them and said, "Okay, sonny. You win. Get your clothes off and have your fun."

Johnny nodded. He still didn't like her hard-nosed attitude, but he had an idea he could fix it. Not taking his eyes from her lush nudity, he began to undress. He peeled his clothing away slowly. Her eyes seemed to widen a little as she saw the muscles bulging on his arms, the band of muscle across his hairy chest. But still she looked cold, still she seemed to be unwilling to give him anything more than the temporary use of her body.

He pulled off his pants. Then his shorts. He let her get a good look at his nakedness. He knew it was an impressive sight, and he knew that even a veteran tramp like this one was bound to be impressed.

Naked, he walked toward the bed and stood above her. She hadn't moved. She still lay there in mocking invitation.

He said, "You're a beautiful girl. Marilyn, and I want to go to bed with you. But I want you to act like you're enjoying it, not like it was an order from the boss."

"Come on. Cut the talk and climb aboard."

"Not yet. Not till I get the witchiness out of you."

"Listen, I'm gonna lose my patience, kid."

Johnny sighed. He reached out for her, as though to caress her breasts, but his hand moved upward suddenly and he knotted it in her rich, lustrous blonde hair. He tugged at it, pulling her away from the bed.

"Hey! What the hell do you think you're doing!"

"Stand up. Stand up, you witch!"

"Let go of me!"

He yanked her to her feet. She started to yell, and he slapped her across the mouth, not hard enough to split her lips and draw blood, but hard enough to sting her and make her quiet down. Still keeping one hand firmly buried in her hair, he slapped her again, this time across the breasts.

"You stinking hick," she muttered, "wait till I tell Lurton you're belting me around! Just wait! He'll get rid of you so damn fast you won't know what hit you!"

Johnny laughed. "You aren't telling anybody anything, girlie. You got to learn, I'm no hick, I'm nobody you can spit on. I'm a big man."

"You're a crud."

He slapped her again. "I'm Johnny Price," he said. "You better remember that name. It's going to be important. Now lay down."

He hurled her onto the bed. She lay there, propped up on her elbows, glaring at him.

Johnny said, "We're going to make it now, baby. You and me. And you're going to enjoy it. You may think you aren't, but you'll be flipping in five minutes." Her only answer was a snort of contemptuous anger. Johnny shrugged off her hostility and joined her on the bed. His hands grasped the incredible rounds of her breasts, caressed the nipples, toyed with the little rigid nubs. Not surprisingly, she was going stiff in the nipples.

The presence of a naked man, her own nakedness, maybe the slaps in the breasts that he had given her—all those things were warming her up despite her hatred of him.

His hands wandered down to her thighs. He touched silkiness. He felt warmth. He caressed, stroking lightly.

Then he put his lips to her.

He took his time. His tongue snaked out, encountered, caressed. He moved around from place to place, exciting her, and he could feel the change in her, the relaxing, the shedding of the chip-on-the-shoulder attitude. Obviously few men bothered to make love to her. They regarded her just as a kind of automatic convenience. Something that you plugged into, instead of plugging in. Probably nine out of ten didn't give a damn about her pleasure.

Johnny did. He gave her the Johnny Price special.

He worked her over for nearly half an hour, until she was sighing and dreamy and half delirious with love. There wasn't any question of anger any more. Her eyes were little slits of passion, and her big round breasts were going up and down in convulsive, jerky breaths, and her entire body was warm and flushed and trembling.

When he was sure she was absolutely ready, he took her.

His body reached hers, plumbed the depths of her, and she trembled and quivered and gripped him tight. Her skin was like satin against his. She felt warm and feverish and delectable. He worked his hands underneath her, gripped her marvelously smooth buttocks, held her up, moved to her with gathering force.

"Oh, God!" she cried.

Johnny grinned. He knew he had conquered her.

He brought her along, higher and higher, heading rapidly toward the peaks of passion.

Then she shuddered beneath him, writhing and wriggling, churning, thrashing. Johnny rode with her, right to the finish line, and then he let go with all he had, slamming to her, and her body arched and stiffened.

And then it was over.

He waited a few moments, until the frenzy had died down for both of them, and then he withdrew from her, and stood up, and began to dress.

She lay with her eyes closed, her face wreathed in a dreamy smile of content, of fulfillment.

"Still angry at me?" he asked.

"No."

"You sorry you were so witchy?"

"Yes! Yes!"

"Okay," Johnny said. "You're forgiven, Marilyn. Only next time, when the Syndicate asks you to hand one out on the house, don't be so chinchy about it. You could get into a lot of trouble." He looked at her, eyeing the superb curves of breasts and thighs. "I'll see you around," he said. "The name is Price. Johnny Price. Remember it."

"I'll remember it, Johnny."

She smiled at him. The smile told him that she wouldn't have minded a second round. Neither would Johnny. But not now. There was too much pride in the girl.

"See you," he said.

He walked out, feeling pretty satisfied with himself, all things considered.

CHAPTER FOUR

Living with Kloss and Lurton was a picnic. It was a kind of on-the-job training in crime, and for the first time Johnny really could see close up the possibilities that the mobster life had to offer. All it took was guts and daring, the courage to climb up a little higher than the ordinary joes crawling around in the mud.

Lurton and Kloss had their fingers in every pie. Because they were important men living in an isolated part of the state, they had a supremacy that wouldn't have been theirs if they had set up operations in some more densely populated area. Out here, they were the biggest fish in the pond, and even though the pond itself was tiny, Lurton and Kloss made out all right.

They were affiliated with a big crime syndicate operating out of New York City. Every week, supplies of reefers and dope arrived at the mansion, to be routed on to individual peddlers, in Troy and Schenectady and the other upstate cities. The smaller towns didn't go in much for strong stuff like that, but the middle-sized cities did. Reefers were a big thing almost everywhere, since thrill-happy high school kids gobbled them up. Heroin only went over in the major cities, but the market was anything but skimpy.

It wasn't long before Johnny found out that Lurton and Kloss were giving the New York syndicate a hard time on the rake-offs, as well as putting the squeeze on the small distributors. It was obvious. Their books were cooked, and they were doing much better financially than they had any right to do. As middlemen they were growing plenty fat.

Johnny filed his discovery away in the back of his head for possible future use.

Lurton and Kloss took care of plenty of other things, too. They believed in a diversified operation, lots of baskets to keep the eggs in. One of their sidelines was the illegal pinball business, which they handled on a local scale, with commissions going to the outfit formerly headed by the late Phil McCarran. Nobody ever found out what happened to McCarran and his two stooges. In little towns like Reesport, the police aren't too interested in what happens when a gangster gets killed in a private squabble. The police are only out to protect the law abiding citizens. It's much safer for them that way, as they well know.

Lurton and Kloss also had a thriving call-girl operation going, too, and a ring of card-sharps, and some pool hustlers, and half a dozen other things. In their small-town way, Lurton and Kloss were masterminds of crime.

But the longer Johnny stayed with them, the more he realized they were nothing but small-fry. They had looked big when he'd been on the outside, but now he was getting better perspective on the situation, and he saw plainly that they were nothing but a pair of local hoods, impressive around here, but not much compared with the big boys in New York.

Johnny didn't plan to spend the rest of his life working for Lurton and Kloss. He could use them to climb over on his way up the ladder, but that was about all. He didn't intend to rot away his best years in towns like Reesport and Rumseyville.

They gave him some little jobs of his own to do. One of them was making collections from the pinball-machine operators in the area.

These were usually local store-owners who kept the machines in back rooms for the benefit of small-time gamblers who liked to pick up an extra nickel or two. Pinball for prizes or money is strictly illegal in New York State. You can't even offer a pack of cigarettes for a high score, according to the law. The only legitimate prize allowed is a free game for a certain score. But that doesn't stop people from running pinball machines as gambling operations.

Johnny's first pinball collection was in the neighboring town of Marboro. Marboro, four miles south of Reesport, was a two-horse town where the pinball concession was run by a joe named Mack Blossom, in the back of his little soda-and-magazine shop.

Johnny stopped around to pay his first visit to Blossom about a month after he had started working for Lurton and Kloss.

Blossom was a plump, middle-aged man who probably saw a way of making a quick buck by operating the pinball setup. He wasn't a crook—just someone who preferred to skirt the law when it served his convenience to do so on the sly.

There were a couple of kids sipping sodas in his store the day Johnny came in. Johnny had grown a mustache to look older, and didn't think of himself as a kid any more. Not after having helped murder Phil McCarran. There's nothing like seeing men killed to help you grow up in a real hurry, Johnny knew.

Johnny walked in and said to the pudgy man behind the counter, "Your name Blossom?"

"Yep. Do something for you?"

"Maybe. How's the pinball business?"

Blossom looked uneasy. He had a little thin straggly mustache, and he nibbled it. He dragged his fingertips down his round rubber cheeks and said cautiously, "What you mean by a question like that?"

Johnny shrugged. "First of September's collection day, ain't it?"

"Who sent you?"

Johnny smiled. "Lurton and Kloss."

"How am I supposed to believe that? They always come themselves."

"Not this time. They hired me to help out."

"That's what you say," Blossom countered. "Maybe you're just a wise guy trying to pull off a shakedown."

"Maybe I am," Johnny snapped. "Does that matter to you, though? One way or another you hand over the dough, so don't chatter."

Blossom said nothing. He looked mean and miserable. Johnny took a folded note from his pocket and put it down on the counter in front of him.

"Read it."

Blossom read it. It instructed Blossom to make the payment for the month to John Price, as official representative. It was signed by Ed Kloss. Blossom studied the note for a long moment, played with the edges of the paper, then put it back down on the counter. Johnny picked it up and pocketed it again.

"Come with me," Blossom said shakily.

He led Johnny through a frayed curtain into the small back room where the pinball machine was. There were two people in it, a boy and a teen-age girl.

Johnny looked at the girl first. She was about seventeen, eighteen. She was slim and pretty, with short-cropped dirty-blonde hair, bright, intelligent eyes, and full lips. Impressive breasts jutted out against the plain plaid flannel shirt she was wearing. She looked interesting, and as he looked her over she looked him right back, with nothing shy about the way she appraised him.

The boy with her was a skinny kid with faded blue jeans and long sideburns down his cheeks. He was bending over the pinball machine like it was a lover, crooning softly to it and caressing its sides and wiggling his hips as the ball ricocheted from bumper to bumper, sending up cascades of light with each hit.

He was counting: "Ten thousand! Twenty! Thirty! Forty!"

Johnny peeked over the kid's shoulder at the placard fixed to the corner of the machine. It was the standard business. If you scored a hundred thousand points, that entitled you to one free game. After that it was one additional free game for each ten thousand points, plus fancy bonuses. If you wanted to, you could cash in the free games for dough, at a nickel a game.

It was strictly small time. But it added up, both for the player and the operator. A good player could run up twenty or thirty free games in an hour, sometimes as many as fifty. That was two and a half bucks in cash for an initial investment of a nickel. Not bad, either. But the proprietor always came out ahead, because there were always plenty of over-eager jerks who tilted out without winning anything at all, and who fed in nickel after nickel until they were busted for the night.

Blossom was sitting behind a counter figuring out how much he owed Johnny. Johnny became interested in the game, and in the girl. The girl seemed very interested in Johnny. Maybe she was bored at having to share her boy friend with a pinball machine. She was sitting there with her knees drawn up, and her jeans were so tight they looked like they were about to split. She wore a funny smile. Johnny liked the gleam of brains in her eyes.

But he glanced at the way the game was going, too. The punky-looking kid had run up to 90,000 with one ball left. He stood to rake in five or six free games, if he played it cagey.

The whole setup was just about as foolproof as they came. If the cops came around and asked questions, all that Blossom had to say was that he was giving away free games, no prizes, no dough. You couldn't prove otherwise. And it was strictly legal to offer free games.

But the cops never came around.

"Let's go, now," the kid crooned. He pushed in the plunger and sent the gleaming silvery ball up the track. He clung to the sides of the machine, body tense as a baseball player's, ready to manipulate the flippers that kept the ball hovering up there in the pay-zone.

He hit the first bumper and picked up a thousand. A light flashed, a bell clattered. Johnny watched the numbers mount, a thousand at a time, once two thousand.

90,000, 91,000, 93,000, 94,000. All the way up to 99,000 now. Just one more hit and the kid had a free game. One more—

TILT!

For a second the boy was stunned. He stared at the board that had gone dead suddenly, and started to mouth vicious curses.

Looking up from his books, Blossom said in a kindly voice, "I've told you a dozen times if I've told you once, son. If you shake the machine she's gonna tilt on you, and there's no denying it."

The boy whirled. His thin face was distorted with anger. "You fat old louse," he spat. "This machine's *fixed! I* was right up at 99,000 when she tilted out, you know that? You fixed it!"

Blossom laughed. "Just because you can't control yourself and keep on tilting it, Jimmy, that ain't no reason to say it's phony. You know that. Go on, now, before you make me sore."

"You lousy crook," the boy muttered.

Johnny stared. Obviously this kid was about to work off a lot of resentments right here, using the tilted pinball machine as an excuse for shooting off steam.

The kid moved toward Blossom, who ignored him and continued to go over the books. Johnny didn't move.

Neither did the girl, who continued to sit in the corner, watching the whole thing as calmly as though it were all just a television show.

Suddenly the kid's hand moved to his waist and came out with a knife.

It wasn't a switchblade—those were hard to find, now that they were illegal. No, it was the new kind of knife that Lurton was pushing through the neighborhoods, the gravity knives that were still legal until they got around to outlawing them the way they had outlawed the switch.

The gravity knife was simple. You held it and you flicked it with your wrist through the air, and the blade came shooting out and fixed itself in position.

The boy whipped the knife into sticking shape and took three steps across the dirty floor toward the cowering Blossom.

Johnny quickly sized the situation up, figuring all the angles carefully. The kid was about eighteen tops, a six-footer but still a couple of inches shorter than Johnny, and a whole lot lighter. He was a mean-looking kid and there was fire in his eyes now. Obviously he'd been storing up a whole lot of resentment that he wanted to take out now on the chubby store proprietor.

Blossom was shielding his face with his arm and mouthing, "Get away from me, Jimmy. Put that knife away. You crazy or something? Get away!"

"I'm gonna slice you up, Blossom." The boy's voice was dull, mechanical, ominous. "Been throwing nickels into that machine all week and you got it rigged. Don't like rigged machines. Don't like you, you fat old slimy leech. Gonna slice you up."

He took a few more shuffling steps forward. Johnny stood to one side, watching the sweat come oozing out of Blossom's pores, wondering if the fat man was going to have a heart attack. The curtain was drawn and nobody in the front room was able to see what was going on. The girl was in the room, and Johnny, but the kid with the knife didn't seem to care that he had a couple of witnesses.

Blossom's face was greenish-white, the way Phil McCarran's face had been the day he had come down to Reesport to collect from Lurton and Kloss.

The kid was very close now.

Johnny figured he had let the little show go on long enough.

"Do something!" Blossom begged.

Johnny nodded. He stepped quickly out of the corner and clubbed down with the side of his hand against the bicep of the arm holding the knife. He brought his hand down with enough force to break a dog's neck. He came close to breaking the kid's arm.

The knife dropped and the kid let out a howl. Johnny kicked the knife into the far corner of the room. Then he turned the kid around and slammed him across the face with the back of his hand. Lips and teeth met and blood started to drool out of the kid's mouth.

All the fight abruptly went out of the kid, but Johnny didn't let up. He rapped the kid smartly in the stomach, slapped him twice more, belted him in the shoulder hard enough to spin him around.

Now it was the kid's turn to cower with his hands up, trying to protect himself from Johnny's ferocious assaults. He looked dazed and terrified.

Johnny finished up with a short chop to the jaw that made him fold up, dizzy.

"No more," he whimpered feebly. "Please don't hit me... no more...."

"You learn to keep that damn knife in your pocket next time," Johnny snapped.

He picked the quivering kid up and carried him through the curtain into the front room, past the soda fountain with its wide-eyed gawkers, and out the front door. He booted him in the rear and sent him on his way. Then he turned and went back inside, to the back room.

The girl was still there. She looked at Johnny with glowing, admiring eyes. There was no trace of any resentment over the fact that Johnny had just reduced her boy friend to a pile of pulp. She smiled at Johnny, a bedroom smile if there ever was one, and slowly walked out, taking a deep breath to show off the high, thrusting hillocks of her full young breasts.

Blossom was slumped over at the table, panting hard. He had found a bottle and was pouring something for himself with shaky hands.

"I'll take a little of that," Johnny said.

Blossom poured it, spilling some. It was some kind of bourbon, probably costing about two bucks a quart. Johnny sampled some, rolled it around in his mouth, and spit it out on the floor.

"Mouthwash," he said calmly.

Blossom said, "I—I don't know how to thank you, Mr. Price. That kid was out of his head. He woulda carved me up for sure if you didn't beat him around."

"Yeah. Would have been too bad, too. Having one of our operators getting carved up with a blade we sold, I mean. How much is the account, Blossom?"

Shakily Blossom looked at the records. "Thirty-eight bucks." He drew out a worn leather billfold and started to count the money out, a dollar at a time. "I'm sure glad you stopped around today, Mr. Price. I'm really grateful. You saved my life, you know. Next time that kid comes, I'm gonna be ready for him."

"Add five bucks to the bill," Johnny said.

Blossom looked up, blinking. "What for? I keep fair books, Mr. Price. I wouldn't want to cheat Lurton and Kloss. Thirty-eight smackers is all I owe them. That's the honest truth, Mr. Price!"

"I believe you. The five bucks is for special services rendered."

"You mean—?"

"Sure," Johnny said with an easy smile. "Risking rife and limb to throw that punk out of here, Blossom. Hell, you don't think I'm gonna act as your bouncer for free, do you? Do you?"

"But—five dollars!" Blossom mumbled.

"Yeah. You object?"

"N-no, sir. No. Here you are."

Johnny pocketed the five, as well as the thirty-eight dollar take from the machine. The thirty-eight would go to Lurton and Moss, but the five was his, and nobody else had to know about it.

He felt good about things.

He was learning the business fast.

CHAPTER FIVE

When Johnny stepped outside, he was surprised to find the girl standing there. He had figured she would go off to see after her battered boy friend. But no. There she was, right outside Blossom's place, leaning relaxedly against an old beech tree.

There was a brazen look in her eyes and a smile on her face. And she had unbuttoned the top two buttons of her flannel shirt.

Johnny glanced at her with interest. She was okay, this Marboro hick. She had a good figure, she was a good height, and he was impressed by those bright clever eyes. But why the hell was she waiting?

"Hi, tough guy," she said.

"You want something?"

"Yeah," she said. "You can give me a lift if you're heading north."

"Aren't you afraid I'll eat you up?"

"I'll take my chances," she said. "Jimmy drove me down here, but he took off like a bat out of hell, didn't even wait for me. So I got to get back home somehow, I live a mile and a half up the road, toward Reesport." She laughed. "You really showed that creepy kid, huh? He thought he was a big man. He waved that knife around like he was king of the world. I bet he won't show his face around here again."

"Were you his date?"

"Yeah," she said. "Sometimes you can't be fussy. You gonna give me that lift or do I have to walk home?"

Johnny pointed to his car. "Get in. I'm heading north anyway."

The girl glanced at the car. "That your car?"

"Sure it's my car. Who the hell's car do you think it is?"

"Nice," she said. "Nice."

The car was a '57 Cadillac. It was old, but it was in good shape. Lurton had had the Syndicate lend it to him. They didn't think it was proper to have a Syndicate man go driving around in a decrepit jalopy. So Johnny's Chevy was in cold storage, and he drove a Cadillac these days, until the time came when he could afford to buy his own new car.

The girl slipped in alongside him. She got close to him. He could feel her thigh against his. He started the car, enjoying the surge of power. It was a ball driving a Caddy. It was like piloting a rocketship, Johnny felt. Even an old one like this had plenty of push.

As he pulled out, the girl said, "My name's Ellie."

"I'm Johnny Price."

"I know."

"How?"

"Everybody around these parts knows you. You're with Lurton and Kloss, aren't you?"

He blinked in surprise. "You know a lot for your age, Ellie. Maybe too much."

"Oh, I'm no fool. And I'm not as young as you probably think I am, either."

"How old are you?"

"Eighteen last month."

"Legit?"

"Want to see my birth certificate?"

"I'd rather see something else," Johnny said.

"You can see that too. Any time. Just stop the car somewhere private."

"Got any suggestions?"

"Sure," she said. "There's a turnoff half a mile up the road. You can pull in there. We'll have all the privacy we need."

Johnny was amused by the out-and-out frankness of the girl. She didn't believe in beating around the bush, and he appreciated that.

When they came to the turnoff, he pulled in and stopped the car. He glanced at her.

"Back seat?"

"Nah," she said. "Into the woods. I told you we'd have privacy."

They got out of the car and she led him past a thicket of close-standing white birch, into a narrow natural amphitheater ringed with towering pines. It smelled good here, and there was a carpet of soft, silky, brown pine needles on the ground.

Johnny flopped down.

The girl came down next to him. Johnny reached for her right away. It was a beautiful September day, the sun high and golden, the sky beyond the pine-tops blue and cloudless. He hadn't expected a little dividend like this, but he wasn't going to turn it down if it happened to come his way. He had plenty of time before his next stop.

He unbuttoned her flannel blouse. She had a pink bra underneath, with little yellow flowers sewed to the straps. He grinned. She grinned back.

"It's an old bra," she said. "I got it when I was just a kid."

"Did it fit you when you got it?"

"Yeah," she said. "I was precocious. I was the first girl in my class to grow boobs. When I was eleven, they started."

"When did you start fooling around with boys?" he asked, as he slipped the blouse off her and unsnapped the bra.

"When I was twelve," she said.

He bared her breasts. They were startlingly beautiful, big and firm and round. The skin was milky white, the nipples small and high-set. They reminded him of Marilyn's breasts. He hadn't seen a pair like this since Marilyn had gone back to New York City.

He put his hands over them. They were warm and satiny to the touch. The nipples were hard. He squeezed, cupping into the firm fleshy globes. Ellie hissed in pleasure and started to move her thighs together.

He reached for the belt of her jeans.

He pulled them down over the fullness of her hips and thighs. The jeans were so tight that her panties came along with them, and he dragged jeans and panties past her ankles and she kicked them off. Then she was stark naked on the pine needles next to him.

She was gorgeous.

She looked like another Marilyn in the making. She wasn't quite as elegant-looking as Marilyn, as citified and sophisticated. But she would do. The raw material was there. The big firm breasts, the lush belly, the tapering thighs and sleek calves, the full buttocks.

"Hold still," she said to him.

Then she was pulling his pants off, baring the manhood of him. She looked at him and smiled.

"Mmm. Nice!"

"It's all yours if you want it, baby."

"Yeah. Let me show you a little trick, huh?"

"Anything you like," Johnny said.

He was lying on his back. She sprawled out on top of him, flattening out over his hips. He could feel the heavy globes of her breasts swaying down onto him.

She began to move.

He felt the warmth, the softness. It was the height of pleasure to lie there with his eyes closed and let himself be rocked to ecstasy between those two big firm sweet boobs.

She knew how to please a man. She waited until he was almost at the moment of fulfillment, and then she wriggled lower, so that not her breasts but her lips were on him, and she engulfed him. She was active and eager. He gasped and knotted his hands in her hair, and bit his lip, and the next moment ecstasy came.

She didn't budge. He could feel her lips still moving, moving, until the last spasm was over, until the final quiver of fulfillment.

Then she looked up.

"How was I?" she said.

"Great. Only you didn't get any kicks."

"That's okay," she said. "I can be patient. I know your kind. It won't be long before you're ready again, and you can take care of me."

"You're sure of that?"

"Sure I'm sure." She put her hand on him. "Look. You're half ready already."

He grinned at her. She was a real minx, a kid with a talent for loving. Her hands continued to toy with him, and his healthy, virile body lost little time in responding.

"Okay," he said, hoarsely. "Now we try it the regular way."

He turned over, topping her. He pressed her down into the carpet of pine needles, and her body welcomed him, and he entered easily, confidently into the warmth of her, and she rose to meet him, and her body moved with steady jolts, and she trembled and locked herself around him and shook with passion.

It was quite a performance.

The kid was a natural, Johnny thought.

He rode with her, upward all the way, and her fulfillment came like the beat of a drum, and his followed right along, and when it was over she lay quietly in his arms, naked, happy, her firm young body fitting snugly against his.

After a while she said, "You think I'm good, Johnny?"

"You're terrific, kid. You must have had a lot of practice."

"Not as much as you'd think. I don't think I've had a hundred guys yet."

He laughed. "You poor kid. You've lived such a quiet life. Not up to your first hundred yet, and you're eighteen already!"

"I'll get there though. Will you give me a job, Johnny?"

He looked at her. "What kind of a job?"

"You know."

"No. Tell me."

"A job with your outfit."

He propped himself up and stared at her. "What the hell do you know about our outfit, anyway?"

"I know you've got girls in it. That the girls go all over the state and make a lot of money. That's what I want. Lots of money. They say a girl can make five hundred bucks a week in New York. But she's got to have the right connections. You can fix me up, can't you, Johnny?" Her eyes were glowing with greed. "You can get me where I want to be. I know it. And I'm good. I just showed you how good I was. You know I'm good!"

Johnny chuckled. He understood the whole thing, now. Why she had waited for him, why she had been so eager for him to lay her.

She had ambitions.

She wanted to be a call-girl. To get the hell out of this backwoods neighborhood.

Well, why not, he thought? She had all the natural qualifications. And she had the ambitions. She'd probably make a hell of a good call-girl.

"Okay," he said. "I'll talk to the big boys about you tonight, and we'll set it up."

He smiled. She was his discovery. His protegé. Lurton and Kloss would be pleased with him. Finding her would show them that he had initiative, that he was always looking out for the best interests of the Syndicate.

He ran his hands lightly over her swelling young breasts, over her firm pale buttocks.

"You're as good as in business," he told her.

A couple of days later, after talking about her to Lurton and Kloss, Johnny brought her out to the mansion, and the big boys had a look at her. They had a look at her with clothes on, and then with clothes off. Ellie stripped with no hesitations whatever, as though she were on a visit to the doctor.

Then Kloss took her inside to give her a performance test. She must have passed it with flying colors, because when they reappeared, Kloss walking hand in hand with the naked Ellie, he grinned and said, "We just hired ourselves a new girl, Mike."

And so Ellie joined the chain of call-girls. Johnny was pleased about it, pleased not only because it meant some fun for him, it had also demonstrated to Lurton and Kloss how valuable he could be to the organization.

He had showed them again and again, in the short time he had been working for them, that he was more than just a mere country lunkhead. And he noticed a change in their attitude toward him, as a result.

They didn't regard him as just a simple greenhorn kid any more. They looked on him almost as an equal, now. They let him in on confidential things, really incriminating stuff. They gave him more delicate assignments to carry out. And they raised his take—from ninety bucks a week to a hundred-twenty, and then in short order to a hundred-fifty.

It was nice dough for a big kid not yet old enough to vote. Johnny gave back the old Cadillac the Syndicate had lent him, and bought a car of his own. Not a Cadillac—he wasn't quite in that bracket yet—but a Plymouth, sharp and shiny, with fins in the back the size of a whale's flukes. He kept it in the mansion's huge garage, next to Lurton's big Cadillac and Kloss' glossy Lincoln Continental. It made him feel good just to see it.

Johnny hit it up big with the girls, too, not that there had ever been a time when he hadn't. Now he had the bankroll, and he had the car. There was an air of mystery about him, these days. Once in a while he'd be in nearby Reesport, and he'd wave at people who had once known him. Everybody was aware that he was now mixed up in the rackets, but no one knew exactly what it was he did.

He saw Beth once or twice. But he didn't date her, didn't even let himself get into a conversation with her. She was part of his past. She was just a flat-nosed little hick kid with big boobs. He could do a lot better than her now, and he did.

He dated the daughter of the County Magistrate, even. This was a girl with class, a college girl, the kind of girl you'd think would be a virgin. Johnny had her first time out. She was tall and slim, with nice aristocratic little boobs, and he had a good time with her, even though he knew her father regarded him as dirt. Somehow that made it all the more pleasant to have her.

But he didn't have to depend on the local girls exclusively. There was always plenty of other stuff available. There were invariably two or three Syndicate girls in the big house—girls stopping off overnight on the way to do a job in Buffalo or Rochester or someplace like that further upstate. Generally the girls didn't mind turning over a trick on the house for Johnny and his two employers.

Lurton didn't seem to have too much interest in the girls, though he took one to his room every once in a while. Kloss, though, had one almost every night. The little rabbity guy had an insatiable appetite for sex. The way it worked when a new girl stopped off at the house was, Johnny had to let Kloss have first crack. That went without saying. When Kloss was through with her, Johnny could have seconds.

Johnny didn't mind that too much. There were only a couple of times it worked out to his disadvantage—when only one girl came along, and Kloss took her, and all night there were groans and gasps of passion coming out the little man's second-floor bedroom, and Johnny had to sleep alone. That was bad, especially when the girl would go padding around naked in the house, tempting him.

But he survived. His day would be coming, he knew. Someday Johnny Price would have his pick of every woman in New York.

It was a damned good life.

And there was better yet to come, he knew, if he only played his cards the smart way.

Meanwhile, he went along doing what he was told. He made the rounds of the pinball joints in the county, picking up the dough and making sure no little-time operator was giving the Syndicate a screwing. Occasionally, Johnny was sent on trips upstate, to deliver some goods or to make a pickup. He ran a lot of heroin up to Buffalo, driving alone late at night, and always boffing a Syndicate girl in the morning before coming home. The Syndicate was obliging that way. They didn't expect a guy to make a long lonely drive, carrying dangerous stuff in his car, without giving him some fun at the end of his trip.

He bought fancy clothes and he lived high. Any time he ran out of cash, he could borrow what he needed from Lurton, as an advance against his next week's pay. When even that wasn't enough to cover his current expenses, he could squeeze it out of the country jerks who rented their pinball machines from Lurton and Kloss. It wasn't hard.

"An extra ten bucks this week," he'd say. "A special commission."

"But I don't have it!"

"You want me to smash your place up, wise guy? Come on. Cough up the ten before I change my mind and ask for fifteen."

He got his extras. Ten bucks here, fifteen there, twenty the other place—it added up. Nobody tried to cross him. He was big and he looked ruthless, and he got his way from the little shopkeepers.

The one thing he took good care never to do was to try to cheat on his bosses. Money that he collected on behalf of Lurton and Kloss went to them, every last cent of it. He had a good deal going with Lurton and Kloss, and he didn't intend to lose out by swindling them.

Not yet, anyway.

There were some pretty good parties in the big house on the hill. With three or four Syndicate girls present all the time, some of them turned into real brawls.

One night about four months after Johnny had gone into the outfit, Kloss called him aside and said, "We're getting some very special company tonight. I thought I'd let you know ahead of time."

"Who?"

"Joe Angelucci and Pete Rizzo and some girl friends of theirs. They're on their way to Syracuse to see a basketball game they rigged, and they're stopping over here for some fun tonight. Go down to the town and get some liquor." Kloss fished a bill out of his wallet. "Here's fifty bucks. Angelucci likes gin. *Beefeater* gin, no other kind. You get any other brand and I'll gut you, you hear?"

Johnny grinned. The threat had been almost a playful one. "Beefeater it is, Ed. You can count on me."

He drove downtown and bought a case of gin, and slung it into the back seat of his Plymouth and headed out to the mansion again.

He felt apprehensive. He didn't need to be told who Angelucci and Rizzo were.

They were Syndicate biggies—not top men, but pretty far up from the ladder. They ran things from New York, and in their eyes Kloss and Lurton were just a couple of local stringers, a pair of hicks. Johnny wondered if Angelucci and Rizzo knew just how much dough Lurton and Kloss had been fleecing them of.

Was that why they were coming?

Johnny knew the inside story. Lurton and Kloss were getting away with the neighborhood of ten thousand a year, over and above their recognized take. Kloss stayed up half the nights, sometimes, juggling things so they could drain off more dough than they were entitled to. Once a week, Kloss sent a report down to Rizzo by special delivery, along with a check.

It was all very businesslike. Crime was organized that way, like a well-run business.

Except that every year a legitimate business has an accountant come in to check over the books. In the crime business it didn't happen every year on a formal basis. It happened whenever the top man decided he didn't trust his middlemen any more, and if the checkup showed any serious discrepancies, those middlemen were going to be up to their ears in hot water.

The way Lurton and Kloss would be if the Syndicate ever found out what was going on up here. Johnny smiled to himself. One of these days he was going to let the Syndicate know. He was going to send in a full report.

But not now. He had to establish himself first, and to strengthen his beachhead. He was still too green to make any move against his immediate bosses. But one of these days he would, and when the Syndicate rubbed out Lurton and Kloss, Johnny Price would be the local kingpin.

Soon. Soon.

Johnny drove back to the big mansion with the case of gin, and stowed the bottles away in the bar. Twelve big, shiny bottles, wrapped in cellophane. They looked nice. He stacked them neatly. The time was half past five.

"They'll be here about six," Lurton said.

Lurton and Kloss were pacing around the recreation room nervously. They were worried. That was obvious. They were wondering, Johnny thought, whether the Syndicate had found out about them.

He played it innocent. "What's the matter with you guys?" Johnny asked them. "You both look so damn jumpy."

Lurton said sourly, "These guys expect a big show. They get annoyed if we don't shell out for them. We've got to give them a good time, or else."

"Yeah," Kloss said. "They can be mean."

Johnny wondered whether Lurton and Kloss were aware of how much he knew. You never could tell, with those guys. You never could tell.

The minutes ticked away.

At ten after six the outside door chimed.

"Go let them in," Lurton said.

CHAPTER SIX

Johnny hopped out and opened the door. Two men and two women stood outside, bundled up against the December freeze in expensive-looking clothing. A European car, maybe a Rolls-Royce, was parked near the garage. It looked about half a block long.

Johnny gave the foursome a big smile. "Won't you come in?" he said, as if they planned to do anything else but.

The four of them stepped in, and Kloss and Lurton appeared. Johnny helped the newcomers off with their coats, savoring the expensive cut of the material with something close to awe.

Lurton said, "Joe, Pete, meet Johnny Price. He's our protegé, so to speak. Heh-heh."

A short, thick-lipped man with savage cheekbones and tightly curled hair stuck out his hand. "Pete Rizzo. Hello, Price."

"I'm Angelucci," said the other. He was very tall, taller even than Johnny, but he was thin, almost corpselike, with pale hollow cheeks and slicked-back black hair. He looked like something out of a horror movie.

The girls introduced themselves as Marie and Agnes. They were quite something, Johnny thought. They both made Marilyn look like a chambermaid, and up till now Marilyn was the high-water mark in his experience.

Both of them wore clinging low-cut wraps liberally trimmed with rhinestones. Agnes, who was Angelucci's chick, was a blonde, long-legged, long-haired, with dark inviting eyes and a high, full bosom. Marie was a slinky dark creature with lovely white arms and firm pale breasts that peeped out of the front of her gown.

Johnny had seen plenty of women around the place in his four months, but these two were something special. They were the New York type of women. Thoroughbreds. The type that high-echelon men like Angelucci and Pete Rizzo rated as a matter of course.

The type that Johnny Price was going to rate, someday soon.

The first part of the party consisted of watching Rizzo and Angelucci consume a lot of gin. They liked it on the rocks, and the supply of ice-cubes dwindled fast as they called for refill after refill. The phonograph played, and the two girls laughed and whispered to each other, and everything was very, very merry.

Johnny served as bartender. He kept the liquor flowing, hardly resting for a minute. Somebody was always ready for more. Most of the gin flowed into the four guests. Lurton and Kloss weren't drinking much. They were too scared to relax, probably afraid to get drunk and lose control of themselves. It was a pretty good bet that the two Syndicate men had come here on a strictly social call, nothing ugly intended, but Lurton and Kloss were apparently bothered by guilty consciences.

Johnny didn't drink much either, just a sip or two to keep in the spirit of things. He found he could manage better if he stayed sober, kept his ears peeled, and listened to everything that was said. There was never any telling when he'd come up with something useful that he could file away for the future.

Most of the talk was about the business—about members of the syndicate who had been carted off to jail, or who had met untimely deaths, and so forth. Neither Angelucci nor Rizzo said anything that was likely to be incriminating. They were smart cookies. Not even the huge amount of gin they had consumed loosened their tongues. Johnny figured that anybody who was tough and smart enough to climb as high in the organization as they had was also clever enough to keep his mouth shut in front of subordinates.

Angelucci complimented Johnny a couple of times, giving him gaunt, cadaverous grins every time Johnny refilled his glass. They both seemed to like him. Rizzo said, "It's good to see some new blood in the organization. He looks very capable."

"He is," Lurton said.

While Johnny was opening the fourth bottle of Beefeater of the evening, Kloss turned to Rizzo and Angelucci and said, "Well, are you guys ready for the evening's entertainment by now?"

Rizzo said, "Any time. What's on tap?"

"You'll see," Kloss said slyly. He turned to Johnny. "Johnny, go get the girls. I'll take care of the drinks while you're gone."

"Right."

Johnny left the room. There were four girls of the Syndicate staying in the house overnight besides Marie and Agnes. They had come in from Rochester that morning, and they were en route to Albany. It was convenient that they had been on tap when Lurton and Kloss needed them, because otherwise they would have had to use local talent to amuse the two Syndicate bigshots.

The four girls were rooming in the guest rooms on the third floor. They bunked two to a room, but all four of them were in one room when Johnny went upstairs. Only two of them, girls named Helene and Meg, were being used in the entertainment. They were fully dressed, primping themselves at the mirror. The other two girls, Joan and Sal, were relaxing. Sal, a full-blown brunette, was nude except for a pair of stockings. Joan wore only panties. They were reading confession magazines.

Johnny grinned at the two nude cuties. They were dumb broads, but sexy, and he was figuring on making use of at least one of them before the night was out. But not right now. He glanced at Helene and Meg and said, "Are you two ready?"

"Ready as we'll ever be."

"Okay, you're on. Curtain's going up."

"We're coming," Meg said.

Johnny chuckled. "Did you have a dress rehearsal this afternoon?"

"Don't worry," Helene said. "We know what it's all about. We won't foul up."

"You better not," Johnny said. "You better put on one hell of a show. Or else."

"Or else what?" Meg wanted to know.

"Or else I'll cut your boobs off," he snapped at her. "Any other questions?"

"Nope."

"Come on, then. We're keeping them waiting."

He led the two whores downstairs and into the living room. The party was still as boisterous as when he had left. Angelucci and Agnes were on one couch, Marie and Rizzo on the other, with Lurton and Kloss sitting rather primly on armchairs in the middle. Angelucci had his hand in the front of Agnes' dress, squeezing the ripeness of her breasts. Rizzo's hand was shoved up out of sight beneath Marie's dress, and from the way the girl was squirming around, it was easy to tell that the hand was busy.

Johnny said, "This is Helene. This is Meg. They're going to perform for us."

The party quieted down. Johnny went over to the hi-fi cabinet and put on the record that he had selected to accompany the performance. It was Ravel's *Bolero.* He turned the volume up high, and set the control on the record changer so that when the record ended, the needle would go back to the beginning and play it all over again.

The first sinuous melodies began to emerge. Johnny found a seat and watched the girls.

This was going to be good. He had been looking forward to seeing it ever since Kloss had told him what kind of a show was going to be staged to amuse the two visiting biggies from New York.

Helene was a statuesque blonde, almost six feet tall, and well over the six-foot mark in high heels, which she was wearing now. Her tight dress hugged the contours of her body, revealing rather than concealing the astonishing lines of her enormous breasts and massive buttocks.

So far as Johnny was concerned, Helene was nothing but a dumb cow. He preferred his girls to be constructed along more elegant lines—like

Marilyn, like Ellie, like Marie and Agnes. Boobs didn't have to be basket-ball-size to please him. The size of softballs was enough.

Meg was a sharp contrast to her companion. She was petite, only about five feet two, with a dark complexion and a delicate build. Johnny had happened to see her in the nude that morning, when she took a shower and strolled around the hall investigating the place, and he had been surprised by her body. It was like a little girl's. Her breasts were hardly more than little pointy nubs, her hips were narrow, her buttocks were flat and boyish. She was as underdeveloped as Helene was overdeveloped.

But, Johnny knew, it took all kinds to make a world. The Syndicate aimed to supply a girl to suit every taste. And obviously Meg filled somebody's bill, just as Helene suited the demands of someone else. Neither of them was exactly Johnny's type, but that didn't matter.

They were dancing, now. Helene was leading, Meg following. They moved in time with the barbaric beat of Ravel's music, body pressed against body, cheek to cheek. Their eyes were closed, their expressions dreamy.

The tempo of the music picked up, now.

The two girls separated. They continued to move in strict time. But now they started to take off their clothing as they danced.

They were dressed to the nines. That was part of the routine. Buttons came open. Blouses came off, and then skirts, and then slips. Still they moved in rhythm, bumping and grinding like the expert strippers that they had been before they decided there was better money in the call-girl racket.

Off came the slips, now.

Helene wore a corset. Meg was down to panties, bra, and stockings. They came together, and Meg's nimble little fingers helped the big blonde off with her corset. It came away like the shell of a crustacean.

Helene's breasts were bare, now.

They were gigantic, great heavy globes of flesh, the biggest breasts Johnny had ever seen. It was almost revolting to see such huge boobs. What was her bust measurement, he wondered? 48? 52? Two tremendous spheres of milky-white flesh sprouted from her chest. The nipples were big too, and were set in dark red aureoles as big across as silver dollars.

Helene laughed coarsely. She threw up her arms and wiggled. Her breasts leaped wildly about.

Strangely, considering their size, they weren't really sloppy. They didn't hang. They had firm muscles holding them up, and they had a perfect shape. They remind him of Marilyn's breasts, blown up to three sizes larger.

Meg was kneeling, now. Unhooking Helene's garters, pulling her stockings off. All Helene wore was a pair of panties, now. Sheer panties. She turned in a pirouette, showing the profile of her monstrous breasts, and it was easy to see the heavy slablike cheeks of her buttocks within the panties.

The music continued to mount in tension.

Helene kept her panties on, for the time being.

Now it was Meg's turn to strip.

Slowly, skillfully, Meg drew her legs up, waggled them at the rapt, fixedly staring audience of seven, stroked them, and began to slip the nylons down. Her legs were beautiful, Johnny thought. Short, but perfectly proportioned, wonderfully contoured.

Off came one stocking. But she kept the other one on.

Helen came up behind her, enormous breasts undulating like continents of blubber, and unsnapped Meg's bra. The dark-haired girl's bosom was bare.

It was a remarkable contrast. Meg's breasts, small and pointy, looked like the unformed bosom of a child next to the voluptuous Junoesque abundance of big Helene.

Meg removed her panties next. The small round bowl of her belly was bare, and the narrowness of her hips, and the darkness of the tiny triangle. All she wore now was her garter-belt and one stocking. The effect of having one leg bare and one encased in nylon was an interesting one, Johnny thought, though he didn't know why it appealed to him in any special way.

Helene removed her panties to reveal the lush quivering mounds of her buttocks, the curving roll of her belly. Meg pulled off her remaining stocking, then her garter-belt.

Both girls were nude now.

They moved toward one another. The music was at its wildest crescendo now, beating with jungle fury. Helene opened her arms wide, engulfing the smaller girl. They came together, breasts to breasts, thighs to thighs, belly to belly. Meg's small dark body stood out clearly against the vast white expanse of Helene.

They kissed.

They caressed one another's breasts.

Then they sank to the thickly carpeted floor and began to make love.

Johnny glanced at the company. Rizzo was staring with hypnotized fascination at the two writhing girls on the floor. His lips were open, dangling stupidly, and there were beads of sweat on his forehead. His eyes seemed to be bulging from his head.

Angelucci, too, was keenly enmeshed in what was going on, it seemed.

The lean, cadaverous gangman had uncoiled his legs and was sitting with both feet flat on the floor, one hand on his knee and the other on the arm of the couch. The stiffness of his position gave away his rapt interest in the Lesbian act.

As for Marie and Agnes, they were less interested. Perhaps Lesbo routines bored them, or perhaps they were pretending boredom to hide the real desires that were churning within them. Johnny couldn't tell.

He looked back at the floor.

Helene was on the bottom, lying on her back. Little Meg sat astride her like a flea on an elephant. Meg was grasping Helene's breasts, but her tiny hands couldn't even begin to encompass those massive mounds of flesh. Helene, grinning, had her hands spread out splayedly over Meg's taut, firm little buttocks.

Meg was rocking back and forth. And now Meg lowered herself, went down.

Helene welcomed her.

There was silence in the room. Helene's hoarse, gasping breathing was the only audible sound. For long minutes, Meg continued to pay homage to the big blonde girl. Helene groaned in pleasure, writhed, moved her hips up and down.

Then they changed places. And it was Meg's turn to lie with legs spread, clenching and unclenching her fists in excitement, as Helene's active lips sent her into transports of ecstasy.

They were going at it with unfaked enthusiasm, Johnny saw. Lurton had once told him that about half the call-girls in the business were secretly Lesbians, but Johnny hadn't been sure whether he was kidding or not. Now he saw the truth of it, at least as it applied to Helene and Meg. What they were doing now, they were doing for the sheer joy of it, and not simply because Lurton and Kloss had ordered them to put on a good show. This was their natural inclination. What they did with men was done for a living.

The two bodies were writhing and churning frantically on the floor, now. Meg worked one slim thigh between Helene's two vast ones, and then a moment later had her entire body between Helene's legs.

Meg began to move.

Both girls gasped. Johnny watched their faces with sharp interest. Faces distorted, faces swollen and puffy and weird-looking. He had never seen anything like this. Lurton and Kloss were suppliers of stag movies, among other things, and Johnny knew that they had a few reels of Lesbians in action, but he had never bothered to take time to watch them.

It was a fantastic sight.

It was astonishing, amazing, to see these two chicks going at it, their breasts bobbing wildly, their hips pivoting and twisting, their entire bodies quivering and flushed with the frenzy of unnatural love.

On and on it went.

There seemed no limits to the girls' endurance. Now and then one or the other would cry out in the frenzy of a climax, but they would pause only a moment and go right on to the next round. They were unaware of the audience that was so avidly watching them. For them, the universe was bounded by their own flesh.

Meg had her mouth over one of Helene's breasts, now. Helene had her hands at Meg's thighs. Both girls were in ceaseless motion. The record had reached its finish and had started again, building up the tensions, but the two girls had long ago ceased to pay any attention to the rhythms of Ravel. They were moving on the dictates of their own inner rhythms of passion.

Higher, higher, higher the excitement mounted. Faster and faster the limbs pumped, Meg's dark slim shape hammering into Helene's fair abundant one.

And then, suddenly, it ended.

Helene let out a long, echoing scream of passion, a banshee shriek of fulfillment. It rose and fell and ebbed away, and Helene lay naked and spread-legged on the floor like a beached whale, and Meg, breathless, panting, sweat-soaked, lay atop her.

Neither girl moved.

The show was over.

For a moment, no one in the room moved. Then Rizzo grinned and began to applaud. Angelucci joined in.

"Hey, great!" Rizzo yelled. "Who are those two chicks, Lurton?"

"They're based in New York," Lurton said.

Rizzo leaned forward. "Hey. You two. Stand up, will you?"

Helene and Meg got uncertainly to their feet. They were both soaked in sweat, their breasts heaving, their eyes bleary from passion. Runnels of sweat ran the length of their bodies, making breasts and bellies gleam.

Rizzo said, "I want you two to stop off to see me when I get back to the city. You hear? I think we can sell the two of you as an act. Would you like that?"

"You bet," Meg grinned.

"Yeah. Sure. No more making men, huh? Just each other?" Helene asked.

"That's right," Rizzo said. "We got plenty girls who can do the making. You two will be performers. Okay? See me in New York."

The two naked girls smiled and walked out of the room, hand in hand. Johnny had one last look at the two pairs of buttocks in the doorway, the flat boyish cheeks and the pale fleshy ones, and then Helene and Meg were gone.

Rizzo yawned and stretched. "Hey, good show," he said. "I really dug that. And now I think I'm gonna go upstairs and sack out." He swished the gin around in his not quite empty glass. "Maybe I'll have one for the road. No. No, the hell with it. I had enough. I'm as tanked as a guy needs to get."

Rizzo stood up. He looked at Marie and said, "Suppose you come along with me."

Marie grinned at him. "Soon, Pete. I want a couple more drinks first. Okay?"

"Okay. Be expecting you."

Lurton said, "Johnny, show Mr. Rizzo to his room."

"Sure," Johnny said.

CHAPTER SEVEN

Johnny escorted Rizzo upstairs to one of the second-floor guest bedrooms that had been laid out for the visitors. Rizzo was weaving unsteadily around. He hadn't seemed drunk downstairs, but he lurched a couple of times on the way up, and had to clutch the banister to keep from toppling back down and landing flat on his face.

The room he had been given was a big, imposing one with its own fireplace and its own little balcony. The bed was a king-sized one. As they entered the room, Rizzo looked at Johnny and said in a thick voice, "Price, you're a goddamn good kid. I like you, Price."

"Thanks, Mr. Rizzo," Johnny said humbly. He knew when to be polite, and to whom.

"You from around here?"

"That's right, Mr. Rizzo. I'm from Reesport."

"Local talent. Well well well." Rizzo laughed drunkenly. "I like you a whole lot, kid. I think you can go far in this business. You got the right attitude." He clutched the doorframe to support himself. "If you ever get down to New York, Price, be sure to stop by and see me, hear? Maybe I can help you out a little. Always willing to encourage promising new talent when I see it."

"That's very kind of you, sir."

"And—and here's something to show how I feel about you, Price. A little token of—a token of—of—" Drunkenly, without tying down the sentence he was mumbling, Rizzo fished in his pocket and came out with a thick stuffed billfold. He reached in almost at random, pulled out a bill, and handed it to Johnny.

Johnny took it and put it away without looking at it. "Thank you, sir."

"Welcome. Good night. And tell Marie to get the hell up here, huh?"

"Of course, Mr. Rizzo. Of course."

Johnny watched the crime magnate stumble into the room and pull the door shut. He turned away and looked at the bill for the first time. It was a hundred, new and crisp, fresh from the mint. Grinning cheerfully, Johnny slipped it into his pocket. He went back downstairs.

Lurton was the only one in the living room when Johnny got there. Lurton was sitting quietly, almost corpse-like, in the big armchair, sipping a drink. There was a strangely peaceful look on his features now, after all the tension earlier in the day.

Johnny looked around and said, "Where'd everybody go, huh?"

Lurton shrugged. "Angelucci and his dame went off to bed. Kloss is conducting them to their room."

"How about Rizzo's chick? Marie."

Lurton shrugged again, this time sloshing half his drink onto his trousers. "She had a little too much booze, she said. Said she wanted to grab some fresh air. She's out on the front porch."

"Rizzo wants her upstairs," Johnny said. "I better go find her before she passes out under a rosebush or something, I guess."

He started toward the door. Lurton got up out of his seat with a speed that was surprising for a man his size, and caught Johnny by the wrist.

Putting his lips close to Johnny's ear, Lurton said quietly, "You were upstairs with Rizzo a long time, Johnny. Maybe five minutes or so. That's a hell of a long time. What took so long?"

Johnny frowned. "He was drunk. He was staggering all over the place. And then he wanted to talk. To tell me what a nice promising kid I am."

"That all."

"He gave me a hundred bucks." Johnny looked shrewdly, coldly at the fat man and said in a voice he would not have dared to use with Lurton three months earlier, "You angling for a cut of it, Mike?"

Lurton shook his head. "Nah. You oughta know that. Whatever he gave you is yours, kid. I just wanted to know if—"

If I squealed to Rizzo? Johnny thought.

Out loud he said, smiling blandly, "Relax, Mike. I didn't give away any trade secrets. You can count on me, Mike."

"Yeah. Yeah. Okay."

"Look, I better go find Marie now, Mike. Rizzo wants her and he's likely to get pretty goddamn sore if I don't get her up to him right away."

"Okay," Lurton said. "Go ahead."

Johnny stepped out into the cool night air. It was early December, but still not too cold. The air was clear and the stars speckled the sky. A big moon brightened things considerably.

He smiled over Lurton. Lurton didn't trust him, it seemed. The booze had brought out the truth. Lurton was secretly afraid that Johnny was going to sell him out to Rizzo.

Relax, Mike, Johnny thought. *It isn't time yet. Not quite yet.*

He looked around for Rizzo's girl.

After a few moments he found her. She was sitting on the swinging bench in the garden, rocking back and forth. He walked toward her.

"You trying to get pneumonia, Marie?" he asked. "Girls with dresses like that shouldn't go outdoors this time of year."

"I wanted some fresh air before I went to bed." She continued to swing. Her breasts bobbed up and down as she moved. "Come here, Johnny."

He crossed over to her.

"Sit down next to me. On the swing." Her voice was low and throaty.

He sat down. The swing rocked back and forth. He smelled the perfume of her, and the finer scent of her own body, and sudden lust rocked him. The little skit Helene and Meg had staged had filled him with desires, and he had figured on satisfying those desires with one of the tramps upstairs.

Now new ideas stole into his head.

Dangerous ideas.

Johnny didn't know whether to risk it or not. A copse of big spruces hid this part of the garden from the house, and in any event Rizzo's bedroom was on the other side of the building, so nobody could see anything that happened to go on down here. But still—

Johnny said, "I just put Rizzo to bed. He's anxious for company. Your company. You better go up there and take care of him, Marie."

"He can wait a few minutes," Marie said. She wrapped herself around him, took his hand and laid it on her warm breasts. He dug his fingers in, covering the firm fleshy breasts and cupping them. His fingertips slid down to feel the rock-hard nipples under her strapless bra.

She said huskily, "I like you, Johnny. I like big men. Not little fat ugly ones like Rizzo."

"Marie—"

"I want you! Let me have you before I go upstairs to him!"

"He's waiting!"

"Screw him," Marie said. She reached out, caught hold of Johnny's zipper, yanked it down. Her hand dove into his pants and emerged triumphantly a moment later. He felt the coldness of the night.

She grinned. "Oh, yes," she said. "Oh, look at that! Oh, momma wants!"

He didn't know whether to trust her or not. Maybe, he thought, this was some kind of trap—that he was having his loyalty tested. A guy who would take a big shot's broad might stoop to selling his bosses out.

But he decided that that was crazy. Nobody was *that* suspicious. He was reading motives where no motives were. Marie wanted love, that was all, and it was cockeyed to think of all sorts of conspiracies.

Besides, he wasn't able to resist her. Not now, with her hot little hands at work on him.

He turned toward her. He slipped his hand downward, to her calf, and brought it quickly up, up over her nyloned knee, up to her thigh, to her bare stretch of soft flesh between the top of her stockings and where her panties began.

He kept the hand climbing.

Only her panties never began. She wasn't wearing any. He followed the straps of her garter-belt up, and the next thing he knew he was at her belly, round and firm and warm, and he felt the silkiness of her, and the smooth satiny flesh of her buttocks underneath, and no panties.

"Isn't it cold that way?" he asked.

"No," she said. "It's hotter. Much hotter."

She was panting now. His fingers found her and enjoyed her, and stirred her. She clamped her thighs tightly together around his wrist. His fingers moved for a moment, and gusts of smoke came from her nostrils as she panted.

"Not the hand," she whispered harshly. "Use something else! I'm ready!"

"Okay," he said.

She pivoted around in the swing to face him, and lifted her dress high, and he took a sideways position and the next moment she was settling down, straddle-legged across him, and he gasped in sudden excitement and ecstasy as the super-heated furnace of her body came down on him.

She began to move.

She eddied her hips back and forth. They sat facing each other, and he grasped her breasts tightly through the cocktail gown, and the swing moved back and forth in rhythm to that of their thrusting bodies.

In another moment he saw her close her eyes, saw her bite her lips as passion took hold.

Then came the spasms, the jolts of ecstasy. He thrust harder, and in another instant there was the searing fulfillment for him, and it was all over.

It had been good, for both of them.

But it had ended much too soon.

They sat together for a while after it had ended, her body still pressing his. He was breathing hard, and so was she, and her eyes were misty. The warmth of her was still wonderful next to him. He hadn't been expecting this at all, this sudden burst of lust, this sudden entrapment by a pantie-less girl on a swing in December, with the bright moon looking down on them.

Finally he said, "We better get back inside before there's trouble. We've been out here ten minutes, maybe more."

"Yeah. Yeah."

She lifted her leg, clambered off him and down from the swing. He watched her as she pulled her dress up, showing him what had just been his, the shrine of passion atop the stockings, still ruffled from his savage strokes of desire.

Then she straightened out the dress and grinned at him. She said, "I like you even more, now, Johnny. Maybe I can get to see more of you someday."

"Maybe."

"Would you like to?"

"You know damn well I would."

"Rizzo can't last forever," she said. "Ever think of coming to New York?"

"Soon," he told her. "I'm not ready for the big leagues yet. But I will be, pretty soon."

Together they walked back toward the house. Johnny felt on top of the world. He hadn't dreamed the evening would end up this way.

As they came to the end of the garden path, he said, "We better not go in together."

"Yeah." She smiled. "See you in New York."

"I hope so."

"I know so. We'll have an encore. Only this time we'll take more than ten minutes for it."

"That's for sure," he said.

He watched her walk into the house. The memory of her body lingered with him—the taste of her lips, the sweet musky woman-smell rising from her breasts, the searing warmth of her womanhood. It all seemed a little dreamlike, that sudden wild encounter in the December night, on the swing. Hoist the dress and away we go.

Didn't she ever wear panties? Or had she taken them off earlier in the evening, just in case something like this happened? Had she known he would eventually follow her out into the garden? Or had she been willing to take anybody who came out there?

No, he thought. No, she had wanted *him*.

He couldn't believe it was any other way.

And there would be a next time, he thought. Soon. Only this time it wouldn't be any ten-minute quickie with clothes on. They would get undressed, and their bodies would come together as man and woman should come together, flesh to flesh, no barriers at all, and they would scale the heights of passion together.

He went back into the house. There was nobody in the living room. He looked around, at the mess of empty gin glasses and half-empty gin bottles, of melting ice-cubes and spilled cigarette ashes.

Johnny felt like a king. Before long, he knew, he would be able to make the jump from small-time to the real thing, downstate in the big city.

He had it all figured out. By informing on Lurton and Kloss, he could win himself a position in Rizzo's outfit. But even Rizzo was only a middle-sized fish, after all. There were plenty of guys as bigger than Rizzo as Rizzo was bigger than Lurton and Kloss. Someday, perhaps, Johnny could pull the same deal on Rizzo, and rise even higher in the organization. The sky was the limit.

And Marie would be his.

The thought of having Marie every night tickled him. Right now, she belonged to Rizzo. But Rizzo couldn't last forever, Johnny thought. Sooner or later, he'd have a humpty dumpty. They all did.

And Marie would be waiting.

He walked slowly upstairs, through the dark, enormous house. Pausing on the second floor, he strolled down the hallway, simply listening.

They were pretty interesting sounds. If he taped those sounds, he could sell the tape for a mint. As a sound track for some of the stag movies that Lurton and Kloss liked to peddle.

The first room he came to was Kloss'. He heard the sounds in there. The creaking bedsprings, the groans, the pants, the gasps.

"How you doing, Meg?" Johnny heard Kloss ask hoarsely. "You getting there?"

So Kloss was banging the slim little Lesbian. Johnny smiled. Kloss had always had peculiar tastes in women. Johnny strolled on.

The next room was Lurton's. Did Lurton have a woman tonight? Yes. Lurton did. Gasps and moans here, too. Cries of passion. Johnny listened for a moment, until he heard the voice of the girl. He identified it as that of Sal, one of the tramps staying in the house overnight.

He continued on.

Now he was in front of Angelucci's room. A funny sound here. The sound of slapping, hand against bare flesh.

Johnny frowned. He decided to do something risky.

He bent down, peered in the keyhole.

Angelucci and his girl Agnes were both naked. Agnes was lying face down across Angelucci's lap, with her plump pink buttocks turned upward toward him. And the tall, cadaverous hoodlum was spanking her. Up went the bony hand, and down, *whack!* across the rosy buttocks. Up, down, *whack!* Up, down, *whack!*

And they both wore a beautiful, beatific smile of pure pleasure.

Johnny straightened up, shrugged. It took all kinds, he knew. Well, if that was how Angelucci got his kicks, and if Agnes didn't mind getting her bottom walloped, who was he to criticize?

He walked on.

The remaining bedroom on the floor was the end one, the one that Marie and Rizzo were sharing. Johnny felt a surge of jealousy as he passed it. In the last half hour he had come to think of Marie as his. It was a foolish attitude, he knew, but he couldn't help it.

He stooped, peered in.

Rizzo was lying in bed, still half drunk. He was naked. And Marie was kneeling on top of him. She was crouched over, with her back bent. Her buttocks were pulled taut, facing the keyhole. He could see everything she had.

She was making love to him with her mouth. And Rizzo was groaning with pleasure.

"That's it, baby. Yes, yeah, yeah! Oh, that's right! Yeah!"

Johnny stared, morbidly fascinated by the service Marie was performing. He was annoyed, but he knew the girl had no choice—that Rizzo must have ordered her to do it, and she had to obey. He was probably too drunk and un-co-ordinated to make love himself right now. He just wanted to lie back and have Marie give him pleasure, and Marie was doing it.

He peered in at Marie's luscious buttocks. He knew it was risky to be out here peeping into a boss's bedroom this way, but he didn't think there was much danger. The other four were all busy raging away themselves right now, so who was there to catch him?

But the things he was witnessing inflamed his own lusts. The encounter in the garden had only half-satisfied him, anyway. It had been over too fast to really drain him of passion. He wanted more.

He couldn't have Marie. But there were others.

He mounted the stairs, raced up to the third floor, the servants' floor where the small fry like him lived. He went down the hall to the guest rooms and knocked on the door.

"Yeah?"

He pushed the first door open and looked in. Helene lay in bed, naked, a true confession magazine propped up on her enormous bosom.

Johnny didn't want her. He wasn't in the mood for taking on a wench that size. Especially after watching her in that Lesbo display.

"Where's Joan?" he asked.

Helene pointed. "Across the hall."

Johnny nodded and knocked on the other door. The girl answered, and he went in.

The girl was standing by the mirror, combing out her long black hair. She was wearing a transparent shorty nightgown that came down only to her hips. The effect was far more provocative erotically than if she had been completely nude.

"Come on," Johnny said.

"You want me?"

"Damned right I do. Let's go."

She didn't argue. She was new, and she was small fry, and in her eyes Johnny was one of the bosses. He led her down the hall to his room. She was a good-looking girl, not very bright, but stacked.

He took the shorty nightgown off her. He came over to her, put his hands on her breasts. They were cool, hard, good breasts. Young breasts. She was about nineteen.

"Lie down," he said.

She went to the bed and took her position. He undressed quickly and went to her. His body throbbed with memories of Marie, and in his mind's eyes blazed the image of Marie crouching naked over Rizzo, her doubled-up buttocks pointing toward the door. With a quick thrust, he forced himself to the warm, yielding depths of the dark-haired tramp's body, and in easy rocking motions rid himself of the tensions of desire, and pillowed himself on her cool, firm breasts, and fell asleep with her black fragrant hair trailing down over his face.

He dreamed of Marie, and the big time.

CHAPTER EIGHT

About seven weeks after that big night, Johnny decided that the time had come to make his move.

He had been with Lurton and Kloss almost six months now. That was long enough to know just about every aspect of their business. He had always been smart, in the things he cared to apply himself to. He figured he could handle the business now without them.

He knew who owed them money, who was likely to fudge on payments if he didn't get prodded, and everything else. He had become an expert in the crime business after only a six-month apprenticeship, and now it was time to get rid of his two small-town mentors and start heading for the big time.

And for Marie.

Johnny had been planning wisely. He had opened up an account with a big New York City commercial bank, and made his deposits by mail. Already, he had managed to salt away two thousand bucks—his income was big, his expenses were small—and he was putting more in the account every week. When he went down there, he wanted to have a backlog of dough waiting for him.

Early in February he said to Lurton, "Mike, I want a couple of days off."

"What the hell for?"

"It's the slow season, isn't it? With all this snow coming down, I can't get anything done. So I figure on taking off. You don't need me."

"Yeah," Lurton said. "But where you going?"

Lurton was still suspicious of him, Johnny realized. He said carefully, "There's a girl in Marboro. I've been breaking down her resistance for the past couple of months and I just about got her made now. I figure I can clinch it if I take her away for the weekend."

Lurton guffawed. "All this free stuff laying around the house and you've got to go seducing broads?"

Johnny said, "You know how it is. If you don't have to work for it, there's no fun in it. Here, I just snap my fingers and two broads come running up with their boobs jiggling. This girl's different. She won't come across unless I play the game."

"She a virgin?"

"I think so," Johnny said. "But I'm figuring on taking care of that this weekend."

"You be careful, kid. Next thing you know, she'll slip a ring through your nose and you'll be on your way to the altar, and won't that be a damn shame?"

"Don't worry, Mike. I've got more brains than that, I think."

"I hope so."

"I know so."

"Where you figuring on taking her?"

"New York," Johnny said.

Lurton's eyes narrowed. New York was where Rizzo was. New York was where the Syndicate had its headquarters.

"New York, huh?"

"Where else?"

"Yeah," Lurton said. "Where else?"

Johnny nodded. "What's a good hotel to take her to, Mike? Gimme a recommend."

"Try the Waldorf," Lurton said. "You can't miss there. It's a cinch."

"Thanks, Mike. You don't mind if I take off for the weekend?"

"Nah," Lurton said.

Johnny left the next day, driving his flashy new car. He had been afraid that a new snowfall would lock him up, but for once the skies stayed clear, and the highway crews had a chance to push the accumulation away.

Neither Lurton nor Kloss seemed very suspicious about his taking the trip, at least not on the surface. He waved good-bye to them and drove off in the direction of Marboro, but after he was two miles from Reesport he changed roads abruptly and picked up the highway that led to New York City.

There hadn't been any girl in Marboro that he was trying to make. Johnny hadn't had trouble making any girl in years, and certainly not lately. The girl in Marboro that he was supposed to be taking to New York for a whirl was strictly mythological.

He was on his way to New York to see Pete Rizzo. He was going to show him a couple of the documents he had in his suitcase.

It was usually a two-hour drive to New York, down the pike. Because there was still some snow here and there, Johnny had to take it slow. He reached Manhattan late in the afternoon, coming in across the George Washington Bridge and running down the west side.

He found a hotel—not the Waldorf, because he valued his dough too much to make that kind of splash this early, but a smaller and cheaper hotel near Times Square. It wasn't any palace, but it was no fleabag either. He didn't need to impress anybody, just yet, so why bother throwing the money out at a fancy hotel?

At the desk he said, "What can I do with my car?"

"Garage across the street's the only thing. You can't keep it on the streets around here."

"Okay," Johnny said.

He took his car across the street and parked it at the garage. Two bucks a day, but what the hell, he didn't have any choice.

It was a cold, crisp winter day. Snow had fallen down here, too, and ugly blackened heaps of it were piled up at the street corners. Johnny didn't mind the ugliness. This was New York, and you had to tolerate the ugliness if you wanted to have the excitement, the sheer high-powered verve of the big city.

He went for a walk in Times Square.

This was only his second visit to New York, and he was just as awed this time as the last. To stand at 42nd Street and Broadway, to look uptown at the welter of neon signs and theater displays, made him realize that he was still just a hick at heart. He hadn't yet shaken all the mud of Reesport from his boots.

Not yet.

He walked around. He passed a movie theater that was showing a nudie film, and wondered what would happen if one of the upstate small-town theaters tried to show a film like that. Bombs would be thrown, probably. He went past the theater, and saw a book store, and poked his nose in there to see what was doing.

The book store was full of men. That was the kind of book store it was: The Kind Men Like. There were about a dozen men in it, some in their twenties, others a lot older. About half of them were thumbing through the racks of paperback books, looking for a hot one. Three men were looking at little cellophane-wrapped packages of photographs.

Johnny picked up one of the packages. All he could see was the top photo, but it told him that the merchandise was nothing much, by Syndicate standards. The photo showed a girl with big breasts, a cow of a girl, a girl the size of Helene. She was wearing a g-string, though. In the photos the Syndicate peddled, there were no g-strings. But you couldn't sell stuff like that over the counter, not even in a Times Square book store.

There was also a heap of magazines. Some of them were girlie magazines, but there was a pile of Swedish nudist magazines. Johnny looked at them. They were a little surprising. The pictures were completely unretouched. And some of them even showed naked men. The magazines were stapled together to discourage browsing, and they sold at a high price.

He put the magazines down. He had never been interested in looking. If he couldn't touch, if he couldn't *do,* what was the good of looking? Who could love a three-by-four photograph? Who could sleep with a nudist magazine, even one with unretouched photos?

Johnny drifted out of the store.

He wandered around Times Square for a while, looking at the people go by. A lot of them were girls. A lot of the girls, he was willing to bet, were for sale. Streetwalkers. He felt sorry for them.

The Syndicate didn't have any truck with streetwalkers. Streetwalkers were the dregs. They were freelancers. When the Syndicate sold a girl, they did it on an organized basis, so many appointments a week, payment in advance, regular medical checkups, et cetera, et cetera. They ran it like a business. These poor kids out in the cold, probably turning sixty bucks a week and getting sick in the bargain, were in the wrong kind of life.

He thought about picking one up, giving her a good time. He decided against it. The Syndicate could supply him with a girl for the night. At least he'd be sure to catch nothing, that way. And he'd save a few bucks too.

He had dinner at a pizzeria on 47th Street. Then he went to a phone booth and dialed Rizzo's number.

As he expected, one of Rizzo's lieutenants answered, a surly, suspicious-sounding fellow.

"Yeah?"

"I want to talk to Pete Rizzo."

"What about?"

"That's between me and him. My name's Johnny Price. You tell him that."

"He's busy now. Try some other time."

"Philadelphia," Johnny said. It was a code word that was supposed to get people to give you their attention, in the Syndicate.

The hood at the other end said, "Okay, so what's your name?"

"Johnny Price. I'm from Reesport, New York. I work for Lurton and Kloss."

"Who in the hell are they?"

"Big men up there. Look, friend, tell Rizzo I've got some dope that he'll find very interesting. If he doesn't remember who I am, tell him he once gave me a hundred-buck tip for helping him get upstairs."

"You wait. I'll see if he's free."

Johnny waited. And waited. It was cold in the phone booth, and people were standing in line outside. But he held onto the phone. He stared through the transparent plastic walls at the bustling New Yorkers outside.

His dime dropped through. The operator said, "Please deposit five cents for the next three minutes."

Johnny scowled and dropped a nickel into the slot. Another minute went by, and then Rizzo's underling came back to the phone at the other end.

Rizzo had remembered.

The underling said, "The boss says it's okay for you to come over. He'll expect you at eight."

Rizzo lived in a swanky apartment house on East End Avenue, in a sixteenth-floor penthouse. A doorman studied Johnny critically as he came in, but evidently he passed the inspection.

The elevator zoomed upward like a missile bound for Mars. Johnny hadn't had much experience with elevators, and never with one like this. It seemed that half a second after he nudged the button, the elevator was rocketing to a halt at the top of the building.

He gulped his stomach back down where it belonged, got out and rang the penthouse buzzer. The underling with the ugly voice came out, and he turned out to be as nasty-looking as he sounded, a hulking, apish kind of guy with little piggish eyes and snaggle teeth.

"Yeah?"

"Johnny Price. To see Mr. Rizzo."

"Come on in," Snaggletooth grunted.

Johnny followed him in.

It was quite a place. Not even the mansion where Lurton and Kloss lived could begin to compare with it. Johnny had never dreamed a place could be so fancy. There were real paintings on the wall, and carved statuary all over, and luxurious couches and sofas and divans. Huge picture windows provided vast vistas of New York City.

One of the sofas was occupied by Marie. She wore a revealing wrap, thin and filmy, showing off the opulent curves beneath to best advantage. On her finger was an emerald ring big enough to choke an elephant.

"Hello," Johnny said.

She smiled warmly, a sizzling smile. "Hi there, Johnny. Long time no see."

"Seven weeks, that's all."

"It seems like more than that. It seems like seven years." She grinned. "Has it seemed like that to you, too?"

"You know it has. How've you been, Marie?"

"Can't complain," she said. "I miss the country air, though. That stroll in the garden—"

They both grinned. Johnny ran his eyes over her, savoring the full curves, remembering that strange little moment of skirt-lifted passion. He wondered what she looked like naked. He wondered if he'd get a chance on this trip to find out.

She said, "What brings you down here?"

"Business."

"Where are you staying?"

He told her the name of the hotel. He wished now that he *had* stayed at the Waldorf, just to make a hit with her. But she didn't seem disturbed that he was staying at a commercial hotel.

She said, "How long are you going to be in town?"

"For the weekend, at least."

"That's nice." Her voice was soft, languorous. She hitched her legs up, letting him see their curved beauty almost to the thigh. " A weekend. That's a whole lot of time, isn't it?"

He smiled and studied her, and felt desire mounting and mounting within him. She just sat there, cloaked in the glow of her own beauty. He forced himself to keep away from her. They had no privacy here.

A voice behind him said, "Hello, Price."

Johnny turned. Rizzo stood there, a squat, thick-lipped, paunchy little figure in an elaborately decorated green velvet dressing-gown.

He said, "Did Lurton and Kloss send you down here, Price?"

Johnny shook his head. "I came on my own. I've got some things to talk about with you."

Rizzo frowned. "What kind of things?"

"Can we go somewhere that's completely private? What I've got is strictly confidential," Johnny said. "I've got some stuff to show you." He patted the pocket of his jacket meaningfully.

Rizzo shrugged. "Okay. Yeah. I suppose we can work it. Come into my den."

They crossed through the apartment and went into a room at the far end. The door of the room was unusual, Johnny noticed—thick, metal-shielded, almost like a bank vault, as though Rizzo had prepared this room as a hiding place in case anyone ever came after him.

The den housed a fantastic gun collection. There must have been five hundred weapons of all makes and ages, mounted in gleaming display cases around the wall. Some of the guns seemed to be hundreds of years old, real antiques of fabulous rarity.

Rizzo leaned against the shielded door, gave Johnny a quick flick of his cold little eyes, and said, "Okay. You brought something to show me. Let's see."

"Take a look," Johnny said.

He drew the little packet of papers from his pocket and pushed them across to Rizzo. The little hoodlum studied the packet a moment, fingering it without opening it. Then he looked inside.

The documents were records of the exact amounts that Lurton and Kloss had shaved off their payments to the Syndicate in the past three months. Rizzo read through them with an ever-deepening frown, his eyes veiled in thoughtfulness. Finally he looked up. His bulldog face was grim.

"What the hell is this, some kind of joke, Price?"

"Yeah. A big joke."

"I mean it. Are these records kosher?"

"I'd swear on my mother's grave."

"Skip the dramatics. I just want to know, is this the straight dope?"

"Believe me, it is."

Rizzo stared levelly at him for a long moment without saying anything. Johnny flinched inwardly, but held his expression rigid. He knew that there was no turning back, now. He had committed himself. He had stabbed Lurton and Kloss in the back but good, and now he had to ride it all the way through to the finish.

Rizzo broke the tense silence by saying, "This is serious stuff."

"I know. It's big. That's why I took a chance and came down here to bring it to your attention."

"Has it been going on since you joined them, or is it something new?"

"From the start," Johnny said. "And before me. They've been doing it all along. I saw the real books. They've been taking better than ten grand a year."

Rizzo drummed ominously with his fingertips on one of the glass gun-cabinets. Dead sober, as he was now, he seemed a lot more menacing than the drunken gin-swiller that Johnny had cuckolded in December.

"If it's true," Rizzo said, "Lurton and Kloss are finished. Finished. But heaven help you if you've faked any of this. You'll regret it to your dying day, and that won't be a very long time."

"I swear—"

"Never mind that," Rizzo said curtly. "We'll check into it all pretty fully. We'll find out, and your mother's grave doesn't need to be dragged in. We can't let jazz like this go on. First thing you know, every local stringer'll start taking off with whatever he thinks he can get away with, and we'll be up Crud Creek."

Johnny was silent.

Rizzo went on, "How come you brought this to me, though?"

"I thought you ought to know."

There was something ugly about Rizzo's smile. "That was very loyal of you. Loyal to me, that is. And loyal to the Syndicate. But not loyal to Lurton and Kloss. If all this is true, you've cooked them."

Johnny shrugged. "I'm loyal to the organization, not to those two punks. I know what's good for the organization, Mr. Rizzo."

"Mmm. Yes. Yes. You also seem to know what's good for you, Price."

"Maybe so."

Rizzo said, "Okay. We'll look into it. You'll be amply rewarded if the information you've given us is kosher stuff."

"Thank you, sir."

"You'll also get flayed alive if it turns out to be just a phonied-up attempt to hurt Lurton and Kloss, some kind of grudge deal."

"I'm not worried," Johnny said.

CHAPTER NINE

Rizzo carefully put the documents Johnny had brought into a cabinet, and sealed it. Then they left the den, strolling back into the main section of the apartment.

"What do you think of the place?" Rizzo asked.

"It's fabulous. It's a palace."

Rizzo grinned. "You know where I was living when I was your age? East Harlem, that's where. Not the nigger part, the dago part. You know New York?"

"Not very well."

"That's the slums. That's the bottom, over there. I lived there till I was twenty-five. How old are you, anyway, Price?"

"Twenty-two," he said, still sticking to the padded age he had given Lurton and Kloss last summer.

"Got your whole life ahead of you, then. You want a drink?"

"I'd like one."

"What?"

"Gin, I guess. On the rocks."

It was Rizzo's drink. That was why Johnny had picked it. Rizzo snapped his fingers at Marie, who was still sitting on the couch.

"Get some drinks, Marie."

"Sure, Pete," she said throatily.

Johnny watched her sweep across the room, but he was careful not to look at her in any way that would arouse Rizzo's suspicion. Marie was wearing nothing under her almost transparent wrap except a pair of equally transparent lounging pajamas. The two layers of fabric hid her nakedness, but not very well. Johnny could make out, without too much difficulty, the ripe hillocks of her breasts, the firm rounds of her buttocks. Enough to give him an idea, anyway.

Marie returned with the drinks. Rizzo said, "How long are you staying in town, Price?"

"Over the weekend."

"Got any girl fixed up for yourself?"

"Not yet, sir. I figured the Syndicate would help me out. I'm a stranger in town."

"Yeah. Yeah. Okay, we'll get you a girl. You want one for tonight?"

Johnny looked past Rizzo to Marie. Marie nodded, as though to tell him that if he didn't accept Syndicate hospitality tonight, he wasn't going to get anything.

"Yes," Johnny said. "I'd like one."

"You got anybody special in mind?"

"Well," Johnny said, "there's a girl named Ellie, Ellie Haines. I recruited her myself, last September. I'd sort of like to see how she's been coming along."

Rizzo snapped his fingers at the apish lieutenant. "Barney, call up Angelucci, find out about this Ellie Haines, if she's in town tonight, if she's free."

The ape picked up a phone. Johnny sipped his drink and stared admiringly at all the admirable things in Rizzo's apartment.

A few minutes later Barney reported, "Angelucci says she's in town, that she's working a trick at the Americana right now. She'll be through at ten o'clock."

"Okay," Rizzo said. "Set it up so that she goes over to Mr. Price's hotel when she's through with that trick. She's going to spend the night with him."

It was quickly arranged. Rizzo grinned at Johnny and said, "Have yourself a ball, kid. I'll be in touch with you about these matters you called to my attention. You can count on that."

"I'm glad to be of service, Mr. Rizzo."

Rizzo disappeared from the room. Johnny started for the door.

Marie came up to him. "What's all this about?" she asked in a low whisper.

"Lurton and Kloss are screwing the Syndicate. I gave Rizzo some information."

"That could be unhealthy," Marie said.

"Yeah. For Lurton and Kloss. I'll make out." He moistened his lips. "You still look pretty good to me, Marie."

"I'll look better tomorrow. I'll be at your hotel room at two in the afternoon. Make sure you get Ellie Whatshername out of there before I come."

"You serious?"

"I'm always serious, Johnny. I said we'd get together when you got to New York. We'll have ourselves a time. Don't use yourself all up on this floozie tonight."

"Don't worry," Johnny said with a confident grin. "I don't use up easy."

He was back in his hotel room by half past nine. He took a shower, got into his dressing gown, and settled down to wait for Ellie.

He felt tense. He knew he was playing a dangerous game, walking a tightrope of intrigue. And he was new at this sort of stuff. He was trying to stir up trouble for a couple of experts. Lurton and Kloss might yet be capable of coming up with a surprise or two.

Could they wiggle out from the evidence Johnny had given Rizzo? He doubted it. It was air-tight, no possibility of denial.

Still, there was an element of uncertainty about the whole thing. He wasn't dealing in a court of law. He was intriguing among crooks, and he was one of them himself, and he knew how easy it was to get dumped unexpectedly.

I'll make out all right, he told himself.

Lurton and Moss were through. He'd be the top man, in their place. And he'd keep on climbing, year after year after year.

There was a knock at the door.

"Coming," Johnny called.

He opened it. Ellie stood there.

"Hello," she said, her voice a soft, sexy purr. "Nice seeing you again."

Johnny gaped. He hardly recognized her. The last time he had seen her, back in September, she had been a country girl in blue jeans and a flannel shirt, rustic and innocent-looking if not exactly innocent.

The transformation was fantastic. She was wearing a sleek, tight-cut dress under a handsome cloth coat. Her hair had been short-cropped, strawberry blonde, but not anymore. Now it was a gleaming platinum puffball, forming a kind of halo around her head. Her eyebrows had been plucked. Her makeup was impeccable.

She didn't have the same rough-and-ready appeal as before. Now there was sophistication, maybe a little too much sophistication. But the old gleaming shrewd eyes were peering at him out of the transformed face. Her six months as a call girl had changed the externals of her appearance, but not the girl herself.

"How do I look?" she said.

"Tremendous. You're completely different."

"I've been having a ball, Johnny. It's such a great life. And you gave me my start. I'll never forget you for that, Johnny. Not as long as I live."

He took her coat from her. The scoop-neck dress revealed curved, enticing breasts. He remembered those breasts from a cloudless day in September. He remembered an interesting trick she had done with those round young breasts of hers as she sprawled on top of his naked body.

"So you're doing okay, huh?" he said.

"Just terrific! You know how much I've got in the bank already? Three thousand bucks! And I've got all these marvelous clothes, and this hairdo, and the loveliest apartment I ever dreamed of, and—"

"I'm glad you're making it okay, Ellie." He grinned at her. "What do you have *under* those marvelous clothes of yours?"

"The same old stuff."

"I remember it was pretty good."

"It hasn't changed any, Johnny."

"Let's have a look."

"Sure," she said. "Sure."

He watched her undress. She had learned things about taking off her clothes, too, since he had last seen her. Then, she had stripped with the simple outdoorsy glee of a country girl. Now, every motion was fluid, everything artful and calculated. He didn't know which Ellie he preferred, the clean-cut farm girl or the sophisticated Manhattan tramp, but he had to admit that both of them were sexy as hell, each in her own way.

Her breasts were bare, now. They swayed delectably as she wriggled out of her panties and stockings. She had put on a little weight since she came to New York, he saw. Not much, maybe three or four pounds. And she had picked the best of all possible places to put it on.

She was nude, now.

Her body was a soft pink thing, supple and curved and inviting. She held her arms outstretched as she faced him in joyous nakedness.

"Well?" she said. "What's the verdict?"

"The verdict is that you look great, Ellie."

"I've come a long way from Marboro, huh?"

"You're terrific."

He came up to her and put his lips roughly to hers, and cupped one hand over the bountiful plenty of her bosom and slapped the other against the contours of her firm buttocks, and held her tight as his tongue slid into her hot little mouth.

Their kiss was a deep, passionate one.

Then she broke away from him.

"Let me go take a shower, okay?"

"Why?" he said. "Don't you feel clean?"

She looked at him steadily. "I just turned a trick before I came here. I don't want to get into your bed with another man's sweat on me, Johnny. I want to be nice and pink and fresh and clean for you. I owe you a lot, and I want to show my gratitude."

"Whatever you say. The shower's in there."

"Why don't you order some drinks from room service while I'm in there? Maybe get some bourbon, okay?"

"Good deal."

She waggled her behind at him and traipsed off into the bathroom. Johnny grinned at the retreating pinkness of her back and buttocks. She was okay, he thought. His own personal discovery, his own recruit into the ranks of fabulous Manhattan whoredom.

She was working out all right, he thought. He started to fit her into the big picture. A Syndicate man of the upper ranks needed a regular broad.

The one he wanted was Marie, but he couldn't have her until somebody knocked off Pete Rizzo.

But in the meanwhile there was Ellie.

Ellie would do just fine. She wasn't as desirable as Marie, of course—no one was—but in her own way Ellie had plenty on the ball. Besides, Marie was three or four years older than Ellie. Ellie still had some things to learn, but she had already demonstrated that she was quick to pick up tricks. Johnny didn't doubt that in a couple of years Ellie would be every bit the woman that Marie was right now.

He picked up the phone, ordered drinks from room service.

He went on planning. With Lurton and Kloss out of the way, he would requisition Ellie for his own use, and she would come to live with him in the big mansion. She might not like the loss of income, but he'd make it up to her. There'd be plenty of Syndicate money funneling into his pocket, and he'd funnel plenty of it on into hers, so she'd be making more as his full-time mistress than she could make down here in New York. And she'd see that he was a man on the way up, that pretty soon he and she would be coming back to New York in style, as top dogs.

He listened to the water running. Ellie was singing in there. He visualized her soaping her breasts, her belly, soaping herself up everywhere. Getting herself nice and clean for him.

Where the hell were those drinks?

She was turning the shower off, now. And finally there was a knock at the door.

"Who?"

"Room service."

Johnny opened the door. A pimply-faced teen-age bellhop came into the room, carrying a tray bearing the drinks. At that precise moment Ellie opened the bathroom door and stepped out, wearing nothing but her rosy pink skin.

The bellhop's eyes widened.

Ellie smiled pleasantly at him without attempting to cover any part of her lush nudity. The bellhop lurched and almost dropped the tray.

Johnny scowled, shot his hands out, caught it. "Easy, buster," he snapped. "Easy!"

"S-sorry, mister."

The boy gaped at Ellie's flamboyant pink-tipped breasts and flawless thighs for a moment. Then he turned and scooted out of the room at full speed, slamming the door hastily behind him.

Ellie chuckled. "Am I that horrifying to look at?"

"Maybe he's shy," Johnny suggested.

"Or queer."

"Naw. Whoever heard of a queer bellhop?" Johnny laughed. "But he sure cleared out in a hurry. He didn't even stay for a tip."

"He didn't need one," Ellie said. "He got an eyefull. On my rates, he had two bucks' worth already." She crossed the room, picked up one of the glasses, and winked at him. He winked back and took the other glass.

They clinked them.

"Here's to old times," he said.

"Here's to new times," Ellie countered.

They put their glasses to their lips. Johnny drank deep, never taking his eyes off the proud hills of Ellie's bare breasts. There was a twinkle in her eyes as she watched him watch her.

He finished his drink a moment before she put her glass down.

"Another one?" he asked.

"Later," she said.

She came to him. She was fresh and clean and sweet-smelling, her pink, well-scrubbed skin warm and soft to the touch. He caressed her breasts and stroked her velvet-soft buttocks and touched the warm, throbbing, palpitating core of her body, and she sucked her breath in a little hiss of pleasure.

Then she slid the dressing gown from him, and he too was without clothing.

It was her turn to look at him.

"Mmm, nice!" she said. She pressed her cheek against his hairy, matted chest, and dug her fingertips into his biceps, and let her body slide down his, until her face was buried in the warmth of him, and suddenly her lips opened and he felt her at work on him.

He reached down to grasp her breasts while her eager, educated mouth was busy. He filled his hands with the rounded splendor of her. And, finally, he lifted her to her feet, and clasped her tight against him.

They moved toward the bed.

She said, "Remember that day on the pine needles?"

"How could I forget?"

"I showed you a trick that day. Want me to show you a different one?"

"I'm game," he said.

She wriggled up against him. The firm cushions of her buttocks pressed against his thighs. She thrust one hand around behind, seized him, guided him.

Johnny frowned. *"There?"*

"Sure," she said. "I like it there just like the regular way."

"Can you feel anything there?"

"If I couldn't, I wouldn't do it. I feel different things there."

"But doesn't it hurt?"

"Only the first couple of times. Not any more. I've been a busy little girl."

"I bet you have," Johnny said.

"Come on! Now!"

He caught his breath and thrust forward, gripping the fleshy cheeks of her buttocks, drawing them apart. There was a sudden moment of resistance, and then there was resistance no longer, and he was gliding forward, forward, and a new world of sensation was opening for him.

He curved around her, fitting his body to hers. Reaching out, he clasped her breasts, trapping the firm fleshy globes in his hands. His body moved in short thrusting jabs, and she moved in answering thrusts, and he drove hilt-deep to her, and her body stiffened and then began slowly to climb the peaks of passion, and he went along with her.

"Am I hurting you?" he whispered.

"No! Deeper!"

"All right!"

"Do you like it this way, Johnny?"

"It's interesting."

"I like it both ways. I'm ambidextrous." She giggled. "Back in Marboro they hang you if they catch you doing stuff like this."

"We aren't in Marboro now."

"I know. Isn't it great!"

And then there was no more time for conversation, as the fires of ecstasy raged high in both of them, and he felt a pounding at his temples and a rush of air out of his lungs, and he clung tight to her and ground his body against hers and drove his way against the firm globes of her buttocks again and again and again, while her white-hot body answered him repeatedly, and then came the final moment, the ultimate crest of passion, and they went up, up, over the top, and Johnny gasped in surprise at the intensity of the emotions he was feeling, the sudden all-consuming furious blaze of fulfillment—

—and then it ended.

Not lingeringly, not slowly. It ended all at once, in a sudden blast of consummation, and all strength left him and he slumped over against her, his body oiled with their mingled sweats.

After a while, he withdrew from her. She turned around to face him. She stroked his cheek lovingly.

"Tired?"

"Mmmmm."

"It takes a lot out of you, that way."

"Mmmm."

"Poor Johnny. You look so tired."

He opened one eye. "Not as tired as you think, girlie."

She grinned. "Ready to go again?"

"Give me five minutes."

"How about another drink?"

"Great idea."

She got him one. He took three sips, then gulped the rest. Warmth and well-being flooded through him. He let the empty glass drop to the carpeted floor.

"Ready now?" she said.

"You bet." He reached for her. "The regular way, this time."

"Whatever your little heart desires."

"It desires you."

"Desire away, then."

His body covered hers. Her legs jackknifed out, locking in place around him. He felt the welcoming warmth of her. He closed his eyes and moved his body, and glided to that coziest of all caverns, that refuge from the cares of the world, and as he took her he heard her sigh in pleasure, and her fingers made little scrabbling strokes against his muscular flanks, and with slow motions he stroked her again and again, and they made the steady ascent toward bliss for the second time that night.

CHAPTER TEN

Johnny slept.

Soundly.

Alone.

He knew she was gone. Some time during the night, she had slithered out of the hotel room. He had been half awake when she left, and he had watched her out of one slitted eye, drinking in the sleek beauty of her. She was such a damned good-looking girl. So vital, so alive. From her rounded boobs down to her firm little bottom, she was a real fireball.

He had watched her slipping into her clothes, transforming herself into the sophisticated girl-about-town again, hiding her growing superb nudity beneath the stylish costume of her trade. And then she had come over to his bed, and kissed him lightly, and whispered, "I'm going."

"Why?"

"Busy day tomorrow. Got to go."

"What time is it?"

"Six in the morning."

Johnny yawned. "Look, I'll be in touch, Ellie. I've got big plans for you and me."

"You'll know where to find me."

She kissed him again. And then he was alone. She closed the door lightly behind herself.

Johnny smiled. It had been such a beautiful evening. He had lost count of the number of times they had made it, and the number of ways. It all was a pleasant blur, a long pinwheeling kaleidoscopic night of breasts and thighs and buttocks.

He dropped quietly back into sleep, still wearing the smile.

He slept on and on and on.

His dreams were very pleasant ones.

Morning came. A trickle of sunlight crept across the sill of his window and hit him in the face. Johnny blinked. He opened one eye, shut it again, opened them both. He reached out for his watch, found it, looked at it.

Ten in the morning.

That was a nice round time of day. A good time of day. He stretched and got out of bed, and opened his window shade all the way, letting in the sun and also letting in the dingy view of Times Square in the morning. He felt great. Considering how little sleep he had had the night before, and what heavy demands he had made on his metabolism, he was in fine shape. Tip-top. He grinned and glanced around the room, and saw the relics of last night, the empty glasses, the overflowing ash trays.

There was something green and gauzy-looking on one of the armchairs. Johnny snatched it up and let out a loud guffaw.

It was a pair of silk panties.

Ellie had left him a little souvenir.

He remembered, now, watching her get dressed He had seen her put her clothes on, and, now that he thought about it, he had noticed her neglecting to put her panties on. He could summon the image up clearly—the deepset navel, the firm buttocks, all naked, framed by the garter-belt and the garter straps and the stocking-tops around her thighs. He had noticed. But he hadn't said anything. In his half-asleep state, it had seemed perfectly logical for her to be putting her skirt on without first donning panties. But now that he thought it over, he realized that he had just been too sleepy to react.

He folded the panties up. They were soft, silky—like Ellie herself. He put them to his nostrils, breathed deeply.

Perfumed. The perfume of Ellie.

He put the panties in his suitcase. A little souvenir from Ellie, he thought pleasantly. Something to remember her by. Not that he stood much chance of forgetting her.

He was in a great mood, now. He bent down, touched his toes without bending his knees—five, ten, twenty, thirty times. Twenty deep knee bends. Twenty situps. Twenty-five pushups.

Into the shower. Good brisk rubdown under the cold spray.

It was a great life, he thought. Girls galore, money in his pocket, excitement all the time. And this was only the beginning.

He toweled off, got into fresh clothes. He was hungry, famished, cavernous. The wild night with Ellie had really burned up energy. And in another couple of hours, Marie would be here. He had practically forgotten about that, in the wake of the session with Ellie.

Marie. At one o'clock, was it? No, two. That's what she had said, "I'll be there at two." Which gave him only about three hours to build up his strength.

He grinned. He'd be ready for her.

Buttoning his shirt, he threw a jacket on, headed down to the hotel dining room. It was practically empty, at this hour. Just a couple of harried-looking travelling salesmen dawdling over their orange juice.

A waitress came up to him. She was a sweet-looking kid, plump and juicy, with a pair of saucy breasts jutting out of the front of her faded green uniform. Any other time, Johnny might have tried to get somewhere with her, just from force of habit. But not now. Not with Ellie to remember, and Marie to look forward to.

"Good morning, sir. Here's our breakfast menu, if—"

"I'd like some brunch," he said. "It's too late in the day for corn flakes."

"Of course, sir. If you'll wait a moment, I'll get you the brunch menu."

"Never mind," Johnny said. "Just get me a sirloin steak, double cut, rare. Lots of blood, too. With an order of hash brown potatoes, and coffee."

The girl looked at him almost in awe. "Yes, sir. Sirloin steak, hash browns. Yes, sir. Yes, sir."

She brought him the steak, so rare it was practically raw. Johnny didn't mind. He carved his way through it in nothing flat, and looked around for the waitress. He spotted her across the room. She had bent over to tie her shoelace, and her short uniform skirt was hiked up so far in back that he could practically see the tops of her stockings. Her buttocks were plump and round against the taut seat of her skirt.

He contemplated the view for a moment. When she straightened up, he said, "Waitress?"

"Sir?"

He tapped his plate. "Got any more steaks in the kitchen?"

When he finally left the dining room, he felt fortified, ready to take on Marie and six more after her. He strode into the hotel lobby and found the bell captain.

"Can you have a bottle of champagne sent up to my room about quarter past two?" he asked.

"Certainly. What brand?"

Johnny hesitated. He didn't know much about champagne. He was still new to this kind of stuff.

He shrugged and said, "Oh, I don't know. Whatever you've got. One of the good French brands."

"Piper Heidsieck?"

"Fine," Johnny bluffed. "That's one of my favorites. Bring it up at quarter past two."

"Glasses for two, I presume?"

"For two," Johnny said.

It was still early. He went for a walk around Times Square. On Saturday at noon, it had a little less frantic quality than it had had yesterday afternoon, but there were still more people milling around than in the entire population of Reesport, Rumseyville, and Marboro combined, with two or three of the other towns of the county tossed in for good measure. Times Square was an amazing sight, Johnny thought. It could really set you back on your ears, if you weren't used to that kind of overwhelming gaiety.

He drifted up as far north as 50th Street, and headed east, past the gleaming new skyscrapers, and back down Sixth Avenue to 42nd. Time was dragging away slowly. The time of Marie's arrival was still more than an hour in the future.

Would she come at all?

How was she going to slip away from Rizzo? Didn't he keep an eye on her? Could she just go out and do as she pleased?

She had said she would come. He clung to that. He hoped she'd follow through.

At half past one, he returned to his room, tidied it up, opened the windows to let in some fresh cold air. He paced around. The minutes crawled.

Quarter of.

Ten to two.

Five of.

She would be late, he figured, if she came at all. In this city, no one was ever exactly on time, especially women. It just wasn't stylish to come on time. Punctuality was a little bit square.

So he was all the more surprised, at two on the button, to hear a light rapping on his door.

"Coming," he said.

He scuffed to the door, threw it open. And there she was.

Marie.

She looked more beautiful than ever. She glowed. Although she was dressed simply, far more simply than Ellie had been the night before, her natural beauty and underlying erotic appeal radiated through. She emanated pure sex. The simplicity of her clothes only highlighted the appeal of what lay beneath them.

"So you made it," he said.

"Didn't you think I would?"

"I didn't know. I thought you might have trouble getting away."

"Pete doesn't keep me under lock and key." She handed him her stole. "I told him I was going shopping, that's all. And I left."

"Just like that."

"Sure. Just like that." She laughed. "Don't tell me you're worried! Afraid to be cutting in on Pete Rizzo? You think maybe he had me trailed?"

"Of course not," Johnny lied.

She grinned at him. "Maybe he did, though. Maybe he sent four hoods after me. Maybe they'll break in any minute, and gun us both down for daring to deceive him."

"Very funny," Johnny said. He walked around her, so that the light from the window illuminated her. "God, you look beautiful, Marie. You don't know how good it makes me feel, just having you here in the room with me."

"And how was your little girl friend last night? Ellie?"

Johnny shrugged. "Why talk about her?"

"I'm just curious. Did you have a good time with her, Johnny?"

"Sure," he said. "I won't lie about it. I had a damned good time with her. But I expect to have a better one with you."

She sprawled down onto his armchair and crossed her legs, crossing them high, displaying a breathtaking expanse of calf and thigh. Johnny stared at her. He was fascinated by every move she made. She was all woman, the most supremely sexual creature he had ever seen. She was Marilyn and Ellie and Beth and all his other women, rolled into one.

And he had never even seen her naked. He had had her, but only furtively, only quickly.

It would all be different today.

She kicked off her shoes. She yawned and stretched, her breasts thrusting out excitingly.

There was a knock on the door.

"You see?" she said. "Here come the gunsels now. They've caught up with us, Johnny. This is the finish." Her tone was a light, mocking one.

Johnny forced a grin. But he was a little troubled as he went to the door. It was a dangerous business, fooling around with Pete Rizzo's woman, and he knew just how risky it was. That didn't stop him from wanting her. But it kept him uneasy.

"Who is it?" he said.

"Room service."

Johnny relaxed. Only the champagne.

He opened the door and found himself confronting the same pimply bellhop who had bolted tipless the night before, flustered by Ellie's nudity. The kid's eyes were wide in anticipation already, and muscles were throbbing in his cheeks, as though this time he were determined to stand his ground.

But there were no naked girls in the room this time. Only a fully clothed and very lovely Marie.

"Your champagne, mister," the boy stammered. He wheeled in a cart, with an ice-bucket topping it. He threw a sidelong glance at Marie. Color flooded the kid's face.

Johnny peeled a five-dollar bill from his wallet and handed it to the boy.

"You want me to open the bottle, mister?"

"That's okay. I'll take care of it."

"Right, mister. Thanks a lot, mister." The boy backed toward the door. Just as he opened it, he blurted, "Jeez, mister, you sure know a lot of pretty women!"

Then he was gone.

Johnny laughed. Marie said, "What was all that about?"

"He brought some drinks up for Ellie and me last night," Johnny explained. "He got here just as Ellie stepped out of the shower. He was so embarrassed he ran away without even waiting for his tip. And now to-day he sees a different girl in my room."

"With her clothes still on," Marie said. "That can be fixed."

"Let's hope so. But first let's have our champagne," Johnny said. "It isn't genteel to drink champagne in the nude. Emily Post says so."

"You've been studying up."

"I have to," he said. "I'm just a hick from hicksville. I've got to learn the ropes."

"Seems to me you're learning pretty fast, big boy."

"I've got a long way to go," he said. He surveyed the champagne bottle perplexedly. "Maybe I should have had the kid open it after all. Don't these things explode if you don't open them right?"

"They only explode if you shake them," Marie said. "Would you like me to open it?"

"No. Just tell me how."

"Well, first untwist that wire. That's right. Take it off. Now, hold the cork, and turn the bottle. Keep it steady and don't point the cork at me. Or at you. They can blow off pretty fast sometimes."

"Hold the cork, turn the bottle—"

Pop!

The cork flipped out. A few sudsy bubbles followed it, but not many. Opening the bottle had been less of a chore than he thought.

"You see?" she said. "Nothing to it."

"It was my first time," he said. "I was a virgin when it came to opening champagne."

"Now you've lost your virginity, poor dear. Which was harder? Your first girl or your first champagne bottle?"

"At least I didn't have to worry about the girl exploding," Johnny said.

"No, but did you ever see a pregnant champagne bottle?"

He chuckled and poured the champagne, carefully, not spilling a drop. They touched glasses.

"Down the hatch," he said.

They smiled at each other as they sipped the champagne. They had two glasses apiece.

Marie said, "Emily Post says it's all right to be partly nude for the third glass of champagne."

"Is that a fact?"

"It's gospel."

"Okay," he said. "I'll take off my socks. I'll be partly nude."

"You can do better than that," she said.

"I can't help it. I'm shy."

He peeled off his socks, grinning slyly at her. Marie improved on his performance by removing her dress and her slip. Only the narrowest of bras held her breasts in place. Johnny felt a trembling in his loins. He had never seen her bare breasts. He had held them in his hands, that moonlit night in the garden, but he had never seen them completely uncovered.

"Pour," she said.

He poured. They each had a sip of champagne.

She said, "Let's play strip drinking. One sip of champagne, one article of clothing removed."

"Sounds like fun."

"Let's find out."

Sip.

He removed his shirt. She peeled one stocking off.

Sip.

Off came his undershirt. Off came her other stocking.

Sip.

He pulled his belt out of the loops. "That's cheating," she said. "A belt isn't a garment."

"Sure it is."

"Okay, wisenheimer." She grinned and took her wristwatch off.

Sip.

He slipped *his* watch off. Marie unclipped her left earring.

Sip.

He took his trousers off. Marie removed her other earring. Now he was down to nothing but his shorts, while she was still decked out in bra and panties and garter-belt.

"Hey," he said. "It isn't fair. You were wearing more than I was."

"Looks like you lose the game then," she said. "You have to remember to check the ground rules before you begin, buster."

He grinned wryly. "Score a point for you. Okay, let's keep going."

Sip.

"You first," he said.

Marie shrugged and wriggled out of her panties. He stared at the whiteness of her rounded belly, at the firm curves of thighs. He had seen all this before, that night in the garden.

"Your turn," she said.

He took his shorts off. He was completely nude, now. His desire rose like a flagpole. Marie saw, and grinned, and winked.

She picked up her glass.

Sip.

She removed her garter-belt.

Johnny held his breath and waited impatiently for the ultimate revelation.

She fumbled with the clasps. A moment later, they came away, and the cups dropped from her breasts, and for the first time he was looking at Marie's totally naked body.

CHAPTER ELEVEN

She was magnificent.

Her breasts were high and round and full and firm, set close together, tipped with little reddish-brown turrets of nipples. When she breathed, her breasts breathed with her, rising, falling, expanding, contracting. Below her breasts, her body swept away leanly, widening again in sudden eye-glazing splendor at the hips.

She stood up. She moved in a slow circle, showing herself to him, all of her. The jutting profile of her breasts, the sweep of her bare buttocks and legs.

He felt a lump in his throat. He was awed. He had seen a great many naked girls in his short life, and especially in the past six months. But they all dimmed in comparison with this one. Even Ellie, with whom he had spent such a jolly night, Ellie who was so satisfying in every respect, Ellie for whom he had such big plans—Ellie had to take second rank to this girl.

Given a few years, Ellie might mature into a Marie. But this was the present, this was right now, and Marie was here, in front of him, nude.

He was shaken.

"What's the matter?" Marie asked. "Scared?"

"Just stunned," he said. "You know how it is when you see the Taj Mahal? That's you. The Taj Mahal of sex."

"Sure. The Taj Mahal is made of marble, isn't it? Nice cold marble. I'm frigid, huh? I'm like stone?"

"You know what I mean."

"Suppose you get your foot out of your mouth, then, and come over here and kiss me."

He went to her. She opened her arms to him, and he gathered her in. The points of her breasts seared him like fire. Her body pressed tight against his, and he felt the throbbing nudity of her, and he put his hands on her shoulder blades and slipped them down, down, down over the mar-velously smooth flesh, down past her dimples to the miraculous swell of her buttocks, and then inward, toward the source of all warmth, toward the fountainhead of pleasure.

He held her tight.

She lifted her head, and he accepted her lips and her tongue, and her kiss was a burning thing.

He gripped her passionately. Suddenly, she was all the women he had ever desired. It was an agony, a pleasurable torment. He felt that if he had to wait another moment before he possessed her, he would explode.

He forced himself to wait.

He explored her body, first with his hands, then with his lips, his tongue. She stood there, statue-still in the middle of the room, while he roamed the geography of her, up hill and down dale, into caverns and crevices. Her skin was cool, except where it was blazing hot. And it was soft, soft as the finest silk, everywhere.

Then it was her turn to make a voyage of exploration, and she wandered over him, touching him lightly here and there, there and here, breathing, flicking the tip of her tongue out for a dazzling tenth of a second at a time, nibbling, kissing, caressing.

Johnny trembled. He shook.

He knew that this was Pete Rizzo's girl, that he could be executed by the Syndicate for what he was daring to do now. And he didn't give a damn, just then. Let them shoot him. Only let him have her first! Let them hold their fire another hour, and then they could do their worst!

After he had had Marie, what else would matter?

He led her toward the bed.

They tumbled down together. Her body surged toward his. Her tongue entered his mouth. Her hands grasped him, probed him. She was so soft, so silky, so good to touch, to feel—

Her legs moved aside.

The warm, throbbing of her beckoned him. Johnny looked down, his own body pulsing eagerly. He moved toward her.

Probed.

Thrust.

Reached.

As he took her, she let out a hissing sob of pleasure. He remembered, from the brief few minutes in the garden, how easy she was to get to, how rapidly she could be brought to a climax. They had had a mere ten minutes together that first time.

It had been enough, and yet not enough. A man can slake his thirst with a sip, but why stop there when he can have a full glass?

He eased himself down, and thrust upward, and felt her body accommodating his, making room for him, welcoming him as though he had been designed by nature to take his place there. She brought her legs up, knees practically touching the tips of her superb breasts, and Johnny bore down, and her body quaked and shook with the excitement that was bubbling and churning within her, and he felt her starting to respond, and then the first eddying upsurge of ecstasy burst from her.

The first of many.

She was the most passionate woman Johnny had ever known. It wasn't so much a matter of appetite as it was capacity to respond. Johnny took her up to paradise, and kept her there for a long moment, his body hammering against hers with relentless fury. Then, since he had delayed his own satisfaction, he let her rest a moment, and then started anew, and she was right with him the second time.

And the third.

And the fourth.

Again and again came the spasms, the contractions, the inner convulsions of the muscles. She was a marvel. She was so torrid Johnny felt himself getting scorched.

He moved with redoubled energy. He felt her hands wandering again, finding, squeezing

He gasped.

He buried his face in the hollow alongside her cheek, and his body rocked convulsively, and then the hammer blows of fulfillment hit him.

He lay still when it was over. He was drenched with sweat, and a dreamy kind of peace had stolen over him, a feeling of being at one with the universe, of having attained nirvana, of having burned away every doubt, every uncertainty in a triumphant affirmation of the power of the flesh.

Marie broke the long silence. "Emily Post says it's extremely appropriate to drink champagne after sexual relations," she said.

Johnny opened one eye. "That so?"

"I read it once."

"I don't believe it."

"Cross my heart and hope to die."

"Come here," he said. "I'll cross your heart, and then you can get me some champagne."

He grinned and stuck his index finger out, and drew a criss-cross X over her breasts, starting from a point just above her right breast, and going on a diagonal over the pale hillock of the breast, stopping for a moment to touch the nipple, continuing on down until he reached the ribs below her left breast. He did the same thing the other way, from above her left breast to below the right. He lingered for a long moment at the nipple.

Then she rose, moving with that wonderful fluid grace of hers, and got the champagne bottle. Johnny lay quietly, watching her, savoring the miraculous way she was put together, the stunning explosion of flesh at her waist, the heavy swells of her perfect buttocks.

She came back to the bed, carefully carrying two glasses of champagne filled right to the brim.

"I killed the bottle," she said. "The ice in the bucket was starting to melt anyway."

"We can order another one later," he said. "How long can you stay here?"

"Till five-thirty."

"It's only quarter to three now. We've still got plenty of time."

"Not nearly enough."

"No," he agreed. "Not nearly enough."

They sipped champagne and watched each other in silence for a few minutes. After a while Johnny said, "How long have you been living with Rizzo?"

"A little over two years."

"And before that?"

"I was the girl of a guy named Flaherty."

"In the Syndicate?"

"Yeah. Rizzo's boss."

"What happened to him?" Johnny asked.

"You ask a lot of questions," Marie said. "What do you mean, what happened?"

"You went from Flaherty to Rizzo. I'm sure this guy Flaherty didn't get bored with you. So why'd you change men?"

"Because Flaherty died."

"Of cancer," Johnny said.

"Yeah. Cancer of the brains. Somebody put a couple of bullets through his head and he got infected, and caught cancer."

"That so?" Johnny finished his champagne, put the glass down. "So a Syndicate man got killed, huh? I suppose they took care of the guy who knocked him off."

"They took care of him, all right," Marie said.

He put his hands on her breasts, then ran one of them down her smooth flanks. "And before Flaherty? Who were you with then?"

"Jesus, you're inquisitive!"

"I suppose I am."

She looked at him, straight on. "Before I was with Flaherty, I was a call-girl for the Syndicate, just like your little girl friend Ellie. I got promoted four years ago when Flaherty liked me. And then Rizzo."

"You must have started young," Johnny said.

"Sixteen."

He figured that made her about twenty-five now.

He said, "And after Rizzo?"

"I'm still Rizzo's girl."

"So why are you here?"

"I'm entitled to step out on him once in a while."

"Once every three years?"

"Once every once in a while." She laughed. "When are you coming to New York again?"

"Soon as I can."

"I heard Rizzo talking last night. He's going to send some boys up to your place to check the books. He's probably going to rub out your bosses."

"That'll be pretty rough on them," Johnny said. "It means he's going to need a new top man up there after he does that."

"Looks that way."

"I wonder who it'll be?"

Marie shrugged. "It could be anybody, lover. Almost anybody."

"Put in a good word for me, will you?"

"Don't worry. Rizzo's impressed by you. He thinks you've got plenty on the ball. And you know something, lover? I think so, too."

"Then why are we sitting here talking?"

"That's what I was wondering too," she said.

She rolled over on top of him. She put her lips to his, and there was the taste of champagne on her. He kissed her lingeringly, cupping her breasts, squeezing them, toying with the rigid, pucker-tipped nipples.

Then she threw one leg over him. She straddled him and sat astride. He saw what she was doing, and he grinned at her, and her hand reached down and guided him.

She rose. And lowered herself.

And began to rock, around and around and around, clockwise and then counterclockwise and then clockwise again, each change of direction sending fresh shivers of pleasure through him.

He looked up at her. Her eyes were sparkling, alert, gay. Her big breasts shivered and jiggled as she moved. Her nipples stood up, stiff and long.

He put his hands on her breasts.

Squeezed.

Harder.

Marie shivered. She lifted herself, lowered the soft cushions of her buttocks to his thighs again, lifted, lowered, lifted, lowered. She bent way back, so that her dangling hair touched his toes, so that all he could see of her face was the point of her chin. The high mounds of her breasts curved upward as her back bent, the rigid nipples stabbing at the ceiling.

He drove his body repeatedly upward to hers. She welcomed him. She was warm and soft and yielding. She quivered, and rocked, and shook.

Waves of ecstasy swept through him as she went from climax to climax above him. Her sweat-slippery body writhed and churned. Her eyes were little slits of lust. Her breath came in gusty bursts.

"Yes!" she yelled, "yes, Johnny, yes, yes!"

He felt the invisible muscles grasping him, the little million unseen hands doing their work. His brain was fogged with delight. Dimly, he was aware of the culmination of his own desires, the surging fulfillment of hers, and then once again they were descending from the heights. She lowered her body, settled down over his without breaking the link that joined them.

"You're okay," she whispered. "You're really something, you know that?"

"It's just that a girl like you brings out the best in me."

"Brings out the beast in you, you mean."

He laughed. "You wait," he said. "You haven't seen nothin' yet."

They rested. He wanted to sleep, but he knew it was idiocy to waste even a moment of his time with Marie. There was plenty of time for sleeping later on.

His eyes drank in the slim nudity of her. He turned to her, put his lips to her breasts, kissed the tender nipples. Went lower, tasted the essence of her, touched the warmth of her.

They pressed tight together.

Marie said, "Maybe something will happen to Rizzo a few months from now."

"Like what?"

"I don't know. Something bad."

"Like cancer of the brain?"

"Maybe. Something like that. He's got his enemies, you know."

Johnny played with her breasts. "What if something did happen to Rizzo?"

"I'd have to find some other way of supporting myself. I wouldn't want to go back to working for a living."

"There must be other Syndicate bigshots who'd want you," Johnny said.

"Oh, there are, there are. That's one of the reasons something might happen to Rizzo. A couple of the higher-ups want me, you see. But they can't just ask for me. That wouldn't be right. So they might take care of Pete to get me free. A kind of Syndicate divorce."

Johnny looked tense. "So you'll shift from one biggie to another, but where does that leave me?"

"Smack in the catbird seat."

"How do you figure that?"

"What makes you think I want to put out for Rizzo's bosses?"

"Because they're on top."

Marie grinned. "Anybody higher than Rizzo in the Syndicate, he's got to be at least fifty years old. And fat as a pig, because they swill down the food all the time. Like that Lurton of yours. The guys who want me, they're as sloppy as Lurton. I've seen them. They belch in your face and squeeze your boobs like they're doing exercise. They aren't for me. I'm not interested."

"But they're rich."

"So what? I'm rich myself. I kept the dough Rizzo gave me. I didn't have any expenses. Listen, money isn't the whole works." Marie chuckled. "Uh-

uh. If anything happens to Rizzo, my next guy is going to be someone young. Young and ambitious. A guy who can cut the mustard."

"Anybody in particular?"

"Yeah," Marie said. She slid her hand down his body and grabbed a solid handful of him. "Him," she said.

"He's attached to somebody."

"I'll take the somebody too."

"You're snowing me," he said. "Why would you want a guy like me? I'm a nobody."

"Right now you're a nobody. A few weeks from now you'll be a small-time somebody. And then a big-time somebody soon enough. You're on your way up, Johnny. I don't need to tell you that. And I want to ride right along with you. I liked you from the start. I'm with you, man. All the way."

"I feel like I'm ten feet tall when I hear you say that," Johnny said.

"You know something?" she said. "You *are* ten feet tall. Compared to the guys I've seen."

Their bodies came close. He felt himself swelling with pride, with joy in his own masculinity. The future seemed unbounded, the horizon infinite.

For the third time, he took her.

He took her like a conquering hero. He marched to her, and he could practically hear the bugles and trumpets sounding, and they headed straight for the finish in one supreme curve of passion.

And then it was all over, for the time being. The afternoon was ended. She had to go. She had to run back across town to Rizzo's East End Avenue penthouse, and go back to being the mistress of a middling-big gangland boss.

"I hate to think of you going to him," Johnny said, as she slipped her bra over the majestic curves of her bare breasts. "Sharing his bed. Sleeping with him."

"Try not to think about it."

"I can't help it. He's such a piggish little louse, Marie. And to think of the two of you together, him on top of you, touching you—"

"If it bothers you," she said, "how do you think I feel? Listen, Johnny, these are the facts of life. So long as Pete Rizzo's alive, I'm his broad, and that's how it has to be. If I left him for you, how long do you think you'd stay alive?"

"I'm not afraid of Rizzo."

"Only a chump would say that. You *better* be afraid of Rizzo. Because any time he feels like it, he could have you dumped in the Hudson River head first. He's got power, Johnny. And I can't leave him. When the time comes, he'll go out of the way."

"When does that time come?"

"Not yet. Not yet."

She was nearly dressed now. Her lovely legs were encased in nylon; her panties hid the splendors of her buttocks. He watched.

Then she was fully dressed. He went with her to the door. She looked into his eyes, and he saw the warmth there, the depth of feeling.

"So long, Johnny. It was a great afternoon. I had a ball."

"You weren't the only one," he said. He moistened his lips. "I'll try to get down to New York again soon. Three, four weeks. And we'll get together again."

"Sure we will."

He kissed her, lightly, on the cheek. She didn't want her makeup smeared. He took her hand, gripped it for a moment.

Then she slipped out of the room, and she was gone, and he was alone.

CHAPTER TWELVE

Johnny Price was in a kind of daze. So many good things had been happening to him so fast that he hardly knew which end was up any more.

The two latest good things were Ellie and Marie. Marie and Ellie. Ellie and Marie.

He sank down limply in his armchair, closed his eyes, and thought back over the events of the past eighteen hours. First Ellie had been there, then Marie. He wondered if the walls of his ugly room had ever seen a display of sex to match what had been going on in here since last night.

He had always known he was good. But, even so, he was a little shaken up himself by this demonstration of his own powers as a stud. To take on two girls of the order of Ellie and Marie, one after another, and to take them both a total of perhaps nine or ten times during one solid span broken only by a short break for sleep and meals, and to have been still full of pep after the last round with Marie—that impressed even him.

Ellie and Marie. Marie and Ellie. He closed his eyes tight and thought back, remembering what he had done with them, all the different positions, the angles and extras and specialties.

Terrific!

And they were just part of the big picture, the picture of Johnny Price's future. Soon, he was sure, Lurton and Kloss would be pushing up daisies, and he would rise to the rank of local supervisor for the Syndicate's activities. That would rate him Ellie as a full-time mistress.

And Marie?

Well, she belonged to Rizzo, and she had made it clear that she would go on belonging to Rizzo until something happened to Rizzo. Johnny wondered. Suppose, he thought, about a year from now Rizzo had an unfortunate accident, and Marie became available. He'd drop Ellie, move over to Marie. And a few years later, when he had risen still higher in the Syndicate, he might pull a reverse switch.

After all, by then Marie would be getting close to thirty, or maybe even past it. And Ellie would just be coming into her prime. So he would pass Marie along to some worthy cause, and take Ellie back.

It was all neat and shiny.

It was a lot to look forward to.

He felt pleased with the way everything was going. Here he was, a little bit shy of his twentieth birthday, and he had money in the bank, more women than he knew what to do with, and the prospect of a great future.

It was a good life, Johnny thought. A damned good life. And the funny thing was, anybody with a little brains, a little guts, could be living it. Why weren't they? Why was he one of the lucky few?

He shrugged. Let the unlucky many worry about that, he thought.

He was hungry again. His bout with Marie had burned up the energy of those two brunch steaks, and the champagne hadn't been enough to keep him going. He took a quick shower, dressed, and left his room.

Saturday night in New York. And he didn't even have a date. He grinned. Right now he was perfectly content to be stag. He had had quite enough female companionship in the last few hours to last him for a while.

He made his plans. A good dinner under his belt, then maybe a show, and a good night's sleep. Then back to work in the morning, a quick drive upstate to wait for the moment of reckoning to come for Lurton and Kloss.

A ticket-broker in the lobby of the hotel got him a seat to the biggest hit in town. It wasn't hard to get a single seat. The theater was only a couple of blocks from Times Square. Johnny ate in the best restaurant he could find, treated himself to a thick steak and three bottles of imported beer, and went over to the theater.

The show was pretty good. But his big meal—and all that sex with Ellie and Marie in the past day—had left him pretty drowsy. He had to fight to stay awake all through the last act.

On his way back from the theater to the hotel, one of the Times Square girlies accosted him. It happened quickly. He was on Seventh Avenue near 43rd Street when a girl suddenly stepped out of a cafeteria doorway and said, "Got a light for me, friend?"

"Sure," Johnny said.

He took out his lighter and flipped it. The girl moved up close. She was around twenty, Johnny figured. A thin kid with wide black eyes and a big nose and thin lips. Her breasts stuck out nicely against her tight sweater, but Johnny wasn't taken in. He knew women, by now. He knew that breasts were mostly fat, that any girl with such thin lips and such hollow cheeks wasn't likely to have a pair of boobs like that. What was being stuck in his face right now was mostly padding, he realized.

The girl puffed on her cigarette. Then she deftly slipped one hand down and ran it over him. The fingers gave him a skilled tweak.

"Want a good time, mister?"

"Sorry."

"You've never had it as good as with me."

"No," Johnny said. "Afraid you don't appeal. I only go for little boys with pink bottoms."

He left her gaping there, and walked away, grinning to himself and thinking about Ellie and Marie, and how pink *their* bottoms were, and what a memorable weekend this had been in every respect.

He got back to his room by eleven, and sacked out immediately. Alone. It was almost a novelty to be sleeping alone. He stretched out in the bed, arms dangling over the sides, and drifted easily into sleep.

When he woke, it was ten o'clock Sunday morning, and he went to the window to see a light cloud of snow dusting down over the gray city. It was a pretty sight—big fluffy flakes dropping out of an oddly blue sky— but Johnny didn't wait around to admire the beauty of it all. He had a long drive ahead of him, and the more time he wasted before setting out, the slicker and more dangerous the roads were going to be that afternoon.

He had a quick breakfast, checked out, picked up his car. By quarter past eleven, he was going up the highway ramp at 42nd Street and heading out of the city. The snow was still coming down in big lazy spirals, but it wasn't sticking to the road.

As he continued north, the snow grew heavier, and up there it was sticking. But it hadn't been sticking long enough to cause him any real trouble. If he had left New York two hours later, it would have taken him half the day to get home. As it was, he made a pretty steady forty miles an hour, even through the snow, and he was back at the house by the middle of the afternoon.

It had been a good trip, he thought. It had set him back almost two hundred smackeroos, but that didn't bother him. He could call it an investment. He knew he had set himself up good in Rizzo's eyes. Before long, he realized, money would mean as little to Johnny Price as it did to Pete Rizzo. He was on his way.

Besides, for his two hundred bucks he had had both Ellie and Marie the same weekend. There were men who'd give two hundred bucks gladly to have either of those wenches for an hour or two, and he had had them both for hour upon hour. Yes, a worthwhile investment, Johnny thought.

He garaged the car and entered the house. A plump, scantily-dressed girl Johnny hadn't seen before let him in. He looked at her and saw round, heavy, dark-nippled breasts peeking through her gauzy chemise.

"Who are you?" he asked.

"Alice. I'm new." She giggled. "I'm going to Syracuse tomorrow."

"Where's Mr. Lurton?"

"In his office."

"And Kloss?"

"Asleep."

Johnny nodded. The girl walked away, shimmying her ample buttocks. Johnny watched her. The world was full of whores, he thought. In the few months he had lived here, he had seen hundreds of girls pass through, literally hundreds, all of them eager to sell their bodies and get rich. He wondered if he would have gone in for being a whore, if he had been born a girl.

Probably I would, he decided. *But not for long. I'd have been a madam by the time I was thirty. I was born to run the show, not to be a grubby employee.*

He knocked on the door of Lurton's office.

"Who's there?"

"Me, Johnny. I'm back."

"Come on in."

The fat man was sitting at his desk, going over his phonied-up account books. He swivelled round to face Johnny. Johnny stared at him, saw the rings of fat on his wrists, the heavy jowls, the layer of blubber at his throat. There was a ring on Lurton's finger, a star sapphire in a gold setting. The band was almost covered up with flesh. Probably Lurton had put the ring on twenty years and eighty pounds ago, and couldn't get it off now. Johnny wondered what would happen to the ring after Lurton was dead. It was an expensive-looking ring. They'd probably have to hack the finger off, he figured.

Well, Lurton wouldn't mind. Not by that time, anyway.

Lurton said, "Well, how was your weekend in the big city?"

"No complaints."

"Did that girl come across for you?"

"What do you think, Mike?"

"It's written all over your face, kid. Got yourself a virgin, huh?"

Johnny shrugged. "I didn't ask her. If she was before, she isn't now."

Lurton giggled. His gross body shivered and jiggled with amusement.

Johnny thought, *Go ahead and laugh, Lurton. Laugh as hard as you know how, friend. Because pretty soon you won't be laughing any more. You're going to be dead pretty soon, Lurton. You and Kloss. You can't get away with swindling the organization forever.*

He said out loud, "Did I miss anything up here while I was away?"

"Nah. Not a goddamn thing. You see the new girl we got in?"

"Alice?"

"Yeah. She showed up yesterday."

"Nothing special," Johnny said. "Kind of fat and dumb-looking, I figure."

Lurton's eyes glowed with satisfaction, "Ah, it isn't what she looks like that's so interesting, kid. It's who she is."

"Who is she, then? A newspaper reporter trying to find out first hand what it's like to be in the life?"

Lurton snorted. "Guess again."

"An observer from the United Nations?"

"Nope."

"I give up, Mike."

Beaming, Lurton said, "She's the daughter of State Senator Sobieski."

"Sure," Johnny said. "And I'm the lost grandson of the Czar."

"No. I mean it. She's Sobieski's daughter!"

"Seriously?"

"I'm not kidding."

Johnny stared at the fat man in amazement. State Senator Edward Sobieski was the leading anti-vice crusader of the east coast. Everything that smacked of pleasure was considered vice, in Sobieski's eyes, and naturally everything that could be deemed vice was fit for denunciation.

So Sobieski denounced. He denounced sexy foreign films, and he denounced magazines that ran photos of the breasts and buttocks of desirable women, and he denounced novels in which the characters occasionally made love with one another. He denounced burlesque shows and he denounced night club routines. He denounced homosexuals, and he denounced suggestive clothing, and he denounced off-color jokes.

"We have to maintain our moral line," he would thunder. "If we give in to the tide of smut and filthy trash, we will be inundated by Communism!"

Naturally, Sobieski didn't confine his denunciations to such tame things as girlie magazines and night club routines. He went after bigger targets, too—organized prostitution among them. He was one of the Syndicate's most dedicated enemies.

And his own daughter was here? A prostitute herself, for God's sake?

Johnny said, "Listen, Mike, maybe this is some kind of gag someone's pulling on you."

"No. She was checked out downstate. She really is Sobieski's daughter."

"If that's true, she must be spying."

"Spying? And getting laid nine ways from Sunday? Look, Johnny, there are other ways of getting information about us besides turning your daughter into a prostitute. Do you seriously think Sobieski would go that far?"

"I guess not. But why—"

"Because she's fed up with her old man, that's why. I had a long talk with her. It seems she's been kept under lock and key since she was old enough to know. So she had this love affair with some guy, and got herself pregnant. She told her father about it. Would he give his blessing to the marriage? Like hell he would! He pulled strings and he got the guy drafted, and he made his daughter have an abortion. So she ran away from home. If you were in that setup, what's the best way you could hurt your father? Right. So she became a whore."

"I'll be damned," Johnny said. "But what happens when Sobieski finds out where she is?"

Lurton giggled. "You know how he's going to find out? By reading her memoirs in the paper."

"*What?*"

"Isn't it a scream? She wants to ruin him politically. She thinks he's a stuffed shirt, and she figures it's time to slap him down. He's got big polit-ical plans. He figures to break up the Syndicate, and run for U.S. Senator, or maybe Governor of New York. And then after that the White House, on an anti-sex platform. She's going to stop him. She's going to publish her memoirs. I WAS A TEEN-AGE WHORE, by State Senator Sobieski daughter. She's already sold the rights to the *Daily News*. And there'll be a paper-back version—oh, she's a sharp one!"

"She looks like a nothing."

"She's got plenty on the ball," Lurton said. "Send for her and you'll find out."

That evening, Johnny asked Alice Sobieski to come to his room. She showed up, still wearing her filmy chemise. Her face was painted whor-ishly. She looked like comic-opera version of a prostitute, a plump teen-age girl with rosy cheeks and wide eyes.

Johnny said, "Lurton gave me a big story about you. He says you're Sen-ator Sobieski's daughter."

"That's right. I am."

"This is crazy," Johnny said. "Suppose you go and sell us out to your father?"

"Believe me, I won't do a thing like that."

"Who hired you?"

"Pete Rizzo," she said.

"And he knew who you were?"

"We talked the whole thing out. He wants to get my father laughed out of office. And I want to show my father I'm an independent human being. So I'm going to love my way all over the state, and then tell my story. The Syndicate won't get hurt. But my father will."

Johnny shrugged. It seemed to him that Rizzo way playing with fire, that in his haste to topple Senator Sobieski, he might upset his own apple-cart as well. It was risky to court public exposure for the sake of getting rid of one admittedly dangerous politician.

He said, "How long have you been in the life now?"

"Two weeks."

"Enjoy it?"

"Sometimes."

"You never dreamed you'd grow up to be a tramp, did you?" Johnny laughed. "Well, let's see how good you are. Let's see if you can fool me into thinking you're a professional. Take off your slip."

She didn't look shocked, or hesitant, or uneasy. She didn't give him any virginal looks. She didn't try to say, "Do I really have to?"

She dropped her slip, quickly.

She stood naked before him.

Smiling, Johnny looked her over. She wasn't bad. There was a plumpness about her that was more baby-fat than anything else, bands of flesh about belly and thighs, a heaviness about her breasts. But Johnny saw that if she lost ten pounds she'd be quite a dish. Her breasts were high and round, and though there was a little bit too much there for her general build, that could be fixed fast enough.

He said, "How old are you?"

"Nineteen."

She was less than a year his junior. But, somehow, she seemed like a little girl to him. He had grown up fast in the past few months. There's nothing like taking part in murder and extortion to help you grow up.

He stripped off his clothes. She eyed his nakedness calmly. He took her hand, led her to the bed.

She smiled and said, "Maybe you won't believe this, but a year ago I was a virgin."

"You've had a busy year, then."

"I sure have."

He pulled her down, cupped her breasts. Suddenly she was up against him, palpitating with passion, her body hot and trembling. She put on a good act, he knew. Here he was, just some kid hoodlum that she hadn't even met yesterday, and she was acting like he was the great love of her life. That was the mark of a successful tramp.

He cupped her soft big breasts. He felt the nipples stiffen. He dug his fingers into the yielding flesh of her ample buttocks.

She panted and tossed and groaned. She clawed at his rigid body in need.

The kid's a kook, he thought. *She's a real nympho. It serves the Senator right.*

Johnny grinned. He put one hand on each of her pale, soft thighs. She arched her back, making his way easier for him.

He plunged.

The moment he took her, she gasped as though speared, and began to writhe and heave herself around. Johnny rode right along with her, right to the finish. She made it there ahead of him, and they lay there, panting, for a long while.

Then she rose from the bed. She walked to the window and stared out at the falling snow. Johnny looked at the white double mound of her buttocks.

She said, "I enjoyed that."

"I'm glad."

"I'll remember you, Johnny. You're something special. I'm a little afraid of you, but I like you. You're hard and cold. You're all death, Johnny. And yet there's warmth about you, too."

"Put me in your memoirs," he said. "Just don't mention my name, that's all."

She laughed. Her breasts and bare buttocks jiggled gaily. Then she put her slip back on, and blew him a kiss, and went out of the room.

CHAPTER THIRTEEN

Senoator Sobieski's merry, memoir-writing daughter went off to Syracuse the next morning, and Johnny never saw her again. It had been an amusing interlude for him, nothing more. He was pleased that her witch-hunting father, with his puritanical, fanatic zeal, was going to get his come-uppance. It was funny to think that every time Senator Sobieski delivered a flaming speech about the moral standards of our time, his only daughter Alice was in an upstate crib ready for a succession of eager johns glad to take their turns on top of her.

There were risks to the Syndicate, though. If, when she published her memoirs, the police worked her over, they could shake all kinds of information out of her—enough to send half the Syndicate up the river. And her father, angry about her shameless conduct and the ruin of his own political career, might just let the cops give her the third degree.

Hell, Johnny thought. Rizzo knew what he was doing. He would never have agreed to let Alice Sobieski work the circuit if he thought she'd turn stoolie.

A few days passed. Johnny forgot about the senator's nymphomaniac daughter.

His mind was absorbed with other problems. Such as when Pete Rizzo would start to take action against Lurton and Kloss. The wheels had been set in motion during Johnny's visit to New York. Presumably Rizzo had his men checking things out right now.

But how long would it take?

Why were they waiting?

A week had gone by, now. That seemed like an awfully long time. The longer Rizzo waited, the more chance there was that someone might whisper a word to Lurton and Kloss, who would lose no time eradicating Johnny themselves if they had reason to think he had sold them out.

An eighth day went by.

A ninth.

Johnny began to sweat and fidget.

Everything was taking much too long. Where was the action? What was Rizzo up to?

There was action on the tenth day after Johnny's return from New York. But it wasn't quite what Johnny was expecting, though when he thought it over he saw that it was logical enough, though pretty nasty.

What happened was the dead body of Alice Sobieski turned up in a motel just outside of Troy, New York.

She was found nude, in the bathroom of her motel room. She had slashed her wrists, and was lying face down in her own blood. Next to her lay a note that explained how she was ashamed of the things she had been doing, how she could no longer bear to go on living. And elsewhere in her room was a bulky document—her "memoirs," the story in her own hand-writing of how she had quarreled with her father over a love affair, how he had forced her to have an abortion, and how in revenge she had gone into a life of prostitution.

It just so happened that a news reporter was able to photograph most of the memoirs before the police confiscated them. And so the text, in an expurgated form, was in print in half the tabloids of the state before Alice Sobieski was in the ground.

"How do you like that," Johnny said. "The kookie kid killed herself!"

Lurton grinned oddly. Kloss said, "It just goes to show. You got to be careful when you play around with razor blades. You can get cut."

Johnny said, "I feel sorry for the kid."

"You made her, didn't you?" Lurton asked.

"What of it? So did you. So did Kloss. So did a hundred other guys. And now she's dead. She killed herself because she was ashamed to look herself in the eye any more after a while."

Lurton guffawed. "I thought you were dry behind the ears by now, kid."

"Huh?"

"Weren't you so worried that this whole deal might backfire and hurt the Syndicate?"

"Yeah, but—"

"Well, now it won't backfire. The girl can't name names. She can't be interrogated. But her memoirs were released, and her father's a dead duck politically."

Johnny's eyes widened. "It wasn't suicide, is that what you're telling me?"

"Now, don't you go putting words in my mouth," Lurton said, but his grin was a giveaway.

Johnny understood.

He felt troubled by it. Now that he thought it over, it made sense to him. Rizzo had never planned to let the girl live long enough to tell her story. From the outset, he had figured on letting her make the rounds, letting her live the life—and then on knocking her off after a few weeks, so no one could interrogate her, so her story would have to reach the public posthumously.

Johnny felt chilled. He was still new enough to the game to dislike killing innocent people. If a guy wanted to assume the risks of being a criminal, and then got killed by other criminals, well, that was his hard luck. But Alice hadn't been any criminal. Just a kooked-up kid with a nutty father. And now she was dead, because it had suited Pete Rizzo's purposes to have her killed.

Johnny could picture the scene in the motel room as it must have happened. Some emissary of the Syndicate must have picked the girl up in Troy, taken her to the motel, telling her that they'd stop here before going on to the next assignment. Alice wouldn't have objected. She knew that it was customary for Syndicate personnel to use the girls themselves, and she didn't mind being used, didn't mind befouling and soiling herself, because every time she parted her legs she was taking another swipe at her hated father.

So she had stripped, and there she had been in all her plump rosy-breasted nakedness, and the Syndicate man had come up to her and given her the choice between murder and suicide. Either she was cooperative and cut her own wrists, or else he would murder her himself.

The Syndicate man must have been graphically vivid about the form the murder would take. It would be slow and lingering, of course. Unutterably brutal. Perhaps he had told her how he would cut her nipples off, first, slicing them away with steady sawing motions of his blunt blade. And then, as the blood spurted from the bloody flesh as though from two rounded fountain-spigots, he would draw the blade down her body, slash at the soft flesh of belly and thighs.

Perhaps, he would tell her, he would slip the blade into a lover's place, cold steel where warm throbbing flesh belonged, and he would turn it, and twist it, needling it through delicate tissues and sensitive nerves, slashing it around until she howled in agony and pleaded for death.

But death would be a long time coming, that way.

She would lie there, blood coursing from breasts and loins, but she would still be alive, and he would flip her over to lie on her belly, and with an artist's skill he would carve the bloody blade between the quivering mounds, drive it deep, raping her with murderous intent. And then she would huddle in a heap, the most intimate parts of her body savaged beyond repair, and as life left her he would begin to carve her even further, lips, perhaps, and earlobes, and eyeballs, until her brain rebelled at the sadism and all life departed.

Syndicate men were good at describing things like that.

They were good at doing them, too.

So the nude and trembling Alice would listen to the details of how she would be murdered. And then, sick with fear and apprehension, she would whisper, "No—don't, please don't do those things to me!"

"There's only one way out. Do it yourself."

"No!"

"Then I have to."

"All right. All right. Give me the razor blade!"

"First write the note."

And she would take his dictation, and write the suicide note. Her mind would, perhaps, have come around to the idea that death would not be such a bad thing now. It would free her from all fear, all doubt, all shame. There would be no more tyrannical fathers, no more babies ripped from her womb, no more slobbering johns ready to plunge to her.

So she would write the note.

And then she would take the razor blade, and would close her eyes, and would tell herself that this was the way it all ended, here in a remote city in a cold motel room at the age of not quite twenty, and she would draw the blade across first one wrist, then the other, quickly, hardly feeling it. And the Syndicate man would stand by, his eyes glowing with pleasure as he watched the blood flowing from her wrists, staining her plump breasts, running over her nipples, down onto her belly, into the deep socket of her navel, turning it red, onto her thighs. The blood of the innocent, the blood of virginity staining the body of this young tramp.

And gradually her strength would ebb. Gradually she would slump forward, to lie half-conscious in the sticky warmth of her own blood, breasts and thighs against the cold tile of the bathroom floor, pink buttocks pointing toward the low ceiling with its dangling fluorescent fixture. And she would die, finally.

The Syndicate man, his job done, would quietly depart.

Police would come, in due time. And reporters, too, who had been tipped off about the sensational memoirs, the document that would shatter the holier-than-thou image of State Senator Sobieski and end his political career as spectacularly as it had begun.

There would be a funeral.

And the Syndicate would go on flourishing.

Another day went by, and another. Wasn't Rizzo ever going to move in on Lurton and Kloss? What were they waiting for? Was it so unimportant to them that they could take this long for their vengeance?

On the weekend, Johnny had a visitor, unexpectedly.

Ellie.

She pulled up in front of the mansion in a sleek, shiny little Corvette. Neither Lurton nor Kloss happened to be around. They were out on business, and Johnny was minding the store, when Ellie came in.

It was early March, and the countryside was still heavily snowbound, but she looked like the first breath of spring. She was dressed in gay, stylish, brightly colored clothes, and the bouffant mop of platinum hair was radiant and glittering.

Johnny was on the phone, talking to one of the pinball operators in Reesport, when she came. A tart named Rhona who was currently living in the house knocked on the door of Johnny's office and said, "There's a girl to see you, Mr. Price."

"Do I know her?"

"She says you do. She says her name is Ellie." Johnny got off the phone in a flash, and rushed out to greet her.

"Ellie!" he whooped. "Hey, you look gorgeous! How come you're here? You should have phoned!"

"It's my vacation," Ellie said. "The Syndicate gave me a week off. I figured I'd come up and see what the old homestead looked like."

"Come on," he said. "I'll give you the best room up there."

"No. I'm not staying here."

"How come?"

"I've got a room at the motel on Route 71. I couldn't stay here, Johnny."

"Why not?"

"Because if I did, I'd just be a Syndicate tramp passing through. And that would mean Lurton and Kloss could sleep with me just by asking. I don't want that. On this trip, I want to be yours, Johnny. I'm not here en route to a Syndicate job. I'm just vacationing."

He grinned. "I get you."

"You come see me at the motel tonight. It'll be a private deal. I'm not putting out for the bosses on this trip. Just for you," she whispered huskily.

He held her tight. His hands stole over the high, proudly curving mounds of her breasts. Taut shivers of desire ran through him. He felt the pounding of a sudden primitive passion for her.

"Look at my car," she said, breaking away from him. "It's right out front."

"It's a beaut."

"Corvette. I bought it last week. I'm really in the chips, Johnny. Some creep gave me a five hundred-buck tip a couple of weeks ago. I used it for my down payment."

Johnny whistled. "What the hell did you have to do to earn five hundred bucks as a tip?"

Ellie winked at him. "Nothing much," she said. "I used my talent, that's all. He was a creep, I told you. Some creeps satisfy easy. I did a good job with this one."

"Will you do a good job with me tonight?"

"You know I will," she said. "Just don't tell Lurton and Kloss I'm here."

"You think I'm crazy."

Later that evening, Johnny drove out to the motel. It was a new one, at the junction where Route 71 met the superhighway. Johnny had planned to come out to the motel in the spring, to talk about putting in some pin-ball machines. The place wasn't run by locals, though—it was part of some big chain, and the Syndicate policy was to go slow when outside manage-ment was involved.

He parked his car in front of the room Ellie had given him, and knocked.

"Door's open," she said.

He went in.

Everything was ready for him. There was a bottle of bourbon on the nightstand, and a pitcher of ice and some soda. There was a nude girl on the bed. What more did he need?

He stood there, looking at her. His gaze travelled up her body, from the small, perfect toes to the lithe ankles and ripe calves, to the firm thighs, to the lush swell of her womanhood, the breadth of her hips, the twin hillocks of her ruby-tipped breasts, the bouffant splendor of her platinum hair.

He remembered the tanned farm-girl he had laid in a pine copse back in September.

She was so very different now. And yet so much the same, in the essen-tial ways.

She rose from the bed, the deep bowls of her breasts swaying excitingly, and prepared drinks for them. Johnny took off his jacket, kicked off his shoes, and settled down in the armchair next to the bed.

Ellie brought the drinks over. He took his from her.

She curled up in his lap. He felt the warmth of her, the sweet-smelling heat of her nudity. He slid one arm around her, cupping it over her breasts. He felt the nipples going rigid. They sipped their drinks in silence for a while.

Then he felt her hand, slipping downward, prying into his pants.

"What are you up to?" he asked.

"You're the one who's up," she said.

"How can you tell?"

"Believe me, I know." She smiled, and the deft little fingers went about their business, and then she began to shift her position on his lap, and sud-denly he felt warmth against him, and he smiled.

"You're a little minx," he said.

"I'd rather be a little mink. Or at least *have* a little mink." She caught her breath. "Oh, now! How does that feel, eh?"

"It feels fine."

"And this?"

"Mmm!"

She continued to wriggle, lowering herself into place. Johnny hadn't moved. But now the warmth of her imprisoned him, engulfed him. She had taken him, quietly.

They didn't move. She remained curled up in his lap, her naked body warm against him, her buttocks against his thighs, his hand on her breasts. But now a link had been forged. Johnny put his glass down, and took hers from her and set it on the table.

Then he went into action.

Gone now was the spirit of relaxation and repose with which they had entered their union. He stood up, now, lifting her with him, driving himself to the depths of her willing, yielding body.

She thrashed against him. He held her aloft, lifting her and lowering her, lifting, lowering, lifting, lowering. The scepter of his passion blazed with sensation. He could feel the throbbing warmth of her.

Another moment and they were both exploding with their culmination.

Then it was over, and they lay entangled sleepily on the bed, and his hand roamed her, toying with her, cupping the full, heavy mounds of her breasts. She was a good kid, he thought. Young and lively and full of juice. They were going to have some high times together before they were through.

She said, "Like me?"

"You know I do."

"I feel so good when I'm with you, Johnny. Everybody else, it's just business. But with you it's special."

He grinned. She bent over, and he drew in his breath sharply as her lips surrounded him. Her head moved busily for a few minutes, and when she lifted it again, he was ready for action. But he held off for a moment, and touched his lips to her sweet-smelling warm breasts, and kissed the stiff little nipples, and then drew his mouth down her body, and found his goal and devoured it, and she trembled and sighed with pleasure as he went to work.

Then he lifted his head again. He smiled at her, and she smiled back, with a glow in her eyes, and he reached for her and she opened for him and he took her again.

Her legs locked tight around him. His pistoning body drove deep to her, and she writhed and surged upward to meet his thrusts, and away they went. It was as good as ever, with them. They didn't understand what failure was. They had only to come together, and magically there was a fulfillment of their passions.

Afterward, they rested again.

"Fix me a drink?" Ellie said.

"Sure."

He dumped cubes into a fresh glass, poured bourbon in generously. He added some soda. She took the drink from him. Her hair was touseled and tumbled now, but it only made her look all the more desirable. He smiled with pleasure at the sight of her lush pink-tipped breasts, her firm athletic thighs. Already, so soon after the last round, desire was rising in him again.

Ellie looked up. She said, "I didn't only come up here for a vacation. I sort of didn't tell you the whole story, Johnny."

"Oh?"

"I didn't want to say anything about it over there. But here I can tell you. I've got a message from Pete Rizzo to give to you."

"What kind of message?"

"He says he's going to be coming up here in a few days," Ellie said. "He says he's checked into the matter you mentioned, and he finds that you've tipped him off to something big. So he's going to take care of it. He'll be here on Wednesday, and he wants you to be sure to stick around when he comes."

Johnny nodded. "At last. At last."

"What's this all about, Johnny?"

"I can't tell you, chick. Not now. But it's big. It's going to be a terrific break for me. For you *and* me. We're going to be moving in high circles from now on, Ellie." He threw a sharp look at her. "Tell me something."

"Mmm?"

"Suppose I asked you to quit the call-girl racket and come live here and be my girl? *Only* my girl, nobody else to touch you? I'd take care of you. I'd give you more than you're making down in New York."

"Of course I'd live with you, Johnny. But how could you afford it?"

"Don't worry about that," he said. "Things are going to be changing fast around here, soon. I'm going to be a very important man. And I'm going to want you right next to me. I don't want you out selling yourself. I want you to be mine, Ellie."

"Sure, Johnny. Sure."

"Everything starts to move next Wednesday," he said. "That's the big day."

Her eyes were glowing. Her breasts and body held a magnetic pull for him.

Jubilantly, he threw himself on her. The warmth of her swallowed him up, and he celebrated his triumph on her body.

CHAPTER FOURTEEN

He thought Wednesday would never come. Johnny had never known that days could drag on so horridly. Monday, Tuesday—they seemed like eternities. Ellie was gone; she had just come up to deliver the message, and, after paying a visit to her family in Marboro, had gone on her way, tootling along in her shiny Corvette. Johnny had told her he'd get in touch with her as soon as everything had adjust itself up here.

He waited out the days.

Wednesday came. And ticked away. Ten o'clock, eleven, noon. This was the day. Some time today vengeance would descend on Lurton and Kloss. By nightfall, Johnny knew, he would be the big man around here.

One o'clock.

Why don't they get here?

The roads were clear. There hadn't been any snow in a long time. It shouldn't take much more than two hours for them to drive up from the city. Of course, he knew better than to expect Rizzo to set out at dawn to get here. But if he had left at eleven in the morning, he'd be here by now, and he wasn't here.

Another hour ticked away. Lurton and Kloss were busy on the phone all morning, heckling local stringers. Johnny had nothing to do. To kill time, he went up to the third floor, routed out one of the floozies in residence, and took out his impatience on her body, romping over her as though she were a toy. She didn't mind when he grabbed her breasts and squeezed. She didn't mind when he dug his teeth into her shoulder. She didn't mind when he clawed at her fleshy buttocks in his passion. She was a slow-witted, big-breasted kid named Carole, whose one function in life was to please men.

She pleased Johnny. But she couldn't drain him of his tensions, of his impatience.

Adjusting his pants, he went downstairs. It was half past two, now.

He heard the doorbell chime.

At last! At last!

One of the girls was going to answer it. "Never mind," Johnny said. "I'll get it."

The girl vanished. Johnny opened the door.

"Hello, Price," Pete Rizzo said.

He was standing squarely in the doorway, looking cold and deadly. Behind him was the towering, gaunt figure of Angelucci, and three other toughs Johnny did not know at all.

"Come in," he said. "Come on in, all of you!"

They came in,

In a chilly voice, Rizzo said, "Are Lurton and Kloss here?"

"They're upstairs," Johnny said.

"Get them."

There was no mistaking the tone of command. This was it, Johnny thought. The day for evening the score had come. The executioners were here, five of them, and Lurton and Kloss didn't stand a chance.

Johnny went to the head of the stairs. "Hey!" he yelled. "We got company! Come on down!" In his nervousness, he forgot all about the intercom system.

Lurton's voice could be heard, bellowing, "Who is it, Johnny?"

"Never mind. Come down."

They came down, Lurton first, moving with slow ponderous stride, and then Kloss. Lurton's jaw dropped when he saw who the company was, and a tinge of gray appeared in the pink fleshy jowls of his face. But he covered quickly, flashing a phony smile.

"Pete! Joe! Hey, why didn't you let us know you were going to be coming this way?"

"So you coulda baked a cake, huh?" Rizzo snapped. He shrugged his shoulders, a quick, menacing shrug. "We just happened to be passing by," he said. "So we decided to stop in."

"God, it's great to see you boys again," Kloss said, his voice taking on an oily, obsequious tone. He emitted a little dry laugh. "I see you didn't bring the girls along this time. Marie, Agnes."

"No," Angelucci said in a tombstone voice. "We brought the fellas this time."

Lurton and Kloss began to look really scared for the first time. Standing to one side, Johnny watched their lips go white as they compressed them in tension. Lurton's fat face seemed to sag.

Kloss said, "There isn't any trouble, Pete? Anything wrong?"

"This we don't know," Rizzo said. "But we're going to find out. We came up here to check up on your books, boys. A little birdie told us that maybe you weren't handling things kosher, that maybe you were hanging on to some dough you were supposed to turn in. We'll see." He made a quick gesture. "Look them over, boys."

Quietly, efficiently, the three thugs stepped around and frisked Lurton and Kloss. They also submitted Johnny to a frisking. Just in case by some miracle Lurton and Kloss escaped punishment this time, it wouldn't be healthy if they knew that he was the informer who had sold them out. Better that they think he was in trouble, too.

The thugs extracted everybody's gun.

Weaponless now, sputtering in fear, Lurton said, "Pete, honestly, you don't think Ed and I would have tried to cut the Syndicate out of money?"

"You know we aren't—" Kloss began.

"Cut the jazz," Rizzo said icily. "Let's see the books. The *real* books. That'll tell us better than all this cruddy blubbering."

It was all over in ten minutes. With Rizzo's thugs keeping careful watch, Kloss opened the safe and silently handed the records over. These were the genuine articles, Johnny knew. They hadn't been doctored.

Rizzo leafed through them. As he read the columns, he scowled, chewed on his fleshy lower lip, tugged at his earlobe.

Finally he looked up. There was a cold, terrifying smile on his face.

He glowered at Lurton and Kloss and said, "According to these records you got here, pal, you haven't been playing so fair with us. We don't like that kind of stuff. We'll have to fix that, won't we?"

Lurton was quivering. It was startling to see a man that big tremble with fear. His whole body shook. Johnny half expected to see Lurton wet his pants any minute.

Kloss was steadier. A muscle throbbed in his cheek, but that was his only outward sign of tension. He said in a tight, thin voice, "Okay, Rizzo. You've got us cold. But how did you find out?"

Rizzo shrugged. "We were tipped off. We never name our informants. You ought to know that."

Johnny smiled suddenly. It was an involuntary smile of triumph, a twitch of the facial muscles that he was powerless to hold back. Lurton and Kloss were going to die, and he was going to take their place, and he couldn't help smirking over the whole thing.

The smile lasted only a fraction of a second before Johnny controlled it. But Kloss saw it. His eyes widened and he said in a hoarse screech, "He's the one! Isn't he, Rizzo? Price told you about us. He knew, and he told you! The lousy little stoolie!"

"Those are harsh words, Ed," Johnny said.

"He admits it!"

"Shut up, Kloss. You're making too much noise," Rizzo snapped impatiently.

Johnny felt uneasy, but he forced himself to meet Kloss' gaze. The little man glared at him accusingly. Johnny looked back, calmly confident now.

Rizzo gestured to his three thugs. "Take Lurton and Kloss outside in back and give them what's coming to them. This place is so secluded that nobody will hear the shots around here."

"No!" Lurton screamed.

Rizzo slapped him. "You stinking chicken, are you afraid to die? You weren't afraid to cheat us, were you?"

Blood and spittle ran down Lurton's face. He seemed about to collapse.

Kloss said, "See? Just the two of us. Not him! Not Johnny! He was in on it, too!"

"Johnny gets a reward," Rizzo said. "He wasn't responsible for what you two thieves did. He was loyal. He tipped us off to you two, sure. And we'll take care of him for it, Kloss."

Kloss foamed with rage. He nearly broke loose from the arms of his captor, but the thug gripped him more tightly. Kloss hurled curse after curse at Johnny. But Johnny was on top of the situation now. He simply smiled blandly at the angry little man.

"You taught me not to cheat the organization," Johnny said piously. "But you didn't practice what you preached. So I had to turn you in. It was the only thing I could do. I had no real choice. I'm sorry about that, boys. But thanks for all the help you gave me."

"You'll fry in hell, too!" Kloss raged.

"Take them away," Rizzo commanded.

The thugs hustled Lurton and Kloss outside of the house and into the back garden, the same garden where Johnny had made love to Marie so many months before. Inside the house, Rizzo and Angelucci stood with their ears cocked, listening for the sound of death.

Johnny listened too.

He felt warm and happy inside. This house would be his, now, and the entire district would belong to him. And Ellie would come to live with him, and every night he'd fondled her lovely hard-tipped breasts and feel the soft sleekness of her body beneath him as they scaled the heights of passion.

And when he was ready to make his next move up in the organization, he'd find some way of getting rid of Rizzo, and climb another notch toward his goal at the top.

And with Rizzo out of the way, he'd have Marie. That was nice to think about.

Suddenly came a hoarse scream from outside: "No! God, no!"

There was a shot. And a kind of a groan.

Another scream, lower pitched. That was from Lurton, this time.

Another shot. A moan.

"The boys are having fun," Rizzo said. "Winging them first. Making them hop around a little."

Another shot. No moan this time.

Another shot.

And then silence.

"They're finished," Angelucci said.

The three thugs reappeared, their guns holstered and out of sight. Rizzo looked at them inquiringly, and they nodded. The job was done. The gangland execution had been carried out in proper style.

Johnny felt the first triumphant pulsation of power. He was on top, now.

Rizzo turned to him. He said, "We owe you thanks for this, Johnny. Those birds were taking us for thousands. We had to put a stop to it."

Johnny shrugged with Boy Scout modesty. "You don't have to thank me, sir. I was just being loyal to the organization."

"Sure you were, Johnny. That's why you ratted on the two fellows that took you in and showed you the ropes. You were loyal to the organization, so you turned them in like a lousy stoolie."

Johnny frowned. He felt the beginnings of a chill running down his back. He didn't like the new tone of Rizzo's remarks at all.

He said, starting to sweat, "I was helping you, Mr. Rizzo. They were stealing the organization blind. How could I let that go unpunished? I had to let you know about it."

"You're perfectly right, Johnny," Rizzo said. But the smoothness of his words contrasted with the new coldness in his eyes. "You sang like a miserable stoolie because you saw a way of climbing over their dead bodies, and now that they're both out of the way you'll be setting traps for me next. I know your kind. The organization doesn't need guys like you, Johnny."

"I saved you thousands! I—"

"Take him outside."

The meaning of the words didn't sink in for a moment. Then Johnny understood, and he had to struggle to keep his knees from buckling.

"No! You're kidding me!"

"You're out for yourself, kid. You did us a good turn, sure. But I ain't going to risk having you do the organization another good turn some day at the expense of my neck, buster. My girl Marie was talking about you. She likes you. She thinks you've got plenty of drive. She says you have big ambitions. Well, we don't like kids to get too ambitious too fast, Johnny-boy. Take him outside."

"No! No!"

He felt them grab his arms. He tried to struggle; but there were three of them, each his size, and he didn't stand a chance.

They hustled him outside, into the cold.

Confused thoughts rushed through his brain. This was why Rizzo had sent Ellie up here, then, with the message that he was to stick around for the execution on Wednesday. It was so they could nail him too. Ellie had been an innocent decoy. But had Marie squealed on him? Or had she just accidentally and unintentionally dropped one word too many?

It didn't matter. Rizzo knew Johnny's plans for getting to the top, and didn't intend to let him live long enough to put those plans into operation. Someone who had squealed once might always squeal again, if there was something in it for him. Something like Marie. He remembered how Rizzo had made a deal with Alice Sobieski, had used her and then had killed her before she could become a danger to him. It was the same here.

Two crumpled bloody bodies lay in the back yard, sprawled by the swing where Marie had once hoisted her dress to show Johnny the nudity beneath, where he had plunged to the palpitating warmth of her body while Rizzo was unaware upstairs. Lurton and Kloss lay sprawled, their blood staining the whiteness of the snow.

Johnny stared in disbelief at the naked guns that had suddenly appeared in the hands of the thugs.

"Don't shoot me," he pleaded desperately, his voice ragged with fear. "I'm Johnny Price. I'm gonna be big some day, and I'll take care of you guys! I'll see to it that you get everything you want!"

"Listen to him," one of them said.

He persisted. "Look—go inside and shoot Rizzo and Angelucci instead! I'll take care of you! I'll give you ten thousand bucks apiece! And you know their girls, Marie, Agnes? I'll let you have them. As many times as you like. Just don't shoot me! Not me!"

They snorted. The hood in the middle said, "That punk kid would sell anybody out. We better finish him."

"No," Johnny whispered. He thought of Ellie's breasts, and the taste of Marie's lips, and all the other good things he had known in these few months, and all the power and pleasure that still lay ahead. He was only twenty. He was on the way up. Life was one big ball for him.

They didn't waste any more time.

The first bullet caught him in the shoulder and knocked him to his knees in the snow, a few feet from Lurton's fat corpse. The second shot went into his lungs. Johnny clung to life, moaning, trying to tell them that it was all a mistake, that he was Johnny Price and on his way up in the gang world, that someday he'd be the top man. He heard Rizzo laughing savagely somewhere nearby, and he knew it would be no use. He had served his purpose and Rizzo was having him rubbed out. Him, Johnny Price! It was good-bye to Ellie, good-bye to Marie, good-bye to sex, good-bye to breasts and thighs and hot heaving loins, good-bye to everything.

He coughed bloodily. Tears welled to his eyes just before the final bullet crashed into his brain.

THE END

Afterword
SIN, SOFTCORE AND SILVERBERG
By Michael Hemmingson

I

It is no longer a secret that some iconic masters in the science fiction and mystery/crime field earned money writing "soft core" erotic novels—sometimes referred to as sleaze pulps—during the paperback's salad days of the 1950s-60s, where books were printed in the hundreds of thousands for the newsstand market. Midwood, Lancer, Fawcett Gold Medal, Ace, Pyramid, Lion, Nightstand, Monarch, Signet, Lion and a number of short-lived imprints are well-known in the paperback fan and collector market. Many of these books, which once sold between 25-50 cents, now fetch anywhere between $100-1000. Lisa Morton's article, "Smart Broads and Tough Guys: The Strange World of Vintage Paperbacks," notes that:

> By the late 50s, paperback originals were firmly established and many writers dipped their toes in the water courtesy of pseudonyms, usually employed on "sleaze" or soft core porn novels. One of the most sought-after vintage paperbacks now is a hot number called *Sex Gang*, credited to one Paul Merchant — who was actually Harlan Ellison [...]. Donald Westlake was only one of several authors who wrote sleaze novels for the "Midnight Reader" series under the name Alan Marshall. Robert Silverberg used Don Elliott, and even horror master Dennis Etchison got into the swing with a late 60s porn novel credited to the punny-if-not-funny moniker Ben Dover. (np)

Ellison wanted to use the pen name D.S. Merchant (for "Dirty Sex Merchant") and publisher William Hamling did not approve. Some of eleven stories in the volume originally appeared in *Gent, Dude, Rogue, Adam,* and other second-tier men's magazines under pen names Sley Harson, Landon Ellis, Derry Tiger, and Price Curtis. Pen names were not only used to mask writing genre works deemed unworthy of a writer's real name, but also for the reason that the one writer could pen the bulk of stories and articles in magazines—Robert Silverberg, for example, wrote entire issues of Hamling's *Imagination SF* as did Randall Garrett, or the two in tandem. This was done for a number of reasons: not enough publishable stories were coming in from freelance writers, while tested writers were consistently professional and would not require much editing, or could easily be self-edited, and the publisher could make a bulk story deal on the price of the work, getting an issue's worth from writers who desperately needed the cash.

Ed McBain wrote as Dean Hudson; Marion Zimmer Bradley as Brian Morley, Dee O'Brien, Marlene Longman, Morgan Ives, and Miriam Gardner; Robert Silverberg as Don Elliott, Loren Beauchamp, David Challon, and Mark Ryan. Don Elliott is fairly well-known these days among Silverberg and vintage paperback fans. The Elliott novels were popular among readers. Silverberg's early style, found in his 1950s-60s science fiction, can be spotted in books such as *Roadhouse Girl, Sin Hellion, Sin Servant* and some of the graphic sex scenes in Silverberg's New Wave science fiction of the late 1960s and the 1970s reflect the atmosphere of the sex scenes in Silverberg's softcores.

∎∎

William Hamling was born in 1921 on Chicago's South Side, a former Irish-Catholic altar boy whose faith was tested during his service in World War II. Gay Talese, in his treatise of the sexual revolution, *Thy Neighbor's Wife*, describes Hamling's growing disillusionment:

In the Army, [his] perspective changed; it was there that he saw the Church, in deference to the war, becoming less celestial, more nationalistic and permissive. Sins that had been called sins for centuries were suddenly no longer condemned as such by the Church [...] and when tons of pinup magazines were transported by the military up to the front as substitute stimulants for the womanless warriors, the Church, once so strict and censorial, was silent. (103)

When Hamling returned to Chicago, he started to write science fiction. He sold his first story, "War with Jupiter," a collaborative effort with Mark Reinsberg, to *Amazing Stories* in 1939. In 1940, he founded a fanzine called *Stardust*. He then landed a job with Ziff-Davis Publications, editing the pulps he had been writing for, working alongside a young Hugh Hefner who, like Hamling, had some lofty notions about branching out as an independent magazine publisher.

In the early 1950's, Hamling established Greenleaf Publishing in the basement of his house on Greenleaf Street in Evanston, Illinois, pumping out science fiction pulps such as *Imagination* and *Imaginative Tales*, which featured an entire novel each issue. The science fiction market was dwindling (as stated by Silverberg in the introduction of this book) and Hamling noticed that there was money to be made in soft core sex books with flashy covers like those offered by Bedside and Beacon Books. Hamling worked out a contract with the Scott Meredith Agency: Meredith would supply new manuscripts for paperback books from a team of writers. Each writer was contracted to churn out a monthly title. The writers were paid six to eight hundred dollars per manuscript, at the start, then a thousand as the market proved profitable. (Later some of the "names" were paid upward to $1,500, which is about the same that erotica writers get advanced today, if not less.) The books were sent to Hamling under pen names; the agency kept the writer's true identities secret.

Hamling began publishing *Rogue*, a low-brow men's magazine not quite in the same neighborhood as *Playboy*, edited by an up-and-coming young writer named Harlan Ellison. Ellison also edited a more mainstream imprint for Greenleaf, Regency Books, that originally published his *Memos from Purgatory* and *Gentleman Junkie* as well as Jim Thompson's classic crime noir, *The Grifters*. Taking the success of Bedside soft core books, Hamling started the Nightstand imprint. Technically, these books and magazines were not published through Greenleaf per se but a shell company called Blake Pharmaceuticals, a failed firm whose shares Hamling had purchased for pennies. After Ellison left, Earl Kemp, a familiar face in science fiction fandom, eventually got the job. Hamling was tired of paying off the cops and the city officials to look the other way of his smut peddling; he soon decided it was time to get out of Dodge. In a *San Diego Reader* article, "Porno Kings (and Queens)," Earl Kemp recounts:

In 1964, William Hamling discovered California. What he found was [...] an elite hideout for the elite, a fantasy in anyone's imagination. Here, everywhere he looked, he saw someone he recognized, someone rich and famous and admired [...] the more he became addicted to California living, the less we saw of him around the Porno Factory in Evanston. Then, much to our dismay, he began making noises about changing the whole focus of the business and moving the operation totally to California where morals were a great deal more relaxed than in Illinois, where the really beautiful people lived, and where the sun always shined. Along with this came his preliminary efforts at alerting certain key staff members to the eventuality of moving along with their jobs. I was one of them. (92)

Hamling fancied himself a publisher of adult literature in the tradition of Barney Rosset at Grove Press and the infamous Maurice Girodias, whose Olympia Press first published Vladimir Nabokov's *Lolita* and Henry Miller's *Tropic of Cancer*. Hamling also published a number of political books under the Greenleaf colophon. In 1963, he released Ben Hass's expose, *KKK*; in 1966, *The Truth About Vietnam: Report on U.S. Senate Hearings*; in 1971, *The Illustrated Presidential Report of the Commission on Obsceni-*

ty and Pornography. The last one was a reprint of the government report accompanied by lewd and shocking (for the times) illustrations that generously filled the pages. J. Edgar Hoover sent his G-men after Greenleaf, which he had a personal loathing for—and he was not alone.

"At times there were as many as half a dozen competing agencies bugging the lines," Kemp states in the *San Diego Reader* article. "We could get nothing but police radio calls on our phones. I remember going out to a pay phone and calling the cops and demanding that they release at least one phone line for business purposes." In 1966, Hamling was served a 25 count indictment out of Houston, Texas for violating the Federal criminal statutes of Interstate Transportation of Obscene Materials. The case was declared a mistrial, much to the chagrin of Federal prosecutors, but "Hamling was ecstatic," Kemp claims. "As he saw it, the courtroom battle that had begun more than 30 years before in the case of United States v. One Book Called *Ulysses*, resulting in a victory for the literary elite, had now ended in 1967 with a triumph for the man in the street."

On March 5, 1971, Attorney General John Mitchell held a news conference on the steps of the Justice Department to announce the indictment of four Greenleaf Classics employees for alleged crimes associated with the "unauthorized" production of the book *The Illustrated Presidential Report of the Commission on Obscenity and Pornography.* They faced a 20-count indictment. One count prosecuted the book on grounds of obscenity, another on knowingly distributing obscenity. The jury was hung on the obscenity issue and the Justice Department tried a secondary strategy: 12 counts of violating post-office prohibitions of sending sexual material through the mail. This had nothing to do with the actual book, but rather with mailing 55,000 copies of a brochure describing it that included a few sample illustrations.

"Petitioners were convicted of mailing and conspiring to mail an obscene advertising brochure with sexually explicit photographic material relating to their illustrated version of an official report on obscenity, in violation of 18 U.S.C. 2, 371, and 1461," wrote Judge Thompson of the Federal Court in San Diego in his ruling. Hamling received one year imprisonment on the conspiracy count and concurrent with that, consecutive terms of three years each on the remaining eleven counts plus a $32,000 fine. Kemp—who had since resigned from Greenleaf—received one year and a day on the conspiracy count followed by concurrent terms of two years for each of the eleven counts. Hamling and Kemp were also sentenced to five-year probation terms following their respective release dates.

In February, 1976, Hamling and Kemp began serving their time at Terminal Island in Long Beach. "We spent three years and one day there," Kemp told me in an email:

This was (at the time) the federal "legal bad boy minimum." As things were constructed then, convicted criminals were the personal possession of the judge who sentenced them for three months and one day. At three months and two days, they become property of the Justice Department so the judge has only that much time, one day, to salvage that criminal from the Justice Department grist mill.

Greenleaf continued publishing books until 1985, fronted by a shell company owned by Hamling's son-in-law, Jack Abey. Kemp now lives in Kingman, Arizona, and is still an active figure in science fiction fandom (with his online fanzine *eI*) and pulp paperback collecting, where he often attends conventions across the country. Hamling lives in Palm Springs and won't speak to anyone about "the old days" and is no longer involved in publishing.

Don Elliott was the most productive author, having only one real person behind the name. Lawrence Block (Andrew Shaw and Andrew Shole), Donald Westlake (Alan Marshall and Alan Marsh) eventually hired ghostwriters to complete monthly manuscripts, cutting young writers in on the pay, as they worked on other things under their own names but still wanted the monthly paycheck. Robert Silverberg, however, penned every Don Elliott novel except one, *Carnal Counselor*, when he was unable to meet the deadline one month (it is unknown who wrote that Elliott for him). Greenleaf, in the later half of the 1960s, assigned the house names to books written by a variety of authors. A few of the early Silverbergs wound up bylined John Dexter, and one as Marlene Longman.

Love Addict, Silverberg's first Elliott, has some historical significance in sleaze book publishing, for Nightstand/Greenleaf/Corinth/Blake Pharmaceuticals, and science fiction history. Silverberg was paid $600 for the book, along with a $200 bonus when it went into a 2nd printing.* For a long time, paperback scholars and fans considered *Love Addict* to be Silverberg's first foray into soft core yet he had been publishing books with Bedside all through 1959: seven as David Challon and five as Mark Ryan. He had been contracted by a science fiction fan who was editing the books for Valiant Publications (which did not pay Silverberg for all the manu-

---

*We must consider the value of the dollar in the late 1950s. $600 was about $6,000 in today's money, not bad wages for quickly written genre fiction. As Silverberg notes in his introduction, he was writing two or three of these books a month, at an average of $1,000 each; essentially he was making $20-30,000 in today's funds for smut.

scripts, some which Silverberg re-sold to Midwood as by Loren Beauchamp, with slight changes but essentially the same novels). *Love Addict* was written in July 1959 and published in October, so Silverberg was a busy guy, typing away. Earl Kemp, in his essay, "Have Typewriter, Will Whore for Food," believes it was Silverberg's idea to have Ellison pitch a Bedside-like series to Hamling:

In New York City, popular young science fiction writer Robert Silverberg discovered Bedside Books. At that point in time (1959), Silverberg had already acquired a serious case of Compulsive Writeritus and was looking for new markets to conquer. Bedside Books looked like a natural.... The new market direction could be the answer to many writers' wildest dreams in the very near future.... Silverberg approached Ellison with the glorious possibilities for the future for energetic young writers and had him all primed and ready for William Hamling so Ellison could lay out the road map to Toon-town in front of him.... Hamling liked the idea of the proposed books and grasped the concept of the throwaway sleazy paperback firmly in his hands. After a bit of formulation, Hamling sent Ellison back to New York City to start the ever-loving money-making wheels in motion [and] Harlan Ellison went straight to Robert Silverberg to report on his success with Hamling in the initial set-up phase of the operation. It was Silverberg, not Ellison, who took the proposal to Scott Meredith that eventually opened the doors to the fabled black box clandestine enterprise that virtually flooded the country with soft core pornography. (np)

Basically, Harlan Ellison and Robert Silverberg started the ball rolling of what is now canonical history in publishing, freedom of speech, obscenity and censorship lawsuits and criminal court cases, and now a niche collector's realm.

Toss out the half dozen rather tame sex scenes, and *Love Addict* is an urban novel about a serious drug addiction in the 1950s: heroin, horse, junk. It is also a doomed love story. Jim Holman is an engineer in the middle of a bad divorce. Pissed after leaving his wife's lawyer's office, Holman stops off at a Brooklyn jazz club to have a few drinks; there is a mesmerized the 22 year-old woman singing with the band, Helene Raymond. He talks to her, convinces her to let him drive her home... she keeps warning him that she will hurt him, she is no good. She tells him she's a junkie, and shows him the needle marks on her thigh. She says she has been off junk for three months but knows she will relapse. He doesn't care; he's in love. Problem: the band leader is an ex-boyfriend and has been since Helene was 17. She has broken it off but he's possessive and does not like her dating and sleeping with this older man (Holman is 29). Helene is manic and goes back on heroin, which her ex-boyfriend is happy to supply. Holman tries to help her quit the habit... he takes her for a two week trip to the Adirondacks. He says he will marry her when his divorce happens. She moves in with him at his upper west side apartment. But her ex-bf tracks her down and gets her hooked again. Holman murders the guy with his own saxophone.

It wasn't just the sex and the cover that mad people buy this book: there was the dark forbidden underside of jazz hopheads, reefer madness, and shooting junk with shared needles, themes already popular in the paperback market.

The second Don Elliott title, published December 1959, was *Gang Girl*, reprinted in this book, which also tackled another popular pulp theme: juvenile delinquents. Only months earlier, Silverberg published, as Mark Ryan, *Streets of Sin* with Bedside, a gang story that is pretty much the male version of *Gang Girl*: criminal teenager in a new city, looks to join the local gang, has to prove worthy of the gang, gets in and tries to move to the top too fast and it becomes their downfall. In 1960, the Elliott *Sex Jungle* was also a gang tale.

Juvies were not as prevalent as other themes in the Elliott books. The more common themes were corporate settings in the offices of Madison Avenue or manufacturing (*Convention Girl, Expense Account Sinners, The Flesh Peddlers*), Manhunt-style noirish crime (*Passion Patsy, Gutter Road, Sex Bum*), grown men getting involved with teenage girls (*Orgy Maid, Flesh Pawns, Sexteen*), couples getting into sexual trysts while on vacation (*Sin Cruise, The Lust Seekers, Orgy Isle*), Hollywood (*Sin Festival, Lust Queen, Backstage Sinner*), prostitution (*Convention Girl, Party Girl, Carnal Carnival*), sado-masochism (*Shame House, The Pain Lusters, Sin Servant*), suburban wife swapping (*Three Sinners, Switch Trap, Take My Wife*), lesbianism (*Alternate Wife, Sin Girls, Diary of a Lesbian*), and in the later part of the 1960s, sports (*Lust League, Flesh Taker*), and even elements of the supernatural (*Lust Demon*). A couple Elliotts were reprints of Midwood Beauchamps, with name changes: *Registered Nympho* is *Nurse Carolyn* and *Orgy on Wheels* is *Sin on Wheels*; likewise, *The Passion Barons* is also Mark Ryan's *Streets of Sin* and *Rouge of the Riviera* is David Challon's *French Sin Port*. Lately, there has been a flurry of reprints of these vintage paperbacks from publishing operations large and small. This edition marks the first Don Elliott reprints authorized by Robert Silverberg, and I'm sure there will be more to come as more readers discover and re-discover these little bright gems of the paperback's sinful past.

Referencess

Kemp, Earl. "Have Typewriter, Will Whore for Food." eI Vol. I, No. 2 (efanzines.com/EK/eI2/index). April, 2002. Hemmingson, Michael. "Porno Kings (and Queens) of San Diego." San Diego Weekly Reader (30 June 2005): 84-106. Morton, Lisa. "Smart Broads and Tough Guys: The Strange World of Vintage Paperbacks." Clarkesworld Magazine (clarkesworldmagazine.com/morton_07_08). 25 Oct. 2008. Talese, Gay. Thy Neighbor's Wife. New York, Doubleday, 1980.

THE EROTIC NOVELS OF ROBERT SILVERBERG: A BIBLIOGRAPHY

Don Elliott (all published by Greenleaf under various imprints)
Love Addict (1959)
Gang Girl (1959)
Naked Holiday (1960)
The Flesh Peddlers (1960; reprinted as The Flesh Merchants, 1973)
The Lecher (1960)
Mistress of Sin (1960; reprinted as Depravity Town, 1973)
Party Girl (1960)
Sin on Wheels (1960; reprinted as The Instructor, 1973)
Passion Trap (1960; reprinted as Carnal Cage, 1973)
Sex Jungle (1960; reprinted as Jungle Street, 1973)
Convention Girl (1960; reprinted as The Man Collector, 1973)
Summertime Affair (1960)
Woman Chaser (1960)
Backstreet Sinner (1961; reprinted as The Bed and the Beautiful, 1973)
Expense Account Sinners (1961; reprinted as Keep the Clients Happy, 1973)
Lust Goddess (1961; reprinted as The Temptress, 1973)
Lust Queen (1961; reprinted as The Decadent, 1974)
The Lust Seekers (1961; reprinted as Till Love Do Us Part, 1974)
Sin Club (1961; reprinted as The Lady from Soho, 1974)
Sin Cruise (1961; reprinted as Fifteen Nights of Love, 1973)
The Sinful Ones (1961; reprinted as Every Night in Rome, 1974)
Wild Divorcee (1961; reprinted as Nowhere Girl, 1973)
Streets of Sin (1961; reprinted as The Untamed, 1974)
Hotrod Sinners (1962)
Kept Man (1962)
Lust Captive (1962; reprinted as The Game Susan Played, 1974)
Lust Cat (1962)
Lust Cult (1962; reprinted as None But the Wicked, 1974)
Lust for Two (1962)
Lust Lord (1962)
Lust Market (1962)
No Lust Tonight (1962)
The Orgy Boys (1962)
Passion Thieves (1962)
Roadhouse Girl (1962; reprinted as No Pleasure So Painful, 1974)
Sex Fury (1962)
Sexteen (1962)
Shame House (1962)
Sin Bait (1962)
Sin Kin (1962)
Sin Quest (1962)
Sin Sick (1962)
Three Sinners (1962; reprinted as A Change for the Bedder, 1974)
Wild Flesh (1962)
Lust Crew (1963)
Passion Patsy (1963)
Sex Bait (1963)

Sex Bum (1963)
Sin Crazed (1963)
Sin Made (1963)
Sin Servant (1963)
Beatnik Wanton (1964)
Black Market Shame (1964)
Flesh Bride (1964)
Flesh Lesson (1964)
Flesh Melody (1964)
Flesh Pawns (1964)
Flesh Prize (1964)
The Flesh Seekers (1964)
Flesh Taker (1964)
Gutter Road (1964)
Lust Burns (1964)
Lust League (1964)
Lust Set (1964)
Lust Spree (1964)
Orgy Isle (1964)
Orgy Maid (1964)
Passion Pair (1964)
Passion Partners (1964)
Passion Trio (1964)
Pickup (1964)
Shameless (1964)
Sin Bin (1964)
Sin Circuit (1964)
Sin Partners (1964)
Sin Service (1964)
Sin Sold (1964)
Switch Trap (1964)
Wanton Web (1964)
Alternate Wife (1965)
Carnal Carnival (1965)
Escape to Sindom (1965)
Flesh Bigamist (1965)
Flesh Boarder (1965)
Flesh Cry (1965)
Flesh Man (1965)
Good Girl, Bad Girl (1965)
Lust Doomed (1965)
Lust Finale (1965)

Naked She Died (1965)
The Nite Lusters (1965)
Nudie Packet (1965)
Of Shame Reborn (1965)
Only the Depraved (1965)
Orgy Slaves (1965)
Passion Killer (1965)
Passion Peeper (1965)
Passion Pusher (1965; cover listed
   as by Don Holliday)
The Shame Protector (1965)
Shame Scheme (1965)
Sin for Solace (1965)
Sin Kill (1965)
Sin Spin (1965)
The Sin Switch (1965)
Sin Warped (1965)
The Sins of Seena (1965)
Teaser (1965)
Would-Be Sinner (1965)
The Young Wantons (1965)
All on Sunday (1966)
Big Blast (1966)
Campus Traders (1966)
Cousin Lover (1966)
Diary of Desire (1966)
Every Bed Her Own (1966)
The Gay Girls (1966)
Initiates (1966)
Lust Demon (1966)
One Night Stand (1966)
Pain Lusters (1966)
The Passion Barons (1966)
Take My Wife (1966)
The Virtuous Ones (1966)
All the Best Beds (1967)
Carnal Counselor (1967; ghost-
   written, author unknown)
Diary of a Dyke (1967)
Flesh Fever (1967)
Flesh Tryst (1967)
Orgy on Wheels (1967)

Registered Nympho (1967)
Rogue of the Riviera (1967)
Those Who Lust (1967)
The Wanton West (1967)

As by Loren Beauchamp
Love Nest (Midwood, 1958)
Another Night, Another Love
  (Midwood, 1959)
Connie (Midwood, 1959)
Unwilling Sinner (Midwood,
  1959)
Meg (Midwood, 1960; reprinted as
  All the Best Beds as by Don
  Elliott, 1967)
Nurse Carolyn (Midwood, 1960;
  reprinted as Registered Nympho
  as by Don Elliott, 1967)
And When She Was Bad
  (Midwood, 1961)
Sin on Wheels (Midwood, 1961;
  reprinted as Orgy on Wheels as
  by Don Elliott, 1967)
The Fires Within (Midwood,
  1961)
Campus Sex Club (Midwood,
  1962)
Sin a la Carte (Midwood, 1962)
Strange Delights (Midwood, 1962)
Wayward Widow (Midwood,
  1962; reprinted as Free Sample,
  1968)
The Wife Traders (Boudoir, 1963)

As by David Challon
Campus Love Club (Bedside, 1959;
  reprinted as Campus Sex Club as
  by Loren Beauchamp, 1962)
French Sin Port (Bedside, 1959;
  reprinted as Rouge of the Riviera
  as by Don Elliott, 1967)

Suburban Sin Club (Bedside, 1959;
  abridged & reprinted as The
  Wife Traders as by Loren
  Beauchamp, 1963)
Thirst for Love (Bedside, 1959;
  reprinted as Wayward Widow as
  by Loren Beauchamp, 1962)
Man Mad (Chariot, 1960)
Suburban Affair (Bedside, 1960)
Campus Hellcat and Other Stories
  (Bedside, 1960)

As by John Dexter
Stripper! (Nightstand, 1960;
  reprinted as One Bed Too Many
  by Jeremy Dunn)
Sex Thieves (Nightstand, 1961;
  reprinted as Wife in Name Only
  by Jeremy Dunn, 1974)
Sin Festival (Nightstand, 1961;
  reprinted as The Goddess Makers
  by Jeremy Dunn, 1974)
The Bra Peddlers (Nightstand,
  1961; reprinted as The Venus
  Affair by Jeremy Dunn, 1974)
The Lust Plotters (Nightstand,
  1962)
Passion Bum (Nightstand, 1962)

As by Dan Eliot
Dial O-R-G-Y (Ember, 1963)
Flesh Flames (Ember, 1963)
Lust Lover (Pillar, 1963)
Nympho (Ember, 1963)
Sin Doll (Ember, 1963)
Sin Hellion (Ember, 1963)
Sin Mates (Pillar, 1963)

As by Marlene Longman
Sin Girls (Nightstand, 1960;
  reprinted as The Tormented,
  1973)

As by Ray McKenzie
The Wild Party (Chariot, 1960)

As by Gordon Mitchell
Immoral Wife (Midwood, 1959;
   reprinted as Henry's Wife, 1961)

As by Mark Ryan
Company Girl (Bedside, 1959)
Streets of Sin (Bedside, 1959;
   reprinted as The Passion Barons
   as by Don Elliott, 1966)

Twisted Love, (Bedside, 1959;
   reprinted as Strange Delights as
   by Loren Beauchamp, 1962)
Savage Love (Bedside, 1960)
Illicit Affair and Other Stories
   (Bedside, 1961)

As by Stan Vincent
The Hot Beat (Magnet, 1960)

www.ingramcontent.com/pod-product-compliance
Lightning Source LLC
Chambersburg PA
CBHW070929190726
48292CB00004B/1161